The Quest of The Land of the Eagle Feathers

The Book of Winter

I0557487

By

Joe G. Morin and Jo Ann Bullard

Copyright©2020

Published by

Lyrics and Books from the Heart

Publishing Company, Inc.

Preface

What is life? It is the flash of the firefly. It is the breath of the buffalo in the wintertime. It is the little shadow which runs across the grass and loses
itself in the sunset.
Blackfoot Proverb

The Keepers of the Yawi are in the last season in the circle of time. They have come far in their quest for the four books. They have learned many things about themselves and the other members of the group. They will need all their special powers and knowledge to locate the last most important book, *The Book of Winter.* If they do not locate the book, **The Land of the Eagle Feathers** will not survive.

They know that they will face many dangers and a great battle. Each character must find the resources within themselves to survive. It is a race against time. Time is running out for **The Land of the Eagle Feathers**.

They have no idea what will happen, but they know they must succeed. They will face each sunset and sunrise with the belief that everything the power does, it does in a circle. They can only hope they survive the journey.

Will they locate *The Book of Winter?*

What will happen to each character?

Will The Land of the Eagle Feathers continue to exist?

Will what they have learned be enough?

What secrets remain to be discovered?

Will the circle be completed?

The Table of Contents

Chapter I
What is Happening?
Why did they kill Them?

The sound of the door closing was the last thing that was heard. The room was dark. All the lanterns were dark. A wind had blown the flame out of each of them. Everyone was puzzled at what they had seen. Lo Ming and Moses had just murdered the old man and his dog. They had burst in and killed them without any explanation and ran back out. Could they had been mad with blood lust from the happenings of the last few days? They had been covered with blood, and their clothes were muddy.

The storm outside was in full force. The old Eagle Train Station rattled with each clap of thunder. The only light was from the lightning flashes. One second, everything was lit, and in an instant, it was dark. Nick clapped his hands together, and all the lanterns lit at once. The group looked at each other as if someone could give them an answer as to what they had seen. Rose got up from her chair and went over to the two victims that were dead on the dusty floor of the lobby.

As she was about to turn over the old man's body, a ruff old voice could be heard. "I see that my plan worked." Their heads turned to see the old man and his dog standing by the station master's door. "They thought they had killed me and my faithful dog. That was their mistake. Well, they paid for it. John, you were right to send Lo Ming and Moses back early to help me," said the old man.

"Who are they?" asked June. "You should know them, Antonio," answered David. Antonio looked a little closer at the bodies. "They are two of the best assassins that Kamir has. The one, playing the old man, is Mano. The other is Fato. They are both known for being able to change their shapes to surprise their prey. They almost killed me once.

Lucky for them that Lo Ming and Moses killed them before I did. I wouldn't have been so quick. I recognized them when we came into the lobby," replied Antonio.

"How did you know?" asked June. "See the small green earring in the old man's ear! It's an emerald. Mano always wore it because that's where his power came from to change shapes. Fato was his assistant. They were inseparable," answered Antonio. "Why did you wait?" asked Rose. "I knew that the old man had this covered. He and his dog are too smart to be killed by them. I presume that this was a trap for the last of Kamir's men to be captured or killed. He had to pretend to be dead to lay a trap for them. His men were to burst into the door and kill us. I guess Lo Ming and Moses were waiting outside to finish them," replied Antonio. As if to make that point, the old front door opened. Lo Ming and Moses were standing wet from the rain with water running down their clothes.

David applauded. "Well, old man, I see that you haven't lost a thing. You were always one for the dramatic. I don't know about anyone else. I am hungry. Where's the food?" A female voice answered that question from the other side of the room. "It's in the lobby of the old hotel. I don't cook just for anyone," said the Red Woman. She had slipped in while everyone was talking. "Lo Ming and Moses, there are dry clean clothes in Room 2 of the hotel for you," the Red Woman stated.

Lo Ming shook her head. "We still have a problem. Some of Kamir's men got away. There were too many of them for us to get. There is one more big problem. Kamir is still alive. I don't know how. Someone must have tipped him off about the trap at David's mansion. He is somewhere up the trail with the last of his men. I saw him when the last flash of the lightning hit a tree beside him," Lo Ming said with anger in her voice. "It's too dark, and another storm is coming in to

5

do anything right now. We will wait till daybreak before making any more moves," said John.

"Don't we need to clean up the bodies?" asked Mary. "Now, honey! You just let me take care of that. They will be gone when you get back here after the storm goes through this morning. You all need to get some sleep after breakfast. Let's say be here at noon. I will have the horses and mules packed for your journey by then. It's a long way to go around them fellows up there. Besides, I have other guests coming who I must get ready to welcome.   Isn't that right, David?" said the Old Man. We all turned to look at David. David had a wicked smile on his face, "I will explain to everyone after breakfast about who's coming for dinner."

They went down to the old wooden clapboard hotel. Inside, the smell of coffee and breakfast being cooked filled the lobby's air. Morning Star met them at the dining room doorway. " Go get cleaned up. There are fresh clothes in Room 2. There are several rooms available for you to change that have bathrooms. Some of you will get your clothes off faster than getting clean ones on. I will have the food ready in 45 minutes. Don't be late!" Morning Star said.

The Red Woman appeared from the kitchen, "David, we have some business to finish before breakfast. Go to Room 24 at the top of the stairs…"   David cut her off in the middle of the sentence, "Yes, I remember where Room 24 is. How could I have forgotten?" Morning Star laughed, "Now, all of you need to get going, you don't have much time to waste. A bad storm will be here in about an hour. June, there is a special person waiting for you in Room 34 in the attic. Take that basket of food with you. You don't need to be back down here until noon."

It wasn't long before everyone found a room to change. Lo Ming and Moses went to one room together. Nick and Shanna went together to another. Antonio and Angela found a room for them near the back of the building. Mary and Rose found a spacious room for them. John found a small room to change from his wet clothes. In each room was a large bathroom with both a tub and shower. There were toiletries that only the best hotel would have. Nobody bothered to try to reason how these rooms got here in this old hotel. This mysterious town had a way of its own.

June picked up her food basket. She headed upstairs to the third floor. She found a ladder on the third floor that led to the attic. There was a door that was at the top of that ladder. June climbed the ladder carefully. She reached up and opened the door. She put the basket inside and climbed into the room. It was pitch black inside except for stars shining where the roof should have been. She let her eyes get used to the darkness. She could feel that she was not in the hotel anymore.

A figure stood in the middle of the room. White Elk walked over to her. He whispered into her ear. "I have decided to give you a reward for your great deeds. There is someone over there that is waiting for you. You must leave this mystical place by noon. You have until then. I will see you at the Council Meeting." White Elk faded into the darkness.

She saw another figure moving toward her. She knew who it was immediately. One Feather pulled her into his arms. He said to her, "Let's not waste any time. We have only a few hours together. This special place allows me to be with you. White Elk will take me back with him to **The Land of the Eagle Feathers**." "Don't worry, I won't waste one second with you, my love," she said before giving him a passionate kiss.

David took the old wooden stairway to the second floor. The old floors and steps creaked as he walked. He liked the sound of old floors creaking. He missed the sound that old wooden floors made when you walked across them. They gave a building a character all its own. Modern buildings lacked the character that the old ones had. They lacked the creaks and sound of people walking.

He reached the second floor. He turned left at the top of the stairs. Room 24 was three doors down on the right. He opened the door to the room. He was pleasantly surprised to see that the room hadn't changed in all these years. It was just like it was over thirty years ago. There was a large full bed with a purple and white quilt with Indian symbols on it. A fireplace was in the middle of the far wall. The bathroom was off to the side. He took off his dirty clothes and put them in a clothes basket. His clean clothes were in a clothes closet.

He went into the bathroom to take a shower and shave. When he finished shaving, he decided to take a bath instead of a shower. The warm water felt good as he lowered his body into it. His thoughts returned to Donna. He liked the idea that she was now known as the Red Woman. It was more fitting for her. He would never call her anything else. She deserved that honor and position to be called The Red Woman. He heard the door to his room open. He leaned back in the full tub of warm water. He was sleepy. He closed his eyes. He must have slept for the few moments.

His body jumped when he felt the touch of a female hand on his face. A voice said to him, "We have some unfinished business." He drew the Red Woman to him and held her in his arms. The rest was a wonderful blur of passion and love.

The Red Woman had waited a long time for this moment. She was not wasting any time on talk. They didn't need to do any talking. This was to be the last time for them to be together until the journey was over. They had a plan, and they would follow it to the end. She needed him more now than ever. She would make this hour special for him and her.

Everyone seated themselves around a large breakfast table except for June. The room was silent. We ate in silence. Nobody was talking. The events of this early morning were still fresh in their minds. It was as if they were waiting for someone to break the silence. People were getting past the killing of the two impostors in the train station. They were now thinking about who took *The Book of Fall*. This was a game changer. This could be a serious problem for all of us.

I decided to wait until someone said or asked a question. They would expect their leader to start the discussion of where we go from here. Finally, Rose spoke, "John, don't you have something to say about what is going to happen? We have questions that need to be answered." I started to speak. I was interrupted by the Red Woman.

The Red Woman rose from her chair at the breakfast table. "I know that you are concerned about *The Book of Fall* being missing. Antonio knows all about that. Just to make you feel better, I know who has it." She had everyone's attention with that announcement. "I have it or I should say Little Wolf has it. I can see that this is a shock to you. Antonio will need to explain how this happened."

Antonio wasn't ready to give a speech about this subject. The Red Woman had pushed it on to him too soon for his liking. He wanted to watch the group to see if he could find who was leaking information to others outside the group. He thought the missing of the book would give him an edge to find out. He was not the only scorpion in this.

Antonio stood up and went to the head of the table. He seemed to be a little nervous before he spoke. That was unusual for him. "It's a long story. Let me go back a little. Little Wolf is a genius in deciphering languages. I spent some time with him in **The Land of the Eagle Feathers.** We worked on *The Book of Fall* together late at night. I was worried that if something would happen to me, all would be lost. When I was satisfied that he could decipher *The Book of Fall* himself, I decided to give him the book after I finished finding the pages in Houston to decipher. I marked the pages in the book and gave it to the Red Woman to take back to **The Land of the Eagle Feathers** to give to him.”

"You had the book, and we were there to protect you. Why did you feel that something could happen to you or the book?' asked Rose. Rose already knew the answer. She had seen that two assassins were after them in her crystal ball.

Antonio answered, "Rico told me in Houston that people were asking about us. Angela and Shanna told me that I had a price of two million dollars on my head, dead or alive. I knew that I was right. Rose, you already knew the answer to that question. I saw that you had your exploding beads ready at the train station."

"How did you know that the Red Woman was in Houston?" Nick asked. "It was simple. The book told me that David and the Red Woman were once married. It told me a lot of things. It also told me not to trust anyone. The Red Woman was the only one I could trust with the book up to a point. The only place that the Red Woman would go would be to David. Everyone knows that the Red Woman was gone when we got back to the sacred mountain.

I had Rico make a copy of the outside cover of the book and used that to fool everyone that I had the book. Rico gave me the false cover. He does do good work. He can forge anything. Remember when Rico came to give us the clothes for the wake for David, I gave him a package to deliver to David's mansion. I told him to give it to David. It was addressed to the Red Woman. I knew that Rico would not look inside the package. His business depends on people trusting him. He also knows that either I or David would kill him if he didn't follow my orders. That is another reason for me trusting him. He still wants the painting we stole from his museum. It is his favorite, and it is worth millions of dollars," Antonio laughed out loud.

The Red Woman spoke up, "David gave me the package. He was surprised to see it addressed to me. I opened it. There was a note inside that told me to take it to Little Wolf. It said in case of my demise. You will be able to save my son, your grandson and the land. David told me that we had no other choice but to take it back. I left that day."

"That's a nice story, but there are some holes in it," said Moses. "I will explain those. Antonio knew that someone was leaking information to Kamir and possibly others. I suspected the same. There is reason to believe that one of us could be that someone. Antonio didn't want anyone to be able to find the treasure map inside the book. I don't think Antonio could even trust himself with that map," said David.

"Rico told me that many people knew about the legend of the treasure map. There were rumors that some people would kill to get the book just for the treasure map. Angela and Shanna told me that there were still people wanting to stop anyone from getting *The Book of Winter*. The two people that Lo Ming and Moses killed were from someone that wanted a chance to kill us for either the book or just to stop us. I do know one thing. Kamir is dead," said Antonio."

"Then, who is the person that I saw?" said Lo Ming. "That would be Red Bear and what is left of Kamir's group and Red Bear's followers. I could sense his presence here. I will have to deal with him later. We have more important things to do. Isn't that right, John? " asked David.

I looked at David and answered, "Yes, we do. You explain our plan to get to **The Land of the Eagle Feathers,** David. There is one more thing that I will add. Everyone here has reasons to want *The Book of Winter* including myself. Remember, scorpions are scorpions. You know what that means." David got up to go over the plan that we had forged together.

"We will be going to the tunnel to get to **The Land of the Eagle Feathers** by a route that is different from what you have done before. Angela and Shanna will stay back with me to meet the next train coming late today. That train will have a professional combat team on it. Benita with assistance from Raven will be leading this combat team. Their objective will be to neutralize the last of Kamir's forces and Red Bear's forces. The reason I chose Angela and Shanna for this job is they are not needed to obtain *The Book of Winter*."

"In other words, we are expendable," said Angela. "In a way, the answer to your question is "Yes." There are other reasons for leaving them with Benita. One is that Raven and Benita are very sure that both of them are loyal to me and them. The other reason is that Angela and Shanna are both skilled fighters. I can trust them to get the job done. They do not have any reason to second guess John and my orders. The third reason is that they will be needed to protect Raven and Benita. We will need Raven and Benita to make sure that they come back and bring the rest of **The Dark One's Army** to the final contest for **The Land of the Eagle Feathers**. Angela and Shanna are to make sure that they gain the confidence of Raven and Benita.

There are two more things. Angela, when the fighting is over, Red Bear is to escape, and Angela and Shanna will have a falling out. That will give Angela reason to leave and join the rest of us at the entrance tunnel. You must make that believable.

Shanna, you will accompany **The Dark One's Army** to the Valley of Death. Remember, your reputation is one that is ruthless in obtaining results. You must assure Benita and Raven that they will win. You must get them to be over-confident about the battle ahead. This over confidence will be their undoing. They will make mistakes. You are not to point them out. You are to reassure them they are making the right moves.

I know that this assignment will be extremely dangerous and difficult. We can only beat them if we play head games with them. Angela must be out of there when Benita realizes that the Red Woman is still alive. They will try to kill her when they find out or suspect that she didn't kill her the first time. I know Lo Ming and Moses would like to go with you. They cannot because we must take no chances in losing them. They have already done their part. They have weakened Kamir's followers and Red Bear's followers. At noon, we will all meet at the train station. That is all for now. John will brief you at the train station for any final questions you might have. You have 3 hours. Make the most of it."

I got up and told them, "Everyone must bring your weapons and other gear to the train station. We are on a very tight schedule. Everyone must follow David's and my orders and not question them. If you don't, you probably won't be alive to see this journey through. Let's hope that everyone is on the same page. We took into account that we are all scorpions or people not to be trusted. I will see you at the train station at noon sharp." I left for my room without taking any questions from anyone. I didn't notice Mary following me. I thought she was going to her room. It would have been better if she had.

Nick didn't like David's plan at all. He was afraid for Shanna. He went over to David to talk to him. Before he got there, Shanna intercepted him. Shanna grabbed Nick by his right hand. "We have little time left before you must go. We have some unfinished business to do," she smiled. She didn't have to say anything more as Shanna led him to their room. Nick knew that he couldn't have changed anything about the plan if he wanted to. If Shanna wanted to do her part, he knew not to try to stop her.

When Shanna and Nick got to their room, Nick couldn't help himself. "It was you and Angela that came up with that plan," he said to her. "Yes, it was. David was a little leery of the plan at first. It was the Red Woman that sold it to David. It takes women to outsmart other women. You men are all babes in the woods when it comes to the deviousness of women," answered Shanna. "Enough said, we've got better things to do," she laughed as she jumped on Nick. They landed on the big four poster bed together in each other's arms.

Antonio was very concerned about what he had heard. He would worry about Angela later. All he wanted was to use the last few hours as best as he could. He took Angela by their hand. He whispered in her ear, "I love you." He kissed her on her lips in front of everyone. Out of the corner of Angela's eye, she could see the Red Woman. The Red Woman was smiling back at her. In Angela's mind, she heard these words, "You two deserve each other. Now go, time is short and be happy for a few hours," the Red Woman spoke to her mind.

David and the Red Woman sat down on an old wooden bench on the front porch of the old hotel. David looked at his first wife with sadness. "I know what you are thinking, David. You can't forgive yourself for marrying Benita. You have nothing to forgive. I don't care about that. I only care about what is now. We are together. We both made mistakes. The one that I worry about is our daughter, Mary. She may not forgive us, especially me," the Red Woman said with tears running down her cheeks. "Don't worry about Mary. She is a very strong woman. I don't know what to do about John. It is up to Mary to decide that. John and I have been enemies for a long time. I fear that at the end of this, John and I will have a reckoning. Whatever happens, don't interfere. It is up to our destiny to see who remains standing." Let's just sit here and watch the sun rise over the mountains. I sometimes forget how beautiful the mountains are," said David. David put his arm around Donna, the Red Woman, and held her close to him.

I opened the door to my room. I felt a hand on my shoulder. I turned to see who it was. Mary was standing behind me. "May I come in to talk to you?" she asked. I showed her inside and closed the door. There were two seats by a small table by the room's window. I motioned her to have a seat.

"John, I don't know what to say to you. In some ways, I hate you. In other ways, I do not. I must have been a very naïve young woman when we met. I sometimes think that you took advantage of my youth. I must have loved you or thought I did. I have no real memory of that emotion. My father and mother deceived you and me. That is not your fault. You saved my life several times. Likewise, I did the same for you. Fate has not been so kind to us. We have a wonderful son, Little Wolf. He is much like you. No matter what happens, I want to have more time with my son. I only ask one thing of you. You must see to it that I and Little Wolf survive this journey," Mary said with her voice shaking.

I looked across from the table at Mary. "You are not that young girl I knew long ago. You are much more. I was a fool to think that I deserved such a woman as you. Whatever you decide about us, I will promise you that I will protect you and Little Wolf with my life. I don't have much time left. But to know that you are alive and Little Wolf is my son is more important than life itself. We have a bond. My destiny is written in the stars. Yours and Little Wolf's are written in the sands of time. Now go and get ready for our journey. This might be our last journey together." Mary stood up. She walked to the door. Then she came back to me. She kissed me on my cheek and left the room.

Rose was sitting by the fireplace in the main lobby of the hotel. She was in deep thought. She felt lonely. Zan was on

15

her mind. Would she get to see him again? "I know what you are thinking, Rose," said Shanna. "You are thinking about Zan. A woman can tell such things," Rose turned to see Shanna standing there. "You know about Zan," asked Rose. "Yes, Nick told me the whole story. Zan must be a lucky man to have someone like you to love him. Nick told me he promised to help you bring him back. I told him, "He had better." I owe you a lot. You have saved him several times. I have no right, but I want to be your friend. I don't have many friends that I can trust. I feel that I can trust you. You are somewhat like me. You are a warrior. Warriors only have their word. That is all they are given. I heard about you many years ago. But that was another time and place," said Shanna with the utmost respect.

Rose stood up. "Yes, I need a good friend. Now, I have two great friends. I will take care of Nick for you while you are gone. That is my warrior's word to you. Now, unlike a warrior, give me a big hug."

Lo Ming and Moses took the events in stride. They knew that this journey would be coming to an end. They had decided to go for a walk among the old buildings of the town. There was an old swing on one of the porches that looked almost brand new. Moses pointed it out. The swing overlooked a small mountain stream. The soft sounds of the water had a calming effect. They sat down in the swing and watched the stream's water flow to the south.

Lo Ming was deep in thought. She wondered why Moses never asked her many questions. "Moses, you never ask me anything about my past. Why is that?" she asked. Moses looked at her. His eyes were dark with thought. "Well, I know what I need to know," he replied. "What do you mean?" she asked. "All I need to know is that you love me. That is enough for me. It is up to you to tell me. It is not up to me to ask. We all have our secrets. I know many things about you. I figure if my mother approves of you, then why should I worry about such little things. You have your reasons. You have lived a long time. My grandfather told me to look to the stars and look at the ground. Our lives are just a short time of the years of the universe. As in the Outback, you make the best of what destiny gives you. For reasons unknown to us, we are together. That is all that matters to me. I hope that answers your question," he softly said looking into her eyes.

She replied back to him, "You are a very special man. I am honored to have your love. Someday, I will explain everything to you. You are the only one that I have met in my long journey of life that can speak to my mind without talking out loud. It is said this only happens to anyone once in a lifetime. Let us hope that we survive to live many more lifetimes together. For now, we have only this lifetime to share together." They swung in the swing together until it was time to go to the train station.

One Feather and June went back to their special room. Their two wolves, Midnight and Snow, greeted them. They sat down in the grass of the small clearing in the middle of the room. They knew this special place would disappear when they would leave. They patted their wolves as they talked. "There is something I must tell you. I am not going with you and the others. I will be leaving soon with the Red Woman. She wants me to go back to **The Land of the Eagle Feathers** with her. I am only here because I am a Spirit Warrior. My body is back in the land. She allowed me to come to see you. She wants me to help her with Red Bear and the others. In a few moments, I will disappear and go with her spirit," he whispered to her.

A voice spoke to them. "It is time to go, One Feather. We must go." It was the Red Woman. "We must protect your mother and Shanna. Red Bear is a very dangerous man. They will need our help. Red Bear has lost his way. We must help him find himself again before it is too late." One Feather leaned over and kissed June and said, "I will see you in The Land of the Eagle Feathers soon, my love." One Feather and his wolf faded and disappeared before her eyes. June summoned her black wolf. "We have much to do," she said as she patted her female wolf. Her wolf looked sad, "I know. I feel the same. We will see them soon. Let's go!"

At noon, everyone gathered in the train station. There were two members of their group missing. "Where is the Red Woman and One Feather?" asked Nick. The old man replied, "The Red Woman told me to tell you that they were going back today up the trail. It is part of her plan. That is all I know. She said that they will meet you at the Council meeting in **The Land of the Eagle Feathers**. That is all I know."

A train whistle blew. David said, "The train is coming with Benita and Raven and their men to finish off Red Bear's and Kamir's men. Everyone needs to go except for Angela, Shanna and myself. You know the plan." The old man told everyone to go to the stables and get going. "I have the mules loaded and your horses ready for the south trail to take you back to **The Land of the Eagle Feathers**. You will be able to bypass the main trail. David, here's a map of a short cut to catch up to John and his group after you meet with Benita and Raven. Don't worry, nobody will be able to see John and his group leave from the stables," the old man said to them.

The old man and his dog watched as John and his group left by the south trail. At the same time, the old train rattled and stopped at the wooden platform in front of the train station. Steam covered the platform. Twenty men dressed for a war got off with Benita and Raven. David, Angela and Shanna greeted them.

"Benita and Raven, I hope you had a good trip. I see you brought our best fighting men. Lo Ming and Moses finished off most of Kamir's and Red Bear's followers. We figure that's there are about forty of them left up the trail. Angela and Shanna will lead you up the trail to find them. Benita, you will be in charge of eliminating the rest of those men. I know you can't wait for a good fight. Remember, you can only use swords and medieval weapons here. Modern weapons don't work in this land," ordered David.

Benita responded to David, "As you see, my men are ready. They are experts with these types of weapons. Raven has been a great help to me. We will finish off those men for you, my love. I have made Raven my second in command. We are ready to start right now."

Angela had seen that look on Raven and Benita before. She knew they were smelling blood. Shanna noticed one thing about Raven. Raven didn't look too pleased to be named second in command. Shanna would use this to her advantage later. Shanna was a little worried that Angela would be in great danger when Raven and Benita found out the Red Woman is still alive. She only hoped that she could save Angela from them. She would follow the plan.

David gave Benita a kiss. "That's for good luck, my dear. You follow our plans, and we will be rich and powerful beyond your wildest dreams. Everyone here will be rewarded with more than you ever dreamed of. Follow Benita's orders, you know the consequences if you don't. I must leave to catch up with the others. It's your show, Benita. I can't provide you horses. It is too dangerous to use them. Have a good hunt!" David said as he saluted everyone by hitting his chest with his right arm. The old man had brought up a black stallion to the platform. David jumped into its saddle and rode off.

Benita and Raven told Angela and Shanna that it was time to go hunting. Angela and Shanna replied, "We can't wait. Follow us! It's time to have some fun."

The old man couldn't help but smile as he sat in the train station watching them go. He looked down at the old hound dog, "I know what you are thinking. I wonder who is underestimating whom. We will soon find out. The best of plans can always go wrong. Benita and Raven are two tough cookies." The old hound dog barked back at the old man. "Yes, I agree. Things are going to get interesting very soon."

Chapter II
Winter is coming
Traveling is getting difficult

It was late afternoon. It would soon be winter. The bare hardwood trees made it easy to see the trail up ahead. The wet fall leaves from the hardwood trees were slippery under the animal hooves. A strong wind had started blowing in from the North. The wet grass and branches were beginning to ice over. Sleet began to fall. The trail was beginning to ice over. Our group had been on the trail for over three hours. It would be getting dark in a few hours. Nick was on the lead horse of our small line of horses and mules. Mountain weather is very tricky this time of year. Nick saw something he didn't like. His senses told him to stop. The sleet was coming down harder. He saw its shine just feet from him.

Nick halted the line of riders behind him. He signaled for me to come up beside him. I stopped my horse right beside his. Nick told me to be careful and stay right behind him. He walked a few feet and pointed at something in the air. It took me a few seconds to make it out. A very fine clear plastic line was stretched across the trail about four feet high. He didn't have to say anything. I knew it was a tripwire. Someone had put it high enough to be tripped by a person walking or on a horse. The reason it was so high was to prevent small animals from tripping it.

"I will take care of this. You tell the others to get off their horses in case something explodes. We don't want anyone getting bucked off their horse," said Nick. I went back to the others and had them dismount. We watched Nick follow the tripwire to the other side of the trail. This part of the trail was only six feet wide with trees on both sides. Nick stopped at a large oak tree on the right side of the trail. He reached up into the side of the tree. He took out his knife and held the tripwire in his left hand and slowly cut it. He took the wire closest to the tree and gently let it slowly go limp in his hands. Carefully, he untied something from the tree. He seemed to cut something in his hands. He walked back to us carrying it.

He placed the explosive in my hands. "This is not something that would kill anyone. It would injure you but not kill you. Someone either wanted to use it as a warning device to see if someone was using this trail or wanted to slow us down by having us treat an injured person. What do you think, John?" Nick asked.

"I think we better get some shelter from this sleet. We can talk about this later. I knew you saw the sign on this trail of someone using this trail. They were good at hiding their sign. They are professionals in what they were doing. Up ahead is an outcropping by a cliff. We can make camp there and dry out. I will lead you to it," I told everyone. I could sense our group's uneasiness about what had just happened. I knew they had questions. There was one thing clear. I had no answers for their questions.

We moved up the trail about a mile in the wet sleet that was turning to a heavy snow. The trail was covering over. It was hard to follow. We had put on our winter jackets with hoods covering our heads. The trees were becoming snow covered. A peaceful silence with only the muffled sound of the horses' hooves could be heard. The valley before us had become a winter wonderland. I took over for Nick and led the way to the outcropping.

I spotted the place to turn off the trail to the outcropping. The old cedar trees in a cedar grove were covered with snow like Christmas trees. This was the landmark that I needed to find. Behind that grove was the outcropping that would protect us from the wet snow. The Native Americans called this place: Shelter from the Storm. The outcropping that created this shelter was at the base of a high cliff. It looked like someone had hollowed out the base of the cliff. You could walk back at least 20 feet from the edge of the cliff. The cedar grove in front of it protected you from the blowing wind and snow.

The outcropping was at least 100 feet long and 20 feet wide. We could put the horses and mules on one side of it and still have plenty of room for us. I told Nick to get a fire ready and the others to unpack the mules and horses. It would be dark in two hours. We would need to dry out our clothes and bed our animals down. Soon, Nick had a fire going. He had started to boil water for tea and coffee. June and Antonio gathered up wood for a fire with Moses. Lo Ming and Mary were attending to the animals and campsite.

Nick and Rose decided to start supper. A good hot vegetable soup with flat bread made from cornmeal would be our supper for tonight. I told Moses to keep a close watch for anything moving from the trail in front of us. Moses asked, "Where are you going, John?" I replied to him, "I'm going to walk up the trail to check on any signs of who might be around. There's a small pass up ahead that could easily become blocked by a landslide. I haven't been on this trail for years. I need to check it out."

I had only taken a few steps down the trail when a whole mountain seemed to explode. I ran back to the shelter of the outcropping. You could hear rocks and debris falling down the mountainside. Luckily, it was down the trail from us. I motioned Moses to follow me. What we found down the trail was not good. The small pass between the mountains was filled in by the landslide. Boulders and trees blocked the trail. This meant that we would have to find another way to the entrance to **The Land of the Eagle Feathers**. Moses said after looking at the pass, "If I had two cases of dynamite, I might be able to blast the pass open. It would take a very well-trained explosive expert to do that. I am good, but I don't know if even I could do it." I told him that we need to get back to the others and talk about what to do later.

We were covered with snow by the time we got back to the campsite. Rose had made a makeshift broom from some sage weed and string. She brushed the snow from off both of us. She also had a clothesline attached to two poles that Antonio had cut from two small trees. She hung our coats up to let them dry close to the fire. It had gotten dark. The snow had stopped. The late autumn sky had cleared. Stars were bright in the sky. The moonlight reflected off the new snow. Each of us got a big bowl of vegetable soup and some flat bread to eat with it. All of us sat cross-legged around the campfire to keep warm.

June had fed the horses and mules some oats and other feed grains. She had tied them loosely to a long hitching line. In the distance, we heard a loud growl of a bear. A couple of wolves howled back at the bear. June laughed and said that reminded her of the legend of the Big Dipper. She said her mother had told her a story about how the Big Dipper was formed. Mary liked listening to June's stories. She asked, "June, I would love to hear that legend. I can see the Big Dipper by the top of the mountain range over there. I have always wondered why it appears to take different shapes during the year."

June loved to tell her tribe's legends. By now, it was almost a tradition that June would tell us some legends each night when we camped out by the stars. June never needed encouragement to tell her stories. Moses couldn't help but say, "June, we are waiting for some of your entertainment. The stage is yours."

June stood up. Not only did she tell her stories by talking, she used sign-in-language at the same time. June pointed to the Big Dipper, "This legend is called,

The Hunting of the Great Bear.

One day during the cold nights, four hunters received a message. A Great Bear was threatening their village. The four hunters with the help of their dog went after the Great Bear. The hunters were all brothers. After chasing a bear for several hours, one brother told the other brothers that he had hurt his leg. The other brothers thought that this brother was just lazy. He was known for not working very hard. However, the hurt brother convinced the other brothers that he really had sprained his ankle. They didn't like it, but they lifted him up from the ground where he had fallen and carried him.

The four hunters, following their dog, hurried up the mountain to catch the Great Bear. They hadn't noticed that they were high in the clouds. Finally, their dog had Nyah-Gwohch, the Great Bear, cornered. The Great Bear didn't think much about the hurt hunter. The Great Bear decided to bite their dog. When he tried to bite the dog, the hunter with the hurt ankle jumped down and speared the Great Bear in the heart and killed the Great Bear. The hurt hunter had used his wits to pretend to be hurt in order to surprise the Great Bear and kill him.

Soon all the brothers decided they would cook the bear and eat him. When they had cooked the bcar, they sat down to eat him. It was then they realized that they had been tricked. They looked down and saw that they were not on a mountain

24

but high in the sky beyond the clouds. This bear was a spirit bear. Their dog started barking. The bones of the bear were starting to put the bear back together.

This bear was magical. Soon the hunters found themselves chasing the bear throughout the sky above the earth. If you look close at the Big Dipper, you can see the bowl has four stars or bear claws. The handle has four stars with a little one behind. The little one is their dog. They have been chasing the Great Bear ever since. Every so often, the Big Dipper changes, that is because the four hunters and their dog are getting closer to the bear. The Great Bear has always managed to stay ahead of them. See the Big Dipper is changing, maybe this time before winter comes. they will finally catch him," as June pointed to the Big Dipper above the far mountain range.

A voice from the dark startled everyone. "That's a good story, June. I believe you are right. I have seen it move, myself," David said as he dismounted his black stallion. "Can we get some food and dry out? We are both hungry." Nick got David some food. Rose took his wet coat. Moses led his black stallion to the other horses and bedded him down. "I bet you have a story to tell us about what happened back at the train station," said Rose. "Well, you can say, I do!" replied David as he sat down to eat.

As David finished his food, the rest of the group joined him around the campfire. David looked up. "I know what you want me to tell you. After you left, the train arrived with Benita, Raven and their select group of mercenaries. I recognized the mercenaries as being from the **Dark Ones' Elite troops.** They are skilled in the martial arts. They never use guns or modern weapons to kill. They are silent and deadly. I pity for anyone that goes up against them.

I gave orders to Benita and Raven to clean-up what was left of Red Bear's and Kamir's followers. They were to have

Angela and Shanna lead them up the mountain to find them and destroy them. Nobody can escape. Everyone was to be eliminated. When that was over, they were to return to the Eagle Train Station and return to Houston.

In Houston, they were to assemble the forces to enter **The Land of the Eagle Feathers** for our final battle to conquer the land. They were to return with Rico. He is the only one that can read the inscription to open the tunnel to gain entrance into **The Land of the Eagle Feathers.** Angela and Shanna were to assist them in Houston.

I met with Benita, privately, in the Old Man's station's office. I told Benita to be careful of Raven. I reminded her to trust nobody especially Raven and Angela. I felt that Angela and Raven might have an alliance of some sort. Also, I told Benita to be careful. In these mountains, things are not always what they seem to be. I could tell that Raven didn't like me meeting with Benita without including her.

I must say that Angela and Shanna were playing their part well. They seemed to be bonding with Benita and Raven. Shanna had done some work for both of them in the past. I could tell that they still thought Angela was on their side of things. The four of them looked like they were going to enjoy going on this mission together. I overheard them talking about who would get the most kills. They had a bet on that. I only wished that I could see all them in action. It would be a wonderful sight to witness them all in battle together.

The last thing I did before they left to go up the mountain trail was to give Benita a big kiss in front of Raven. I told Benita in front of everyone that we would finally get everything we always wanted. Raven turned red with jealousy. I knew that Benita and Raven were more than co-workers. Now, I know it for sure. Everyone knew that I had to leave to catch up with you. I saluted everyone and left."

Nick asked David, "How did you know about Rico being able to decipher the symbols at the tunnel entrance to the land?" David replied, "I always knew that he had many talents. Who do you think taught Antonio? However, I must admit Antonio is much better than Rico will ever be. John knows that it was Rico that assisted me in getting my army into the land long ago. He was able to decipher the symbols on the tunnel then. Too bad they made it harder after that. Don't be upset with Rico. He is a scorpion just like many of you. Isn't that right, John?"

I could feel everyone looking at me. David had a way of making people distrust each other. He was working his skills on our group. The problem was that he was right. This group had its share of scorpions. The only thing I could say was, "It is getting late. Moses, you have first watch followed by Nick, Antonio, Lo Ming, Rose and Mary. We still have someone out there that might give us trouble. We will have to figure a way around the pass in the morning." David laughed and asked, "Why didn't you choose me to be on watch?" I replied to him, "Because you are the biggest scorpion of all."

Rose looked at everyone, "From now on, things are going to get interesting. There is one important fact that we have learned on this journey together." Mary interrupted her by stating, "Everything is not always as it seems. That fact especially applies to everyone here." June smiled and said, "A wise medicine man once said, after all, a starving man will eat with the wolf ."

The night went uneventful. As morning came, a thick fog covered the valley. They could feel the warm wind coming in from the South. The snow was quickly melting. Nick and Rose had fixed a breakfast of powdered eggs and corn cakes. Everyone could feel that something wasn't quite right. There was no sounds of animals or birds. Then, it happened. Three blasts of some type of explosions up by the pass in front of them. "That's dynamite. It had to be at least three cases of dynamite. I would know that sound anywhere," said Moses.

Out of the fog, they could make out a figure on horseback with some creature beside them coming into their camp. Everyone grabbed their weapons. A familiar voice said in a gruff voice, "Now, is that a way to welcome old friends. I see that you have breakfast ready for us. Mind if I have some?" the old man with his hound dog asked them. The old man was on his beautiful stallion with the black silver trimmed saddle. He was leading a big black mule behind him.

John motioned him to have a seat. Nick got him some breakfast and found some treats for his dog. Moses gave his horse some oats and grains from a feed bag. "I see that Nick found my tripwire. I knew that the first snow would bring down the mountain. I hoped you would stop here before it did. I guess that trick worked. I sure like my coffee. Do you have any, Nick?" asked the old man. Nick poured the old man a cup of coffee and handed it to him.

"Well, I thought you would need a little help getting through the pass. Three cases of dynamite did the job. Now the pass is open enough for you to get through," said the old man. The old man ate the rest of his breakfast quickly. He mounted his horse. He looked at us and said, "You all better get going. The sound of that dynamite will attract some people. I hope the rest of your journey goes well. May the spirits be with you. You will need them." The old man tipped his ragged old brown cowboy hat. He rode off with his mule and dog following him back to the train station. The fog had cleared by then. Everyone saddled up.

Moses whistled when they got to the pass. The old man had blasted it open. "The old man knows his stuff," was all Moses would say. David replied, "He knows more than just dynamite. He is right. The blast will attract others. We need to hurry." David took the lead. He set a fast pace. I figured that it would take a day and most of tomorrow before we would get to the tunnel's entrance. I had Nick scout ahead of us to make sure the way was safe.

We had no problem all day. About two hours before nightfall, we set up camp for the night by a small crystal-clear hot spring. The weather as always in the mountains this time of the year can change from one extreme to another. It was now getting rather warm. I told everyone after they ate, they should take a dip in the spring. It would be the only chance to clean up for a few days. I would take the first watch while they did. The rest of the night watches would be the same as the night before.

Lo Ming and Moses couldn't wait to jump into the spring. They wore only a little as possible. They used the water to wash their clothes. The others followed suit as well. It was nice to see that they were all having some time to themselves. David didn't go with them. Instead he decided to come and talk to me. "What do you want? I asked him. "I know that you have your reasons to dislike me," he answered. "Just about a thousand reasons," I sarcastically replied.

"I reckon you do." David said. "If you were trying to save **The Land of the Eagle Feathers**, why did you invade our land twelve years ago? Wasn't it you that led **The Dark Ones**?" I asked. "That's a long story. I put off coming here for several reasons over many years. Some of the reasons were good, and some of them not so good. I did take out several organizations that would have tried to invade by using the excuse of them being competition against **The Dark Ones**. Finally, I didn't have a choice.

Raven, my boss, accused me of not being trustworthy. She put me in a tight spot with **The Omen.** Raven ordered me to either invade the land or she would kill Mary. I was blackmailed to do her bidding. I had no choice but to try. I made a good show of it. John, your troops were very

29

powerful. Raven was watching my every move. When you tried to save Moses' father, I had to try to kill you or Raven would have killed my daughter. You know the rest. I used your death as an excuse to retreat saying with you dead it would be much easier to take the land later. We were too weak to do it then. I had lost too many troops to win. Luckily**, The Omen** thought I made the correct decision. Raven had no reason to kill Mary because I proved that I could be trusted by killing you, the great general of **The Land of the Eagle Feathers**," David answered back.

"There is one more thing. I thought you took great pleasure in killing me," I said. David looked me straight in the eye. "Yes, I did. I won't lie. When I found out that Mary had a lover that got her pregnant, I wanted to kill him. When I found out it was you, it gave me great pleasure in doing just that. I made a mistake by not doing it then. Your future is now in the hands of Mary. Her mother, the Red Woman, and I decided to let Mary decide what to do with you. If she wants you dead, then we will help her do that. Your fate is in her decision. There is no way you can beat both the Red Woman and me. With that said, David turned and left.

Moses took over my watch about two hours later. The night was warm for being just a few days before winter. The weather had made a complete change from cold to warm. I got my dirty clothes and headed to the spring to clean-up.

Everyone had pitched their tents and were sleeping. At least that was what I had thought. I washed my clothes. The air was a little cold, but I could stand it. It was not a dark night due to the moon and stars. Antonio had put more wood on the campfire to add more heat so the clothes on the clothesline that Rose had made would dry everyone's clothes by morning. I noticed that David had set up his tent close to Mary's.

The warm spring water felt good on my sore back. I had taken off all my clothes and washed them. I placed them in a neat pile on the spring's bank. I would put them on the clothesline later. Looking up at the stars, I wondered what the next few weeks would bring. We were getting closer to finding *The Book of Winter*.

I thought about our group: **The Keepers of the Yawi**. Many of the members of our group could be thinking the same thing I was. If they got their hands on the book and claimed it, they would be the most powerful person in the world. I needed the book to save myself, protect the land and the world. The other members of our group could do the same things. They could still protect the land and then gain all the power they would ever need.

I didn't need riches or power. I had had those things many times throughout my life. Now there were three things that I needed more: my son, his son's mother and time to spend with them. I would pity anyone that stood in my way to obtain those things. *The Book of Winter* would be the key to ensure I might get those things.

Trust is a funny thing. You think you can trust someone with your life, but they may have other reasons to betray you. I looked back at the camp. My existence depended on a few people. My world depended on a few people. The Big Dipper was low in the northern sky. Maybe I was like the four brothers and their dog chasing the Big Bear. Their problem is that they catch the bear, but he always gets away. There is no end to their hunt. My problem is that I must catch the bear and never let him go. I need to end this hunt.

Nick was talking to Rose by the campfire. "It was less than a year ago that we started on this journey. I remember the first time I saw you, Rose. I knew you were something special. I was a lonely and depressed young man. More than anyone in the world, you saved me from myself. I have done many things that I am not proud of in the last few years. This is my chance to redeem myself. I can only hope that I will. The power of the final book is very tempting," said Nick.

Rose looked at Nick and smiled. "You remind me of my Zan. He was young and full of life. I guess that I was lonely too. That is what drew us together. We had lost a special someone. You are a lucky man. You got Shanna, your love, back. This is the first time I have felt hope to see Zan again. I sense that you will help me get my true love back also. I do have a fear within me. We have some members of our group that I wonder about," said Rose.

"Yes, I know. I don't have to name them. They have their own agendas. Even us, we have our own agendas. Temptation can cause some people to do what they least expect. The temptation to have the book that could change everything is something we will all have to deal with. Do I trust everyone? The answer is no. I don't really know if I can trust myself. There is only one thing that we must worry about right now. We must get that book. What happens after that is anyone's guess. We better get some sleep. I will see you in the morning, Rose," Nick said softly.

Rose got up and looked at Nick. Nick was right. Could anyone trust anyone here? Rose did have another agenda besides getting Zan back. Revenge is best served cold. Something in the way Nick talked tonight told her more about Nick. For the first time, she sensed that Nick had another agenda that he was hiding. What he was hiding, she didn't know. She would keep a watch on him. Nick would help her get back Zan. As he said, when we get the book back what will happen after that. A woman can change a man. Shanna could do that. Shanna has always played by different rules. No, it was not Shanna. It was something else. "Sweet dreams, Nick," Rose said as she turned to go to her tent.

Antonio was having difficulty in getting to sleep. He was exhausted. His mind kept going over the events of this past year. He had been persuaded to go on this mission. No, he had been blackmailed by The Council of Religions to go on this mission. He didn't have any choice. He smiled. He would have taken this mission anyway, if he had known that he would be with Angela again.

His plan to double-cross The Council of Religions was not going as well as he had hoped. Things were getting much too complicated. Finding out that Angela and he had a grown son was one thing. John and David were another problem. It appears that everyone has reasons for wanting *The Book of Winter* that included his superiors. His superiors wanted more than just the book. He would never let them have what they wanted.

He had given up one of his friends to The Council of Religions once. He was not going to give them John. He would never do that because they were blood brothers. There was also another reason. John was the only friend he had left. All the others were dead. Then Antonio realized that he was worrying about nothing. John was a legend. John had always kept one step ahead. John wouldn't have survived these many years if he didn't. Antonio was good at being devious. He just knew that John was better at it. Antonio knew why he couldn't sleep. His mind was telling him something. It was simple. He should have seen it coming. It was more a question than a thing. What was John planning? It had to be something big. Not just big, it had to be greater than that. That is why The Council of Religions wanted John.

David decided he needed to talk to Mary. He went over to her tent. She wasn't there. She must still be at the spring. He would talk to her early in the morning. He needed to know if she still was going to follow their plan. It was important for their future. David was uneasy about things. There were too many people involved with getting the last book. He didn't trust any of them. Angela and Antonio were one problem. He wasn't so worried about them.

John was another matter. Something about the way John was conducting himself. John seemed too calm. He knew John was planning something. He just didn't know what or why. It would be nice to distract John from John's plans. He knew just who that would be. If anything would distract John, it would be his daughter, Mary. Maybe they would accidently meet at the spring. That would distract John. Mary would be David's ace in the hole.

Moses was on his watch. He didn't mind taking his turn. Lo Ming would be waiting for him at their tent. They would be together. That should have been enough to satisfy him. It wasn't. He was still upset with his mother. He was upset with John. He didn't know if he could keep his feelings about John inside. He would try. He heard a noise behind him. He didn't have to turn around. Lo Ming told him to his mind that she was there. She came up close to him. She had two blankets. "It will be getting cool tonight. I told the others that I would take their watch tonight. That will give us more time together. Don't worry about anything being around. I had Rose check the surroundings with her crystal ball. There's nobody close," she told Moses. Lo Ming carefully spread the blankets on the dry grass. Moses watched as she slowly undressed.

Lo Ming took her time. Moses was a person she never expected to find in her life. He never questioned her past. He didn't care. Their minds would touch each other. She knew that Moses knew she had another agenda. She only hoped that her agenda would always include him. She had her reasons for being here. One day, everyone would know. She needed *The Book of Winter*. She needed it to answer some questions for her. She needed it for other reasons. Those reasons were why she was on this journey.

June was sleeping in her tent. Most of her clothes were drying on the clothesline. She didn't like the feeling of being alone. She wanted to feel One Feather close to her again. She took off what little clothes she was sleeping in and covered herself with one of One Feather's deerskin shirts. He told her to hold it close to her whenever she got lonely for him. She loved the way it made her feel closer to One Feather even though he wasn't there. Little did she know that the shirt had powers of its own.

A soft voice spoke to her, 'I see that you are lonely. I am glad you did as I asked. My shirt told me to go to you. I am a Spirit Warrior. I can transport myself to you. I am back with the Red Woman. She told me that I could go to you. She doesn't need me until morning. I can only come to you in spirit form. You will not be able to see me. You will be able to feel me. I am mostly energy. I will try not to use too much, or I could cause you harm. Do you want me to make love to you?"

"Yes, my love, make love to me, One Feather. I long for your touch. I can feel your energy. It is like a small charge of electrical current. It feels wonderful.

The next thing June could feel was Rose shaking her. "I see One Feather visited you. Don't be embarrassed, the energy from your lovemaking cast a golden glow over the whole camp. I told them all to get some sleep and not bother you. Now, you go to sleep. You need your rest," giggled Rose like a little girl that had gossip to tell. Rose smiled at June and left

When she woke in the morning, a letter from the Red Woman was lying next to her. June tore open the letter. It was not what she expected. The note said, "June, you must tell David the truth about why Red Bear wants to kill you. If David finds out from someone else, there could be severe consequences for you. Included is another note that is in this letter for him from me. It is the one with bees' wax sealing it. You must give it to him.

One other thing that everyone needs to know, Red Bear escaped and is coming for you tonight. At midnight, you and David must meet him at the clearing by the Roaring River Falls. You two must be alone. David will protect you. He may not want to, but he will do it for our mission. Tell everyone about what you did to Red Bear's youngest son in a meeting before you leave this morning." There was a wax stamp on the bottom of the note. It was a red wax engraving of the Red Woman.

It was early morning. The sunrise wouldn't be up for an hour. At the edge of the camp, David was talking to Mary. "I take it that you and John must have had a long talk," David said with a little annoyance in his voice. "Yes, we did. We had a lot to talk about concerning Little Wolf," she replied. "I hope that you are still on board with our plans for *The Book of Winter*," stated David. Mary thought for a minute before she answered. "I have given it long thought. There is or was nothing that John could say that changes that. I just want to know one thing. Is my real mother in agreement with our plans?" asked Mary. "Who do you think formulated the plan with my help?" replied David back.

David asked, "Why did it take all night to get things settled with John?" Mary looked at David, her father, "We had to clarify some issues to settle about Little Wolf. John wanted to know what would happen to Little Wolf if he dies or we both die." David still wasn't convinced of Mary's explanation. "Well, what did you come up with?" asked David. "After arguing half the night, we decided to leave that up to his grandparents, believe it or not," she answered. "I bet that took some convincing speech from you, Mary," David said with surprise in his voice. Mary looked David straight in the eyes, "I didn't convince John. He convinced me. John said a child

36

needs to be with his next of kin." Before David could say anything else, Mary walked off to her tent. She could hear David say out loud, "Well, I'll be damned!" Mary said to herself, "You and the rest of us scorpions will probably be. That's just our nature."

They were all gathered at breakfast. Nick and Rose had fixed pumpkin pancakes. Nick had found a small wild patch of them growing by the spring. The coffee and tea added to the breakfast along with honey that Nick brought along. About the time breakfast was over, June got up and told everyone that she had to talk to everyone, especially David. June gave the note to David that the Red Woman had sent.

June told everyone that she had news from the Red Woman. One Feather had left her a note last night. He was here last night. Rose laughed, "Well honey, we sort of guessed that. You woke us and half the forest up." June turned red with embarrassment. "Let's get serious for a few moments. What I must tell you and David is very important. It will explain what is going to happen next. It will also explain why Red Bear wants me dead or worse. This is a long story. I will give you only the highlights. You can judge for yourselves," said June. David interrupted June, "There is no need to tell them. This situation affects me more than anyone of them."

David's concern did not stop June from telling her story. Mary started her story about Red Bear and her. "A few years ago, I met a young Indian brave. I was home on summer vacation from college. He was a handsome young man. He said his father had sent him to our tribe to learn more about Native American life. He was charming and very personable. He said his father had heard that I knew much about the different tribes and their customs. I would be one that could teach him about such important aspects of Indian life.

I was naïve. I didn't even ask him his father's name. He said his name was Red Sparrow. I was flattered that he

37

wanted me to teach him. I spent about two hours each day for about a full moon's worth of days with him. I grew fond of him, much like a teacher to their best student. One day, he asked me to show him some of my powers. He said his father told him that I had such powers. I was surprised that anyone knew about them. I had taken great caution in not letting anybody know about them.

I told him that I could not do that because it would hurt my powers to show anyone what I could do. I could see that Red Sparrow didn't like my answer to his question. He became mad and walked away. I had always been somewhat suspicious of Red Sparrow. He asked a lot of questions. I thought more than what most people would. Many of his questions were about the powers of medicine men and what I knew about them. I pretended not to know that much.

When I asked him who his father was, he would only say a great medicine man that I probably never heard of. He said his father didn't want anyone to know that he was his son. His father had many enemies that might try to hurt him.

One day towards the end of summer, Red Sparrow said that it was time for him to leave. He said that he must go home. He would leave early tomorrow morning.

He asked if we could spend his last day near a river about two miles from our tribe's village. I thought that was fine. I liked walking there. The river was wild and swift with many rapids. It was a beautiful place between two mountains. We decided to make what you call a picnic.

I fixed some food for us to eat. Red Sparrow brought a blanket for us to use for the picnic. I remember the path to the river had late summer flowers blooming on both sides of the path. It was one of those days that seemed perfect. We got to a good place to have our picnic. I had noticed that Red Sparrow seemed to have a lot on his mind. He had been silent most of the way there. He did ask some questions about plants and some legends. There was something different about the way he looked at me.

We sat down on the blanket. I got out the food that I had brought. Red Sparrow didn't say anything while we ate. When we finished our lunch, I asked Red Sparrow what was bothering him. "I was sent here by my father to spy on you. I told you that my father was a great medicine man. My father had heard that you were a very gifted medicine woman. I am to go back and report to him about what I saw being with you," he said.

I replied, "I didn't know anybody thought that of me. "How did he hear about me?" Red Sparrow repeated that his father was a very powerful medicine man. "You never told me his name," I asked. Red Sparrow replied, "I have become very fond of you. I think, I am in love with you. You have been so kind to me. Nobody has ever been that kind to me because of the deeds of my father. I will tell you who my father is, if you promise not to hate me. I am my father's son. I would do anything for him. I love him very much. I will tell you that I have a brother. He hates his father. He left many years ago. He believes that my father is wrong to do what he is doing. I don't. Please don't judge me too harshly."

Again, I asked, "Who is your father?" Red Sparrow was silent. He stood up. I stood up beside him to listen to his answer. We were right by the riverbank. The current was very strong there with lots of rapids and rocks. Red Sparrow looked at me and gave me his father's name. "His name is Red Bear," he said. I looked at him. Red Bear's name has been associated with evil deeds for a long time. I felt betrayed that his son would not tell me about him. Red Sparrow grabbed me by my shoulders to hold me. I told him that I could not forgive him for being so devious. I had welcomed him into my village while all the time his father must have been plotting a plan of some sort. Red Sparrow saw my anger. He became very upset and angry.

"I thought you were different than other women I have known. All I have to say is my father's name, and they hate me," he said. "You are just like them. I should throw you in the river. That should make my father happy. He is the only one that cares for me." Then he did the one thing I didn't expect. He kissed me and tried to make love to me. I told him that I didn't feel that way about him. I pushed him away from me to run away. Red Sparrow lost his footing on the slick bank of river. He fell into the river. The next thing I saw was him being carried by the swift current down the river into the rapids.

I panicked and ran back to my tribe. White Owl got some braves and went to look for Red Sparrow. They never found him. They presumed that Red Sparrow was dead. When Red Bear heard that I had killed his son, he wanted revenge. He told everyone that he just didn't want me dead. He wanted me to suffer. He has been after me ever since.

The Red Woman sent me word that Red Bear has escaped. They had captured him. They could not hold him. . As he was escaping, he issued a challenge to me. He knew if the Red Woman had heard the challenge, she must honor it. The Red Woman cannot stop a challenge once it is given. That is why Red Bear will be waiting for me and David at the Roaring River Falls tonight at midnight. David is to see that I come alone. None of you must come with me. This is a fight to the end. Only one of us will live."

Lo Ming asked, "Why is David to come with you?" "It is simple. David is the opposite of Red Sparrow. David is Red Bear's eldest son. Red Bear knows that he will follow his instructions. David will see that it is a fair fight. David is to witness that it was fair. Red Bear also knows that David will not kill him because Red Bear is his father."

I looked at the group. "I know what you are thinking. Why don't we all just go and kill Red Bear. It doesn't work that way here. When a challenge is given from one medicine man to another, nobody can intervene. It is written in the stars that June must face her enemy. So be it, we will head for the Roaring River Falls. Let's get on the trail. Red Bear will be waiting."

Everyone silently packed their things and put the equipment on the mules. We rode out in single file. I put David in the lead. He knew these mountains as well as I did. He played here as a boy. I could tell that the others in our group were not happy with the situation with Red Bear. They understood it. They were warriors and understood the ways of warriors. I knew they were surprised to find out about David being Red Bear's son. They looked at David a little bit differently. It didn't take much thinking to reach the conclusion that David must have powers that he inherited from his ancestors.

We reached a good campsite about dusk near the Roaring River Falls. I had everyone set up camp. We ate, talking very little. We were worried about June. The moon had risen over the mountains. There was a chill in the air. We sat and watched the flames of our campfire. I looked at my watch. I nodded to David. He got up. June had changed into a white buckskin dress covered with precious gems. Rose had braided June's hair. Mary gave June a necklace with diamonds and jade. Mary told her that it would help protect her.

June and David left for the falls shortly after that. Lo Ming, Moses and Nick saluted her. Antonio did something unusual for him. He pulled out a golden ring. He said, "One Feather gave me this for you. He wanted me to give this to you if I thought you were in trouble. It will give you strength." June kissed Antonio and let him put it on her finger. I went over to June. I gave her a hug and whispered into her ear. "Don't worry, the spirits are on your side. I will see you when you come back. Now go with the great spirit."

We could only wait for them to come back. David led June to the clearing near the waterfalls. The noise from the falls made it easy to find. When they arrived there, Red Bear was at the other end of the clearing. There were several poles with torches burning to give the clearing light.

David sensed that this was a trap. He could feel two other warriors near. "I thought that this was to be a fair fight," he yelled at Red Bear. "Now, you know me. I am your father. June is a great medicine woman. I will defeat her but just in case I don't, I want her dead. They will see to that," he replied back to David. "Well father, I know you. I brought along some of my friends," he laughed. David motioned. One by one, we appeared around the clearing with our weapons. "You see. This will be a fair fight. If your men make a move to help you, they will kill you and your associates."

"My son, I always knew you had a little of my blood in you. I expected nothing less. You can't blame an old man for trying," laughed Red Bear. "Now let's get this started. The night is cold." Red Bear walked to the center of the clearing. Red Bear was dressed in his best ceremonial clothes. The clothes were of a great medicine man. June moved to face him.

"We do not have to do this," June said. "Oh yes, we do," replied Red Bear. Red Bear moved his hand. He started to strike a blow of lightning toward June. The lightning bolts just died in his hands. He looked startled. A painted pony appeared from the forest with a young woman on it. "No, you don't have to do this," she said.

She was dressed in red buckskins with a full headdress of eagle feathers. She rode into the center of the clearing. She carried in her right arm a white wooden warrior's lance with eagle feathers attached to the whole length of it. "I have come with a message from the Great Spirits. This must stop at once. We know that Red Bear made a sacred oath to his mentor, Grey Fox, to stop anyone from obtaining the sacred books. It was Grey Fox who hid the books. Red Bear was his student. Even though Red Bear did know where the books were hidden, he was to protect them at all costs from others. That was Grey Fox's dying wish.

Things are different now. We had decided to strike your sacred pledge to Grey Fox. Red Bear, you have followed your pledge to Grey Fox with honor. It is now time for you to stop. You must do the opposite. We suggest you assist **The Keepers of the Yawi** to find the books."

Red Bear asked, "Why should I do that? I have lost a son to them. June killed my son." "No, Red Bear, your actions and deeds killed your son. June was only trying to get away from Red Sparrow when he fell into the river. Your son was misguided. You never taught him how to handle rejection. He had trouble with right and wrong. He did June wrong. Because your son was so misguided in his thoughts, we didn't let him die. We wanted to save him from the sins of his father. We took him and sent him to The Land of Nightmares. If you ever want to correct your wrongs, you will go with them and face your son and tell him. If June believes that your son has changed for the better, she can release him from his captivity. If she does not believe he has repented, he will remain there for eternity. The choice is yours. What will it be, Red Bear?' the young woman asked.

Red Bear had tears in his eyes. "I have lost my way. I was not a good father to my sons. I had one son, David, run away from me because he hated what I had become. My other son, Red Sparrow, has become like me. I will accept your wise and gracious offer. I will follow **The Keepers of the Yawi**. That is all I can say, I will pledge my life to them. My pledge is my bond. As I have shown to my mentor, Grey Fox," said

Red Bear. Red Bear knelled on the ground and lifted his arms to the sky to show respect to the Great Spirits.

The young woman on the painted pony took her lance. She threw it at the ground in front of Red Bear. "This is Grey Fox's war lance. It is to show you that he honors you and respects you. Your men must leave here and go home. You must go back to John's camp and smoke the peace pipe with all of them. Red Bear, it is time for you to come home," said the young woman.

The painted pony reared up on her back legs. The painted pony leaped into the sky. It disappeared with its rider into the dark night's sky. Red Bear got up slowly. He took turns nodding his head to everyone there as a sign of respect and service to them.

David said to his father, "I did not know about your pledge to Grey Fox. I could have looked at things differently. All I knew was that my father was doing evil things. He had disgraced my family. Maybe I should have talked to you. Maybe, we could have stopped what you became. What I have witnessed today has changed much of my opinion of you. To go against your tribe and fellow braves is exceedingly difficult. I am not one to judge you. Now, I understand why you did some of the things in the past. I have done some of those things myself. It will take time for me to adjust to this. It will take some time for me to welcome you as a father. The Great Spirits are wise. Now, it is time for you to come home."

June and Red Bear walked back to our campsite. We and Red Bear followers followed them. When we arrived at our campsite, we were met by White Elk. He held a peace pipe in his hands. The pipe stem was made from a thigh bone from a large deer with a fired river clay for the bowl. The bowl was in the shape of an eagle head. Attached to the bone stem were eagle feathers. Several animal shapes were decorated on the stem with stars and planets.

White Elk had June and Red Bear stand between him. He had the rest of us sit in a semi-circle around the sacred campfire. White Elk had put white sage on the fire. White Elk explained the peace pipe ceremony. "The white sage was added to the sacred fire. White sage purifies and cleanses the body and spirit of negative energy and thoughts. The smoke of the sage attaches itself to negative energy and carries it away with it. Then the negative energy was recycled into positive energy. Sage was very important to the peace pipe ceremony.

The peace pipe was the link between the physical, Mother Earth with the spiritual, Father Sky. The peace pipe was prayers in physical form. The smoke becomes our words. It goes out and touches everything and becomes a part of all that was. The fire in the pipe was the same fire in the sun which is the source of all life. The reason why tobacco was used is to connect the worlds. The tobacco plant's roots grow deep into the earth, and its smoke rises high into the heavens."

White Elk loaded tobacco that was mixed with several herbs and willow bark. "This tobacco was from a tobacco plant that is much stronger than what white men use. It is said that nobody could become violent or disruptive from smoking it. It would bring peace and calm to whoever smokes or inhales its smoke."

White Elk had everyone seated in a cross-legged fashion. White Elk took a twig and lit it from the sacred fire in front of him.   He lights the pipe. He points the peace pipe to the west. The west is the power of the spirit. He then points the pipe to the east. The east is the power of the rising sun. It brings knowledge. He turns the pipe to the north. Its powers are endurance, strength and honesty. He turns the pipe to the south. Its powers bring bounty, great medicine and growth.

White Elk points and touches the pipe to the earth to be acknowledged by Mother Earth. He says, "Mother Earth, I seek to protect you." Then he holds the pipe toward the sky. He says, "O, Great Spirit, I thank you for the six powers of the universe. " Lastly, he holds the pipe up to the Great Spirit.

"We are here to send our prayers of peace to the Great Creator and Great Spirits. The smoke of each of these two enemies will carry their prayers of peace to the Great Creator and Great Spirits. Their prayers of peace cannot be broken when they smoke the pipe of peace. That is the promise of those participating in this ceremony." White Elk gave the peace pipe to Red Bear. He took a puff and blew it out quickly, His smoke carried to the sky above him. Then he pointed the peace pipe to the sky. White Elk took the pipe and gave it to June. She took a puff and blew it out quickly. Her smoke carried to the sky above. She then pointed the stem of the peace pipe toward the sky to carry her prayers of peace.

"Red Bear represents himself and his followers. June represents herself and **The Keepers of the Yawi**. They have agreed to peace between them and their followers," said White Elk. "In the east, the sun rises. In the west, the sun sets. In the north, snow comes to cover the earth and cleanse it. In the south, the wind blows the warmth that starts the cycle of life. Mother earth brings us life. Father sky carries our prayers. This is our life that we share for our short time here. May peace between these two great medicine men and their people be forever."

The sacred fire rose high above its hearth. There were the sounds of drums beating and ancient flutes singing their songs of peace. Above the fire, the young woman that was on the painted pony appeared. She floated in the air. "To have unity among you, David must smoke the pipe of peace with his father, Red Bear."

David stood up and walked over to take the peace pipe from White Elk. He looked at Red Bear, his father. He took a puff from the pipe and let it float out of his mouth toward Red Bear. He sat down next to Red Bear.

The young woman nodded her head as to bless the ceremony. "So be it. I will take your prayers and go to the Great Spirits and Great Creator with them". She turned into a bald eagle and flew up into the sky. When the fire died down, White Elk was gone.

"Come and eat together, I have fixed you food to eat. White Elk told me to come with food. You must all eat together. You need to rejoice in your peace," said Morning Star. Nobody ever asked Morning Star how she got there. There were lots of food that Morning Star had spread on some blankets. Red Bear took some cornbread and broke it. He gave it to June to eat. June took some of it and gave it to Red Bear. They both ate it at the same time. Everyone looked at the sky. Shooting stars lit up the sky. It was a sign that the Great Creator and Great Spirits were pleased.

Morning came too early. When we got up, there was fresh food waiting for us. Morning Star was gone. David saw his father, Red Bear, sleeping on the ground between David and Mary's tents. Red Bear asked if Mary was his grandchild. David nodded. "I knew that she was. I also know that Little Wolf is my great grandchild. David, my son, I have much to catch up on. I only wonder how this is going to turn out. I sense that many of the people here have much on their minds. They are unsettled about what to do. I will send my followers back to my people. They will have orders to join Black Panther and his tribe and come and help us. Do you have a fresh horse for me to ride? My horse is very tired and worn down," asked Red Bear.

"He doesn't, but I do," I told him. "Well John, I do appreciate that. This must be difficult for you. We have fought for many circles of the sun over the books. You have lost many people, and so have I. I am at your service. I take my pledge very seriously," said Red Bear. I looked at Red Bear and David, "It won't matter unless we get *The Book of Winter.* All will be lost if we should fail in this mission," I replied. "We both have very good reasons to succeed. I have one son back. I hope to get the other one back. You have **The Land of the Eagle Feathers** to save and your son. I hope that the others are just as motivated as we are, John," pointed out Red Bear. I looked at David and replied, "We all have various reasons to succeed. Don't we, David?" David never answered my question. He smiled and got him something to eat.

   We got saddled up and left about an hour later. I let Red Bear lead us back to the entrance tunnel to **The Land of the Eagle Feathers**. Moses asked me why I let Red Bear and David lead us. I told Moses because I could watch both David and Red Bear that way. Moses laughed, "That reminds me of an old saying: Keep your friends close and your enemies closer." Moses nodded his head in approval.

   We arrived at the tunnel's entrance about two hours before dark. Angela was waiting at the entrance. She looked tired and hungry. Her left arm had a big bandage on it. Antonio jumped off his horse and ran to her. She gave him a big kiss and hug. "I see you survived. How is Shanna?" I asked. "I guess she is fine. I will tell you more later. I see you captured Red Bear," Angela stated. "Not really, he is one of us now. It's a long story. I will tell you later," I told her. "That should be some story," replied Angela.

   I told everyone to dismount. "We will be taking our horses and mules into the land this time. Angela will be going with us," I told them.   Antonio went over and looked at the symbols inscribed in the rock. He said the inscription out loud. The entrance opened. We led our horses and mules inside. We would be camping on the other side of the tunnel.

Angela would give us a briefing tonight after supper. That should be an interesting story.

Chapter III
Back in The Land of the Eagle Feathers
Will Angela and David be welcomed?

It didn't take long to reach the end of the entrance tunnel. We camped for the night by a hot spring at the end of a big grassy field. Everyone got to work. It didn't take long to set up camp. I gave Red Bear one of our extra tents that was stored in a supply box. Rose helped Red Bear set up the tent. She gave him a blanket to sleep on. Angela didn't need a tent. She would be sleeping with her lover, Antonio.

Moses and Lo Ming gathered firewood for the campfire. Nick rubbed his hands together, and a flame shot out from them and started the wood on fire. Mary and David went out to gather some walnuts and hickory nuts. Nick and Rose started the evening meal. He made a stew out of jerky, wild potatoes and carrots. Rose took some flour and made some fried flatbread to go with it. David and Mary returned with several wild winter squash, walnuts and hickory nuts. Nick cut open the squash and cooked them on the coals of the fire. David and Mary cracked the walnuts and hickory nuts and took out the nut meat.

Moses and Antonio picketed the horses and mules after letting them graze on the last of the fall grass. Rose yelled for everyone to come to supper. It seemed everyone had a large appetite. It wasn't long before all the food was gone.

It would take Angela some time to get used to Red Bear being on our side. Antonio and she ate together as far away from Red Bear and David as they felt comfortable. When everyone was finished with supper, they sat down around the campfire. It was starting to get a little chilly at night. The fire felt good. It cut the chill of the coming night.

Angela got up to talk about what happened to their group of Benita, Raven and Shanna. Angela started her story. "I assume you know from David what happened after you left. Shanna and I greeted Benita and Raven like we were old friends. That's hard to do when dealing with those two. Benita loved being in charge. David did a good job of convincing Benita that he loved her. Raven was more than a little jealous. If looks could kill, David would have been the first to go.

After David left, Benita started barking out orders. She had everyone on the trail in less than 30 minutes. I can't help it. I must say I was impressed. Shanna and I took the lead. I told them to hold the main force of 20 warriors about one half mile behind us. Raven and Benita did as they were told. I think if Raven and Benita had their way, they would have left their warriors behind. You could see that they wanted blood and a good fight.

We traveled up the main trail until it started to get dark. Shanna found a good spot to camp by a mountain stream. We had boulders on every side of us to give us protection from any enemy. We didn't light a fire to cook or keep warm. Benita put up two guards in front on boulders and in back. We camped in the middle of all the boulders.

We ate our rations. Shanna and I set up one tent. We figured that we could stay warmer that way. It started to snow. It was a wet, cold snow. Benita gave orders to the Captain of the Guard to assign guard duty. It was a miserable cold night. Benita and Raven stayed in the same tent. They must have stayed pretty warm. They seemed to talk a lot or something like talking. Shanna seemed to get along well with both of them.

Late that night around midnight, one of the guards reported seeing a woman dressed in a woman's Indian dress in front of our position. There was a young Indian male with her. When they sent two warriors to investigate, they found nothing. Not a single track was found. This made the warriors a little concerned. Surely, they would have found some tracks in the soft three inches of snow. The men started talking about Indian spirits and other things.

Shanna and I left camp at first light. Raven and Benita left an hour later with their warriors. The wet snow made traveling difficult. You would take one step forward and slide two steps backward. We were worried that this would make an ambush easier for our enemy. It was about noon when were first located two of Kamir's men. They were hiding behind some boulders and cedars off the trail about 200 hundred yards ahead of us.

Shanna had an idea. She would go back and tell Benita and Raven where Kamir's two men were. She knew that Benita and Raven would come quickly. I made sure to keep the location of the men in case they moved. Shanna told me that Benita and Raven couldn't wait to come up and fight. Soon, they left their men behind and came up to my position. I pointed out the location of the two men to them. Benita wanted to take the man that had moved to the left side of the trail behind a large boulder. Raven wanted to take the man on the right side of the trail behind two large fallen cedar trees.

I told them to be my guest. I also told them to watch out for an ambush. It was starting to snow again very hard. I could not see behind the men. I felt that they had made it too easy for us to locate them. Shanna told them the same thing. Benita watched and waited for an hour before deciding to take out the men ahead of us. I knew that Benita and Raven would be too impatient to wait it out.

When Benita and Raven left us, Shanna told me that we should be ready for an ambush. She could see better than me. She pointed out that four other men were waiting covered up with snow about 100 yards ahead of us. It must have been Shanna's training with Special Operations that made her able to see what I could not. Shanna told me to go to the right side into the brush. She would go to the left side. We would back up Benita and Raven when the men would spring the ambush.

I moved up into the thick brush on the right side of the trail walking very carefully. I had pulled out my short sword to be ready when the combat would begin. I must say both Raven and Benita was very skilled in stalking their prey. Raven was holding a Roman short soldier's sword. Shanna was following on the left side of the trail using evergreen trees as cover. She had her throwing knives at the ready. Benita had a crossbow and a long dagger in her belt.

Benita signaled for Raven to stop. Raven was about 20 feet from her man. Taking aim with the crossbow, she let her arrow fly. The arrow silently hit her target in the neck. He could not even cry out. He fell silently into the four inches of snow dead. Raven, not to be outdone, ran and jumped on her man. She cut his throat with one stroke of her sword. He, too, fell dead. Before Benita and Raven could congratulate each other, the four men sprang their trap.

Jumping up behind them with their long swords raised, they attacked Benita and Raven. I yelled at them to turn around. Benita had not reloaded her crossbow. One warrior was closing on Benita. Benita didn't have a chance. The tall warrior swung his sword at Benita. To Benita's surprise, the tall warrior missed and fell dead at her feet. He had Shanna's throwing knife sticking in the middle of his back. Another warrior dressed in white was closing in on Benita. He swung his sword. Benita was able to block it with her crossbow.

Benita took out her dagger in one swift motion and stabbed the attacker through the heart.

The two warriors that were after Raven were on her. I jumped on one and soon had a sword fight on my hands. Raven turned and faced the last warrior with her sword. I was too busy with my opponent to watch how Raven was doing. Shanna later told me that Raven and the other warrior had a great sword fight. It took both of us a few minutes to dispatch our foes. When we got through killing them, Raven and Shanna applauded us. Benita went over to Raven and gave her a kiss. "You are a great swordswoman," she told Raven. Raven smiled and replied to Benita, "You are pretty good with that Scottish Dagger."

Then they did something out of character. They both thanked us for helping them. I looked at both and said, "I knew you two would get the job done. We just helped a little. It was a great pleasure to see both of you in action. You are very skilled. I suggest we go and set up camp for tonight. The snow is too heavy to go on today. Our enemy will probably be waiting for us in the morning further up the trail. I think I know just the spot they will be waiting for us." Benita agreed, and we went down the trail. We set up camp in a small grove of cedars about 50 yards off the trail.

That night about dusk, Raven pointed out to Benita that she saw something that she couldn't believe. Raven thought we saw David's wife, Donna, up the trail from us through the heavy snow. Benita laughed at Raven. Benita sent two of her men up the trail to check it out. Again, they came back to tell Benita and Raven that they could not find anything, not even a single track. Benita looked at me and said, "Angela, I know that you said you and your men killed Donna several years ago." I replied back, "Yes, I did. I got several small scars to prove it." I pulled down my jacket and showed her the small scars on my left side just below my bare left breast. I noticed that Raven and Benita took their time looking at them. Benita even touched them to see if they were real.

Benita decided to go up the trail herself and check it out. She took Raven with her. They came back about 30 minutes later. Both were upset. They thought they had seen Donna, David's dead wife, with a young Indian brave.

I immediately drew my sword and started to swing at Raven and Benita. Shanna blocked my swing with one of her throwing knives. Raven and Benita had their weapons out. I ran and jumped over a small cliff into a large fir tree. I fell down the tree about 50 feet below. I played dead. Before Raven and Benita could try and get to me, I got lucky, and a small avalanche rolled down the mountain. I was able to use it to run away and cover my tracks. The boulders and snow covered up where they thought I was located by over thirty feet of snow and rock.

From where I hid, I could hear, Benita and Shanna thanking Shanna for saving their lives. Shanna told them, "I thought Antonio and Angela couldn't be trusted. Angela must have saved Donna to have her help her obtain the sacred books. I know David thought his wife was dead. He told me so. He said that he was lucky to have found another wife that he could trust. He felt that you, Benita, was the woman he could trust.

Don't worry, I won't say anything about you and Raven. Benita, I don't blame you. Raven is a beautiful woman. You know me, I have done things for you in the past. I am loyal to you because you have always paid me well. Let's just keep it that way, David is your problem not mine." Benita replied to Shanna, "You are very wise, Shanna. Your discretion has always been your strong suit." I could hear Raven say, "Why don't you join us in our tent tonight?" I couldn't hear Shanna's answer.

I followed Benita and her warriors the next day. With Shanna's help, they killed all of Kamir's men except for one. He escaped. They captured Red Bear and his two followers. They decided to take Red Bear and his two followers back with them. That's when Donna and One Feather helped them to escape.

Benita and Raven were satisfied that Red Bear and his two followers would not be in a position to be any danger to us. Shanna told them they should be getting back down the mountain before the weather turned any worse. They left after burying the dead men and went back to the train station. I could tell that Raven and Benita now trusted Shanna. They let Shanna lead them back. I think David's plan is working out fine."

Antonio motioned for Angela to sit by him. Angela whispered in his ear to control himself. She would join him later. She had some other things to do. Out of the darkness, the Red Woman and One Feather walked into the firelight. The Red Woman spoke to everyone, "I have come to give each of you an invitation to our Potlatch except for Red Bear, Angela and David. They must meet with the Great Elder before going any further in **The Land of the Eagle Feathers.**

For you that don't know what a Potlatch is, I will inform you. The Potlatch is a major Native American ceremony. It is usually held in the winter months. This year it will be held in your honor. It is a ceremony where possessions are given and distributed throughout the tribe. There will be a feast, storytelling, gift giving and entertainment. It is a great honor to be invited to our Potlatch. Finally, after the festival activities are over, you will be meeting with the Great Elder and our Council. I will explain more when we reach our village."

Antonio looked at Angela. He was worried about her meeting with the Great Elder. Angela had told him that The

Great Elder had forbid her from ever coming back here. She had disobeyed him by leaving this land without permission.

The Red Woman pointed to Angela and told her to go to the big Red Oak tree at the far end of the field. Sit down cross legged near a fire One Feather built there. The Great Elder will meet you there. She told Red Bear and David they would have to wait their turn to see The Great Elder. The Red Woman's news didn't come as a surprise to Red Bear or David. They suspected something like this. They would wait.

I told the rest of the group to rest and relax. "There won't be any need for us to have a watch. We are safe here in this land. I know you are tired. I suggest that you get cleaned up tonight and bathe in the pool. In a supply box over there, are some scented soaps and detergent to clean your clothes if they need it. It is an honor to attend the Potlatch. You should look your best. If you want more privacy, there are two more hot springs further down the field to the right of one I showed you late today. The night is warm. Take advantage of it."

I looked at Mary. "We didn't finish our talk. I know a place where we can finish our talk. Nobody will disturb us. Get your clothes and follow me. Don't worry, I won't do anything." The stars and planets were bright in the night's sky. The moon was a dark red. It felt like all you had to do was reach high enough and you could touch the moon. Mary stubbornly grabbed some of her clothes, a towel and washcloth and joined me. I had put some on my best clothes in a bag. I motioned for her to follow me. Mary looked at me saying, "Don't worry, I won't hurt you tonight. Tomorrow may be another story."

It took Angela about 20 minutes to get to the big Red Oak tree. She sat down cross legged by the fire. It wasn't long before the Great Elder walked out of the shadows. He seated himself across the fire from her. "I see that you came alone," he said to her. "Yes, I can do as I am told," she said back to him. "It has been a very long time since we have talked last. I have felt you come and go into this land. You are a hard woman to figure out. Don't worry, I will not punish you. I forgave you long ago when you saved the Red Woman. You are very courageous. It almost cost you everything to save her. I understand you still have the scars from that. Do I trust you? The answer is No. Perhaps, a little time in our village will change you. You are welcome to attend the Potlatch. Now, go before I change my mind. Antonio is waiting for you. I hope you and Antonio change your plans. I will be upset if you don't. When you get back, tell David to come to see me." said the Great Elder.

Angela didn't reply to the Great Elder. She thought to herself, "It's just like him. He never has changed. You can never get a final word with him. She didn't care. Tonight, she would be with the one she loved. The only thing that mattered to her was Antonio and her being together. There was a special place for them that she knew. She would take him there. It was a hidden hot spring with soft mossy banks. It would also cure her cut arm. She would take the lead in their lovemaking. Antonio was a good lover. She knew she was much better.

It wasn't long before David reached the big Red Oak tree. The Great Elder was seated by the fire across from him. "It is good to see you again. I thought I had lost you to the evil side of things. You must be mad and angry at me for not telling you that your wife was alive. If I had told you, your destiny would not be fulfilled. I knew your anger at your loss would turn to action. You have destroyed many great tribes and secret organizations that would have come to destroy this land," said the Great Elder.

David looked into the Great Elder's eyes. "I went to the outside world to save this land. More than just save this land, I wanted to save my family's name. My father had become an evil man. I know that wasn't always the case. In his own way, he thought he was saving this land from those that wanted to get the books. I guess, you never know what to think. We sat across from each other. I do understand your reason. What I don't understand is why you have treated John so harshly? I had my reasons for hating John. You did not have any reasons. He was only a man trying to help you and our tribe. Don't get me wrong, I have not forgiven John for what he did to my daughter. He should have left her alone. He was old enough to know better."

"You are right. It is somewhat my fault. I sent John to assist your daughter in the great Southeastern Desert. What I didn't tell John was who he was helping? I thought he wouldn't help Mary if he knew who she was. John has traveled many places in his lifetime. I was foolish to let him help Mary find the artifact that protected our land. His wife had died many years ago at Wounded Knee along with his children. He was lonely and lost. Your daughter was a very naïve young lady. As you know, the desert can have effects on one's judgement. I will only say one thing more about him. Losing one wife is terrible, but to lose another great love has more pain than anyone could bear.

After he lost Mary, he went crazy. He did many things through time travels. Some of them were for good, while some not so good. Somehow, he survived it all. Don't take John so lightly. He is a dangerous man. Through the years, White Elk had taught him many things. He had also learned from others. He has a great following among the tribes of the world. This is his only home. He will not let anyone destroy it.

He knows he is dying. That makes him dangerous to both of us. He has nothing to lose. I fear I don't trust him. He has other agendas. He has two weaknesses. One is Mary, and the other is Little Wolf, his son. If anyone gets in the way of either, he will not hesitate to kill. He knows if he kills anyone here, he will die before the new Indian year comes. That won't stop him from killing anyone to protect them. After all, he has nothing to lose. He has seen more death and killed more than anyone should ever have been allowed. It is his destiny. Think about what I have said. Then you will know what to do with John, your grandson's father. You must go to the Potlatch. You might learn something. Your heart can be very cold. That is why I picked you. You might be the only one that can save us from what John is planning! Now tell Red Bear, your father, to come see me."

Red Bear was very nervous when he sat down to face the Great Elder. "Don't say anything to me. You have lost your way. I am glad you have found your way back. Destiny has a life of its own. I have an assignment for you if you accept it. I want you to promise that if you think John is out of line and needs to be stopped, you will finish him with the help of your son and the Red Woman. This will be difficult because nobody knows what John is planning to do with *The Book of Winter.* I think he will do right. Other council members are not so sure, even the Great Spirits are unsure. What do you say, Red Bear?" asked the Great Elder.

Red Bear took his time to think. "I will do anything to get the chance to get my youngest son back. John is very powerful. He has nothing to lose. That makes him an extremely dangerous man. Why choose me for such a thing, Great Elder?" asked Red Bear. "It is simple. You are a very loyal man to a fault. Grey Fox knew that, and I know that. What do you say, Red Bear?" "There is another matter. What do I do to the others if they are a danger to us?" asked Red Bear.

"You will stop them too, Red Bear," said the Great Elder. Red Bear thought about it . He answered the Great Elder the only way he could. He could only nod his head in agreement.

"Then it is settled. You will accompany them to the Potlatch and then to The Land of Nightmares. Only you, David and the Red Woman will know your mission," said the Great Elder. Red Bear left the Great Elder with as many questions in his head as answers. Red Bear knew only one thing: things were getting out of hand. Red Bear gathered his thoughts. He had to answer one question. Who is the greatest danger to **The Land of the Eagle Feathers**? It took him only a few minutes to decide the answer to that question.

Mary was somewhat relieved that she was not at the camp. She was having a hard time seeing David and the Red Woman, her parents together. Her mind was blank. She didn't remember anything about her mother. It was like someone had erased her from her mind.

The moonlight was bright enough that John and Mary could see well enough without a torch or flashlight. The Milky Way flowed like a river of stars in the night's sky above them. The lonely howl of two wolves could be heard in the distance. Mary smiled. She knew that June and One Feather had released their wolves to be together. Midnight and Snow were singing their love song. That meant that One Feather and June must be together. Mary was happy for them. To be in love and to be so young must be a wonderful feeling. Mary wondered if she ever felt that way toward John. Tonight, she would try to find out. Maybe something would jar her memory of them together.

John took Mary by the hand. He told her that there was a special place that he used to go to be at peace. It was not easy to get to because of boulders and brush. Mary reluctantly took hold of John's hand. She was surprised how big his hand felt to hers. It was warm and strong. His hand made her feel safe. She could feel his rapid heartbeat. She laughed out loud. John looked back at her. "What is so funny, Mary?" John said. "I must be having an effect on you. Your heart is beating so fast. It is like you are nervous being around me," Mary replied.

John didn't say anything. Mary knew she had more control over this situation. John must had been deeply in love with her once. Judging by his heartbeat and nervousness, Mary knew he must still be. She wondered how long it took John to realize who she was. After her accident in the Amazon, she had a facelift. She was told by her father that she looked completely different from before her accident. Mary had never seen a picture of herself before the accident. Her father and stepmother, Benita, had all pictures of her destroyed. They said that it would be easier for her not to know what she used to look like. They were probably right.

It took about 30 minutes to arrive at John's secret place. There was a small waterfall about 10 feet high. Below the waterfall was a crystal-clear pool of water. She couldn't believe that the fall flowers were still in full bloom. They covered all the ground and boulders that hid this place. There was a path of smooth round stones that led around the pool to the base of the waterfalls. Night birds sang in the trees. The grass was still green from the mist of the falls.

"I know what you are thinking, Mary. Is this place real? It is like something out of a fairy tale. I hope you read some when you were little. I come here sometimes to think about what I have done in my long life. I am not a saint by any means. Tonight, I want you to experience some peace. You deserve some. This short year has given you much to think about. The warm spring that feeds the waterfall and pool is said to have healing powers. Not so much physical healing powers, but more to heal your soul. You must be wondering where the light is coming from that gives this place its special glow. The stones on the walking path are called Glow Stones," I said.

Mary looked at me. "This place is like a fairy tale scene. I like it. I can see why you do. It is too bad that my life hasn't been much like a fairytale except that I have a wicked stepmother. John, I am not a little girl in a fairytale. I am a grown woman."

"Yes, I know. You are a very lovely woman. You are strong willed. You are more than you will ever know. Your parents are very powerful. This means that you must have those powers and more. I hope you someday find what you are looking for. We are both different from what we were. I am sorry that I can't help you more. I am going to leave you here. I will be back in a few hours. Enjoy the warm waters. If you get tired and want to sleep, there are some blankets and towels in my bag," I told her. "Oh, there is one thing more. See those beautiful red and blue flowers over there, they are very powerful. It is said that if you smell their scent, they will take you on a journey of discovery."

"What do you mean by that?" Mary asked. "It takes you on your journey. That is all the Red Woman would tell me. She is the one that took me to this place many years ago. She said that this place could cure me of many things. I must say it did help. It never cured me of one thing," I replied to her. "What was that?" asked Mary. "One day, I will tell you," I answered back. I turned and left Mary standing there. It was up to her to find out more. You can lead a horse to water, but you can't make it drink.

Mary watched John walk down the stony path until he was out of sight. She turned around and took a good look. She could feel the mystical energy of this place. It tingled in her body. She opened the bag that John left. In it was a bar of scented soap. The scent of the soap was familiar. She had smelled this scent before.

A memory slowly formed as she stared into the pool of water. The movement of the water from the falling water sparkled and danced across the pool in the moonlight. In the pool, a vision formed. A little girl about 5 years old was playing with her mother in a beautiful flower garden. The mother's face was away from Mary. She couldn't see the mother's face. "I wish we could be this happy forever," the mother said. The little girl laughed and said, "Yes, mother, I would like that." The vision faded into the pool. Mary could feel the warmth of the mother's love for her daughter. It felt strange to Mary. Mary had not felt such a feeling for a long time.

Mary decided to take a shower and a long bath in the pool. She tested the water. It was warm. The night air was a little cool to her skin as she took off her clothes. She walked into the pool. She was surprised that the end of the pool by the waterfalls was shallow only about six inches in depth. She walked into the fall's water. It felt warm and silky on her bare skin. She took the soap and covered her body and hair with its rich white suds. The feeling of being free from any restraints and cares was amazing. Slowly she walked into the waterfalls and stood. The water gently flowed down her hair and then her body. She could feel each drop against her body. It was like each drop washed some care away from her.

She liked the feeling of the warm water contrasting with the cool mountain air against her body. Taking a few steps back from the waterfalls, she settled herself down into the warm pool. She had never felt so relaxed. After lying in the water for several minutes, she got out of the pool. She took a towel and dried her body with it. She put a blanket on the grass by the pool.

She was curious about the beautiful flowers that John had pointed out. She plucked one of the blooms from the flowers. She sat down on the blanket. Carefully she put the bloom to her nose. Taking a deep breath, she inhaled the scent of the bloom. She became very sleepy. Lying down, she fell fast asleep. The dreams came. The visions came. A hand reached out, and she took it. She followed a young woman into a dream world. Her journey had begun.

Mary wanted to ask the young woman in front of her several questions. The young woman led Mary to two long tunnels. One tunnel had a sign on it. Mary could read most Indian signs. The first tunnel indicated that it was The Tunnel of The Past. The second tunnel indicated it was The Tunnel of the Future. The young lady said in Cherokee, "You can only go into The Tunnel of the Past. Your future has not been settled by the Great Spirits. You can only go in for a few minutes. You will not learn everything about your past. This is only the beginning of your journey. Be careful, your mind will only take so much. Now, go. May the spirits be with you."

Mary took a few steps. Suddenly the young woman pushed her all the way into the tunnel. An invisible force pulled her down the tunnel. Far in front of Mary, she could see some bright light. The force speeded up. In a blink of an eye, the force pushed her into a room. On the walls were several pictures. Walking very carefully, Mary tiptoed over to the first picture. She recognized one of the people in the picture was David. The young woman looked familiar, but she couldn't tell who she was. After looking closer at the picture, she could see that it was like a movie. You could watch it. The subjects of the picture moved from one picture in the room to another.

In the first picture, there was a baby crib. The young mother had picked up the baby and was holding it. David was standing there by the young mother. He bent down and kissed both mother and baby. Mary looked at the young mother's dress. There was a symbol of a wolf and a moon on it. The woman had dark hair and a dark complexion. The woman seemed to know that Mary was watching. She looked at Mary and mouthed the word, "You." Mary knew instantly that the young woman was her mother, Donna. The Red Woman seemed very proud of her newborn.

On the next wall was another picture. It was of a little girl playing with her mother in a beautiful mansion. David had just come home. He looked worried. It appeared they were arguing about something.

On the next wall was another picture. It was of a newspaper's front page. The heading on the front page of the newspaper said, "Young mother dies in Wreck: Car leaves Road into a Lake. Below that picture was a picture of a young girl crying for her mother with David holding her crying."

On the other wall was a picture of a couple getting married. Mary looked at that picture very carefully. It was David marrying Benita. A little girl was crying for her mother. Benita was looking at the camera. Benita's face said it all. She was frowning. Benita was looking a David's daughter.

On the right-side wall was a picture of a young woman lying in a hospital bed. There was caption that said, "Young Woman Shot in Accident: Lies in Coma! Will her baby Survive?" She could make out the newspaper story. It said that the young woman got shot by a stray bullet during a fight between father and daughter's boyfriend. Mary could not make out the face on the woman. She just knew it had to be her.

The young woman appeared to take Mary to another room. It was just down the hall. When they got there, there were only two things in that room. There was a table and chair. On the table were two objects. One was a turquoise necklace trimmed in silver and gold. Mary went over and picked up the beautiful necklace. On the backside of the necklace was an inscription that said, "To Mary, I will always love you! From John"

Next to the necklace was a diamond ring. The ring was an engagement ring. The band was gold and silver with several small black diamonds around its band. The main diamond was nothing like she had ever seen. That diamond was bright red with several white diamonds around it. There was an inscription inside. It said, "Forever." There was a letter next to Forever. The letter was a capital J.

Nobody had to tell her who J was. In her mind, she saw him. Her emotions flooded her. They became too great for her to bear. She woke up crying. I was holding her. I had put a blanket over her nude body. She put her arms around me. All she could do was cry out loud. Memories started to come to her. Some were good of us together. Then one came that changed everything.

Mary pushed me away. I looked at Mary. The only thing I said, "They told me you were dead when I woke up three days later in a nearby hospital with two bullet wounds. They said I went crazy." "What do you mean by crazy?" asked Mary. "I wanted to die. I became a mad man. I did things that I am not proud of. No matter what I did, I couldn't forgive myself. I thought that I had killed you," I said with tears running down my face. "Who shot me and who shot you?" Mary asked. I looked Mary and said, "Your father, David, I can't tell you anymore."

Mary pulled me close to her. She said, "The first time I saw you at the Eagle Train Station. I was drawn to you. I didn't know why. I still don't have my memories straight. I know one thing. I once loved you. I don't know if I can love you. We have a son. You must have loved me very much. I believe you still do. I don't know about us?" Mary said. "I am so lonely and confused. I am a strong woman, but I am human. The only thing I ever wanted was someone to love and love me back. Little Wolf loves us. He told me that late one night. Maybe that is enough for me now."

I looked at Mary. I could tell by her eyes that she was still questioning our relationship. Maybe, she was right. We have Little Wolf. That just might be enough for us now. Mary is trying to find herself. This year has changed everything for her. It would be very selfish of me to renew a relationship.

"It is enough for me. I don't have much time left. This whole thing is not fair to you. Until you find out who you really are, we must put us on hold. I can't even promise you or Little Wolf that I will be there for either of you. You must promise me to take care of our son. In your pack, I put a book with a map. If I die, or live, take the map and follow it. You will find more wealth than David or anyone has ever seen.

It is yours. I have always wondered about us. You were so young, and I was old in so many ways. I want you to be free to do anything you ever dreamed of doing. You don't need your parents. You have a great career. You are a free spirit. Little Wolf is a lot like you. He is smart and learns fast. Like it or not, I know your mother has taught him well.

I left a note to the old man and his dog. They will assist you in getting my wealth to you and Little Wolf." I told her. I don't know why. Mary pulled me to her and kissed me. "Please don't leave. Just hold me for a while. This whole thing is new to me. Your arms around me seem so familiar. I will do as you wish. It will be for our son and not for me," Mary replied. "Yes, I know. You can't promise me anything more," I answered.

The next few hours I held her in my arms as we watched the Milky Way flow by in the late autumn sky. The bright yellow Harvest Moon was slowly traveling toward the morning horizon announcing the change of seasons. "Yes, I see the Harvest Moon. It means that things will be changing. Don't you feel the change coming?" Mary asked. "Yes, it already has started," I softly whispered.   We smiled as we listened to the love song of two wolves howling in the distance as the last of the moon fell below the horizon.

Nick and Rose sat by the campfire. Nick was upset by not having Shanna here. He looked at Rose. Without asking, Rose knew what Nick was thinking. "I know what you are thinking, Nick! You are a good friend. You are lonely for Shanna and worried about her. It didn't stop you thinking about my situation. You are worried about me. You know how it feels to be without the one you love. You know I am lonely and worried about Zan. It is our destiny to help each other. Don't worry about Shanna. She is probably better than both of us at protecting herself. Remember, whatever she does to stay alive, she is doing it for you and me! She knows we are close.

In fact, Shanna made me promise something for her. She asked me to promise to always be there for you if something happened to her. She also said that she would do everything to help me. She knows I am good for you and, that we are good for each other. I made her promise to do the same for Zan if Zorn kills me. You are a lucky man to have Shanna. When she makes a promise, she will keep it even if it kills her. Angela knows that when she saved Antonio. Don't worry, she won't run away if you ask her to marry you. I saw the ring you looked at in your pack the other day. It is beautiful. I know it was your mother's ring," Rose said with a smile.

Nick replied, "Yes, I know. Shanna left me once long ago. I never recovered from that. She is a free spirit. Much like a wild bird, she can't be captured. She must always be free. I don't know if she could settle down with me." Rose laughed at Nick. "Men are so stupid. Nick, you could never settle down. It is your destiny to fly with wild birds. Shanna is like you. She wants something that will never be. I see you two having great adventures together. You settling down is impossible. You only have to tell Shanna that she must be willing to have some company. You both are addicted to adventure. That will be the secret of you two being together the rest of your lives."

"I think you have a harder road than me, Rose. You have not seen Zan for years. I feel you worry. You don't know what to expect. Will Zan still love you after all this time? Will both of you have changed too much? I will tell you a secret. I don't have a crystal ball to tell the future. I am a man. No man would ever forget his love for someone so special as you. Any man that was willing to leave everything for you will always love you. That is why Zan has lived so long in a place that torments him every day."

Rose looked at Nick. "How do you know that, Nick?" she asked. "Because I lived it every day for years. Even one so wonderful as you, couldn't change my feelings. You don't have anything to worry about."

The Red Woman walked towards them. She said she wanted to talk to them. "I have never known two people so close as you and Nick that are not married. You are both special. The Great Spirits are pleased. For that reason, I have a gift for both of you. Because you are great warriors, they will make you spirit warriors for one night. That means you can transport yourselves anywhere tonight. I suggest you waste no more time talking. Go to your tents and I will transport you to your love for this one night. Tomorrow, you will continue on your journey." Rose and Nick stood up and nodded in respect to the Red Woman. She smiled as they ran to their tents.

Rose laid down on her sleeping bag. She could feel electricity within her body. She started to float above her physical body. She looked down, and her body was asleep. The next thing she saw was a floating portal next to her.

She took a step into the portal. The portal sucked her body into it. It was pushing her into space and time. She was moving at light speed. Planets, solar systems and stars went by her. She felt the sensations of being part of the universe. In a few seconds, she found herself standing in a grassy field. It was dark. In the distance she could see volcanos erupting, throwing lava into the air.

Looking around, she saw a man standing by a straw hut. She knew who he was immediately. He was a little bigger than she remembered him. His dark hair had a streak of grey in it. His shoulders were broader and more muscular than she remembered. She ran to meet him. She threw her arms around him. He seemed startled by her. She kissed him passionately. "Rose, is that really you. How did you get here? Hurry, let's go to my hut before anyone sees you," Zan said in disbelief.

When they were safely inside Zan's small wooden and grass hut, he asked again, "How did you get here," "I have a friend. She granted me a special favor to come here," replied Rose. "Is she called the Red Woman?" asked Zan. "Yes, but first let me know how you are," said Rose.

Zan replied, "Well, my father forced me here. They call this place, The Land of Nightmares. This is because every night you have the same dream of being taken away from the one that you love. In my case, it's because of my father being the one that sent me here. You must figure out how to conquer those dreams to get released from here. How my father had the power to send me here, I don't know? He comes back to torment me often. He says that if I recant that I love you and promise not to marry you that he will release me and take me back to New Orleans. No matter what he does to me, I will not do that. I love you so much, Rose.

"Yes, I love you. I have been trying to find a way to get you out of here. I will be back in a few weeks to get you out of here. I have friends that will help me. You must have faith. We will get you out of here," Rose replied back to him.

Zan put his fingers to Rose's lips, "We must be careful. My father may sense you are here. He might try to kill you if he finds you here," Zan whispered to her.

Zan picked her up as if she was a feather. Rose could feel his hard chest muscles and arms as he laid her down on his rope bed with blankets covering it. "How did you get so strong, Zan" she asked. "Life is very hard. Everything that I have, I had to make myself. I cleared this land with my bare hands using tools that I made myself. The garden beside my hut is where I grow my own food. My father laughs at me. He is too powerful for me to fight him. But one day, I will be strong enough to take him. I have been practicing my magic. Every day, I get better. I let my father think I am weak in spirit. It won't be long before I figure out the dreams."

Zan was lying beside Rose. "How have you been?" he asked. Rose started to cry. "Not so good. I have missed you so much. I have a little shop for mystics in New Orleans. Your father comes by once a year to tempt me to try to get me to promise not to love you and not to marry you. I try to throw him out. He is a very strong wizard. He laughs at me and leaves. I tried everything to find you. Finally, I was offered a chance of a lifetime. An invitation was sent to me to join an expedition to **The Land of the Eagle Feathers**. I knew that this was the only way I would ever find you. We are trying to find the last book of the seasons. It is supposed to be somewhere in this land."

Before Rose could say anything more, Zan interrupted. "Yes, I know the story about **The Land of the Eagle Feathers** and the books. It is said that the last book is full of great powers. My father says he and some others have been looking for those books for many years. Nobody had ever found any of the books. How did your group find three of them?"

Rose looked at Zan's eyes, "It wasn't easy. It's a long story. We have only tonight. Let's don't waste it by talking. I want you. I have waited too long for this moment. Rose pulled Zan into her arms as tight as possible. She smiled and said, "What are you waiting for?"

It was about midnight when Nick floated into Angela's apartment. "This must be where Shanna is staying," he thought. As Nick landed on his feet, he looked around the dimly lit apartment. He couldn't help but admire Angela on her taste. The apartment was furnished beautifully. There was some soft mellow music playing in the background. He could hear three female voices talking in the living room. Nobody could see him. He was almost invisible. Only a faint outline of his body could be seen. Using the dark hall to his advantage, he moved carefully to the sound of those voices. Peering around the corner of the living room, he could see Raven, Benita and Shanna seated on the wrap around sofa talking to each other.

Raven and Benita was sitting on the long end of the sofa with Shanna between them. They must have come in from a night of partying at local clubs. They were all dressed to the nines. Nick had to keep from staring. He could not help it. They were all very sexy in their own way. Naturally, he kept his eyes on Shanna. Her dress was very low cut and short. It showed her feminine assets. He hoped that Shanna would get rid of Raven and Benita soon. He felt like a little kid peeking through a window at three lovely girls. It did seem exciting to watch them.

Raven leaned over and whispered something into Shanna's ear. Shanna laughed and whispered something back to Raven. Raven had a wicked smile on her face. Benita must have gotten a little jealous of the attention that Shanna was getting from Raven. Benita then took Shanna and pulled her into her arms and kissed her.

Shanna kissed her back and told both that she needed to think about this. She was afraid that this was getting too complicated. They were both so lovely and sexy. She told them that there was a spare bedroom in the back of the apartment that was very lovely with its own spa. They were welcome to use it.

Shanna pointed to her stomach. "It sometimes bothers me. Besides, I couldn't choose which one of you are the sexiest. You are both such a lovely pair. You are made for each other." Raven and Benita enjoyed her compliment. They told her that they appreciated the offer. Before they could decline her offer, a couple appeared in the hall behind them wearing only white robes.

"Shanna said you were a beautiful couple. We asked if we could be of any assistance to her while she was in town. She told us that she was not feeling well and asked us to be of service to you tonight. We are good friends of hers. We owe her a lot. We will do anything for her," said the blond, curvaceous woman with her companion, a dark tanned male bodybuilder. Benita took a long look at them. You could see that both she and Raven were pleased by what they saw.

"I guess, Shanna, you thought of everything. We accept your invitation to stay. We hope we don't disturb your sleep," Benita smiled. "No, I don't think so. I took some sleeping pills to help me sleep. I hope you enjoy yourselves," Shanna replied to them. Shanna turned and left the room on a run for her bathroom. "Too bad for Shanna, I thought she didn't look well. She will miss the fun," said Raven in her most sexy voice.

Nick had moved to Shanna's bedroom bathroom to hide. Shanna laughed as she entered the spacious bathroom. She didn't notice the faint outline of Nick hiding in the shower. Nick knew that the clear glass of the shower gave him little to hide behind except it did keep him out of anyone's way if they entered the bathroom.

To his surprise, Shanna went over and turned on the shower. She turned to take off what little makeup she had on using the marble vanity. Nick was getting wet. He decided to open the door to the shower very slowly. He took off his wet clothes and shoes very silently. The hot water from the shower caused the mirror to become clouded over. Shanna couldn't see him in the mirror.

Nick stepped back into the shower. Shanna was taking off her clothes to get into the shower. Nick watched her undress. She seemed to take her time. "Boy, was she sexy," he thought. "I am a lucky man." Shanna opened the shower door. She stepped back for a second. She took a long, hard look at the figure in the shower with her.

"I saw you in the mirror above the sofa. I see you liked the little show I put on for you," she said to him. "How did you know I did?" asked Nick. "I don't know how you got here. I don't care. By what I see, you must have enjoyed yourself," she said as she looked below his waist. Nick could only respond, "Be careful, I am faint because I am mostly energy." Shanna pulled his wet body to her and replied, "I hope you got enough energy to last." Nick laughed as he moved his hands over her body, "As you see, I am already up for the occasion."

Rose and Nick arrived back to camp at the same time. They floated down into their bodies. They both woke with smiles on their faces. Nick opened his tent and walked out. Rose was standing by the fire. When their eyes met, they both turned red. They laughed at each other like two teenagers knowing what the other did last night. Rose said, "I see that you had a good time. I have some cream that will cover that bite on your neck." Nick answered back with a smile, "Well, you better use some yourself. That hickey on your left breast shows you had a good time, or should I say, Zan did." Rose immediately

74

buttoned her blouse one more button to hide it. Rose told Nick that whatever happens on this journey, they must always be close. Nick nodded in agreement. "We just have too much fun laughing at each other. Don't we?" he replied.

After breakfast, everyone got mounted on their horses. They noticed that One Feather and the Red Woman were missing. David said, "John, you will have to ride one of the pack mules. My wife and One Feather took your white horse back to the Indian village. They have much to get ready. They will send your horse back to you tonight. I hope your ride today won't be too hard."

Everyone laughed until I replied. "I will ride old Petunia. I rode Petunia across the country scouting for John Ross and the Cherokees in the Oklahoma territory or what became known as the Nations a few years back. She is gentle but a little ornery." I called for Petunia, and she came running up to me. Moses smiled at Petunia as I saddled her. Moses put his hand on Petunia. "She says that you have gained a little weight. However, she says it's like old times. She sure loves you, old man. I always wondered why you took her along." Petunia nodded her head in agreement.

John figured they were about two days from the meeting place for the Potlatch. They would camp by a sacred spring. It is said that the spring has the powers to make you ten years younger. John had used it numerous times. How many he did not know? He looked at Antonio. It took John a while to realize he had seen or met him many times over the years. Antonio must have found such a spring himself. That was why he didn't place Antonio at first. He finally remembered seeing him in the background at the meeting place for The Council of Religions. The Council never called anyone of its agents by their real names to protect them. All he could remember was Antonio went by Andrew then.

John cursed himself. He should have been smarter. Antonio must have met Angela on one of his missions. The only thing that he knew about the agent called Andrew was that he was never trusted by the Council. His reputation was one of always bending the rules. It seems the last time he did that, he was cast out of the Council. The Council did not like his relationship with Angela especially when he got Angela pregnant.

John was given the job of taking their son back to be raised with Angela's people. Angela had given him up for adoption to the Catholic orphanage in Italy. The Pope assigned him to do that. He remembered how the Red Woman looked at One Feather for the first time. It was obvious that the Red Woman knew who the boy belonged to. The Red Woman agreed to take him and teach him the ways of his people. She had made John promise to never tell anyone who the boy's mother or father was. She also made John promise not to tell Antonio or Angela about the boy. He wished he had never agreed about not telling them.

He was surprised that Antonio didn't kill him for not telling them. Antonio had the right to do that. He figured that Antonio and Angela would somehow realize that they were One Feather's parents.

The Red Woman was afraid if she didn't tell them what she had done, they would take it out on John. The Red Woman told them that she had made John promise not to tell them. She did tell them that John helped raise One Feather like he was his uncle. They asked the Red Woman what had she told One Feather about his parents when she was asked by One Feather? The Red Woman told One Feather that one day his parents would come to **The Land of the Eagle Feathers** to help save the land.

June had confronted the Red Woman about who were One Feather's parents. Being a great medicine woman, June could see it in One Feather's eyes. June told the Red Woman that she should tell One Feather. It took all the courage that the Red Woman had to finally tell the truth to One Feather. One Feather didn't need to be told. He had figured it out the first time he saw Antonio and Angela together. He had felt a connection to them. They had come to save the land.

John worried about Antonio, Angela and One Feather. They would have to somehow get over everything that had happened to them. It would take time. Angela had never had the role of being a mother. Antonio didn't have any idea how to be a father. One Feather didn't know how to be a son. They would have to work this out. Nobody could help them do that.

It seemed strange that Antonio and he were blood brothers. That meant that they could do no harm to each other. They had both exchanged blood to save each other. John hoped that Antonio would keep his oath as his blood brother. Now, Angela was another matter.

Angela was thinking about what her future could be. She had been outside of **The Land of the Eagle Feathers** for a long time. When this was over, it would be easy to take *The Book of Winter* for herself. She could still protect the land and have the power that the book contained. She had talked to Shanna about doing just that. She really liked Shanna. She did have one misgiving about Shanna. Shanna was a freelance mercenary. Could Shanna be trusted? Shanna sure seemed friendly to Benita and Raven.

Angela smiled. Everyone here couldn't be trusted. If anyone hurt One Feather or Antonio, she would kill them. She would protect One Feather with her life. She knew Antonio would do the same. John was unfinished business. The book was another matter. Angela had made other possible arrangements if all did not go as Antonio and her had planned.

77

Nick missed Shanna. He was getting tired of playing along with everyone. Shanna knew who he really was. She had seen him in action during the war in Middle East. He could be as ruthless as anyone here. He had been very careful in not showing all his powers that he had learned from his grandfather. His only worry was that John knew who he was.

He would never hurt John. John had saved his life in that god forsaken desert. John had done what John had promised him. He had reunited Nick with Shanna. He would follow John to the ends of the earth because of that. He wondered what he would do if he got his hands on the last book. He knew what Shanna would do.

He liked this land, but he could never stay here. He would do what his grandfather wanted him to do. He didn't like it. Nick was no fool. He had seen what power and money could do to people. Even the best of people could be lured to their dark side by money and especially power.

Rose didn't care about the last book, except for the possibility it could help her get Zan back. She knew why she was here. Zan was the only reason. She couldn't help that she enjoyed the company of the other people in her group. **The Keepers of the Yawi** were special. If they stayed together, they could conquer anything. She was afraid that the scorpions in the group wouldn't be able to stop themselves from trying to take the book for themselves. She decided if that happened, she would destroy the book herself.

Moses had given his wanting revenge on John much thought. He didn't like feeling he was a fool to have trusted John. John should have told him about his father and mother and their relationship to John. Lo Ming made it clear that John was here to save Moses' father. Maybe, he would only deck John by hitting John on his chin. That would be fitting for not telling him all those things. Lo Ming wouldn't leave him over doing that.

Lo Ming rode in silence. She was deep in thought. She had seen much in her long lifetime. She had lived all over the world. A monk had taught her the martial arts. That seemed like centuries ago, when she was a little girl. It was the Chinese Mystics that taught her other things. She loved Moses. He was unlike any man she had ever known. He didn't question her. He never asked her about her past. He just loved her for what he saw. She would teach Moses many things after this adventure was over. She knew Moses had already taught her many things.

Lo Ming was here for many reasons. Not even John knew why she accepted his invitation to come. Lo Ming had a score to settle. She had promised herself she would. It was a thing of family honor. Perhaps, after this was over, she would meet Moses' grandfather again. She would pay her debt back to him. She would also pay back the debt she owed to the Great Elder's father on that cold road long ago when his father gave her a blanket that saved her mother's life.

David was in deep thought as he rode his black stallion. It had been a long time since he had been here. He wondered about what he would do after this was all over. Would Red Woman and he stay here? He knew that his wife would like to because of their grandchild, Little Wolf. He would have to be careful.

The Great Elder had sent him on a mission to destroy **The Dark Ones** long ago. David had even led **The Dark Ones** into **The Land of the Eagle Feathers.** David had no choice. He had to do that. He made sure that **The Dark Ones** would lose the battle at the Valley of Death. He remembered John on his white horse. John was wearing a suit of armor that was for a Roman General. John had on a gold helmet. He couldn't see John's face because of the helmet. He only knew that the man in the Roman armor looked magnificent on his white stallion.

John led his troops like a Roman General against **The Dark Ones**. John's forces were outnumbered 5 to 1. Julius Caesar couldn't have done any better in battle as John did. David couldn't help but marvel at the sight of both armies facing each other. David's **Dark Ones** were dressed in Black Chinese armor in straight columns of 20 to a row.

John's forces were much smaller. John's troops were dressed in many different styles from Native Indians on their mustangs to the Dog Soldiers carrying bows and arrows and colorful lances. John had put at least 50 horsemen with lances in a straight row across the front of his troops. Then John placed his archers behind his horse men. David couldn't believe that John's warriors were so disciplined. They didn't move until John gave his orders to charge. John didn't charge until his archers were in range. After two volleys of arrows that seem to cover the sky like a swarm of hornets, John, leading his horsemen, charged. John had the sun at his back. That gave him an edge because it was difficult for David's troops to see with the bright sun shining in their faces.

The battle lasted for several hours. When it was over, over two thirds of David's army were destroyed. Many of John's warriors were killed or hurt. David pulled his troops back out of the valley. He knew that **The Dark Ones** would not be in any shape to fight for several years against **The Land of the Eagle Feathers**. Raven was blamed for the loss. This gave David time to come up a plan to finally destroy **The Dark Ones**.

The only regret that David had was that the battle had cost many brave warriors of **The Land of the Eagle Feathers** their lives and many others serious injuries. David did give John credit. John died trying to save several of his warriors by charging into a group of **Dark Ones**. He fought like a man possessed killing at least 20 by himself. This turned the tide of the battle. That gave David the reason to retreat. David was surprised when he heard that the Great Spirits had given John his life back. David wondered what it was like for John to be half man-half ghost. Time was running out for John. David would let fate decide. David's mission was to destroy **The Dark One's Army** for once and for all. With *The Book of Winter*, David could destroy anything or anyone he wanted. John wouldn't stop him from getting the book.

Chapter IV
Attending the Potlatch Ceremony
What surprises await us?

The day went by fast. It was about dark when we arrived at our campsite. We set up camp quickly. After supper, everyone took turns bathing in the warm spring. The water of the spring was very refreshing. It did make us feel like we were younger. We were sitting around the campfire when a rider on my white stallion arrived. It was the Red Woman. She told everyone that she would lead them in the morning to the great lodge for the Potlatch.

The next morning, I had the Red Woman ride my white stallion to lead the way the Potlatch. I saddled Petunia and followed in the back of the line. Old Petunia liked me riding her. I thought it was fitting for me to ride her. Petunia had been to several of the Potlatches throughout the years. Petunia seemed exited. It was hard for me the hold her back. The Red Woman laughed when she saw me riding Petunia. She rode back to me and said, "It's been a long time since I saw you riding Petunia. I was a little girl the first time I saw you ride in on her many years ago. I am glad that you chose her to come with us. It is fitting that you ride her. This might be your last Potlatch." I thought I saw a smile and tear in her right eye as she turned my white horse to ride back to the front of the line.

It was late afternoon when we arrived at the meeting place for the Potlatch. A large wooden lodge had been specially constructed for the Native Indian Ceremony called the Potlatch. The Potlatch was scheduled to start in the late afternoon just before sunset. The Red Woman pointed to two other small lodges. "The lodge on the left is for you men to change clothes and clean up. The lodge on the right is for the women. If you do not have suitable clothes that you brought with you, we have laid out some in each lodge. You can dress in clothes that represent your tribe or ones that represent ours. This is a formal affair as you would call it," she said.

We unpacked our mules and extra horses by each lodge. One Feather took our animals to the big field to pasture for the night. Each of us took our belongings to the proper lodge to dress. The Potlatch would begin in a few hours.

The women were surprised with the furnishings in their lodge. I had Moses and Nick carry two large boxes to the women's lodge and two large boxes to the men's lodges. I went into the women's lodge. "The old man and his wife packed these boxes with each of you in mind. You will find what is best for you. Some of you may have brought proper clothing that represents you. June knows what would be suitable for you to wear." As I left the lodge, I could hear Mary say after they opened the boxes, "These clothes are beautiful."

I had Moses open the two boxes in the men's lodge. They contained several different articles of clothing. I went over one of the boxes and pulled out a bag and gave it to David. "The old man said to give this to you. It was your great, great grandfather's ceremonial dress. He said that it is yours to have. Something about your ancestors would want you to wear it to represent them at the Potlatch ceremony." David opened the clothing bag. The outfit was a white deerskin robe covered with precious gems and shells. The marking on it had scenes of great battles and tribes smoking peace pipes under the stars and moons. The pants and leggings were of white buffalo hide. A vest of red leather and held together with white small animal bones completed the outfit. His ancestors must have been great chiefs. Red Bear had brought his own outfit of a great medicine man. He looked at David and nodded his approval. David just stared at the honor to wear such a ceremonial outfit. We all could see him show emotion for the first time.

After everyone dressed in proper attire for the Potlatch ceremony, One Feather lead the men to the Great Lodge to be seated. Little Wolf led the women to the Great Lodge to be seated.

Moses dressed as an Outback Medicine man. Nick dressed to represent his tribe, The Others. His outfit was a western Indian Chief's with eagle feathers, representing his grandfather. Rose was dressed as a Voodoo Priestess with colorful headbands and a flowing purple dress covered with moons and planets and sparkling gems. Lo Ming wore a red Chinese and Tibetan dress of a high Priest that was her grandmother's. Antonio wore an ancient dress much like an Italian aristocrat from the 1400's. Angela wore a simple white elk skin dress. In her dark hair she wore a headband with a single eagle feather. White Elk said that the Great Elder had given it to her because she saved the Red Woman long ago. She was a true warrior and deserved to be treated that way.

I was surprised by what the Elder wanted me to wear. It was my golden Roman General suit of armor. He said that I deserved to wear it. It was to represent all the warriors that had died to protect our sacred lands. It still had blood stains on it from past battles that I had fought in many lands. June wore her beautiful Medicine Woman's dress that she wore meeting the various tribes on our journeys. Finally, Mary was dressed as a Native Indian Princess covered with gems. She had on a large gold and silver turquoise necklace. I recognized the necklace as the one I gave her.

We must have been a strange sight for many of the other guests. When we walked into the Great Lodge, we were treated with the utmost respect. Everyone here knew we were representing our tribes and heritage. It didn't matter where we came from only that we respected our ancestors.

The Great Lodge was already filled with various guests that represented all the tribes of **The Land of the Eagle Feathers**. There were over a hundred tribes represented. They were all the tribes of North and South America. Everyone was seated as they entered the lodge. There were three tables in the very front of the lodge with a separate table for the Great Elder who would act as the Master of Ceremonies. The Great Elder wore his formal dress with a full head dress. Everyone would be seated as to their importance at the three head tables.

At the first table, the guests to be seated were: White Elk, Antonio, Angela, June and One Feather. At the middle table were to be seated Red Bear, David, Red Woman, Mary, John and Little Wolf. At the last table to be seated were the old man and his dog with Rose, Nick, Moses and Lo Ming. I could see the surprised looks of our group when they saw the old man and his dog in such a seat of honor.

After everyone was seated, the Great Elder stood. He spoke with soft words, "We would like to welcome our guests to our Potlatch. We honor the traditions and beliefs of our forefathers. For many moons, our people have had Potlatches. I will share a story with you. When the white man tried to ban Potlatches, Chief O'waxalagalis of the Kwagu'l tribe made a statement:

"We will dance when our laws command us to dance, and we will feast when our hearts desire us to feast. Do we ask the white man to do as the Indian does? It is a strict law that bids us dance. It is a strict law that bids us to distribute our

property among our friends and neighbors. It is a good law. Let the white man observe his law. We shall observe ours. And now, if you come to forbid us to dance, be gone. If not, you will be welcome to us."

The room was silent. The Great Elder looked around the room. Everyone remained in their seat. This speech was an unspoken law to indicate that anyone could leave if they were here for the wrong reasons. He especially observed the three tables in front of him. He questioned some of their reasons to attend. Nobody left their seats or moved. The Great Elder raised his right hand. A loud drumbeat echoed throughout the lodge. This was the signal for the Potlatch to begin.

The Feast began. Many braves carried in large carved wooden dishes. The carvings on each dish represented the different spirit animals and clans of the various tribes such as eagles, bears, stars, moons and other sacred objects. Even the spoons and ladles were decorated. The braves serving were dressed in red buckskins with white beads. It was an honor to serve the guests present. The first tables served were the three tables up front. Naturally, the Great Elder out of respect was served first. Then every table was served by the status of the people at each table until all tables were served. It should be noted that the tables were made of wood with stone legs. People were seated on stone benches by each table.

The food served could be dipped in several sauces that were on the tables. These various dips were of honey, fish oil and wild seasoning with hot peppers, onions and made from other natural plants. Fried breads made of different grains were served. The foods consisted of venison, elk, fish, buffalo, beef chili and pork pie with campfire ribs. Corn stew and other dishes were served. Elderberry honey was served with the fried bread. Maple cornbread and fried yam cakes were the desserts.

After everyone was served and had eaten, the Great Elder announced that dancers would perform. They would perform an ancient dance. This dance was called the Hoop Dance. Guests knew this dance. They were excited to see it.

This dance was to be performed by One Feather. It begins with one hoop. Hoops are added to represent all the elements of life. Hoops were chosen because they represent the circle of life and the never-ending cycle of life. Hoops are slowly added with each representing the different elements that come together to support life. Each hoop is made by hand and elaborately decorated in various colors.

One Feather stands up. He picks up a hoop. He looks at the Great Elder to nod his head to give him permission. Everyone in the lodge starts pounding on their tables to signal they want the dance to start. They know that this dance could become a challenge dance with different dancers challenging each other. One Feather had the reputation of being a very skilled dancer. Surely, nobody would ever challenge him.

To everyone's surprise, White Elk stands up to challenge One Feather to a dance. The Great Elder smiled. He was pleased by White Elk's challenge to One Feather. The Great Elder knew that many others could join in the challenge. Now, he doubted if any others would. White Elk was a legend. For him to dance was a great honor for everyone here. This would be a dance of the ages.

The Great Elder pointed to the drummers to start the dance. By this time, guests were shouting, and war hoops filled the great hall. Everyone was feeling the energy and excitement of the music. The music controls the dance. One Feather nodded to accept White Elk's challenge. The hall went wild. The Great Elder nodded for One Feather to start his dance.

One Feather starts to dance. He feels the energy and spirit of the room. He jumps and dances to the music. The faster he dances, the more hoops he picks up. Soon everyone is dancing by their tables following One Feather's movements. One Feather moves with the grace of a deer. His movements tell a story of a great warrior. He adds more and more hoops until he has 50 hoops on his arms and body. Finally, exhausted, he ends his dance with one great leap and tosses the hoops toward White Elk. Everyone applauds their approval of One Feather's Dance.

The music stops as White Elk walks over to One Feather to begin his dance. The room is silent as White Elk picks up one hoop. Everyone is wondering, how could anyone top One Feather's performance? White Elk looks for permission from the Great Elder to begin. The Great Elder points to the drummer to start the music. White Elk tosses his hoop into the air as high as it could go without touching the lodge's roof. He jumps so high that he grabs it in mid-air high above everyone there. He twists his body around so fast that he is twirling like a top. He is a blur. The hoop in his hands looks like a much larger circle. The guests start shouting White Elk's name with the drumbeats, "White Elk, White Elk, White Elk."

White Elk lands on his feet in the middle of the lodge floor. He moves like a panther ready to strike. He leaps and jumps back to the other hoops. He takes several and tosses them into the air. In one leap, he collects each hoop and tosses them into the crowd below as he dances in mid-air. He moves his arms and flies like an eagle over the crowd below. The crowd cheers him on as he flies down and picks up the rest of the hoops. He lands on the center of a table in the very center of the lodge. He leaps down to the stone floor. He gracefully dances around several tables performing leaps and twirling his body. He dances up to one of the guests. He has the guest put their hands on his back and invites them to dance behind him. Soon he has everyone joining in behind him.

White Elk points to the hoops. The hoops fly into the air and rotate above the crowd as they dance around the great hall. War hoops and shouting fill the air as the crowd goes wild and dances until they come to a complete circle around the lodge's floor. White Elk signals for the drummers to stop their drumming. He points to the hoops suspended in the air. The hoops become sacred animals dancing above them. He points to the great doors of the Great lodge to open. The sacred animals dance out of the Great Hall and disappear into the dark night. Everyone cheers and dances to their seats and stops as the Great Elder signals for the dance to stop.

The Great Elder motions for White Elk and One Feather to come to him. He starts to hold his hands above One Feather to have the guests applaud to gauge who won the challenge. One Feather asks the Great Elder permission to speak. One Feather points to White Elk and bows his head and body to show his respect. Everyone knows that White Elk has won the challenge. They explode in applause.

The Great Elder announces that the storytelling will begin. Storytelling has always been a part of entertainment at Indian festivals and ceremonies. Great Elk states that there will be three storytellers.

The old man and his hound dog stood up. They moved to a raised platform set up near the east middle side of the building. The old man and his dog jumped up on the platform. The old man was dressed in a long black coat with black woolen pants. He had on a gold vest that shined in the porch light of the Great Lodge. He had several gold and silver rings on his fingers. He had on a black derby hat with an eagle feather in the band around its crown. The old man looked like a gentleman of the early 1830's.

Storytellers did not always speak when telling a story. They often used sign language to tell their tales. That was the universal language of every tribe. That allowed everyone to understand the stories no matter what language the tribes or white men spoke. Fur traders would say that it was not unusual to have total silence when a story was told. Sometimes laugher, applause or other approval would break the silence.

The old man took off his hat. His long gray hair spilled out and fell almost to his waist. His gray beard was trimmed about four to six inches. He put his hat on the floor in front of him. The old man nodded in respect to the crowd. Everyone was silent. Many people believed that the old man and his dog were spirits.

Not a sound could be heard in the Great Hall. The old man began his tale. The old man held his hands up high above his head. The light made a large shadow on the wall behind him. Everyone in the Great Hall could see the shadow of his sign language behind him and understand his story.

The old man began his story. It was called,

The Little Boy and the Hoop Dance.

The Hoop Dance came from a little boy who preferred to be alone. He was shunned by his father because he did not have the same interests as other little boys. Nobody wanted to be his friend or have anything to do with him. The little boy earned the name, "Pukawise or the unwanted."

The little boy having no friends didn't mind. His friends were the animals around him. They didn't care that he was different. They didn't care that he was little for his age. The little boy studied the animals and birds. He studied their movcmcnts and language.

The audience started to notice that the old man and his dog had started to become younger. The old man's hair became darker and shorter as was his bcard. The old man was slowly becoming a little boy before their eyes as he told the story.

The same was happening to the old dog. The old dog was becoming a puppy.

As the boy studied the animals more, he soon started copying their movements. He could spin like an eagle in flight and run like a deer. He could jump like a panther and climb trees like a squirrel.

Word soon spread about the boy that had great knowledge about animals and nature. Many people wanted to know what the little boy knew. The little boy decided the best way to teach others what he knew was to make hoops. Each colorful hoop represented an animal and its movement. He taught others to use each hoop to express the animal's movements in dance. It was in the movement of the hoops that people learned the ways of each animal or bird.

 He taught others to dance like the animals. This dance became known as "The Hoop Dance." The people soon realized that nobody should be "unwanted." All creatures including mankind should be wanted and respected, even the little boy called Pukawise.

When the old man finished his story, he and his dog were a little boy and a puppy. Thunder and lightning could be heard outside the Great Lodge. In a brief moment, all the torches went out. It was completely dark in the Great Hall. A bolt of lightning flashed through the center of the hall relighting the torches. When the light from the torches lit the hall, the old man and his dog were old again. The old man finished his story by signing, remember that is why **The Land of the Eagle Feathers** exists.   It is like the hoops of the Hoop Dance. It is to keep the knowledge and ways of all the tribes from being lost. Nobody should ever feel "unwanted" here.

As the old man and his old dog moved back to their seats, the guests stood up and nodded. They drummed on their tables to show their approval of the old man's skill in storytelling.

The Great Elder introduced Red Bear. Everyone knew that Red Bear had his issues. He was known once as a very wise medicine man. They knew if the Great Elder invited him, they should respect Red Bear. They were curious to what Red Bear would pick as a story.

Red Bear got up to tell his story in sign language. The story was called

The Raccoon's Lesson.

Long ago, there was a great fire. The forest was filled with many wounded and sick creatures. A mama raccoon decided to help these animals. She worked day and night to supply food for them.

The mama raccoon worked so very hard for the other animals. She was soon exhausted. The other raccoons knew that mama raccoon was close to collapse. She fell over, hardly alive. The other raccoons took her to their burrows and nursed her.

In her lapses of sleep, she had dreams. In one of those dreams, Mother Earth said to her, "Mama raccoon, you give all of your strength to others. You forgot to weigh the consequences. Your life has lost its balance. In order to regain your balance of life, you must see the errors of your ways. You must not rob yourself of all your energy for others and give it away. You will leave yourself with no energy. Then you cannot help yourself or any others."

Mama raccoon learned her lesson. Soon she got well. She now works to the best of her abilities but saves her energy so that she has enough to help herself and her family. She does not rob all her energy to help others. If she would rob all her energy, she could not help anyone.

Make sure that you take care of yourself first. Then take care of the others. Do not rob yourself of all your energy or you will not be of any use to your tribe or others. You only have so much to give to others.   We need to all share our resources. Don't be like mama raccoon was, we all need to work together. If we do that, we can survive anything.

That is why we have the Potlatch. We need to share our energies and resources with others. It is to remind everyone that those that have more than others should share their wealth. That way everyone has the resources they need. It is the way of our culture. May Mother Earth and Father Sky bless us all. Several guests nodded in respect to Red Bear's wise story.

White Elk introduced Little Wolf to the guests. Little Wolf did not seem nervous to tell his story. When he got to the platform. he announced his story in sign.

The Dream Fast

In some tribes, it is the custom for a boy when they reached a certain age to go to the forest and wait for a dream. The boy would build a small lodge and wait for a visit from a sacred spirit for such a dream. A good dream would give the boy much power.

A boy named Opichi reached that age. His father was determined that he would have the most perfect dream fast. He insisted the boy go on his dream fast before the last snow left the ground.

His father said, " My son is strong." Opichi wanted to please his father. So, he went into the forest and built himself a lodge. His father said he would come every morning and visit him. A black bird warned his parents not to let their son stay out too long on the dream fast. If he has a dream, he should come home. His father did not listen to the bird's advice. His father wanted his son to have a very powerful dream. His son would become more powerful.

On the first morning, he told his father he had a dream about a deer.

His father wanted him to have a dream of the more sacred powerful animal.

On the second morning, the boy told his father he had a dream about a beaver. His father said, "I want you to have a better dream." His father decided that his son should stay several more days before he would get him.

Finally, on the seventh day, Opichi's mother said "Enough, we should go get Opichi." When they got to the forest and the lodge, they did not find Opichi.

A gray and black bird with a red chest flew out of the lodge. It perched on a branch above them. It said, "My parents, you see me as I am. Your son is gone. You sent me out too early and asked me to wait for power too long . Now, I will return each Spring, my song will let you know it's me. It will sound like opi, chi. Your greed for power has its cost."

Little Wolf made the sound of the bird, opi chi, opi chi. Little Wolf looked at the guests. "Please repeat with me, opi chi, opi chi," said Little Wolf. The audience started shouting, "Opi chi, Opi chi, Opi chi." Little Wolf held up his hands and pointed to the ceiling. Everyone stopped shouting at what they saw. A small object appeared near the Great Hall's ceiling. It flew down and landed on Little Wolf's outstretched arm. It was a gray and black bird with a red chest. Little Wolf let the bird fly away. It circled the room and flew out the main doors. The room was silent. The only thing that could be heard was the bird returning its call, "Opi chi, Opi chi, Opi chi."

When the audience hear the bird's call, the audience couldn't contain themselves. The guests drummed on their tables with their approval. They shouted their approval as Little Wolf went back to his seat. They started shouting, "Little Wolf, Little Wolf, Little Wolf." It took several minutes before their shouting stopped.

The Great Elder told everyone to continue eating and enjoying everyone's company. After about an hour, the Great Elder got up and announced that the gift giving would start. "We of **The Land of the Eagle Feathers** consider this to be a sacred act. The spreading of our wealth to all is a symbol of our responsibility to each other. Your gift to others is a symbol that you care for others. No matter how great or how small, the gift should be something special to that person."

The Great Elder motioned to members of his tribe to bring in the gifts to the guests of the representatives of the many tribes that attended. "As you, our guest, our tribe had put together special gifts of food and other gifts such as specialty designed blankets, baskets, dried fruits, flour, pottery, leather goods, bolts of cloth, knives and other items. Our tribe has prospered over the years. We are happy to be able to spread out gifts to you and your tribes."

A great chief stood up in the audience, "I represent several tribes from the Sioux to the Blackfoot. Your tribe has given to us so generously. There will be a great blessing to your tribe. The Great Spirits will honor your tribe. It is the way of the Potlatch."

All the guests stood up. They bowed to the Great Elder to give their respect for the honor of attending the Potlatch. They silently moved to the great doors in the back of the great lodge to receive their gifts. When the last guest left, the Great Elder signaled for his tribe members to come.

The members of the tribe filled the Great Hall. "When the Great Hall is cleared and cleaned, you should take a seat. Then, we will continue our gift giving to our tribe," said the Great Elder.

It didn't take long before everyone was seated. The Great Elder stood up and raised his hand for silence. "It is the custom of the Potlatch to have those that were most prosperous to give to the those that are less. It is our belief that the more one gives of their wealth, the greater the blessing and the higher the rank in the tribe. I believe that everyone here has prospered. Everyone in this room has special skills and crafts that they can give to others less fortunate. I will go first," said the Great Elder.

The Great Elder raised both arms and made a big circle pointing to all in the room. On each table in front of each member a necklace made of silver and gold appeared. Precious stones were woven into each that symbolized something important to each member there. "These necklaces are to be worn by each of you on New Year's Day. They will give you strength for the coming year," said the Great Elder. The people knew that the Great Elder must have given all his wealth away to give such a gift.

Red Bear stood up next. When you leave, my two assistants in back, will give each of you a basket of herbs and healing potions. These should cure all your illnesses and injuries in the coming year. This is to show my gratitude to you for welcoming me back into the tribe," said Red Bear.

The gift giving went on with individuals giving gifts to each other. After the last of the gifts were given, the Great Elder rose from his seat. "I am very proud to witness what I saw tonight. You have been so generous to each other. The Great Spirits of this land will be blessing all of you. You know that we have special guests with us. They will be given their gifts later. I have called a special Council Meeting. Council members should remain here,"

As the Great Elder was about to close the Potlatch, White Elk stood up. Everyone was silent as they listened to him speak. Few people had ever seen White Elk, let alone heard him speak. "I have only one gift to give everyone. It is not of a material thing. It is onc of knowledge. I will let you see the universe that surrounds us all. Please remain seated! After the show is over, you should take your gifts and leave. Only a few have seen the things I will show you. Take this knowledge and give it those that will come after us."

White Elk pointed his staff to the ceiling. All the torches were extinguished. The Great Hall was completely dark. Soon one star appeared and then another. A sun appeared with nine planets circling it. Scenes of supernovas and black holes appeared. The Milky Way and galaxies far away moved through the Great Hall. Secrets only known to great scientists rose and fell away before their eyes. Finally, scenes from earth from many years ago followed. Animals, birds, plants and creatures of all types including the fish in the seas moved about the ceiling. They saw the wonders of the universe and beyond. A big flash of a supernova ended the show. Everyone was amazed by what they had seen. The torches were lit. The audience left in wonder and silence. This gift was one of the greatest of all.

After everyone had left, the Great Elder had everyone move to the Council Hall for the meeting. When they arrived there, they saw that a large round table had been placed in the middle of the chamber. The Great Elder had everybody seated around the table. "Today was the first day of Winter. As you know, you have less than one moon to obtain *The Book of Winter* and return here to meet the army of the **Dark Ones**.

"Antonio, do you have *The Book of Fall* to give me?" asked the Great Elder. Antonio answered back, "No, I don't." "Where is the book ?" the Great Elder asked. "I gave it to someone for safe keeping," replied Antonio. Before the Great Elder could ask another question, Little Wolf walked into the room. All Antonio could do was to point at Little Wolf. "I had to give it to someone I could trust. The only one that I knew I could trust was Little Wolf. I think you can see my reasoning," Antonio smiled. "I am afraid that I see your logic. As far as I can see, your logic is correct. Now, Little Wolf give it to me," said the Great Elder. Little Wolf looked at

Antonio, "You were right about the passages. I deciphered them. Don't worry about anything. I memorized them all just in case something happened to you, Antonio." Little Wolf handed *The Book of Fall* to the Great Elder.

"Before we get the meeting started, we must finish the gift giving part of the Potlatch. We have gifts that will mean a lot to each of you. These gifts will tell you why some of you were picked for this journey by John and the old man," said the Great Elder. Everyone at once looked at John and the Great Elder. They were somewhat surprised by that announcement. They had wondered about the old man's part in all of this.

The old man and his dog walked into the Council Chambers. The old man had a large box in his hands. The old hound dog had a small pack on its back. "Well, now it is time for you to understand that each of you have a link to one another. You will see that once I explain the gifts that I have brought you and the stories behind them."

The old man walked over to Moses. He handed him a dark brown leather mule whip. Moses looked at the whip. It felt familiar in his hands. He went to Mary and gave her a charm bracelet made from silver and turquoise. Taking a package from the old hound dog's pack, he gave it to Lo Ming. He told Lo Ming not to open it until he told her. He did the same for Antonio. He told him not to open it until he was done. The old man looked at Nick. He threw a large hunting knife at Nick. Nick caught it and put in on the table in front of him. "I see that you are just as skilled as your ancestor," said the old man. "I have an old ivory pipe shaped like a riverboat and a small compass to give you, Rose," The old man looked at Angela. He handed Angela a small necklace with a gold nugget attached to it. "Now June, this is an old Indian blanket. It saved one of your ancestors long ago. Now John, you got your gift long ago, you have always kept it. Petunia saved you on that long march, didn't she? Now it is time to tell you why everyone of you is linked together. It is a thread in time. It is everything or nothing. It is fate."

The old man looked at the old hound dog. "I guess it is time to tell them. What do you say?" The old hound dog barked back at the old man. "I agree, with you. You always get the last word," laughed the old man.

The old man looked at the group, "It's a long and sad story. It explains why this land is so important. It explains your past and just maybe your future. Let's get started with this, I need some whiskey and a chaw of tobacco first. I'm glad I brought them both. I sure would have never found them here."

"The story is one of the saddest and most brutal events of all. I was in the Cherokee Territory in the 1820s and 1830s. I was a young man that fell in love with the Indian culture and way of life. Living in what is known today as the Smoky Mountains was a wonderful experience. I had many warrior friends. I knew most of the great Medicine men, Red Women and Chiefs of the Cherokee Tribes. It was like paradise to me. But like all things good, there was those that destroyed it."

The old man pointed to the Council Chamber's ceiling. The ceiling disappeared. Being the first day of Winter, the early morning sky was still dark. A warm breeze was blowing a small scatter of white clouds across the dark blue sky. The stars in the sky became brighter. There were thousands of them. Some were big and bright, and some were small. They moved together to form a large circular cluster in the eastern part of the sky. Soon from the circle, a line of stars started forming. The line had big stars and little stars scatter in it. As the line made its way toward the western skyline, many of the stars became shooting stars. Some of the shooting stars were small and some big. Each shooting star had a face to it. The small shooting stars were faces of Indian children and elderly Indians. The bigger stars had faces of adults both men and women. When the line reached the Western sky, it reformed into a circular cluster. This time the circular cluster of stars was much smaller.

"You see that over five thousand stars have died out of over 15,000 stars that started across the sky. The small stars are the young children, babies, and elderly that died. The bigger stars are the women and men that died during their journey west. Here in **The Land of the Eagle Feathers** every early morning on the first day of winter, the stars form and cross the sky to commemorate and honor those that had fallen during **The Trail of Tears.**"

This time period in the history of southeastern part of the United States was a time of great upheaval. Nearly 125,000 Native Americans lived in the land from Georgia to Florida. Now, most of them are gone due to the horrendous events that happened in the period from 1820 to 1840. For those of you that do not know the history, I will be brief in telling it. Later we will have some visitors or spirits tell you what happened to them. This is where you will find why you are here today."

The old man took a long sip of whiskey and a bite of dark tobacco before he started the rest of the story. You could tell that he had trouble getting the words out. His voice was trembling and cracked in spots. Tears were starting to form in his eyes. His old hound dog gave out a mournful howl as he started. It echoed down throughout the valleys of the land. It was a sign to those who were lost that they were being remembered. The wind started to blow from the east. Clouds moved in from the east to cover the sky in a grayish black blankct.

"I remember the events that happened like it was yesterday. We, Native Americans, had claimed millions of acres in the southern United Statcs as our own lands. I can say that because I was adopted and married into the tribe. We had lived on these lands for thousands of years. It was our birthright. We were born, raised our families and buried our ancestors on these sacred lands. We had our disagreement over territories, but we settled them in our own ways.

Then everything changed almost overnight. A great tide of people called Americans started to take our lands. We fought against them and even helped them take some of the lands from our enemies. Two great civilizations clashed over these lands. As more and more settlers came, we lost more and more land to them. It didn't matter. We were no match for them.

Many wars were fought. The Cherokee fought with one man and his army against the Creeks. We thought that this would settle our problems, but it did not. The American general, Andrew Jackson, with our help of over 500 braves from our tribe, Cherokees, won the Creek War at the Battle of Horseshoe Bend. Our great Chief Junaluska saved the general's life at that battle. He would have died at the hands of a Creek warrior. We thought the general would honor us. We found out later that he had no honor for us.

In 1828, Andrew Jackson was elected President of the United States. We, Cherokees, elected John Ross as our Chief. Problems between the white settlers and our tribes became more and more heated. The one thing that we couldn't fight was the discovery of gold on our lands. Greed can conquer more than any battle. The settlers took more and more of our lands. There were clashes between us. Andrew Jackson decided that the only way to settle this problem was take our lands and move us away to lands across the great Mississippi River. He and his friends wanted our lands. They made a law called The Indian Removal Act in 1830. We would receive money and land west of the Mississippi for our sacred land.

Chief John Ross fought this law in the white man's courts. Other tribes were forced to sign treaties and were removed

from their lands. Many of those died on their way to the west.
We refused to sign.

We thought that by adopting the white man's ways we could
all live together. We were wrong. We farmed and built
homes. We traded and learned their ways.

Several of the other tribes did the same thing. We became
known as the "Five Civilized Tribes." To the white men, we
were just Indians. We were never equal.

We even won our case in the white man's great court called
the Supreme Court. Andrew Jackson, their President, did
nothing. He said, "Let the Supreme Court enforce their
decision." He did nothing for us.

A group of Cherokees decided that we could not stop the
whites from taking our lands. They split off from the main
Cherokee Tribe and signed a Treaty of Echota, and it was
Ratified on December of 1835 by Congress. Two thousand of
the Cherokees left, but over 16,000 of us stayed. Chief John
Ross fought this treaty in white man's courts as being false
because they had no right to sign it.

Chief John Ross even sent an envoy, Chief Junaluska, to see
President Andrew Jackson to try to stop this removal. Surely,
he would listen to him and do honor to us. President Andrew
Jackson listened to our plea. He did not honor the man and
people that saved his life. He had no honor for us. He
dismissed Chief Junaluska and said, "Your audience is ended.
There is nothing I can do for you."

In May of 1838, the next President sent an Army of 7000
soldiers to take our land and force us to leave. My family was
one of the first. They walked into my home and grabbed my
wife and three kids by gunpoint. We were not allowed to take
anything only the clothes on our backs. Like many, we were
forced into the stockades. That was the start of the horrors
that we faced."

The old man started to weep. Tears fell like rain from his eyes. He couldn't talk. His appearance changed into a great Cherokee warrior. He looked at the sky above like he was searching for someone. A great warrior appeared by his side. He was more spirit than man. He took his hand and touched the old man on his shoulder. The only words that the old man could say was a faint whisper, "Thank you for coming, Chief Junaluska."

"My blood brother, you have so much sadness in your heart. I will tell what happened to your family and the others on that trail. Go sit by the Red Woman. She will try and console your grief. I know what is in your heart," said Chief Junaluska. June went over to the old man and led him to have his seat of honor by the Red Woman.

"I have come to be a witness to you about how important **The Land of the Eagle Feathers** are to all the tribes. It has a lot to do with **The Trail of Tears** and other events that deeply affected all Indian souls and spirits.

I saw many dreadful things on that journey. I always wondered if it was better to have died on that journey than live with its painful memories. Those of us that survived lived with the pain of it every day. We saw too much suffering and pain. We witnessed too much dying especially the deaths of the babies and children. We were never the same after it.

I remember the little children's faces looking back at the mountains they were leaving that had once been their home. You could sense that they knew it was forever. We could never come up with answers to their questions of: Why? What did we do to deserve this? Why are we suffering? How do you answer that when you had the same questions? I never saw a smile on their faces again.

The Trail of Tears started with many Indians being forced by soldiers by gunpoint and bayonet point to leave their homes without any warning. We were forced to leave behind our homes, prize possessions, or even food and clothes. We were not allowed to take anything of value.

I saw a family getting ready to bury their child when soldiers came and took everyone away. They didn't let anyone bury the child. They made them go and left no one there to bury the child. I never knew if the child received a proper burial. This was the start of the emptiness that I felt. Every time I saw something like this, I died a little. We all died a little each day until there was nothing left inside.

We were taken to stockades and housed like prisoners. Food and clothing were in short supply there. The conditions made for disease to infect many people there. People did not have proper clothes or blankets to keep them warm. The children and their mothers cried each night from hunger and cold. Some were scared of what could happen the next day. For many, it was death.

The first to die were the young babies and children. Then the elderly got sick. The last were the adults. Many of the soldiers took advantage of the women and children. Over two thousand of us died in the stockades before starting the long journey to the Indian Territories in what is now Oklahoma. Each death left a mark on our souls. Each death made us ask, "Why?"

One of the Chiefs said it best, "I watched as my people suffered, and I could not understand why. What is in the hearts and souls of the white soldiers? How could they do such evil acts? We had done nothing to them. My eyes saw it. My ears heard the cries of the mothers for their dead children. I did not understand, nor do I ever want to understand. They can keep the evil within their hearts and souls. It will always belong to them, and they called us savages."

Many of us started the journey in such places as Georgia, Tennessee and North Carolina. The journey took months in brutal conditions. Many of my people were forced to march in the cold and muddy conditions with little protection from the cold weather and rain. In some of the places, we waded across cold streams. I remember the cold. It was a deep cold. You tried to get warm. I carry that coldness in my heart. I wish it would go away.

   If a child or adult couldn't keep up, they were left to die by the roadside. Many were not even buried. Sickness took its toll. With food and medicine in short supply, many died of lack of food and clean water.

   People carried their children or took their hands. We knew if they fell behind, they would surely die. Each day seemed worse than the next. We became numb to the pain. Our souls did not.

   Death was our constant companion. If a child or adult died, we would bury them in unmarked graves alongside of the road. The graves would be shallow because we did not have shovels to bury them with. We often used broken knives to dig the shallow graves. Did the officers have no respect for the dead? We should have known that because they didn't have much respect for the living. The horses and mules got better treatment than us.

   There is a legend that for every death on The Trail of Tears flowers would grow. It is said that when The Trail of Tears started, the mothers were grieving so much that they were unable to help their children survive the journey. The Elders prayed for a sign that would give the mothers strength.   The next day a beautiful rose began to grow where each of a mother's tears had fallen.   The rose is white for the tears that were shed. It has a gold center that shows the gold stolen from the Cherokee and seven leaves that represent the seven Cherokee Clans. The wild Cherokee Rose grows along the route that The Trail of Tears took to Eastern Oklahoma. When I returned from the end of that journey many years later, there must have been thousands of flowers growing along the trail. For the four thousand people our mothers had shed tears for on that terrible journey.

No family was spared a loss. Chief John Ross's wife, Quatie, died on the trail. She gave up her only blanket to a sick child during a sleet and snowstorm. She became sick with the fever and died of pneumonia in a bleak winter night. Too many of our mothers and children had died for no reason. It was an honorable death. Without her, the child would not have survived. No warrior was ever as brave as her. It was the first time I felt pride in a lot time.

Some of children and women were allowed to ride in wagons, but there were too few of those wagons. A few soldiers would sneak us food and give us parts of their uniforms to keep children warm at nights. This didn't help much. These kind soldiers would often get in trouble for this kindness. You could see it in their eyes. They were ashamed to be part of this.

The old man's children became weak and died. His wife became distraught. She gave up and died in his arms a day later. We heard he snuck out that night and carried her body back to her two children's graves and buried her by their sides. When he returned late the next day, a soldier beat him. Another soldier stopped it and beat that soldier. The good soldier was threatened with court martial and put into the stockade. Too bad, there were so few like him.

I lost both my wife and children to sickness. I was like a wild bird with two broken wings. I became like a soul lost in the winds of timc. I thought I had nothing left in me. I was wrong. Memories follow me every day. It's the memories that haunt you. Time helps the sadness. It does not cure it.

One memory will not leave my mind. A woman had strapped on her back her baby child and took her other two kids by the hand. The mother was too frail to endure the journey. Her heart soon gave out and she fell and died with the baby on her back. The last we saw of them was her still holding the two children's hands. We were forced to move on. We never knew what happened to the children.

When I witnessed this, tears flowed down my cheeks. I lifted my cap and turned my face toward the heavens and said, "Oh my god, if I had known at the Battle of Horseshoe Bend what I know now, American history would have been differently written."

Why I survived I do not know? I went back some years later to North Carolina. It was as close to home as I could get. I got a new chance and married and had three children. I was rewarded for my service to Andrew Jackson in the Creek Wars by given some land there. Fate has some strange ways. The spirits have their ways."

The old man had recovered. He went over to Chief Junaluska and bid him farewell. The chief disappeared. "After The Trail of Tears, I went back to the Smoky Mountains. I wandered the mountains for many years. I tried to find myself. I would sit on the mountaintops and listen to the spirits of the wind blow by me. Some days the pain was too much. My heart was dead. My soul was cold.

One day I heard a faint sound of a whisper in the wind. It said all had not been lost. There is sacred land that you need to find.

I sent word for several of the great medicine men of the Cherokee Tribes and other tribes to come to the mountains. There is a legend about the Smoky Mountains. There was a hidden land full of game, food and riches. Very few had ever seen it. With the help of the sacred medicine men, we found it. We hid it so nobody would ever see it. **The Land of the Eagle Feathers** is that place.

I became the guardian of the entrance to it. I took the riches I found and bought all the land around it including the abandoned train station and town. I learned the secrets of magic, mysticism and other secrets of the spirits to protect it for all the generations of Native Indians to preserve their traditions forever. **The Land of the Eagle Feathers** is a living, breathing monument to all the tribes. It is to keep our way of life alive. We would sometimes send people from this land to make sure that all tribes would learn their traditions and culture better.

I met John on The Trail of Tears. We have both tried to protect this sacred land for many years. As much as we have tried, we had only been partly successful. We never got a group of people that could finally save it until now. We both worked on who we would need to save it.

We had failed with many people several times to find the books. You are the only ones that can do it. Without the books, the land will never be saved. The gifts that I gave you tonight will tell you why you were chosen. The Trail of Tears is the answer why you are here. You are all linked together like a chain with it."

The old man was now himself. He had changed from a warrior back to an old man in bib overalls with his railroad hat and a flannel red shirt. "Well, where were we?" he asked. "I guess we should start with Moses. The dark brown whip that you were given belonged to one of your great grandfathers. He was a freighter. He had a team of mules and helped on The Trail of Tears. Besides carrying women and children, he would give them food and clean water. Sometimes when they stopped for feed for the mules, he would take his own money and buy extra corn meal for the women to make hoecakes for their children to eat.

One day, another freighter used his whip on a small boy because he was in the way of his wagon. Your great grandfather took his whip and cut that man to pieces. He told him if he ever did anything to anyone else, he would finish the job. One of the officers tried to put him in the stockade. He thought better of it. He knew that your grandfather had great skill with keeping the mules and horses in good health. The officer just said to the other freighter. " I need him more than you. The animals come first." He had a son with him. I heard his son became a great medicine man.

Rose, the ivory pipe carved in the shape of a riverboat and compass were one of very close relatives. He ferried many of the Cherokees across the Mississippi River during The Trail of Tears. It is said that he turned his riverboat around to save a young Indian boy who fell out of the riverboat. The young boy survived. Several soldiers tried to persuade him not to turn around. One soldier put a gun to his head to stop him. The Riverboat Captain told him, "If you shoot me, who will pilot the riverboat." He knocked the soldier overboard. Then, he said, "Should I turn around and get you, or should I let you drown?" Nobody argued with the Captain again. After the Cherokees left the area, I heard he took his boat to New Orleans. He had all he could stomach. He sold his boat. They say he took a map and compass and went into the dark swamps.

The old man looked at Nick. "Nick, that old hunting knife that I gave you was your great grandfather's. It seems that he was able to evade capture by the soldiers. He followed one small captured group of Cherokees for several days. The only weapon he had was that old hunting knife. Late one night, he crawled into the camp and cut the ropes that the soldiers had tied up the men, women and children. He cut the ropes where the horses and mules were tied. He knocked out two guards and slowly knocked out several of the other men one by one.

There was a great thunderstorm approaching. He waited until it was almost on them. He took some gunpowder and lit it. A big flash lit up the camp. All the soldiers woke up. The lightning flashed and only the warrior was standing. The warrior had covered himself in white rock dust. "I represent the great spirits of the Cherokee Warriors. If you follow your prisoners, I will return. I will show you mercy for now because you treated them well. He pointed to a wagon of supplies that had weapons and gunpowder in it. A ball of lightning hit the wagon and it exploded. The soldiers did not move. They watched as the warrior led the group out of the camp. The soldiers were too scared to follow them.

The warrior was smart instead of heading east, he took them to the west. It is said that this group made their home in the Southwestern deserts. They are now called, "The Others." They have come to the aid several times of **The Land of the Eagle Feathers.** Nick, your power with fire comes from that Great Warrior."

The old man turned to June. "June, you have become a great medicine woman. The blanket that you received is the one that was given to the young child by Quatie. It has found its rightful place with you.

The little boy survived the long march. He became a Great Shaman. You are the great granddaughter of that little boy. His spirit is within you. His powers have been passed down to you. You have already shown that you are selfless and brave. You are the one chosen to lead your people back to **The Land of the Eagle Feathers.** They left a battle long ago because of the kidnapping of their children. They did what they had to for their tribe to survive. They have nothing to be ashamed of in our eyes. Because of you, they are coming to help us. Because of you, they are coming home."

Mary looked at the silver charm bracelet in the white box. She recognized several of the charms on it. There were others that were stars and planets. She did realize that many charms had to do with plants and minerals that medicine men had used to cure people of various illnesses. In her studies of ancient medicine, she knew that silver was a powerful metal. It was often used by powerful medicine men throughout North and South America. It was not hard to think that her gift was related to healing people.

"On the Trail of Tears, medicine was in short supply. Many of the medicine men were scattered throughout the different groups on the march. In one group, there were no medicine men available to help the sick. A young woman of mixed blood was in that group. Many thought she was a white woman. She told them, "No."

Her father was a white fur trader. Her mother was a Cherokee medicine woman. She had been rounded up with several other Cherokee women. She tried to tell them that her husband was a white citizen. They said that didn't matter. Her husband was somewhere in the upper Missouri trading for furs when she was captured. He wasn't due back until sometime in the Spring. The soldiers didn't believe her. That was how she was in the group.

There was one thing on her side. One of the officers asked her who her husband was. When she told him her husband's name, the officer just stared at her. The army had used him as a guide and scout. If she was telling the truth, they were in for a bunch of trouble. Her husband would kill every one of the soldiers that had taken her. He was not a forgiving man. Even the Blackfoot feared him. The officer told his men to take the best of care of her. This allowed the young woman to assist the other women and children if they got sick. She could go freely in the camp.

The young woman cared for many of the sick throughout the journey. She saved many lives. It was said that she had special powers that allowed her to use a silver charm bracelet to cure several diseases. One Cherokee woman told the soldiers that the young woman had the power of the Great Cherokee Medicine Spirits. If any harm ever came to her, they would pay dearly. The soldiers witnessed her healing powers. They treated her with respect. She arrived in the Nations with most of her group alive thanks to her.

When her husband found her, he wanted to kill all the soldiers that had captured her. She stopped him. She told her husband that it was the Great Spirits that wanted her to come on The Trail of Tears to save many of her people. The soldiers did not know. It was her destiny to be here.

Her husband being a blood brother to a great war chief believed her. They lived a long life together and were blessed with many children. It was said that this bracelet belonged to your great grandmother. I can only give it to you because you have many if not more of the healing powers that your great grandmother had. This bracelet finds you, not the other way around. May you pass it on to another worthy person when your life on this Mother Earth is over," said the old man. Mary took the silver charm bracelet out of the box. The Red Woman came over and put it on Mary's right arm. The bracelet started glowing. It had finally found its rightful owner.

Angela touched the silver necklace with the gold nugget that she had put on her neck. "Angela, you are a little different than the others. You are very brave. You showed you bravery by saving the Red Woman. You almost died doing that. Sometimes you act without considering the consequences of your actions. There were several things that caused The Trail of Tears. The major thing was "greed." Settlers wanted the Indian lands. The thing that tipped the scales was one thing, "gold." In 1828, a young Indian Boy is said to have traded a nugget of gold to some white men. This led to a gold rush. Soon many gold seekers came to the Indian Territories to seek the gold. They killed and took Indian land. They were not satisfied until they had all the gold there.

The nugget on that necklace you have on it is that nugget of gold. It is to remind you that simple things can cause many serious consequences. Greed is something that can control people. Angela, you are a great warrior. But you are more than that, your father says you have skills you do not know. The necklace is to remind you of that. Money and wealth are not the only things that are important. They are a weakness of many. It is a lesson for you. The knowledge of man's weakness will do you well in your destiny. I do not know what that will be. It is up to the Great Spirits. Touch the gold nugget when you must make a big decision. I hope it will help you make the right one soon." Angela knew the old man knew more than he said about her.

"Antonio, you are a very complicated man. Open the small package I gave you," said the old man. Antonio opened the small package. Inside he found an old leather pouch. He knew what was inside. His face grew pale. He opened the small pouch and pulled the gift out. It was an old string of rosary beads. Antonio just stared at the rosary beads. "How did you get these?" asked Antonio. The old man replied, "From someone you will never guess. She got them as a gift for saving several Cherokee warriors near the Georgia state boundary many years ago.

There was a story of a Catholic Priest that was sent to help the Cherokees and other tribes during the roundup of the Indians for The Trail of Tears. The stockades were a very harsh place. Many people died of disease and hunger. A priest was seen at several of these stockades helping with what he could save some of these Indians.

The Priest had a reputation as being a man that could be hard to get along with especially when innocent people were hurt or killed. After several months of non-stop missionary work, the priest became more and more difficult to work with. He was angry with what he saw. A fire started building inside him.

It was at one of these stockades that one soldier went too far. The soldier got mad at a little Indian girl and hit her. The injured girl started bleeding very badly. When the priest started to give her first aid, the soldier told him to not help her. The priest pleaded with the man to let him help her. The soldier laughed in his face. The priest had had enough. They say the priest had a string of rosary beads in his right hand. Before anyone could react, the priest hit the soldier in his face with every bit of his strength. The soldier fell to the ground unconscious.

The priest stopped the child's bleeding very quickly. It was as if his hands were those of healer. He gave the beads to the little Indian girl. He ran out of the stockade before any of the other soldiers found out about what had happened. On a branch of a Dogwood tree the next day, soldiers found a priest's robe and other clothing. The priest was never seen again. The soldier that hit the little girl was never the same. He had a mark on his face that never healed.

Stories were told of a man that helped Indians and aided them along The Trail of Tears. Many thought he was a ghost that came in the night and was gone before morning. Some people said that the priest had lost some of his faith that day. Some believed he was doing penitence for that day.

I thought that you should have these Antonio. They should mean a lot to you. The little girl made it through The Trail of Tears. She said that whenever she thought she could not make it. She held these beads in her hands." Antonio did not say anything. He looked at the sky above him. An old woman appeared. She waved at him. Antonio stood up. He threw the rosary beads at her. She caught them in her hands. "These are yours." That was all he would say. She smiled at him, "My great grandchildren, my grandchildren and my children thank you." She tossed the beads back to him. "I am giving these back to you. They are to go to your son, One Feather! That is the way of my tribe. They must stay in your family. I can give them back because you just loaned them to me." She nodded her head and slowly faded away.

Antonio put the rosary beads back into the leather pouch. He walked over to One Feather and placed them in his hands. One Feather knew the significance of the beads. They held special powers. Only a father could give such a gift to his son. Antonio sat down by Angela. Angela took Antonio's hand. You could see the pride in her face. The Council members nodded their heads in approval.

Everyone's eyes turned to Lo Ming and her package. They wondered what Lo Ming would have to do with The Trail of Tears. The old man took Lo Ming's package from her. "Not all of the Cherokees stayed on The Trail of Tears. Several escaped. Some had help and others just took their chances by jumping into rivers and swimming to the opposite shores. Some hid out before they could get caught in the high lands of the Smoky Mountains. It is said that a female warrior from another land was seen briefly several times before some people escaped from the wagon trains on The Trail of Tears. Rumors had it that it was a spirit from another world that followed the trail. We know it was not. Lo Ming had her reasons for following the trail.

Lo Ming was trying to find her mother. Lo Ming's mother had ventured to America. She had heard in China about the new land to the east. Lo Ming's mother was tired of the fighting in China. She knew about the Indian way of life and wanted to be part of it. Lo Ming's mother blended in with the Cherokees. She loved the life and their traditions. Lo Ming's mother married a young brave. They were very happy for several years until the problems started with the white settlers. Lo Ming's mother and her husband had a son. They were captured and put into a stockade. Soon they were on the journey west on The Trail of Tears.

Lo Ming was in America trying to find her mother. When she located the village where her mother lived, everyone had been rounded up. Lo Ming started on her quest to find her. Lo Ming searched almost every wagon train along the trail. She helped Indians escape. Soon she found the train that Lo Ming's mother and her family were on. It was what she witnessed there, that changed everything."

The old man looked at the package in his hands. His hands started to tremble. His voice was faltering. He looked at Lo Ming's name on the package. With a grieving voice he said, "I am not worthy enough to do this." The Great Elder stood up and took the package from the old man. The Great Elder said, "You are worthy enough, please let me do the honor." The old man and the members of the Tribal Council nodded their head in agreement.

The Great Elder began to speak, "Lo Ming, we know that you were there at The Trail of Tears. You witnessed Black Wolf and his entire family being shot. They were shot by their own people. The General wanted to show what would happen if any more people tried to escape. He would have other families shot.

It was in the early morning on a cold day. The wind was blowing from the North. The grass on the prairie waved in the wind like waves of water in a large lake. Everyone in the camp had to watch. Black Wolf, being the main Chief of this wagon train, was chosen to be made an example of to the rest of his tribe. There was to be a firing squad. Chief Black Wolf and his family were lined up facing the camp. Several of his warriors were given guns to shoot them down. To ensure that they didn't try to shoot anyone but Black Wolf's family, soldiers stood behind them with rifles trained on them. They also knew if they tried anything their families would be next.

Chief Black Wolf was a very brave warrior. In all the years of battles, he would never do such a thing. Innocents should not die for what others had done. How could these soldiers turn on the Cherokees that had been their allies in the Indian War with the Creeks? Cherokee Warriors do not do that to others that fought with them. He looked at the Commanding officer with disgust. "Doesn't American warriors have any honor? We fought and died with your soldiers. We do not understand. This will be a stain on your people. It will not be the only time that Americans will do this. I will die as a warrior. My family will be brave. We are Cherokee."

The Commanding officer gave the order to fire. Cherokee warriors made sure that their shots were true. They did not want anyone to suffer. The camp moved on without burying Black Wolf's family. His wife with his children were left where they fell. He lay next to them. You watched this from a hill far from the camp. You were helpless to do anything.

When all was gone, you rode your painted pony over to the sight. You were at least going to give them a proper burial. Black Wolf was still barely alive. You took him in your arms. Black Wolf whispered to you, "Give my family a proper burial on that hill over there. I want to see them buried proper." You carried each member of his family one by one in your arms. You buried them on that hilltop that overlooked the prairie.

You went back to get Black Wolf. You were surprised to see he was still alive. We know he said to you, "Thank you for burying my family." He had in his hand a silver coin. "This is payment for burying my family. Please let me die like a warrior and bury me next to them. Let me die in pride." You said, "I will take it as a gift from one warrior to another. You are a great warrior. I will honor your request."

You summoned your painted pony. You put Black Wolf on your saddle. You gave him your bow and knife to hold in his dying hands. With his last dying breath, he rode your pony to the top of the hill. You saw him raise your bow and knife. He

116

fell from your pony dead in the middle of his family. He died as a warrior. You buried him where he fell. You put the coin in his right hand to take with him. You wanted him to know you honored him and his family. You let him die with his pride. He tried to protect his family until the end.

"Open the package, Lo Ming." Lo Ming opened the small package. Tears filled her eyes as she picked up a silver coin and held it in her trembling hands. "The Great Spirits gave this coin to us many years ago. They said that you would return to us one day. That a great warrior from the East would come to help us once more." As Lo Ming held the silver coin that had an eagle on it, it started to shine. It cast its light into the sky above. Lo Ming looked above her in the sky, Black Wolf and his family looked down on her. Black Wolf said, "The coin is now where it should be. It was my honor to have met such a great warrior. My family thanks you. May you live long and die as a warrior." Black Wolf and his family were on painted ponies. They turned their painted ponies and rode them across the night's sky toward the heavens.

"There is more to your story," said the Great Elder. "When you found your mother and her family one night in their camp, your mother refused to leave the camp with you. She did not want to be responsible for anyone dying if she escaped with her family. She made it across the prairie, but her husband and your brother died. My grandfather tried to help her live by giving her his blanket. He died of sickness many years later. They say it was from sickness he got on the trail. Your mother left after they arrived at the end of The Trail of Tears. Nobody ever saw her after that."

Lo Ming turned around and picked up a leather package she had brought. She gave it to the Great Elder. "This has come back to where it belongs. It belongs to your family not mine." The Great Elder and the Council were surprised by her gesture. He opened the leather package. He unfolded an

Indian blanket. It had the symbol of the Great Elder's clan on it. The Great Elder could not speak. He buried his face in it. He could not contain his emotion. The Red Woman spoke for him. "You have honored us with such a gift. Now the blanket is home where it belongs."

I got up and asked for permission to talk. The Red Woman nodded her head. "Yes, John, you can talk," she replied. "The old man and I thought about how to save this land for many years. We have fought hard and lost many lives in doing so. As you know, special powers do not always work in this land. The Great Spirits do not allow us to use them in **The Land of the Eagle Feathers** to kill. This is especially true in fighting with the **Dark Ones** or with any other invader. After studying this matter for many years, we have reached a conclusion. Fighting and killing is not the answer. Killing only brings more killing. Fighting only brings more fighting.

Finding *The Book of Winter* and its power is very important, but it will not be the answer to all our problems. Little Wolf deciphered some passages that suggests that only good can conquer evil in this land. If power could conquer the **Dark Ones**, then we would have conquered them long ago.

I am telling my group and all that will help us defeat the **Dark Ones** that we must not kill anyone during the final battle. We must use our special powers and the power of the book to change **The Dark One's Army** from an evil force to one that no longer wants to fight. The old man and I have worked on a plan for years. It will take careful planning, cunning and strategy to pull this off.

I am tired of fighting and killing. It had gotten us nowhere. If we destroy the **Army of the Dark Ones,** they will just be back later. If our enemies find out that they will lose their armies by their men refusing to fight any more, they will never venture into this land again. We still need to find the book because it has answers to how to do this final step.

I have little time left. I must get the power of ***The Book of Winter*** before the end of the first day of our New Year, January 15th. If not, I will not exist but fade away. The Book will protect this land from our enemies only if we defeat our enemies first. If we do not defeat them, they have right to the book, and all here is lost. They will have unlimited power to destroy any one in their path. That was written in ***The Book of Fall***. Wasn't it, Antonio?" Antonio nodded his head.

"**The Keepers of the Yawi** have fought many battles and hardships to get to this point. I remind them that we have forged a bond in our battles that must not be broken. I ask only one thing of the Council and my Warriors. You must trust me one more time. You and I have no other choice. To defeat this enemy, we must take a new direction. The old ways will not work."

I could see that my announcement was hard for many of the Council and our group to comprehend. White Elk rose to speak. "I can see why you picked the people you did for the journey to find the books. They all have a thread or link to The Trail of Tears and other events that have shaped us. You are wise in what you say. Life is so easily taken from people. Hate is easy to store in your heart. Forgiveness is the most difficult thing to do.

John, it will be hard for warriors to change. Your group have very battle harden veterans. What you say has been written in the stars. We have been waiting for you to find a way to protect this land without bloodshed. I hope you are right."

The Great Elder stood up, "We have this land as a refuge for all. We acknowledge your deeds and those that have followed you. We have waited for answers to our fate. To do as you asked, will not be easy for those that have followed you. We know that the last book that we need is in The Land of Nightmares. Very few have ever found this land or returned from being sent there. I hope that you are successful. Your group must know, they will never be the same after they go there. They will be changed forever by their experience there. You cannot take anyone there that is not totally committed to our cause. They must choose their fate themselves. The Potlatch is over and so is our Council meeting. May the spirits be with you. We will see in the morning who is going to go. You will need everyone to be successful."

Chapter V
Preparing for The Land of Nightmares
Is everyone brave enough?

It was late when the meeting broke up. The Great Elder had arranged for everyone to have their own quarters. Angela and Antonio went to be together in a room set aside for them. They had much to talk about before morning. June and One Feather decided to take some blankets and spend the night with their wolves. They watched the stars on a nearby hillside. Their wolves howled at the moon before jumping on them and laying close to them. The Red Woman and David went to her home in her long house. Naturally, Moses and Lo Ming had a room fixed for them.

Red Bear went back to the male quarters. He wanted to be alone. His thoughts turned to what he would say to his son when he found him in The Land of Nightmares. Rose was very apprehensive about finding Zan and confronting his father. Nick could sense her feelings. Rose asked if Nick would spend the night in her room to keep her company. Rose said that she needed a friend. Nick agreed and took his things to her room.

Little Wolf had studied *The Book of Fall*. He knew that going to The Land of Nightmares was very dangerous. It was said you could go mad or crazy in that land. The second thing was it was going to be very dangerous in obtaining the last book: ***The Book of Winter***. This was his Vision Quest. If he was successful in helping them get the book, he would have fulfilled his Vision Quest. He would come back a full-grown man in his tribe's eyes.

At this moment, he still felt like a little boy that had just found his parents. His mother and dad were here. He wanted for once to know what is was like to have one night together with them as a boy like many of the other boys had around him. Little Wolf followed Mary out of the Council hall. He knew what he would ask would be difficult for her. John, his father, told him what had happened years ago. He wasn't upset at John or Mary, his mother. They didn't know about him. He was very upset with his grandmother, the Red Woman. He knew that his grandmother was trying to protect him. He thought she didn't handle it correctly. He had a right to know who his mother and father was. His grandmother never lied to him, but she never told him the truth. He would have to settle this with her later.

Little Wolf asked Mary if he could talk to her. They went into Little Wolf's wooden small hut. There was a small fire in the middle of the hut. The smoke rose to the opening in the ceiling. She noticed that there was a large bed with blankets on it. "I fixed my hut so that I could have my family stay with me. I never knew what is was like to have a mother and father. I am asking that of you and John, a favor for your little boy, I want to know what it was like to have a family for one night. I want to be a little boy for just once with a family together. All I have known is my grandmother and great grandfather.

If or when we come back from The Land of Nightmares, I will no longer be a boy but a man.   Is it too much to ask that my mother and father be with me tonight?" asked Little Wolf. He had tears running down his face. Mary pulled Little Wolf to her. She couldn't help it. She started to cry. The years that she had missed with her son were gone. She would never get them back. How could she not ask his father not to be with Little Wolf and her tonight? Their problems were small compared to their son's.

   She was about to answer that question when there was a knock on the door. Little Wolf opened the door to his hut. Standing there were John and the Red Woman. John had changed back into his buckskins. The Red Woman had Mary's belongings with her. The Red Woman only said one thing, "This is the Potlatch's gift to Little Wolf. You can't refuse to give it to him." The Red Woman left the hut without looking at them. She stopped briefly to give her grandson a hug. For one night, they were a family. Little Wolf slept between his mother and father.

   Moses and Lo Ming lay together in each other's arms. Moses was not one to talk much. "What you did for the Black Wolf was true to the warrior's code. What you did for the Great Elder was different. It was a side of you that I had not seen before. I was very proud of you for returning the blanket to him," said Moses.

   "Moses, I have lived a long time. I have seen many things and lived many lives. In all my travels, I never met a man like you. I don't want ever to lose you. Some people like John, Antonio and myself can live longer than others. Some people think we are time travelers. I cannot explain it all to you. I have learned to live for the moment. This moment is ours," she said as she kissed him and held him tight against her. In the back of Lo Ming's mind, there was a fleeting thought. Maybe, *The Book of Winter* could change some things for them. Just maybe, John could grant me one wish.

   Antonio and Angela had finished their lovemaking. They laid underneath a blanket. "I always wondered why you and John had this tension between you. I know that John can be sometimes very difficult to deal with. He has always, around me, shown you respect. I know he thinks very highly of your skills. He once told me that you saved his back several times. He is very fond of you. He told me I was lucky to have someone like you. What is that you have against him?" asked Antonio.

Angela paused for a while. "He did save me many years ago. We traveled a lot together on various adventures. He once said I was like a little sister to him. One time he left me with a lady for a couple of years to learn the finer things of life. I got bored and ran away. I got a boyfriend. I guess you could have called him a bad boy.

We did some work for David. We found several artifacts that he wanted in Africa. One day, my boyfriend went to sell some of these to David. I waited, and he never came back. The next day I took the rest of the artifacts to David myself. I asked David if my boyfriend had come by with some of the artifacts to sell to him. David said, "I never saw him. There is word on the street that a man had killed him. I think the man's name was John that did it."

"Well to say the least, I went ballistic. When John showed up a week later, I was so mad that I tried to kill him. We had a big fight. John finally won, but I did hurt him. You have seen that faint scar on his face. I did that. It gives me pleasure to know he will wear it forever," said Angela in a very sarcastic tone.

"May I ask the name of your boyfriend?" Angela replied, "His name was Mark Simeon." Antonio got quite for a moment. "Did this man have white hair with a line of black hair down the middle of his head? Did he speak with a French accent?" asked Antonio. "Yes, on both accounts," Angela answered.

"Yes, he was a very bad boy. He had a bad habit. People didn't like dealing with him. He was a dangerous man. In

123

fact, I almost killed him myself many years ago. John must have beat me to it. He killed a friend of mine," Antonio stated. "I can't believe you. He always treated me nicely," said Angela more than upset. "That was his reputation. His bad habit was that he would double-cross his partners and then kill them when he got something of value to sell. You were lucky to be alive. I bet when John heard that you were running with Mark Simeon. He killed him. I heard it was a bloody affair. Mark did cut up his attacker before he died. That is why you almost got the better of John," said Antonio.

Angela looked at Antonio. "All these years, I thought John killed Mark out of spite about me," Angela said with some shame. "You are lucky to be alive. He would have killed you like he did my female friend. That is why I wanted to kill him. She was dear to me. He did both of us a favor. I guess, I owe my blood brother another favor," Antonio whispered into Angela's ear. "Let's forget about John and such things, we have little time to waste," said Antonio as he pulled her to him. "Yes, I will make sure that we don't waste our time together," whispered Angela in her most sexy voice.

Early the next morning, Angela decided to find One Feather. It was a beautiful morning for this time of year. A warm wind was blowing in from the south. You could see the snow tipped mountain in the distance.

The bright sun was starting its way over the eastern mountains. This caused fog to lie in the valleys below. It made several of the mountaintops look like small islands with the fog being water around them.

Angela found One Feather with June and their two wolves enjoying the views around them where they had slept the night before. June looked up at Angela. June said to One Feather that she needed to get ready and went into the Great Lodge. "May I talk to you, One Feather?" Angela asked. One Feather smiled, "Yes, mother. May I call you mother?" One Feather asked. "Only if you want too," Angela replied caught off guard by the word: Mother.

"I guess I should tell you why I gave you up for adoption. I was very young. Antonio didn't know I was pregnant. He had left to go on another mission for the Pope. I couldn't find him. I was alone and frightened. I didn't know what to do. I couldn't go back here because I left without permission. I panicked. A nun where you were born suggested that I give you up for adoption. At first, I said no. She told me that you would be well cared for and safe. She told me that several bad men were looking for me. There were rumors they wanted me dead. When I saw one outside the hospital, I took you and fled.

These were very bad people. I was supposed to protect an evil priest, but instead I turned him over to the Catholic Church. They wanted revenge for that. I had to protect you. The only place that I thought you would be safe was at the Catholic Orphanage in Rome, Italy. Apparently, the Pope had taken interest in me because I didn't stop Antonio from doing his job. I was promised that you would be safe. I gave you up for adoption to the Orphanage. After a few months, I killed the men that were after me. By the time I realized that I had made a terrible mistake, you were already adopted from the Orphanage. The nuns told me that the Pope had a man take you to a place where you would be safe. They did not know where. I had looked for you for many years. I never gave up. I never had the courage to tell Antonio until he guessed you were his son," cried Angela. "I feel so ashamed and guilty about what I did. Please don't hate me for that, One Feather. Please forgive me."

One Feather could not help it. He took Angela in his strong arms and held her until her sobbing stopped. "One day long ago, I asked White Elk about who my mother was. He had told me that he was my grandfather. He was very protective about me. He said you were a very brave young girl. He explained why you left this land. He also told me that you risked death to save the Red Woman.

This act of courage made me proud to have you as my mother. White Elk told me not to tell anyone. I kept this secret until I told June about it. White Elk told me that my parents were someday coming back to help save this land. I have waited ever since," said One Feather.

"Don't worry, you are not a disappointment. You are a great warrior. John told me that when I asked him about you. He said that you were the only one that ever got the best of him in a fight. He pointed to that scar on his face. I think he was proud that he taught you so well.

He said my father had his good days and bad. I would have to judge that myself. John and my father are blood brothers. They both share the same blood. That is good enough for me. It is the way of this land. I have always treated John like an uncle. Now he is truly my uncle.

This has been difficult for all of us. As they say, destiny is a strange companion. It is our destiny to be here together whatever happens. At least, I will have my family with me, mother. Nobody could ask for more."

Antonio was standing near a tree out of sight of Angela and One Feather. He could hear their conversation. There were tears in his eyes. He had forgiven Angela. He had never forgiven himself. He knew that one day he would have to tell One Feather about him and his past. That would be very difficult. He had done many things both good and somewhat questionable.   He turned and went back to the Great Lodge for breakfast. This day would be for Angela and her son to spend together.

Antonio found June waiting for him at the lodge. She asked him to sit by her. "Well, I see that One Feather is having a good talk with my future mother-in-law. I think, I should have a talk with my future father-in-law. I took some time back home when I realized who you were to find out some things about you.

It seems that you have as the White Men say, "a checkered past." I saw that in the sacred waters by my tribe's camp. You have lived many lives. You had done many things. You have much mystical and magical knowledge. I couldn't find anything more. You will need someday to pass that knowledge on to your son and your grandchildren. I do plan to have children. It will be your duty to do so. I only ask one thing of you: Be a good father to your son! That will make him happy and will make me happy. If you fail at that, I will make you pay. A daughter-in-law can be a very frightful person to have if she is upset. Have a good breakfast future father-in-law!" said June sternly to him. As Antonio watched June leave the lodge to join Angela, he smiled proudly, "And I thought Angela was a handful."

Nick and Rose were eating breakfast. I could tell that both were apprehensive about our journey to The Land of Nightmares. Rose knew that to get Zan back she would probably have to face down Zorn, Zan's father. She had worked and studied all the magic and mysticism that her parents, Big Daddy Crawfish and Sheba, had given her. Nick was not only worried about Rose's welfare he was worried about Shanna. Shanna was taking a big risk in working with Raven and Benita.

I told them not to worry so much. I had full confidence in Shanna and Rose. Both were very good at their skills. We had things to do before we could leave tomorrow. The Red Woman had called a meeting to start shortly. It will be held in the Council Hall. You need to bring your medicine bags to be smudged and cleansed. Only **The Keepers of the Yawi,** Little Wolf and One Feather will be allowed to attend. David,

Red Bear and Angela will need to wait for the ceremony to end to come.

The Red Women was waiting for them in the Council Hall. She had everyone seated around a fire in the middle of the room. The Red Woman greeted everyone. Then she started the ceremony about the medicine bags.

"I hope that your medicine bags are filled with your own spiritual objects that will give your great strength, courage and powers. If you have chosen your spiritual animal, stones, plants and crystals well, they will be of great assistance. You will need them to be successful. Little Wolf, soon to be a man, will go with you. His completing this Vision Quest will make him a man. He is an important key to obtaining *The Book of Winter*. Without Little Wolf, you will not be successful.

Being the Red Woman, the Great Spirits have given me permission to perform sacred rituals. There is a ritual that we must perform before your medicine bags can be used. They must be smudged or cleansed. First, you must be purified by the sacred smoke. Every one of you must empty your medicine bags and put their contents inside the red cloths that I have placed in a circle around the sacred campfire. Each of you including the One Feather and Little Wolf must also stand in the circle around the fire.

Doing as directed, everyone placed the contents of their medicine bags on a red cloth provided and bundled them in that red cloth. The Red Woman next told us to take our hands and pull the sacred smoke from the campfire over our faces and bodies to cleanse ourselves. You must then fan the smoke in all four directions. Then fan the smoke toward Mother Earth, Father Sky and finally to the center for the Great Spirit. You must keep your medicine bags open so it will be smudged and cleansed.

Everyone took their medicine bag and made sure it was opened in their right hand. The Red Woman took out her eagle feather and waved it toward the fire. Smoke started to billow from the fire. Each of us fanned the smoke in the four directions then toward us and then to Mother Earth, Father Sky and to the Great Spirit. The Red Woman smudged our bags to purify each of our bags by touching each bag with her Eagle Feather both on the outside and inside of the bag.

After she completed this task with all of us, she placed in our bags the following items: a small tobacco bag, a small bag of corn pollen, a piece of animal bone and a piece of flint. Then she told us to put the items that we had smudged with the red cloth back into the bag. No one must touch your medicine bag, or you will need to have the bag smudged again. You do not want to lose the powers of your medicine bag. Now each of you have been cleansed and your bags.

The Red Woman spoke again to us. "There are powers in this universe that are greater than us. They are the seven Chakras. Each Chakra is related to the body and soul of each of us. They can provide you with fields of energy to be used when you need them.

Some of you may have had a Chakra before. I will tell each of you what your Chakra is now for this quest in **The Land of the Eagle Feathers**. June, your Chakra is the Heart Chakra which relates to spirit and form. Lo Ming, your Chakra is the Throat Chakra which relates to choice and willpower. Moses, your Chakra is the Solar Plexus Chakra which relates to self-confidence and control. Antonio, your Chakra is the Sacral Chakra of the ovaries and prostates which relates to relationships and social control. Rose, your Chakra is the Brow or Third Eye Chakra which relates to intuition. Nick, your Chakra is the Crown Chakra of the head which relates to guidance. Mary, your Chakra is the Base or Root Chakra of the Coccyx with relates to personal survival. Remember each of these Chakras is powerful but when put together they are overwhelming. To harness the total power for you to survive you must become one.

The Red Woman told us to protect Little Wolf. He is the key that will open the hiding place of the book. I have taught him our ways. He is brave and wise beyond his years. Your group is small, and your hardships will be great.

You can take One Feather with you to assist you. Remember it will take all your collective powers to successfully complete this quest. Every one of you has a purpose. Red Bear and David will need to go. They have a special purpose I do not know. Angela will need to go but must come back when you find The Land of Nightmares.

You either succeed or you fail. Failure will be the end of you and the end of this land. The eagle will not fly, and the spirits will not rest. Everything will be lost. If you succeed, you will be rewarded. Then she looked at Mary and said, "Many of you have suffered enough.

Now is the time to become free. Your journey starts tomorrow. You need to be here with the sacred *Book of Winter* no later than three days before the New Year of this land or January 12th.

The only clue I must give you is the first one to find The Land of Nightmares that *The Book of Fall* told you where you would find *The Book of Winter*. Look to the first light of winter, and that light will start you on your journey." The Red Woman started to leave. "One Feather will tell you the rest as he was told by White Elk. I must leave now. I must talk to David and Red Bear. The Red Woman took one more look at Mary. It was like she was saying be careful. She left the Council Hall in a fast walk like she couldn't wait to get out of there.

The first one to speak was Moses. "Besides the problem of locating the book, why is this quest going to be so difficult?"

Moses asked. That's when Little Wolf and One Feather replied, "Because the deeper you go into **The Land of the Eagle Feathers** the more primitive it becomes."

One Feather said, " White Elk told me about the legends that were handed down. There was one section of **The Land of the Eagle Feathers** that was left wild and not tamed. Our forefathers wanted it that way. This section is very dangerous. It had been off limits for what white man would call centuries. The animals are strange creatures. They are dangerous. There are lost tribes that are not civilized. There are spirits that roam the forests and jungles that will try to kill you. Some of these spirits will drink your blood while you sleep.

The weather is unpredictable. In one area, you could have deserts and another you could have jungles. If you were to hide something, you never would find it in the place that you would hide it.

The legends about those that hid the final book says that 40 of our best warriors found this land. They were accompanied by a great medicine man and his apprentice, Red Bear. They went in to hide the book only five came back alive. Those that came back were never the same. They said that they were like crazy men.

They spoke of horrible animals, spirits and demons. In some places, the ground was on fire. There was one place where the mountain would spit rocks and melted rocks flowed like rivers. The great medicine man called this place The Land of Nightmares. Everyone that went there had their memories erased as to where it was located and where the other three books were located.

The only way to find this land was written in *The Book of Fall* that the great medicine man had written. To find that book, the great medicine man wrote three other books. You all know about those. Another thing you must know, time does not work there like here. Time slows down there. Each day inside will seem like a week. We will have plenty of time inside to explore. Even though the time is short for us to return.

It is said what drove the men crazy was that they had to face their most terrible nightmares. Most of them could not handle that. We need to be aware of that. We need to remember what the Red Woman told us that tomorrow will give us at first light the direction where to start our journey. Then we must rely on the passages to get there and find the book."

Rose stood up, "I brought some precious stones and gems for your medicine bags. I will go and get them from my belongings." In a few minutes she returned, "I feel that it is time for us to have as much protection as possible. I put together a special pouch for each of you. Each of these contains several precious stones, gems and crystals

All these pouches have been cleansed and purified. In each pouch are the following: Turquoise for luck; Hematite to make you invisible to your enemies; Onyx to protect your powers; Green Jade to guard against misfortune; Red Jasper to protect against things in the night and the energy of your body, fire to your powers; Pink Halite to dissolve confusion and doubt; Amazonite for stamina; Snakeskin Agate for healing; and Agate for protection. Also, I put in each pouch a precious stone that only you can use to intensify your special powers.

In Little Wolf's pouch, I put a diamond. This is due to Little Wolf being the key to obtaining *The Book of Winter*. He is the only one that can harness all our powers at once. We must all guard him and protect him. I know this because I saw a diamond shaped birthmark on the back of his neck."

Mary then got up and gave each of us pouches she had prepared. "In each are plants with healing powers. There is snakeroot for fever, milkweed for stomach problems and for skin problems, Tassel Flower for cuts, Bloodroot and several others for sickness. These are all in your pouches that I had the Red Woman cleanse for you. In my study of ancient healing powers, I know their powers, Remember, that you are the only one that can touch these healing plants to cure yourself. Don't let anyone else touch them. Keep them in your medicine bag. I am afraid that some of us may need to use them. I have kept most of my knowledge in healing arts to myself. I have been blessed by the healing spirits of many tribes in my travels. I know that many of you have heard the legends and myths of The Land of Nightmares. My father, David, told me about such a place when I was a child. I thought it was a strange fairy tale. He told me that his father told him about it when he was a child. He told his father that it was only a story. His father said it wasn't. David asked his father how he knew. His father said, "I have been there."

I looked at the group in front of me. "Now you know why Red Bear is so important. He may not know how to get to The Land of Nightmares or even where the book is hidden. I only hope that he remembers some of the things about The Land of Nightmares that could help us locate the book such as landmarks or trails. I asked the Red Woman if Red Bear could come and talk to us about what he knows. I hope he does. We will wait for a few moments to see if he comes. We will need to be ready to leave at sunrise tomorrow. Be ready to ride out at first light, tomorrow."

Red Bear and David came into the Council Hall as I finished talking. "John, you wanted to see us," said Red Bear. "Yes, I do. I was wondering, do you remember anything about The Land of Nightmares? I understand you were once there. It would be a great help to everyone here to know more about it."

"I can only recall very little. Perhaps when I get there, I will be able to recall more. If my mentor, Grey Fox, did hide the book there, I have no idea where. He was very secretive about his actions. He would leave the main trail several times without telling where he was going. Some of the things that I do remember are that it is a very dangerous place. You must watch your every step. There are primitive tribes that will kill you if they get a chance. If you kill any of the animals, they will kill you in return. None of the plants were good to eat. They were poisonous to outsiders. We will have to take our food along.

Spirits and demons roam the night sky looking for prey to kill. Along the main trail will be buildings or places familiar to different members of our group. These places try to entice people to go in. The reason is that they remind a person of something that is unresolved in their lives. Usually, it is an event that was very sad or terrifying that happened to them. If they are successful in overcoming that event, they are safe. If they fail to conquer it, they must remain in the land or die until it is resolved. I saw men go completely mad in that land.

There is another aspect of this land. The Spirits have sent people to this land. Those that are sent there must stay until they resolve some issue. There were rumors that they can be released from the land if they or the people who sent them there feel that they have recanted their deeds. People can assist them but usually this only gets them in more trouble. Remember if you help someone and you fail you must take their place. My mentor told me those things. The only other thing I remember is he telling me: **"Only fools would ever go there. Anyone who goes there usually dies, remains there, or goes mad."**

I suggest that everyone going be prepared for anything. I am going because of my son. Some of you have other reasons such as lost loved ones. Most of you feel that your mission to find *The Book of Winter* to save this land is enough reason to go. The first thing you must do is ask yourself, "Is it worth the price to go?" I will leave you to think about it. If the book is there, will you be able to resist its power? It can change you for the better or the worse. **Is it worth the price?**"

The Red Woman came into the hall. "Red Bear is right. You must ask yourself. Is it worth the price? Some of you may not come back. Some of you might go mad. Some of you might die." Little Wolf looked up at the Red Woman, "There is another option. We all might come back and save everything we love." June said, "I agree with Little Wolf. We are **The Keepers of the Yawi**. It is our destiny to complete this, failure is not an option." Everyone nodded their heads in agreement.

The Red Woman said, "I will see you in the early morning. Have a good day and evening! Spend your time wisely. Starting tomorrow, each day may be your last. Nobody can ever say you are not brave."

It was a sunny warm day. The afternoon was more like autumn than Winter. A gentle breeze blew the fallen brown leaves around the pasture below the camp. The horses were grazing on some late green tall grass. The sun felt good on your face. It was a lazy day. Nick appreciated days like these. In the pasture below about a mile away was a tall oak tree. There were still a few brown leaves on its high branches. The wind moved the branches back and forth. He thought it was inviting him to come. He wanted to be alone. He had already packed his things for tomorrow's journey. The oak tree kept beckoning him to come.

Nick walked down toward the old oak tree. It was a pleasant walk. The dry grass made a slight crunching sound under his light brown desert military boots. He had put a sandwich in one of the side pockets of his brown cargo pants and took a canteen full of water with him.   He watched several eagles floating on the up drafts of the mountain winds. "Yes, it is a good day to be alive. I only wish Shanna was here to enjoy such a day with me. If there is a heaven, this is as close as it gets," he thought.

Taking his time, it took him about 30 minutes to reach the old oak tree. He sat down. He leaned his body against rough, dark bark of the tree . He gazed down at the valley below. He watched several squirrels run up the tree trunk and grab acorns. They would get as many as they could carry in their mouths and run back down the trunk. They were taking them to a smaller hickory tree about 100 yards away. Some buried the acorns in the ground for winter ahead, and some put the acorns into the hollow of the tree. They would chatter at each other like they were arguing about where to put the acorns. It reminded him of times when Shanna and he would disagree on things.

His thoughts returned to Shanna. He couldn't help it. He worried about her. Being around Raven and Benita could be very dangerous for her. He wondered if she would be able to pull off such a double cross on such devious and evil characters as Raven and Benita. Shanna was a good actress. The CIA wouldn't have hired and trained her if she couldn't play the part of a double agent.

Nick had an acorn hit him on his head. A squirrel chattered at him. Nick could swear that the squirrel was laughing at him. "Yes, this is a beautiful day to be alive," he thought before he fell asleep with the warm sun on his body.

Nick started dreaming. It was like he was there in Houston. Shanna was exercising at the gym in Angela's building. It was early morning. She was working out with some weights. A woman was spotting her. "Now, Shanna, that's a lot of weight to put on the bar," said Raven. Raven was dressed in tight, red short gym shorts and a sports bra. Raven's long auburn, reddish hair flowed down her back. "Have you given any more thought about what we asked you about our plans?" asked Raven. Shanna gave that wicked smile back at Raven.

"You know if you double cross David, he will kill you. I have seen him do that to the most dangerous of enemies. He seems to take great joy in killing his enemies. I have only one problem with your plans. Can we trust Benita? After all, she has almost everything she wants being David's wife."

"Don't worry about her, Shanna. Benita and I go back many years. We killed David's first wife. We have been planning this for a long time. Besides, I am a woman, and David can't compete with me. Benita likes both men and women. She still prefers women," laughed Raven.

"We will have to be careful of Benita," said Shanna. "She could get jealous of having me around." "Don't worry about that. Maybe you can loan Nick out to her. Your boyfriend is a handsome young man. Some would call him a stud. Wouldn't we all make a great team? Besides, you like living dangerously. It turns you on," Raven said as she kissed Shanna and left.

As Shanna watched Raven walk to the gym's locker room, Nick could hear her whisper, "Not as much as being with Nick. Raven will be fun to play this game with. I will only have to play a little more with Benita. Jealously will be the end of these two."

Shanna got up and posed in a very sexy way into the full, length mirror behind her. "I can see you very faintly in the mirror, Nick, my love. I hope you liked the show. You are not the only one that has some magic. I could feel that you were lonely. Me, too. Don't worry about me! You know me, I'm having lots of fun. Don't girls like to have fun!" Shanna kissed the mirror. Nick could feel her kiss. "You be very careful. We still have our back up plan if this doesn't work out. Bye, my love, see you soon! Oh, one more thing, I will be with you in your dreams tonight. We will have some fun then," Shanna whispered as Nick woke up.

When Nick walked back to the camp, Rose met him. "Did you enjoy your time at that old oak tree? You look satisfied. They say day naps are good for you," Rose said with a wicked smile. "Why, Rose, you look a little jealous?" asked Nick. "Only as much as you are of Zan," she replied. "That's why we are such great friends," said Nick.

"Don't worry about tonight. I am not so anxious. We have better sleep in separate rooms. I don't want to disturb your dreams. I have some dreams that I must catch up on. I think you do, too. Don't you, Nick?" asked Rose. "How did you know?" replied Nick. "Don't girls like to have fun!" Rose said with that wicked laugh of hers. "Rose must have gotten that laugh from her mother, Sheba. Zan must be something to be able to handle a woman like Rose," thought Nick.

Everyone was saddled the next morning. Rose couldn't leave it alone. "How were your dreams last night, Nick? asked Rose as they gazed at the Eastern sky for the first sign of light. "Probably better than yours, Rose," Nick answered. Rose replied, "I doubt they could surpass my dreams. But knowing Shanna, she tried very hard." They both smiled at the sun coming up over the Eastern Mountain. The first beam of sunlight hit the peak of a faraway mountain. Red Bear frowned. He looked worried as he said, "That's what is known as Moise Mountain. It only appears in Winter."

Moses asked," What does that mean in English?" David answered, "Crawling Mountain or Mountain that Crawls." June added, "It's said there's lots of spirits and demons that crawl around on it." Lo Ming said, "At least, it lets us know what we are getting into." Antonio said sarcastically. "I can't wait until we get there." Angela replied, "We have got to get there first." John said, "Red Bear, be my guest, you get to be the lead horse." A smile on Red Bear's face formed as he replied, "With you and June behind me, how can I refuse?" Red Bear turned his horse around and headed in the direction of Moise Mountain. Nick laughed, "As Shanna would say, just another day in paradise."

Chapter VI
The Journey to The Land of Nightmares
Is it worth it?

The day was turning colder. Red Bear looked at the dark clouds in the sky. He pulled his buffalo cape around him. "I must be getting old. A little cold never bothered me before," he thought. They stopped to give the horses and mules a rest at midday. Red Bear had seen a small clearing that had Cedar Trees covering three sides of it. It would shelter them from the cold wind that was blowing in from the North.

Nick lit a small fire and boiled some water for hot tea and coffee. He fixed some soup for everyone. June was starting to worry about bad weather setting in before they would reach a place to camp for the night. I told June not to worry. We should be at our campsite in four hours. We would be alright until then.

We only stayed in this spot for about an hour. We pushed on down the trail. The trail was getting narrow and rocky. Our horses were having a hard time as the trail turned to mud. I had everyone get off their horse, or mule in my case, as a safety precaution. This slowed our progress. I asked June to summon one of her hawks. When the hawk flew down to land on June's arm, I tied a small note to it. I made sign language for the hawk to find Morning Star. The note was to tell her to camp at the hot spring.

I told them that we would be having a good meal soon. We only had about three miles of this before we would be camping for the night. It would be about dark by thc time we got to Morning Star's camp.

This was exhausting travel. You would take one step forward. and it seemed like two steps back. Finally, we got out of the muddy, rocky trail. We mounted our animals and headed toward the hot spring. A mile later, we found Morning Star. She and her two boys had a fire going. She had a large string of mules with her. As we dismounted, I told everyone to hurry and pitch camp. It wouldn't be long before we would be getting a light snow.

We ate Morning Star's evening meal quickly. Snow had started to fall. Morning Star's boys had moved the mules and horses into a thicket of pine trees to give them some protection from the weather. Nick asked why Morning Star had brought so many mules. "Well, you saw how the horses had so much trouble with the muddy and rocky trail. We will be riding mules tomorrow. We need animals that are more surefooted and tougher than our horses. Tomorrow, you will see why Petunia is my favorite riding animal in rough terrain.

Morning Star will be taking our horses back with her tomorrow. She and her boys will be returning and waiting for us when we get back here after our journey to The Land of Nightmares."

I told everyone that behind the boulders was a small spring of very hot water. " If you need to wash up a little, it's a good place. For some of you, it may be a little too hot. You ladies may think it's just right, but I guarantee the men will not. Get some sleep, it will be a long day tomorrow. Red Bear says it will take us two more days to get to Moise Mountain or Crawling Mountain. One other thing, this is bear country. I have been here before. These bears are larger than any other bears you have seen. Be careful! Moses and I will be taking turns on guard tonight."

The snow had stopped about an hour later. There were at least three inches of snow on the ground. I saw the women go to the hot springs to bathe. I had Moses and Nick bring in the horses and mules closer to the camp. Antonio and Morning Star's boys had collected enough firewood for three campfires. I had Nick light them around the campsite. I hoped that the fires would keep the bears and other animals away for the night.

I was taking over watch at midnight when a loud roar of a bear shook the camp. Moses was on guard duty. He pointed to the campfire at the south end of the camp. A very large dark brown bear about two times the size of a large grizzly bear was approaching the camp. Before I could stop him, Moses walked up to the bear. Moses held up his hand and pointed toward the stars.

The large brown bear seemed perplexed. The bear looked up at the stars to where Moses was pointing. The large bear shook his head liked he understood what Moses was trying to tell him. The bear stood on his back legs and roared at Moses. By now, everyone was out of their tents and watching the scene before them.

Moses roared back at the large bear. Again, he pointed toward the stars. The bear nodded his head. The large brown bear walked over to Moses on its back legs. Moses walked toward the bear. The bear moved his paw as if the strike Moses. Moses stretched out his right arm and touched the great paw of the bear. For several minutes they touched each. They seemed to be talking to each other. Moses would say something in a strange language of grunts and roars. The large bear would grunt and roar back at him. After a while, the bear grabbed Moses and gave him a big hug. We held our breaths. Lo Ming picked up her silver spear to throw at the bear. Moses motioned for her to not throw it. Soon the bear stopped its hug. Its large jaws opened and gave Moses a big lick on his face. Then, the bear landed on all four of his fect and walked away toward the forest behind us. You could hear the large bear roar several times as it disappeared into the dark woods.

Lo Ming ran over to Moses. "You could have been killed," she yelled at him. "No Lo Ming, we all could have been killed," answered Moses. We all gathered around Moses and Lo Ming. Moses told us that the large bear was the leader of all the Great Bears around here.

"The Great Bears do not like that we were in their territory. They thought we were here to hunt them. They were going to rush the camp and kill us. Moses told the leader that we were here to save their land from evil men. The reason that he pointed to the stars was so he could tell the bear about the story of *The Bear and the Seven Sisters.* He told the bear to look at the sky and see the seven stars and the bear chasing them. That would be what would happen if he tried to harm us. His tribe would be chasing us forever in the skies above. He believed Moses when he saw a bear chasing them across the night sky."

Moses said, "I promised them that nobody would ever to allowed to hunt them if they helped us." Antonio asked, "What did you mean by helping us?" Moses replied, "I told them about why we were here. They said that two wolves had already told them about us as the moon came out tonight. They also recognized John. They said if he agreed to protect their territory, they would help us. They would follow us back and fight the **Dark Ones."**

David asked, "Why John?" Moses replied, "Because he is a legend in this territory. He saved a baby bear long ago near here. He fought that man over there to save the baby bear." Moses pointed at Red Bear. "It seems the large bear was that baby bear. The Great Bears also know that John is the one they call **The Gray Ghost.** He saved this land once. It is their turn to help him save it again. They said if John ever dies, they will let him ride the bear that chases the Seven

Sisters across the skies." David looked at John and said, "Well, I'll be damned." Mary sarcastically said, "And so will John."

I didn't worry about having people on watch for the rest of the night. The Great Bears would not let anyone bother us. June and One Feather called their wolves back to the campsite. The Great Bears would protect us for one more day. After that they would go back to sleep until we came back this way. Things would start getting very dangerous when we get closer to Moise Mountain.

The weather changed again. A warm breeze came in from the South early the next morning. Morning Star had breakfast fixed of hoe cakes made from cornmeal with honey. Her two boys had the mules saddled. They tried to pick mules that would match the personality of each rider. I called up Petunia from the field. She came running up to me. Don't ask me why? I loved that old mule. Why she loved me I will never know. We had lots of adventures throughout the years.

I had to smile when I saw the mule that they picked for David. The mule's name was Old Waco. He was a very stubborn and obstinate mule. It would take someone that was a hard case to get him to move. David recognized the mule for what he was. When the mule tried to buck him off, David told the mule he was just as stubborn as he was. We watched and laughed as Old Waco tried to buck off David. I had to admit that David could have been a good rodeo bucking bronco rider. After five minutes, Old Waco settled down. David gave Old Waco a pat on his side. He whispered to Old Waco, "You and I are going to do fine together. We see things the same way." Old Waco "hee ahh" back at David, Moses said, "Now that's a good match if I ever saw one. They both are as stubborn and bad tempered as each other."

Red Bear led the way as we left our horses and Morning Star at the camp. The mules traversed the trail without any problems. The country was getting more wilder in appearance. There were herds of elk and bison in the distance.

Antonio stopped his mule and pointed out that several of the mountains in the mountain range in front of us were volcanos. They were erupting. "I have not seen such eruptions since Mt. Vesuvius covered Pompeii," Antonio said. Nobody knew if Antonio was just kidding or telling the truth. I thought the latter was true.   We took a few minutes to watch them. Red Bear kept a good pace when we headed down the trail again.

The hilly and rocky trail was beginning to fade away. This fact didn't bother Red Bear. He seemed to know where he was going. About midday, we gave our mules a break in a green field of grass with a small clear mountain stream. Morning Star had made us some of her famous cakes of cornbread with nuts and dried berries for a light lunch. After we ate, I decided it was time for me to unbox one of the large boxes on our pack mules.

Moses and Nick placed the box on the ground. Nick took out his large KA-BAR military knife and plied opened the wooden box's top boards. June reached in and pulled out a Cherokee blowgun. There were several in the box with many darts. June said, "I have not shot one of these things in years." I told everyone to be careful in touching the darts. The darts are coated with a drug that will instantly put you to sleep. They are not to be used to kill anything. They are to be used to put an animal or human to sleep. There are some practice darts for you to use to practice. Also, there are several blunt arrows or arrows with a small drug coated needle for knocking out animals or humans for those that would rather use a bow and arrow.

I walked out about 15 yards or meters and placed one of the boards for a target. June said that she was never that good with a blowgun, but she would give it a try. June took a deep breath and gave her blowgun a strong hard blow. Her dart hit the board dead center.

Mary asked to go next. She seemed very confident. Taking aim, she shot her dart directly next to June's dart. Lo Ming laughed and said, "Mary, that was just a lucky shot." Mary's face got red. "Move that target back another 10 yards," Mary said with some anger in her voice. Antonio moved the target back another 10 yards. He took out a small piece of red cloth to put on the board as a target. As he started to put it on the board, Mary shot it out of his hand with another dart. Antonio turned and gave Mary a stern look. A wide grim came across his face. Antonio gave a bow and nodded his approval for Mary's marksmanship.

Lo Ming asked, "Mary, where did you learn to use a blowgun?" David answered for Mary, "When she was a child, her mother taught her. She also learned to become a better shot in Africa and South America."

Everyone took their turn at using the blowguns. David, Red Bear, One Feather, Angela and Little Wolf were very good with them. Lo Ming didn't bother. She said she preferred a bow and arrow. Rose said she didn't need them because she had her exploding beads. Antonio said he preferred the fine sword he saw in the bottom of the box. It was a rapier with a sharp fine point coated with a knockout drug. Moses pointed to his bullwhip.

Nick was another story. He asked Antonio to throw a large walnut into the air. Nick shot it out of the air. He started to say, "I have not shot one of these since Iraq..." Nick stopped in midsentence. He looked away and walked back to saddle his mule. Rose started to go after him. Antonio stopped her.

Angela told Rose, "Nick must deal with his past." David said, "Nick will tell us one day who he really is. He is a good cook. I know he is better at other things." David looked at me and continued, "I once heard of a young lad. He had a nickname. They called him **The Angel of Death** in the Middle East Wars."

"That's enough David! You are just trying to disrupt things," I yelled at David. Red Bear interrupted, "I saw it in his eyes. He has the eyes of a hunter. I am glad he is on our side. We will need him."

We packed up the box and put it on the pack mule. I asked Red Bear if he knew the way. His words were, "How can I forget? I may have been crazy when I left there. Now that I have gotten close enough to remember, I wish I had never been there. There is both evil and good in that land. I only saw the evil. It will take more than a few blowguns and hand weapons for us to survive there."

When it was about two hours before dark, a Great Bear greeted us. Moses dismounted his mule. He put his hand on the Great Bear's front paw. Soon the Great Bear turned and started back toward where we had come. "He said that this is a good place to camp. There is clean water and good wood for a fire. We should be fine for tonight. He said, "Good luck. You will need it tomorrow," said Moses.

We pitched camp for the night. Nick and Rose fixed the evening meal. We ate in silence. The mules were let to graze on the dried grass in the small meadow nearby. As darkness fell, I told Petunia to gather the mules and bring them in for the night. The mules followed Petunia into our camp. Moses picketed them in front of our camp with a rope tied to two trees. Petunia was not tied. I always let her roam around campsites. She is good to have around if something or someone tried to attack us. I used her this way many times on the prairie and in the Rocky Mountains. She saved me many times from unwanted guests. Many a mountain man were saved by their mules stomping unwanted guests.

I asked One Feather and June if they would let their wolves stand guard. Snow and Midnight seemed to like that idea.

They ran up a small hill in sight of the camp. The moon had just come out. It was only a quarter moon. That was enough for the two wolves to howl at it. "Don't worry! The wolves howling serves two purposes. One is that we know they are watching us, and the other is that they are warning others to stay away," said One Feather.

Everyone was sitting around the campfire in the middle of the camp. Moses asked me to finish the story about the riverboat captain on The Trail of Tears. "Oh, the one you met on the boat the other day when we came back with *The Book of Fall* with his wife." I said. "No, John, the one on The Trail of Tears," said Moses.

I could see that got their interest. "As the old man was saying, the riverboat captain had had enough of what he saw. After carrying passengers across the Mississippi River, he took his boat and went to New Orleans. He sold his boat. In those days, New Orleans was a wild place. It was a wide-open city. All sorts of people found their way there.

A former riverboat captain with lots of money would be a target to be robbed. One day the captain got drunk in a bar. Three strong men decided that he would be an easy mark to rob. I guess he was only acting to be drunk. Drunk or not, he jumped up and beat all three of them senseless.

This is where he met a tall, dark woman. People were very afraid of her. They said she was a Voodoo Priestess. Some say she was looking for a strong brave man. Others say she was looking for a husband. She was beautiful. Her skin was as dark as midnight. Her features were of a goddess. Her white toothy smile would melt the coldest hearts.

While he tried to talk to her, two policemen tried to arrest her. The captain didn't take too kindly to that. He knocked both out cold. He had told them that that wasn't the right way to treat a lady. Four more policemen came to arrest both of them this time. Between the captain and the lady, they took quick care of all of them. She told him they had better get out of there.

  She took him to her hotel room down the street. She fixed him a drink. He passed out on a table. The drink was drugged. When he came to, the next morning, there were a compass and a map on the table. A note was attached. It said, "If you like what you saw, follow this map into the swamp. I will be waiting for you. I liked what I saw too. Bring plenty of supplies, you have a lot to learn." It must have been love at first sight. The captain didn't hesitate. He went straight into the swamps.

  People thought he died in the swamps. Nobody saw him for many years. Occasionally, he would bring in a load of crawl fish to sell. He was a big man. They heard he had a beautiful daughter. So, people gave him the nickname of Big Daddy Crawfish.

  It is said that he became a great wizard. His wife, Sheba, had taught him many things. He also learned a lot of things from the swamp people. They have helped a lot of people throughout the years especially Native Americans. They became famous in New Orleans.

  The police put a bounty on their heads at one time many years ago. Several bounty hunters tried to capture or kill them. Many of them never came back from the swamps. Those that did said they would never go back. Their daughter followed in their footsteps. She was just as wild as the swamps. I should note one thing for you. Big Daddy Crawfish and Sheba have risked their lives many times for **The Land of the Eagle Feathers**. Now, their daughter is doing the same thing.

  Moses asked about whatever happened to the tribe members that signed the treaty that caused The Trail of Tears. Antonio replied, "Many of those members were found dead during the years after The Trail of Tears. Nobody knows who did that for the most part. It was many years later that there was peace between the Eastern Cherokee and the Western Cherokee. It was much like a Greek Tragedy. I think I will turn in for the night. I don't want anyone asking me any questions." The group broke up and headed to their tents.

I noticed that One Feather was following Angela and Antonio. I could tell that One Feather did have questions to ask Antonio. Knowing Antonio, One Feather would never get all the answers he wanted.

Rose and Nick still used the same tent. Rose and Nick were good for each other. They had experienced much the same thing. Both had lost the love of their lives. Nick was lucky. He had found his. Rose had yet to find hers. If Nick had anything to do with it, Rose would get her love back.

I went to my tent. To my surprise, I found that Little Wolf had put three tents together. He had put his, mine and Mary's together. I asked Mary if I could come in. Mary replied, "Yes, you can. We have plenty of room for you." Mary was already in her sleeping bag on one side of the large tent. Little Wolf was on the other side of the tent. My bag was somewhat in the middle. A candle burned in the middle of tent. I blew it out and said, "Have pleasant dreams." I fell fast asleep.

One Feather and Antonio walked over to the campfire. They seated themselves facing away from most of the camp. One Feather didn't want anyone to hear want they were talking about. "You are my father, Antonio," asked One Feather. Antonio replied, "If your mother, Angela, says so I am. Angela is a lot of things, but she always tells the truth when asked," Antonio answered.

Antonio asked, "I know that Angela, your mother, had a talk with you. Were you satisfied with her answers? One Feather stared into the flames of the campfire. "I guess so. This whole thing is strange to me. I know that destiny plays a lot in my life. We are all here because it is our destiny to be here. I

149

may be angry with John and my grandmother. I cannot be because they were only doing what they thought was best for me. I know that you did not know I even existed until this year. I cannot blame you. I can only blame destiny. That is something nobody can ever blame."

Antonio looked at One Feather, "I know you want to learn more about me. I have done a lot of good and bad things. I have lived a long time. I have known many people. I spent most of my time working for a council called The Council of Religions. I was a Priest in the Catholic Church and worked as an agent for them. This included doing some very hard and dangerous work. I found that in doing this work it challenged my faith in the church. I left the church. I continued assisting them in their work.

I met your mother on one of my missions for them in Rome, Italy. She did not know that I was working against her. She was guarding a Priest that had embraced the Occult. We fell in love. It was the most important time of my life. I loved her very much. When she found out about me being a former Priest, she left me. I was recalled back to my workstation. A few days later, the police arrested everyone that Angela was working for. They arrested her and sent her away. I didn't find out until many months later that Angela was actually working for my employers. She was the one that turned in the people to be arrested. Her arrest was to cover her.

She never told me about being pregnant. We both tried to find each other. I never located her. She had you while she was in Sicily. She was lost without me. I was lost without her. She was very depressed. She asked to place the child up for adoption. She was not in shape to properly raise a child. The Pope felt a little responsible for all that happened. I found out from John this year that he was ordered to return you to your mother's people. John took you to **The Land of the Eagle Feathers** to be with your grandmother.

150

John had already left working for the Council. He had been working to save **The Land of the Eagle Feathers**. The Pope knew that John was once responsible for Angela. John took you more out of his responsibility for Angela's well-being than anything else. You know the rest of story.

One Feather, I know that this is all new to you. I have gotten to know you. You are a brave warrior. I don't say that lightly. I have known the best in my time. You make me proud. You are unselfish, forgiving and do the right thing. Your grandmother and Uncle John taught you well. If you let me, I will gradually try to make up for lost time.

I have much I can teach you about the outside world. There is one more thing. You have my blood in you. You will probably have some of my traits in you. You will live many, many years. You will need to think about that. It may have an effect with your relationship with June. My plan is to ask John for one wish. That wish would be to give your mother and your future wife the gift of longer life. He can do that if we get *The Book of Winter.* If he does not do that, I will take the book from him.

I don't think that will be a problem for him to grant that for us. It was written in *The Book of Fall* for those that survive this quest will be needed again. **The Keepers of the Yawi** will be needed to save others in the future. It is our destiny.

The only problem is that we must keep John alive. He is the only one that can grant us that. He is my blood-brother. This makes him your Uncle. He must grant you that wish. You see it is our destiny to be together: You, June, Angela and me. You are my son, and June will be my daughter-in-law. I will die for my family. You all are my family. The family I never had." Antonio got up and left. One Feather stared at the campfire trying to take everything in that Antonio said.

June found One Feather by the campfire. She was worried about One Feather. She knew that he was having a difficult time. His world had been turned upside down by the events of this past year. One Feather had to be confused to find out that Antonio and Angela were his parents. Furthermore, he had to be very upset to find out that the Red Woman and John never told him about them.

One Feather looked up at June, "I know you are worried about me. I can sense that you are wondering how I am dealing with all of this. I have two things that I am dealing with: one is that I have gained two parents, and the other is that I have the love of my life standing in front of me. I must deal with the two wolves. I could be upset and mad or I could be happy to have found everything that I ever wanted. I have thought a long time about this. My parents are not perfect. They did the best they could. They are both warriors. They have lived lives of adventurers. You know them better than I. What do you think about them? They will be a big part of our family."

June answered One Feather, "Both of them are brave and have true hearts. I have fought with them. I would trust them with my life. Angela has proven herself by saving Moses and the Red Woman. She would have made anyone a good mother. Moses said she watched over you and Moses like a mother hen. She will do the same for our children. Antonio has finally found himself. I have witnessed that myself. He seems to have a purpose. I saw him take many dangerous chances in the events of this last year to save us. He even gave his blood to Shanna while she was in the hospital. He is very protective of those he loves. He does love both of us. Besides, imagine the stories that Angela and Antonio would tell our children."

"I will follow the good wolf. What you say is right. Since you feel that you would trust them with your life, then I will. I never had a mother or father. Destiny choses our parents for us. I did have other people. I had John, the Red Woman and

White Elk, my grandfather. In many ways, I have been blessed by the Great Spirits. You will have you hands full to have Angela as your mother-in-law," laughed One Feather.

"Don't be laughing so much at me! You have my whole tribe to deal with. They have been wanting to meet you. They are very protective of the members of our tribe. You will meet them soon. They are coming for the great showdown with **The Dark Ones**. They want to see if you are worthy of me. Beware of my four uncles, they are great war chiefs. They can be very harsh on strangers if you don't measure up to their standards," smiled June. June could see a frown come over One Feather's face. One Feather realized that he had more to worry about than his parents.

June took One Feather's hands and pulled him up to her. She gave him a big kiss. One Feather whispered into June's ear. "We will get married when this is over. White Elk will do the honors and so will your grandfather. It will be the biggest wedding ceremony that has happened in **The Land of the Eagle Feathers**. I know that I should have asked you long ago. I knew that you knew it the first time we saw each other. I saw you as my wife the first time I looked at your lovely face. Your eyes lit up like the brightest dawn of a new day," One Feather said with tears of joy in his eyes.

June nodded her head. One Feather took out a golden ring from his medicine bag. "Antonio said that you should have it. It was his grandmother's wedding ring. He said you are the only one that deserves to wear it. His grandmother was a great mystic. She was much like you," said One Feather. "But what is Antonio going to give Angela? I can't accept this ring," asked June. One Feather replied, "He told me that he will give Angela his mother's wedding ring. She was some famous queen from a continent named Africa. I know this is a white man's tradition. I should follow my father's and mother's wishes," said One Feather as he slipped the ring on June's finger.

Red Bear had everyone up early the next morning. After a quick breakfast, the mules were saddled. Red Bear told everyone that this would a long day. We should arrive about sunset at The Land of Nightmares. "Keep your eyes open, there is a herd of huge bison that roam these woods ahead of us. They are very dangerous. They don't like humans. I suggest that Moses follow directly behind me. His gift to talking to animals may save our lives," Red Bear informed us.

The sky was dark with clouds heavy with snow. The mountains pikes in the distance were covered in white. They had only traveled a short distance in a dark pine forest when the snowflakes begin to fall. A cold wind from the North was dropping the temperature. Red Bear stopped and told us to get on our heavy coats and winter gear. "The temperature is known to drop very quickly in these parts. I am worried about the snow. It can mount up and cover the trail which will make it difficult to travel. We are fortunate to be riding mules. Horses would soon tire in heavy snow," Red Bear related to us.

Antonio opened one of the supply boxes. He found enough winter gear for everyone to wear. He was surprised to find that each wool coat had a name stitched on it or a symbol. Red Bear had a Red Bear on his coat. Little Wolf had a brown wolf and One Feather had one eagle feather on his. This made handing the wool coats out an easier task. Antonio was glad that each coat had a hood to protect your head from the wet snow and cold wind.

Soon everything was turning white. The pine tree branches became heavy with snow. Occasionally a gust of cold wind would blow snow off the heavy-laden branches. If you happened to be under them, you and your mule would be covered in white. The forest was thinning out of trees. Red

Bear was glad to finally get out of the thick forest. Branches had started to break away from the tall pines. It had become dangerous to be in the forest.

It was midday when we got out of the forest. Ahead of us was a small prairie of tall dead grass and brush. I called a halt to give the mules a rest. We dismounted our mules and let them roam and forage on the dried grass. The mules kicked off the snow and ate the grass as best they could. Nick passed out his homemade fruit and nut bars to everyone. "This is my grandmother's recipe. They contain a lot of calories and protein," he told them.

In the distance, Red Bear pointed to some black objects moving toward us. I summoned Petunia to roundup the mules and bring them back to us. As we watched, the black and white objects became a dark river coming from the mountain ahead of us. It wasn't long before they covered most of the prairie before us. Moses pointed to the dark objects. All he said was, "Buffalo." I had only seen these once many years ago. They seemed bigger this time. They were three times the normal size of bison most people ever see. The snow was coming down harder. That didn't seem to bother these huge critters. Steam rose from their bodies into the air like a huge cloud over them.

Red Bear said, "I suggest that we turn back and circle around them. They will charge us, and we will have no chance of surviving that charge." Moses shook his head, "They are too big and fast for us to outrun them." I told him, "I agree. Moses and I will have to go and meet them. If we are not successful, then turn your mules around and run."

I got on Petunia. Moses didn't want to take his mule. He was afraid his mule might break and run. I had Moses follow me as Petunia broke a trail through the deep snow. We traveled about 1000 yards across the field. At least several hundred bison met us. I dismounted Petunia. I told her to go at least hundred yards behind us. Petunia shook her head. She refused to go even after I pushed her away.

Petunia moved over to Moses. She bit the hood of Moses' coat. She half-way pushed and pulled him toward the biggest bison ahead of us. I could see that Moses was not too happy with Petunia. Moses kept telling Petunia to let him go. Petunia didn't obey him. "John, tell Petunia to let me go," Moses yelled back to me. "Moses, you should know better. You can't tell a mule what to do, especially Petunia. Just follow her lead, she knows something we don't," I yelled back to him.

Petunia pulled the wool coat off Moses. She took her head and pushed him directly in front of the large white bison in front of the herd. The large white bison stared directly at Moses. The bison's eyes glared at Moses. Moses not to be outdone stared straight back at him. It became a staring contest. Moses knew if he lost, the leader would stampede his herd at us.

After several long minutes, Petunia gave a loud mule's cry. She walked over to the large white bison and motioned for Moses to follow her. The large bison shook his head and moved toward Moses. The bison lowered his head and started to butt Moses. Moses lowered his head as to butt the bison back. Petunia watched them butt each other. It wasn't a hard butt. They both only moved back a little after the butt. Petunia moved between them and did something I never ever seen Petunia do. She turned and bit Moses's left ear. Then she turned and bit the large bison's right ear.

Moses reached out and touched Petunia and the large white bison. He was connecting them to each other. The white bison and Petunia seemed to be communicating with each other. After several minutes, the white bison moved and gave Moses a friendly head butt. He turned and moved his herd back over the trail that they came from. Petunia turned and went back to me. Moses followed her after picking up his coat. I mounted Petunia. She let out another loud cry. We went back to join the others.

Moses had a smile on his bearded face. Moses had let his hair and beard grow. Moses reminded me of one of his great grandfathers. He was in the U.S. Cavalry. The American Indians nicknamed them "The Buffalo Soldiers" because of their black curly hair and their fighting skills.

It didn't take long before we were back with the others. Red Bear greeted us. "I never saw anything like that before." Moses replied to the group, "I wish I could take credit for saving us. I must give Petunia all the credit. She is one smart mule.

She had a plan. She took off my coat on purpose and pushed me toward the leader of the bison herd. She knew that I would not back down from their leader. The leader of the herd had never seen anyone do that. He knew I was not scared of him. When he could not stare me down, he decided to try the scare me with a head butt. That's when Petunia stopped us. Petunia bit my ear and the leader's ear. Petunia wanted to show that she was greater than either one of us. We needed to listen to her.

I touched them at the same time. They began communicating with each other through me. The leader wanted to know our business here. Petunia told the leader we needed to get to The Land of Nightmares to save this land from being taken over by evil humans. If we did not get *The Book of Winter*, they and all of this land would be in great danger. Evil would destroy them and the other animals in this land. The leader asked Petunia, "Who were these evil beings? She told them it was ruthless people called **The Dark Ones** that wanted all the riches of this land for themselves. They were greedy. They wanted everything in this land.

The leader then asked Petunia, "Why should we trust the humans that are with you?" She told them that most of our group were **The Keepers of the Yawi**. The leader said that they had heard of such a group. There are legends about them coming here. The leader asked, "Why should I believe they are members of such a group. Petunia told him about me. She said, "Look at the one I brought to you. See his hair and color, one of his great grandfathers was a member of the famous Buffalo Soldiers named after your ancestors. He is a great warrior. He has powers to talk to animals. You know that he is not afraid of you.

The leader than asked about **Red Bear** and the **Dark One** riding with us. Petunia told them that our leader, John, is in charge of seeing that they would help us. The leader asked how could they help us? Petunia told him that tonight John would tell him what they could do to help save their land and his herd at the entrance to The Land of Nightmares. The leader told Petunia that the Great Bears had told them about us. They just wanted to be sure. Moses is already known throughout this land as a warrior and friend of the animals. If he hadn't passed his test, the leader would have had all his herd kill us.

There is one more thing that the leader said. Don't trust **Red Bear** or the **Man in Black.** They will let them pass only because of John and Moses. If they feel that those two do anything to keep the book for themselves, they will kill them. Also, the leader said that we are so lucky to have Petunia leading the humans. She is much smarter than humans are. The bison will break the trail to The Land of Nightmares so we can get there tonight."

Red Bear smiled his wicked smile and said, "Now, I know why John always had Petunia around. She is the brains of the outfit." I replied to Red Bear with a sarcastic grin, "Nobody would have believed me if I had told them. Everyone laughed except David. David asked, "Why or how did the leader of the herd know I was a **Dark One**?" Moses replied, "The leader said he could smell evil and darkness. He also said that it is written that a **Dark One** would come with **The Keepers of the Yawi**. I suggest, David, that you stay close to John for your own good. The leader of the herd does not like you." Nobody laughed this time.

The snow was getting heavier. The trail was easy to follow to The Land of Nightmares. The bison had trampled down the snow enough that the trail was more a road than trail. We arrived at the entrance to The Land of Nightmares at dusk.

I told everyone to pitch camp. They should put some pine needles branches under their tents to protect them from the snow. It would keep their tents warmer. Moses, Red Bear and Antonio were assigned to gather firewood. Nick, Rose and Mary would cook supper. I had Nick open one of the supply boxes. It was filled with food. "I heard that Mary was a good cook. She once showed me a book of recipes she had written long ago. You help her cook supper tonight. I brought all the fixings she would need," I told them.   Mary's face turned red. "Why do you think I would cook for you, John? she asked. I tossed the book at her. She caught it and looked at the inside cover. There was a surprised look on her face as she read the inside cover. "No, Mary, you are going to cook for your son! Nick and Rose will cook for the others," I replied back. "Lo Ming and June come with me. I must tell you something in private. Little Wolf and One Feather are to send for me and Moses when the great leader of the herd comes." "What am I supposed to do?" asked David. "As Moses said, "Stay close to me."

I had just finished talking to Lo Ming and June when Little Wolf and One Feather came to get me. They had Moses with them. I sent Lo Ming and June back to camp with Little Wolf and One Feather. I had Moses and David come with me.

We met with the leader of the bison herd outside of camp. Moses translated for me. Petunia had come with the leader. The leader trusted her more than us. The leader asked me through Moses, "How could they help?" I told him that I needed them in the fight with **The Dark Ones**. His herd would be more for show than fighting. There was only one thing that they had to agree to. That was they must not kill anyone. It is very important that they must not kill anyone. If they did, we would never be free of **The Dark Ones**.

The leader agreed to my terms. The leader said, "There is one more thing. Petunia needs to take the mules back. The snow will be too high for them to take you back in a few days. I will have my herd and let you ride back on our backs to the campsite where the battle is to take place. It will take many bison to open the trail back." I nodded my head in agreement, "Petunia and I had discussed that before we left. You are a wise bison. It would be an honor to ride back with you," I replied. "No, you will not be on my back. I am too old for someone like you. I want the little one called "Little Wolf to ride on me. It will impress his grandfather. He knows that I only let great chiefs ride on me. His grandfather did long ago. Petunia told me Little Wolf is a brave warrior. It would be an honor for me to do that," said the leader. I nodded in agreement. The leader left with Petunia.

I told Moses to untie the mules and summon Petunia early in the morning. Petunia needs to get our mules back before winter hits or they might be stuck here. Moses nodded in agreement.

We got back at camp in time for supper. Mary had a plate of food for Little Wolf to eat. She told him that it was a special plate of food that ancient warriors were allowed to eat before battle. Little Wolf smiled at her and sat down beside Mary.

Antonio got up in front of everyone that were seated on logs around the fire. "I need to talk to everyone here. Tomorrow, we will enter The Land of Nightmares. The passage from **The Book of Fall** that I was assigned is important for all of us. We will see and experience things that are real or not. Take heed of the passage I will recite to you."

Your Mind Lies

You see with your own eyes
My brother and sister, the mind lies
You must look beyond you
To know what is really true

You hear with your own ears
What you hear may be your own fears
You must listen to another voice
To know what is the right choice

You feel with your own soul
What you feel you may not know
You must feel with another's heart
To Know which place to start

You think with your own mind
What you think may be blind
You must think about what others say
To know what is the right way

You must think, feel and see like another
To find the right way, my brothcr
You must see with another's eyes
My brother and sister, your mind lies

Remember the words of this passage. They may save your life," said Antonio as he sat down.

"Tomorrow will come too soon. Get some sleep. Eat a good breakfast tomorrow morning. I will be at that far tree over there with the supplies packed for each of you. You know what weapons are allowed. You know the rules. Red Bear will lead us to the entrance. Tomorrow will change your lives forever. Now go and get some sleep," I told them.

Chapter VII
Entering The Land of Nightmares
What will we find?

Moses had gotten up early. Lo Ming asked him where he was going. He told her that he was feeding and releasing the mules to go back with Petunia. " How are we going to get back without them?" she asked. Moses replied, "We are going to ride the bison back. They will do better than the mules. They can break the trail of heavy snow by taking turns. We will travel much faster that way.' Lo Ming smiled, "It's cold out there. I will stay in the tent. I will warm you up when you get back." Moses laughed as he turned to go out of the tent, "I will be taking you up on that."

The snow had crusted making it easier to walk. Several inches of snow had fallen during the night. Moses threw some wood on the embers of the campfire to start it up. Moses gave each mule a large cup of oats to eat. He untied each mule. He left the saddles off the mules. They could be used for the ride back with the bison. He had wondered why saddles had extra-long chinches. John had thought of everything or was it Petunia.

Petunia nodded to Moses. Moses touched her forehead and told her to be careful. He tied two sacks of oats to her back. "These should help you feed the others on your way back. Just bite the sacks open when you need to," he told her.

Petunia being playful, waited until Moses had turned his back to her. Then she pushed Moses in the back and knocked him down into a large snowbank. Moses got up and threw a snowball at her head. Petunia ducked and "heed hawed" back at him.

Petunia gathered the other mules and left the campsite. Moses watched them trot out of sight as he brushed the snow off his clothes. "Lo Ming told me that I should never take my eye off any female. I guess that goes for female mules too," he said out loud. "You should have listened to me," Lo Ming said behind him as she threw a snowball and hit him.

Nick and Rose had a very hearty breakfast fixed for them. After breakfast, they packed up their tents and took their backpacks over to John. John collected their packs and put them in supply boxes. He gave each one another backpack filled with food and lighter tents.

"Remember, take only your bows, blowguns, clubs and knives. You cannot take any other weapons that would kill. You cannot kill anything in The Land of Nightmares, or you will have to remain there," I told them.

Red Bear spoke, "Antonio's passage is correct. In this land, it is hard to tell what is real or not. You will see images of things from your past that others won't see. Many of you will be tested. Be very careful, you will need to defend yourselves. Real or not, what you see may be able to kill you.

Those of you that were given passages from *The Book of Fall* must tell me what the clue means. I know The Land of Nightmares very well. I was trapped there for several years. I will lead us to the location that your clue directs us to find. There is a price for finding each clue. You will know it when you see it. Follow me, we will be going to the entrance to the land. It is behind the trees over there."

As they followed Red Bear, they noticed that the temperature was getting warmer. By the time they reached the end of the tree line, the temperature was more like summer. The snow had disappeared. There was a small clearing at the base of a mountain. An arch of stone marked the entrance. A figure stood in the middle of the arch dressed in purple with a purple cape.

As they approached the arch, they could see that the person was an older woman with flowing grey and black hair under her hooded cape. She held up her hands motioning them to stop. "I have been waiting many long cycles of the sun and moon for you to join me. It is written in the stars. **The Keepers of the Yawi** would come to find the last most important book.

The Book of Winter is very powerful. Only you will be able to find it. I warn you. You may not survive this journey. I congratulate you for making it this far. I will take your winter coats and other heavy clothes that you are wearing. You won't need them. There are clothes over there that you can change into. Leave the clothes you got on there. It is summer in The Land of the Nightmares. It is very hot. The volcanos have been very active. I am glad you brought your medicine bags. I wish you well." The woman pointed to the clothes attached to the wall behind her. She walked up the trail behind her and faded away.

The clothes they found were much different than they imagined. They were in bags hung on hooks attached to a stone wall. Each bag had their name on it. Rose was surprised that in her bag were a purple skirt and a blouse decorated with stars with matching long necked moccasins. Lo Ming found in hers a red silk martial arts uniform decorated with dragons, a black belt and moccasins. Both One Feather and Little Wolf didn't have to change much, theirs contained an Indian warrior's vest of bones and a loin cloth. June smiled at One Feather until she saw hers. June's outfit was a short white leather dress covered with precious stones, gems and mystical symbols, even her moccasins had gems and stones.

Red Bear and David didn't have any bags. They were dressed as they should have been. They were both wearing the clothes from the Potlatch. Mary looked into her bag. She pulled out a Red Leather Dress covered with symbols of the moon and stars. This was a dress only powerful Red Women wore. Angela pulled out a dark brown and black short elk skin dress with mystical ritual symbols of a powerful mystic. Angela started crying. All she would say, "It's just like my mother's. How did they get this?" Nobody could answer her question.

Moses pulled down his bag. In the bag was an aborigine's medicine man dress. It had a loin cloth with necklaces and beads with ceremonial precious stones with body paint. Lo Ming smiled at him. Moses smiled back at her. Antonio pulled his bag down. As he put in his hand, he was cautious as if sometime was going to bite him. He pulled out a Templar's shirt and pants. He looked at these very carefully. There was a blood stain in the left shoulder. Angela said, "Now I know where that scar came from on your left shoulder." Antonio's face turned sour. He didn't say anything back. There must had been some bad memories associated with those clothes.

The only bag left was John's. He could tell that they wondered what was in it. John put in his hand and pulled out a leather whip, a large Australian Bush Knife and a Roman military sword. The sword had the Roman words for "Commander" engraved on its blade. Its handle was lined in gold. The sword had dried blood on it. There was a note attached to it. John gave the note to Moses along with the whip and Australian knife. Moses read the note. He looked at John in disbelief. Moses attached the whip to his belt and put the knife through his belt in front of him. Nobody asked Moses or John what the note said.

The only thing John said, "This sword was a gift of mine to your father for his service to **The Land of the Eagle Feathers**. Take it and give it to him when we see him later. It is up to you, Moses, if he will be released from here. If he gets released and I don't live, your father is in charge. Do you understand Moses?" Moses didn't answer John. John asked in a louder voice again, "Do you understand Moses?" Moses showing anger in his voice said, "I most certainly do!"

John looked at everyone, "Change into your clothes and leave the ones that you have on in the bag you got your new ones in."

The old woman in purple appeared. "Here are the gowns and clothes you will wear if you find *The Book of Winter.* You will need them for the Chakra to release the book. Lo Ming, you are to guard this bag with your life," the old woman said as she handed the bag to Lo Ming. The old woman walked down the trail and disappeared again.

After everyone changed, John asked Antonio who had the next passage. Antonio looked at Lo Ming. Lo Ming had everyone stand around her as she recited her passage.

Everything is a Part of the All

There is no joy without pain
There is no growth without rain
There is no false without true
There is no me without you

There is no hate without love
There is no below without above
There is no courage without fear
There is no far without near

There is no death without birth
There is no sky without earth
There is no day without night
There is no wrong without right

There is no low without high
There is no star without sky
There is no weak without bold
There is no warm without cold

Everything is a part of the reason
Everything is a part of the season
The answer will come with a birth of a fawn
The day is darkest just before the dawn

The darkness will give way to the day
The deer will come out to play
The crow will let out a caw
Remember everything is a part of the all

Lo Ming looked at Red Bear, "Do you know of a place that is at the base of a volcano where deer roam, and it is very dark? Also, does this place have many crows that caw before the dawn of each day? This place must be near here. The volcano must be active to blot out the sun and stars." Red Bear thought for a minute or so. "There is such a place. We called it: Volcano land of opposites. You must be very careful. Everything is not as it should be there. It is only a short distance from here. It will take us two hours to get there." Red Bear motioned for everyone to follow him.

After two hours of hard hiking, they arrived at a small valley at the base of a large volcano. Smoke and ash were flowing from the volcano. You could not tell if it was day or night. Lo Ming told everyone to stay at the base of the volcano.

Caws of crows could be heard in the distance. A young white deer stood in front of a trail that looked like it led up the side of the volcano. "You need to wait here until I return. It will be early in the morning at first light that I will return. I must go and face my master. I know what he wants of me. This is the right place. It is much like the place that I fought my master or teacher long ago."

Moses said, "I should go with you." Lo Ming replied to Moses, "No, this is something that I must do alone. Don't follow me, any of you! If you do, this journey will end right now!" Lo Ming gave Moses a kiss. It was the first time Moses saw fear on Lo Ming's face. Lo Ming didn't take any weapons with her as she ran up the trail.

Red Bear told everyone not to set up camp. "Remember, this place is one of opposites. What we think of a long time is short here. She will be back in a couple of hours." Red Bear did not say the last part with a sense of confidence. I had everyone sit down and rest.

Lo Ming ran for several minutes up the trail. The trail rose gradually up the side of the volcano. Lo Ming was getting hot in her martial arts robe. She stopped running as soon as she came to a small plateau about 2000 feet above the valley. On the far edge of the plateau was a small hut or cabin. An elderly man in a white martial arts robe was standing near the door to the hut. He motioned Lo Ming to come toward him. Lo Ming took a long breath. Slowly, she walked toward him.

"It has been a long time, Lo Ming," he said to her as she approached him. "Yes, it has. It feels like centuries since we have been together," she replied. "What do you want of me? Lo Ming asked. "It is simple. I want a rematch. We didn't get a chance to finish what I started long ago," her master teacher of martial arts replied.

"If I remember right, you tried to kill me in our last sparring match. I only defended myself," Lo Ming said without emotion. "Yes, I guess I did. You knew the rules. You left without my permission. When I found you, I had no choice but to find out if you were worthy of my teachings. I intended to kill you. That is the punishment for leaving without permission, Lo Ming," the master said.

"I was afraid when we were fighting," said Lo Ming. "Were you afraid I would kill you?" asked the master dressed in black. "Oh no, master! I was scared that I would lose my temper and kill my master. I knew I could defeat you. I was young and angry at you. I would have if we continued our match," Lo Ming expressed with remorse.

Lo Ming's master laughed, "I have never been defeated by any of my students. What makes you think I would be defeated by the likes of you?" Lo Ming answered, "Because I defeated your best student, The Italian, in Rome in the Gladiatorial Area. I killed him and his partner, Gladiator, at the same time. If you don't believe me, Antonio, my fellow warrior will tell you, he was there. He is at the base of the volcano with my fellow warriors.

I know what I can do if I lose my temper. It is my one weakness. You always seemed to exploit that weakness. That is why I left. I was afraid I would kill you if you made me lose control in a sparring match."

"Yes, I saw you in that Gladiatorial fight. It still does not give you reason to leave my teachings without my permission. You know that the only way that you can leave now is to beat me. I have been waiting here for a long time for this chance. We will find out if Lo Ming is as mighty a warrior as she confesses to be," said the master.

The master walked toward Lo Ming. They both bowed their heads to each other. They both took two steps back. The death match began. Lo Ming was graceful like a cobra fighting a mongoose. The master was still better. He knocked Lo Ming down several times. She jumped right back up. Lo

Ming was patient. She would block the master's blows. She wouldn't strike back. The master was impressed. Lo Ming had learned much since she had fought him last.

The master decided to end the match with a swift kick to Lo Ming's head. Lo Ming saw it coming. She ducked her head and kneeled at the same time driving her fist into her master's loins. Her master fell to the ground in pain. "There is no joy without pain," she said to him. "There is no me without you!" she said with respect.

"You were right, Lo Ming. I now give you permission to leave. You could have killed me. I would have killed you. You have learned to control your temper. That was the only thing that you needed to learn from me. Who taught you that?" he asked. "An older Chinese master, the mother of my lover, long ago," Lo Ming replied. "Ah, I know her. She is the only one I have never defeated in a match. She is a great master. Have you defeated her? he asked. "No, we always had to stop. We are equals in battle. Her son needs more work. I am teaching him," Lo Ming replied.

The master bowed his head to Lo Ming in a sign of respect. "Here is a piece of the puzzle to find what you are looking for. I only hope that your friend knows the patience that you have learned. If he does not, he will never get his father out of here." The master turned. He flew like a bird away from The Land of Nightmares. Lo Ming was honored. She turned and went back down the volcano to the others that were waiting for her.

It was like Red Bear said Lo Ming returned in two hours. Lo Ming went over to Little Wolf and gave him the first piece of the puzzle to find *The Book of Winter*.

Little Wolf put it in his medicine bag. They realized that each of them would be responsible to come back with a piece to a puzzle that would show them the location of the book.

Red Bear asked Antonio who has the next passage. Antonio pointed to Moses. Red Bear asked Moses to recite his passage. Moses appeared to have dread on his face. Moses knew that if he was unsuccessful in defeating his nightmare, he would never see his father again. Lo Ming whispered into Moses' ear, "You have no choice. You must confront your nightmare." Moses nodded his head and recited the passage.

The Mountain Loves Only the Sky

The misty fog makes love to the mountain
The lonesome frog waits in the fountain
The river is destined to cry
The mountain loves only the sky

The river makes a mournful sound
There is no other river around
It doesn't even try to pretend
Its tears are carried in the wind

The wind will tell you why
The river is destined to cry
It may not speak or shout
You hear it at the river's mouth

Where the river kisses the land
You find a way to understand
You will a way to know
The answer is in the river's flow

The sky will make love to the mountain
The tears of the river will flow to the fountain
You will know which way to go
Hey, Yi, Hey, Yi, Hey, Yi, Yo

Moses asked Red Bear, "Where is there a tall mountain that is surrounded by fog and mist from a river? A river must start at the base of a mountain. There must be streams of water coming down the mountain to form that river. A green stone that looks like a frog will lie in the middle of a small pool of one of the streams that feeds the river. The pool is a formation that looks like a fountain. It has several holes that lets the water form a mist when the wind blows. The water that flows through the holes will make a mournful sound."

Red Bear looked at Moses, "Yes, I know of such a place. It is a very dangerous place. The fountain that you describe is located above the fog near the top of the mountain. It rains most of the time there. We gave this place a name." Moses asked, "What name is that?" Red Bear said, "The place of the whispering dead. The sounds of the river and streams are like people whispering to you that you know are dead. It is like they are trying to tell you something. Several of my people went crazy in that place.

There is one other thing about that place. The first name that you hear is a person you must take with you up the mountain to face whatever is there. I will only take you to a hill that overlooks this place. You must go there alone. Remember when you hear the name of the person that you must take with you, you must take them with you to the top of the mountain. I must warn you the person you take with you will be in great danger."

"What do you mean the person will be in great danger. What type of danger?" asked Moses. "Not what, but whom! They will be in danger from you. One of my people went up to the fountain with another person. Only one came back! He said that he killed the person he took. Then he went mad and drowned himself in the lake at the mouth of the river."

Red Bear told everyone to follow him. He would take us to a place near the place called "The Whispering Dead." After about three hours, we arrived at a small meadow covered in green grass and flowers. Red Bear told us to make camp here. He warned us to be on watch. I asked Red Bear what he meant by that? He said, "There are demons and animals here that are unlike anything you have ever encountered." Red Bear took Moses with him to a hill that overlooked the land he needed to enter. You could see Red Bear point down at the other side of the hill.

There was a very tall mountain on the other side of that hill. It was covered with fog and mist. You could not see its top. We watched Moses descend the other side of the hill until his head was out of sight.

Moses didn't like where he was going. It was very damp and windy. He found the river at the base of the mountain very quickly. He could hear the mournful sounds coming from the tall mountain at the source of the river. Streams of water came cascading down the mountain side. The strong wind blew the water in the streams forming a wall of mist. As the mist flowed upward to the mountaintop, the mist turned into a water creating a show of raindrops. This must be the tears that the passage said. The fog on the mountain reminded Moses of a woman holding her arms around her lover. "Yes, he thought. Red Bear has the right place."

Moses turned to follow the river. After following the riverbank for a mile or so, Moses could see a lake ahead of him. The wind was blowing. At first, he could only hear mournful sounds like someone crying out for help. It was a man's voice. As the riverbank stopped at the mouth of the river flowing into the lake, he heard the man's voice louder. It was like a soft whisper of the wind on a summer's day. "Bring John with you. We need to finish this once and for all. Bring John with you I am dying. Only you can save me for my fate. Moses, my son, I am running out of time. Bring John with you."

Moses watched as the river reversed its flow. It was flowing back to the mountain to the fountain on the mountain. The sounds told him to hurry. The mournful cries became louder. Moses ran as fast as he could to get me.

As we were waiting for Moses to return, we pitched camp. Rose took out some white salt and circled the camp with it. Antonio took out some sulfur from his medicine bag. He sprinkled it around the camp. I guess they were not taking any chances. "Think only good thoughts, in your nightmares there are many bad monsters," warned Red Bear.

Moses raced down the hill to our camp. I didn't have to ask. I got up to go with him. "How did you know, I would take you?" asked Moses. "Because I was the one who sent him here. We don't have much time. Let's go!" I told him. Lo Ming looked into Moses' eyes. What she saw frightened her. Moses' hate had returned for John and his mother. Lo Ming thought, "This place is dangerous. It magnifies any little thought. Even one hidden inside you that you don't want others to see appear. Lo Ming ran over to me, "Be careful, Moses's blood is up. He may try to kill you." I looked back at her, "Yes, I know, but I have a friend waiting to help me." I told her.

Moses and I ran until we got to the base of the mountain. There was a faint trail going up the mountain. Moses started running up the trail. I had to tell him to slow down. The trail was moss covered and wet. The rocky stones were very slippery. I had to grab Moses by the shoulders to slow him down. He became angry at me. "If you fall off this mountain, you will never get your father back," I told him. "Who says I want my father back? He and my mother caused me great pain all because of you. I hate them as much as you," he yelled with red in his eyes.

I could hear the mournful sounds of the fountain getting louder. The mist had turned into a gray, deep fog. The only thing that kept you going was the sound up ahead. Moses was the first to reach a clearing with the rock fountain attached to the side of the mountain. A large muscular black man was standing by the fountain. He looked tired and exhausted. He pointed to Moses. It was my friend, Moses's father.

Moses went up to him. "Why did you lie to me many years ago? For years, I thought you had died in an accident. You never told me about John and the dangerous things you were doing. My mother told me you were dead. I feel betrayed by my parents and John." Moses turned around and looked at me. "John, you could have told me. It has taken me years to find him. You are the reason he is here, and I have lost years of him being with me. I curse you for your lies."

"Moses, John never made your mother and me go with him to fight. It was our choice," said Moses's father. "I don't care. John should have told me. I will lift this curse on you by taking the life of the person who sent you here," yelled Moses. Moses drew his knife and whip. He pointed his knife at me. He drew back his whip and snapped it at me. The whip hit my cheek and cut it. This place was making Moses lose his sanity.

Moses lifted his big bush knife to face me. I could tell that he was almost past the line of sanity. As he was about the throw the knife at my chest, a woman's voice could be heard. It was soft as a songbird in spring. "Moses, my dear, come back to us. You must forgive us. It was wrong what we did. We should have told you. John saved me, but he had to make a choice. It was either me or your father. Your father made him save me. It cost John his life to do that. You must forgive us and John. He had no choice. Destiny has strange ways. Go to your father, Moses!" mother cried. Her tears were flowing into the fountain like a river.

Moses was starting to break down. He fell to the ground. We could hear him say with much difficulty from his crying.

"I forgive you all. I don't care about the past only the future."
Lo Ming touched his shoulder. She had followed us. Moses
turned over and saw her face. "Do you forgive me. Your
mother told me long ago. It was after a match. She knew that
you had many issues about what had happened long ago. I
promised if I ever had the chance, I would help you find your
father. I owed that to John. He saved my mother many years
ago on The Trail of Tears. He never knew that until now," Lo
Ming said as she kissed Moses on his wet cheek.

Moses got up slowly. He motioned for his father to come to
him and Lo Ming. He put his strong arms around both of
them. "I have to leave now, Moses," mother said. "White
Elk's magic is fading. I will see all of you soon." Moses'
mother faded away.

The green stone frog leaped from the fountain. The frog
changed into the old woman in purple. Moses, you have your
father back. Your nightmare is over. Your hate is over. You
have earned this. It is a piece of the puzzle to find the last
book. It takes a lot to forgive especially for a warrior like you.
You have shown that today. I wish you well, Moses," she said
as she faded away.

They say that this day was the only day that the fog ever
lifted over the mountain. It took several hours before we were
back at the camp below. It was good to have my friend back
with me. I cried almost as much as Moses did. It was a good
day to be alive. I only hoped that we would survive the night
ahead.

We arrived back at the camp. It was getting dark. Nick and
Rose had fixed a stew for the evening meal. David was
uneasy with this place. He could feel the lost spirits and souls
of men and women floating around. The salt and sulfur were
keeping these outside the camp for now. When David saw
Moses's father, he was taken off guard. He never thought he
would see that man again. He wondered if Moses' father

would want to kill him for all the things he had done in the past.

David decided that he must confront Moses' father. He wasn't going to keep looking over his shoulder to worry about what could happen. It was best to get this out of the way as soon as possible. After supper was over, David asked Moses to introduce his father to him. Moses took both aside away from the others to talk.

"This is my father. I know that you need to talk. I am not part of this. It is between you and my father. I have learned that you two will have to work this out between you," Moses told them. " I will leave you to yourselves." Moses walked back to sit by Lo Ming. It was the first time since his childhood that Moses felt that a great weight had been lifted from him. Moses wanted to be with the ones he loved. Moses looked around. "Yes, this is my family. Like every family, there are those that you get along better with and those that are just family for better or worse," he thought.

Nick sat down beside Moses and Lo Ming. Moses had felt a kinship to Nick. Nick had looked at him in a different way than the others did. "There is a way you look at me. It is like a brother looking at his brother. Why is that, Nick?" Moses asked him. Nick got up and went to his medicine bag that was in his tent. He returned carrying an old photograph. The photograph was getting worn. You could still make out the figures in the picture.

Nick sat down and handed the picture to Moses. Moses took one look at the picture and stared. Lo Ming asked to see the picture. In the picture were two soldiers. One was Nick and the other was a man that could have been Moses' twin.

"Who is the other man in the picture?" asked Moses. "He was my best friend. We fought many battles together. He once saved my life. He died in my arms on the battlefield. He was a great warrior. Before he died, he said that he once met a man in the Australia Outback that looked exactly like him. He had been on R and R from the Army and on leave for a month. Maybe it was fate or his destiny to find himself with his twin.

He said he met you in a bar in the Outback. You must have been a wild man because someone had mistaken him for you. He had to fight half the people in the bar. He said that they were getting the best of him when you walked into the bar. That's when the fighting stopped. He said one man said we can beat one of you, but two would be impossible. It turned out well. He said you owned the bar. Your miners would drink there for almost nothing. It took two days before you got through partying. Then you and he spent a month together visiting your grandfather in the desert. He did say something strange to me. I would meet that man one day. It was my destiny."

"How do you know I am that man?" asked Moses. Nick rolled up his right shirtsleeve. There was a small tattoo on his inside forearm. Moses rolled up his right shirtsleeve. He had the same small tattoo. It was an image of the Rainbow Serpent. "You know soldiers, they do like their tattoos," smiled Nick.

"My grandfather said that destiny had brought us together. He was much like me. It is one on my best memories. We were like brothers. One night at my grandfather's place, we sat around a campfire. My grandfather was very serious. He looked at the fire and then at the stars. There was sadness in his eyes. He said that your friend would not live to be an old man. Destiny had another fate for him. He said that a friend of his would come one day to have great adventures with me. Your friend's mission in life was to save that friend. He fulfilled his destiny. You are here. Don't let our friend's death be in vain. You have much to think about tonight," said Moses. Moses got up and took Lo Ming by the hand. They went to their tent to get some needed rest.

Nick stayed up to watch the fire. Rose came over to sit by him. "I couldn't help it. I listened to your talk with Moses. I am sorry about your friend. You must get over his death. He knew it was his destiny. He is happy that he fulfilled it. Most people don't get to know their destiny. I will need your help tonight. There are many lost souls around this camp. We will need to keep them away. You know much about such things."

Nick nodded. "Yes, unfortunately I do." I could feel them wandering a few feet from the salt and sulfur line outside the camp. I suggest you take the far side of the camp, and I take this side." Rose patted Nick on the back. "Have fun," she said as she left. Nick knew that she was being sarcastic.

Nick went to everyone's tent. He told them no matter what they hear, they should stay in their tents. Rose and he would protect them tonight. Nick could see the dark shadows of their souls moving about. He knew the secret on how to keep them away. If you were not scared of them, they would leave you alone.

The first one to try to break into the camp was an old Indian warrior. Nick went over to where the spirit was standing. The old Indian warrior looked at Nick. Nick started chanting an old warrior's death song that his grandfather taught him. The old warrior seemed to settle down. He stopped pushing against the barrier of the salt line. The warrior started dancing. He sang the song along with Nick. They sang for several minutes together. They were joined by several other lost Indian souls. They were playing drums and flutes.

Nick kept singing. Nick would point to one soul at a time. That warrior's soul would sing their own death song. Many Indian warriors believed that unless they sang their death song before they died, they would not go to the other side. They would be trapped between life and death. Each time a warrior's soul would finish, another would take his place.

The chorus of souls accompanied by drums and flutes music filled the valley. Their agony of the years trapped here could be heard in their songs. Rose came to assist Nick. She sang along with the group. As the last of the warriors' souls finished, several loud drumbeats sounded. The night skies above were filled with warriors. They were welcoming their fellow warriors home at last.

The earth shook with the music and chanting. A young Indian woman on a painted pony appeared as the music ended. She looked down at Nick and Rose. She waved her white eagle feathers covered warrior's lance. It was a signal for the warriors to follow her to the land above. There was great rejoicing as they faded out of sight. The sunrise had begun. It had taken all night to release the warriors' souls. Rose looked at Nick. Nick was proud of what they had done. On the ground before them were two eagle feathers. They were a gift from the warriors to each of them.

Nick and Rose woke up everyone. It was time to move on to the next stop on their journey. Antonio and Angela asked what all the noise was about last night. Nick would only say some unfinished business for some lost souls. June noticed the eagle feathers that Nick and Rose had. "Where did you learn about death songs?" ask June. "As a young child, I lived many years in the Southwestern deserts with my grandmother and grandfather. There was an old warrior of my mother's tribe that lived in a sacred cave. He taught me the ways of my mother's people. I only sang my death song one time. I was in Iraq. I thought I was going to die. I had been wounded in battle.

In my tribe, a warrior's death song can save you. If the Great Spirits are pleased, they might save you to fight another day. I still remember the heat of that summer day on my face and body. The sun had been beating down on me all day. I was tied up on the ground spread eagled. I had just started my death song when two shots rang out. The shots cut the bindings of my hands. The next thing I remember is being carried out of the battle. They say it was an old man wearing an old cavalry hat with a faded seven on it who saved me."

David was sitting down eating his breakfast of pancakes and dried green eggs. Moses's father sat next to David. They were talking to each other. I didn't know if that meant that they had called a truce or that they were keeping an eye on each other. At least, they were not trying to kill each other.

Everyone was seated eating in a circle around the campfire. Antonio got up and pointed to Mary. Mary knew what Antonio wanted. "It is my turn to recite the passage I was given from *The Book of Fall*. I had difficulty in reading this passage. It is very personal to me.

What Happened to Me

Who's that looking back at me
Who's that person that I see
It's someone I don't know
Where did that other person go

I don't know that person with dark hair
Who's that person standing there
I have never seen this person before
It doesn't look like me anymore

Who am I looking at today
She doesn't look like I did yesterday
Someone's taken my place
What happened to my face

Why do I see pain in her eyes
Maybe it's the mirror that lies
Surely this can't be true
What happened to the girl I once knew

There's someone I don't know
Where did the other person go
Who's that person that I see
I don't know what happened to me

Mary asked Red Bear if he knew of any place in The Land of Nightmares that had mirrors or sometime that could reflect light. Red Bear nodded. "Our group traveled to a place high in the mountains to the west. We found a cave that had light coming out of it. An old man dressed in black buckskins guarded that cave. When our Great Medicine Man, Grey Fox, asked him about the cave, he told him that the cave reveals the true self of any that dare to go inside. He warned Grey Fox that to go inside could change his soul. He would see a mirror three images of himself. It would reveal his past, present and his future. You may not want to see the truth of who you really are. Grey Fox went inside anyway. When he came out two days later, he was a changed man. Shortly after that, he left us one night and we never saw him again. That is why I don't know the location of where he hid *The Book of Winter*."

David and I looked at each other. I knew what he was thinking. Could Mary face her past, present and future? She had been through a lot in her life. She never knew the whole story of her life. It could be too much for her. Mary was dressed in the red dress of a great medicine woman. We only hoped that would give her the power for her sanity to survive what she would see.

Red Bear shook his head. "I don't know if I want to take anyone to that cave. If my mentor, Grey Fox, couldn't survive the time in the cave, I wonder if anyone could. "I want to go there. I have no memories or very little of my past. I need to know who I am! Besides, we have no choice if we are to find the book," said Mary sternly. "I will take you there on only one condition. Everyone must promise not to go inside except

Mary. Everyone must say "I" right now," said Red Bear. Each of our group said "I" one at a time. David hesitated before finally saying "I".

Red Bear told us it would take most of the day to get to the cave. It would be a hard, long day hike. The day turned hot and dry. The heat was becoming unbearable. The terrain turned into a jungle. There were many snakes and lizards near or on the trail. Moses walked in front of us following the directions of Red Bear. We reached a river about halfway there. Moses had us stop on the riverbank. The river was full of all types of dangerous animals, snakes and man-eating fish. Getting across safely seemed impossible to anyone that tried.

David studied the situation. He asked Red Bear how his group got across the river. Red Bear replied that this river was not here when he was last here. It must be a test of survival that Grey Fox had put here to stop anyone from obtaining *The Book of Winter* that he had hidden.

David asked Moses if there was anything in nature that could stop these animals and fish. "The only thing that would slow them down would be extreme cold or ice. I don't think the weather would change that much on such a hot day," said Moses. David looked at his father, Red Bear.

Red Bear told David not to even think about it. That magic on such a hot day would kill you. It would take too much of your powers to produce. The river is too wide. David took that as a challenge. He reached into his medicine bag. He pulled out several black diamonds.

Rose had seen such black diamonds before. Antonio told David he was flirting with a dangerous magic. David laughed. "You know the legends about me. I am a cold man. I have my powers. We will have to wait until the sun goes behind the mountains. I must meditate for two hours. I want everyone well rested. I figure we will have only three minutes to cross the frozen bridge. I will be the last to cross. Leave me alone and get some rest," he ordered.

After two hours, the sun had crossed the sky and went behind the western mountains. The temperature started to cool. It had dropped at least thirty degrees. Red Bear lined up everyone. He told them to have the fastest people in front. They could help by pulling the slower ones across the frozen bridge faster.

It was still hotter than Red Bear liked. He told David that he did not believe he could do it. David was not having anything to do with that kind of talk. David looked up into the sky. Storm clouds appeared above. David took several of the cold black diamonds into his hands. His eyes had turned into big red. With just his hand, he crushed all the diamonds into a black dust. In one motion, he threw the dust into the air. He pointed at the dust. He took a deep breath and blew the dust across the wide river. He then pointed at the storm clouds. A cold rain began to fall. As the raindrops hit the black dust, ice began to form.

David pointed at the ice and shaped the ice into the shape of a bridge. When the last part of the bridge reached the opposite shore, Red Bear yelled for everyone to run. Nobody looked back. Everyone ran at once. The bridge was slippery, but everyone made good progress. The snakes, fish and other flesh-eating animals moved away from the frozen bridge. David's strength was fading.

Moses' father had stayed behind to help David. He picked up David like a light doll. He ran with him to the middle of the bridge. Then Moses took David. David was about to pass out. The ice bridge started to melt behind them. When all except David and Moses was on shore, it looked like the bridge would collapse. Antonio ran out to the end of the bridge. He blew some black dust behind them. The rain started to fall again. The bridge stopped collapsing. Antonio

184

slowly walked behind David. When they stepped on the other bank, the bridge collapsed into the river.

David asked Antonio how he knew to do such a thing. The only reply Antonio gave, "We must have had the same mentor. I did better this time. The last time several of my Celtic Brothers almost drowned."

They pushed on because it would be dark soon. Red Bear told them there would be a full moon tonight. In this land during Winter, most of the time, there was always a full moon. Darkness fell as they cleared the last of the jungle. The trail climbed slowly up to a mountain pass. There were not many trees dotting the landscape. The mountains on both sides of the pass were snow covered. Small mountain streams fell down the mountainsides. Moses noticed the mountain sheep on the sides of the mountains grazing on the green grass that grew in small clusters. Deer were plentiful. Next to the trail was a roaring mountain stream. Antonio thought this reminded him of the Italian Alps long ago.

The moonlight was brighter here. It gave a soft yellow tint to everything. Mary thought you could envision this as a land of fairy tales. It was late when Red Bear stopped them in a small grassy meadow at the base of a high mountain.   We pitched camp. Nick gave Mary some energy bars that he had made for her to eat. Red Bear told her that she must follow him up the trail about 100 yards. He would lead her to the cave.

Little Wolf was worried about Mary. He was afraid she would come back changed from the mother that he had gotten to know. David and I had our misgivings about how Mary could react if her memories returned. As Red Bear motioned for Mary to follow him, Little Wolf ran up to Mary and gave her a hug and kissed her on the cheek. Mary patted him on the back. Little Wolf had grown this last year. He was now as tall as his mother. Mary whispered to Little Wolf, "I can take

185

care of myself. No matter what, I will come back and still love you. I promise you that will never change."

Red Bear couldn't help but worry. He had seen what the cave could do to the strongest of medicine men. David had told him about Mary's life. This was the first time he thought of her as his granddaughter. Red Bear shook his head. He wished that he had spent more time with his son. He had wasted precious time. He felt guilty. He should have been helping his son and his daughter-in-law. Maybe this could have been avoided. He knew one thing. He wanted to have a family again. He wanted to be at peace with the world. He would do anything to protect his new family. He was angry with himself and the fate that destiny had given him. He could change all that.

The cave had light glowing from it. It had a large circular opening. Mary asked Red Bear what the symbols meant above the cave's entrance. Red Bear replied, "It took me several years to finally decipher them. It says, "Warning to those who dare to go into this sacred place. You will find the truth. The truth can set you free or destroy you. Nobody that enters is the same as before. May the Spirits be with you."

Mary turned to ask Red Bear another question. Red Bear had tears in his eyes. "My grandchild, you are a strong woman of my blood. You have a family waiting for you. I am proud to have you as my granddaughter. I only hope that one day you will be proud to have me as your grandfather. Now go, you must remember, whatever you find, you have a child that loves you. That should be enough for you to survive."

Little Wolf went over to sit by me. "John, did you love my mother?" Little Wolf asked. I looked at Little Wolf, "More than the world itself. She was young, beautiful and full of life. I must tell you one thing. She looked much different than she does today. That is why I wasn't sure who she was when I first met her this year. She was in a terrible accident in the Amazon jungle. It changed her appearance. I do know one thing. She loves you very much. Do not worry about me, whatever happens on this journey you must protect your mother. You and she must spend time together. She can teach you many things. Things a mother teaches her son."

Rose came over to John with David behind her. John stood up. He collapsed. David caught him before he would have hit the ground. Rose knew she must get him to her tent. John was close to dying. She would use her voodoo powers to keep him alive. John's time was growing short. David carried him to her tent. Rose told him to get June and have her bring John's medicine bag. Rose told Little Wolf not to come back to her tent until she sent for him.

It took all the nerve that Mary had to walk toward the entrance to the cave. She wanted to know the truth. She had wondered about so many things. She had to have the answers.

Mary was anxious as she stepped into the cave's entrance. The only light she carried was a moonstone in a necklace that Red Bear had given her in case the lighting went out. The moonstone would lead her back to the entrance. She walked several hundred feet into the cave.

Crystals lined the walls glowing a pale white light. The cave's tunnel stopped in a large room. There was a cold draft. She was getting cold. Her imagination was getting carried away. This room had a foreboding feeling to it. Had she made a mistake in coming here? Would she be able to deal with what she was about to see? She had no choice. There was no turning back now.

There was a big mirror like crystal at the far end of the room. A figure dressed in a black hooded cape motioned her to come toward the large crystal. The figure took her hand and placed her directly in front of the large crystal. The old woman's cold bony finger touched the crystal.

Mary did not move a muscle. She stared straight ahead. As she stared at the crystal, three lights in the crystal moved around in a circle. The light started moving faster and faster. Mary's mind went blank. Visions started appearing. There was a little baby in a crib. It must have been a girl. A woman was bending over the baby. "My sweet little baby girl. One day you will be a great woman of my tribe. We will leave this place and be happy in the land of my forefathers," said the woman. The woman picked up the baby and turned.

Mary saw the face of the woman. It was the Red Woman. It was her mother, Donna, as known to others. David appeared next to her mother. "How is our little girl, Mary?" he asked. "She is fine. It would be better if we were out of this place. I wish we could take her back to the land," her mother said. "I know, but maybe someday. We have a mission to complete. We must destroy the **Dark Ones** first." Her mother replied, "I only hope that it doesn't kill us or our child first."

The next scene was a little girl playing in a big yard. The little girl must have been about six years old. She was wearing a pink party dress. It must have been her birthday. Mary knew that she must be the little girl. She felt warm and happy for the first time in a long time. Her mother called for her to come and let her brush the little girl's hair. Mary noticed that the little girl's hair was black as coal. Her skin was light copper tan. The girl couldn't be her. Mary's skin was pale, and her hair was light brown.

Memories started pouring into Mary's mind. She remembered her father playing with her in the yard. He was teaching her to ride a painted pony. Her mother was teaching her magic tricks. She remembered how much her father loved her mother. They were always kissing each other goodbye in the mornings. It was a wonderful life.

It was hard for Mary. Her father was so different from the loving father in the visions. Things could have been different if she only knew. She was sad, angry and full of regret. How could her father have become the man he was? She had seen him be very cruel and unkind. He was the opposite of the memories that were coming back to her. Mary was becoming more confused.

The scene changed. Mary felt a sense of dread come over her. A very pale white woman with white hair was talking to her mother. It was Benita. "You know that Raven wants to kill you and your little girl. I can save you both, but it comes at a price," said Benita.

"What price is that?" said her mother. "Raven has sent hired killers to kill you and your daughter. I can fake your death. I have a person that can save you. There are some things that you must do. You must never come back. You must never ever see your daughter again. I will take over caring for your daughter. I may be hard on your daughter, but she will need that to survive. If you don't do these things, your daughter and David will not survive Raven's wrath. The car is coming to do this any minute. Take your car and run. It's the only way!" Benita pleaded with her mother.

The next scene in the crystal mirror was a funeral for her mother. Mary was crying. Benita was holding her hand. The casket was closed. Her father was beside himself with grief. Benita told him that she would help care for Mary and keep her safe. Raven was standing near them. She was smiling at Benita. Benita winked at Raven.

Mary was starting to understand her past much clearer. There were many questions that rose their ugly heads. Did Benita do this to help or get rid of her mother? Was it part of Raven's plan? Did Benita use taking care of Mary as a way to get her father to marry her? There were some memories of Benita being kind to her. She once gave Mary a dark-skinned doll to play with. Benita told her that it looked just like her real mother. Mary had another deeper question. Why did the little girl look so different than what she is today? The visions didn't make sense,

The next scene was a young woman in the desert. She was with an older man. They were trying to find a lost relic from the Mayan civilization. The man took the young beautiful black-haired Woman in his arms. He kissed her passionately. He told her that he loved her. He wanted to take her with him to a land that was only known as **The Land of the Eagle Feathers**.

The young woman was excited to hear that and kissed the man back. Mary could feel those kisses. When the image showed the man's face, she couldn't believe what she saw. The handsome older man was John!

Memories of their relationship came back to Mary. She was that lovely young lady. John was her lover. They would take walks in the desert at sunset. They would joke and tease each other like lovers often do. She could feel the warmth of their relationship. John always treated her with respect. In one scene, she asked John if he would find a tattoo artist to put a small butterfly on the top of her breasts. It would give her good luck. That must be why he once said to her that he knew a woman that had the same tattoos. That's how he started figuring out who she really was. She couldn't help it. She could feel the love that they had for each other.

The next scene made her heart stop. It was an Indian wedding ceremony in the desert. A Native American man and his wife with several others had gathered around her and John. She recognized who they were. It was Nick's grandmother and grandfather with elders of his tribe. Nick's grandfather must be a great chief. He took John's forearm and cut it slightly. He then took hers and cut it. Nick's grandfather bound both of their cut arms together. "We witness today these two in marriage. They are now one forever," said Nick's grandfather. Doves were released into the air. These scenes were followed by their honeymoon. It was a short time before everything went wrong. Mary looked at her forearm. There was a faint scar of a cut. This shook her.

The next scene was very different. Mary was trying to tell her father, David, that she loved John and was going to have his baby. David was so mad that he took out a gun and shot at John two times. He hit John and when she stepped between them, he accidently shot her. David picked her up and put her into his pickup and raced to the hospital.

Mary was in a coma in bed. The doctor delivered her baby while she was still in the coma. Benita was in the hospital room with her. After she gave birth, Benita held the baby. She gave the baby to a woman. The woman took the baby and left. Benita went to another room. She told John that both Mary and his son had died in childbirth. She had a certificate from the doctor to show that. "You better leave before David gets here. He must never know that you were here. He will kill you. Mary wouldn't have wanted that," Benita told him. John left. She could see that John was heartbroken. Nick's father helped John get to Nick's grandfather's pickup and took him away.

David arrived, and Benita told David that the baby had died. She told him that Mary would survive. It would take a while. David seemed to be both relieved and sad there was no baby. How could her father feel that way? She was becoming more upset with her father. How could he be so cruel?

The scene changed. Mary was with her father. She was in the Amazon jungle looking into a cure for cancer. She and Benita were with some natives in a dugout canoe. They were riding down a wild river. The boat got caught in some wild rapids. It was tossing and turning. Mary started to fall out of the boat. Benita either tried to grab her or push her out of the boat. It was hard to tell.

The next scene was David arguing with John in the jungle. "I wouldn't have come if I knew it was you," John told him. "This woman is near death. I need your help to find a witchdoctor to save her. If anyone would know of one, it would be you, John," David yelled at him, "Forget our differences."

John looked down at the battered face of the woman, From the woman's battered face or what was left of it, you could not tell who she was. "You are lucky that I had been here on other business. I should have killed you, but Mary would have stopped me. This woman, you say, was a very good friend of Mary's. Then, I will help you."

There is a witchdoctor near here. He can help her. There is a cost to his help. She will need the blood of a woman. He will transform her into the likeness of that woman. Much like the likeness of you and Benita here, if she was your child. Also, it will erase all the woman's memories. Are you willing to pay such a price for her?" asked John. Benita spoke, "That should be my decision. After all, it is my blood. I know this woman well. I once promised her mother that I would look after her."

John had several of his people carry the litter with the woman to a jungle clearing. An old man dressed as a witchdoctor took Benita and the Injured Woman into his hut. John told David that he would kill him if he asked for any more help. "I only do this because of your daughter who would have wanted me to do it," said John as he left.

In the next scene, the witchdoctor came out of the hut. He asked David to come and see his daughter. "I told your wife that this could kill her, but she said a promise is a promise. It will take them both several weeks to get well enough to travel." David went over and kissed Benita, "I don't know why you did this. I will be forever grateful." He turned to Mary who was lying next to Benita.

The look on David's face was one of shock. The face of the woman lying there was Mary's face. She had been transformed. She had both the features of her father and Benita. Her skin was white, and her hair was light brown. David looked at her. "I don't care if you have changed, I will always love you," he said to her.

Mary just stared at that scene. This was the reason she looked so much different from the young girl and woman. She always wondered why Benita had treated her so well after her accident. She could not remember much before, but she knew that Benita was not always that kind to her. Benita never said another harsh word to her. She treated her more like a daughter. Was this side of Benita real? She thought about it more and more. No, Benita must have cared for her. She could have let her die. One thing was for sure. She could not kill Benita. Benita had saved her life. Benita is much more than anyone would have thought. Is she the biggest scorpion in this whole group of people? Mary realized that Benita was a different breed of woman.

The crystal's light turned off. The woman in the dark hooded cape spoke, "Before we go any farther, you must make a decision. Your future will depend on your decision. An image of a lovely Indian woman with dark copper skin and black shiny hair about Mary's age appeared next to her reflection. "This is your image as it would have been. The picture to your left is your appearance today. Now, you must make that decision of who will you be in the future. Are you the Indian woman or the white woman? In a way, you have two mothers. Which way do you choose? You cannot leave here without choosing," the woman instructed Mary.

Mary had been shown too much. Her mind raced. Would Little Wolf be affected if she changed? What about Benita, who protected her? What about David and John? Who does she want to be? Mary had a hard choice to make. She thought hard and fast. She asked the woman for a few moments to make her decision. She understood most of her past. John was truly in love with her. She was once in love with him. The fact they were married was a big blow to her. John had never mentioned it. She had to give credit to him. No wonder she had felt drawn to him. The others were not of much consequence to her except Little Wolf. It was an agonizing decision. No matter what her decision, she would never be the same. It was true what Red Bear said, "You will never be the same after visiting this place."

The two images reached out to her. The image of who she is now, a white woman with a life back in Maine, and with her dad in Houston, started shouting at her. There were visions of her teaching at the college and doing research all over the world. Her friends, co-workers and all the people she knew would be gone or changed if she went with the image of the Indian woman. Her life as she had known for years would be gone. She had worked so hard to get to her position. The vision of her life now would be no more. Her life would be changed forever. Would she want to lose all of that? She and her father had plans that would take them to the heights of fulfilling their wildest dreams. Would changing be worth that? It was like being torn into. She wanted them both. Why would she want to change into a person she didn't know? Arms from that vision started reaching out to pull her into that image. A voice could be heard. It was Benita saying, "You can have it all. Remain the same! We are part of each other. I love you!" Mary took a step back.

The vision of her as an Indian woman with a son and husband tried to get her attention.   She saw visions of the friends she had made this year on her journey to the land. Little Wolf and her mother and all the people of this land she had met were pictured before her.   Most of all, she saw the images of **The Keepers of the Yawi,** her closest friends**.**

These visions were so new to her. Had **The Land of the Eagle Feathers** changed her? Could she go back to her life knowing she was not that woman, she once thought she was? Mary was confused and distraught. She loved Little Wolf. She had a mother here. They were her people. Could she face the fact that she had a husband? What would life be for her? She would have to start over in the outside world. David and she had made plans. Would it be worth it? The decision was tearing at her mind. Which one is she? Which door should she walk through? She thought of the famous story, The Lady or the Tiger. A hand reached to pull her into the image. The hand was warm, soft and caring. A voice called out to her. It was her mother, "Come and join your true family. Another voice called, "Mother, I need you." Tears rolled down Mary's face as she listened to the voices from both visions.

Mary had only one question to answer. "Which decision can I live with for the rest of my life? She fell to the floor of the cave weeping and sobbing. Her life had been turned upside down. "Who was she?" After several minutes, she dried her eyes. For better or worse, she made her decision. It was the only one she could live with. She stood up and grabbed one of the arms that reached out to her. The arm pulled her into that image into the crystal.

The old woman said "Now, I will show you, your future. You would see if you made the right one." Mary would see what the future could bring to her. There would be no turning back. The old woman touched the crystal with Mary caught inside its embrace. Soon Mary would know! It didn't matter. It was a decision she could live with for the rest of her life.

Red Bear had stood for hours watching the entrance to the cave. A hooded figure with Mary appeared at the entrance. Red Bear had tears in his eyes. "You have made the right decision. I was worried. I want you to meet your grandmother. I asked her to go to assist you," he said. "I sent her to this land before she would have died. You have not only saved yourself, but her as well." Red Bear ran to hold his wife in his arms. "We have only one more thing to do to be a complete family. We must get Red Sparrow. We must get him back. Your grandmother has something to give you," said Red Bear. Her grandmother gave a piece of the puzzle to Mary.

Everyone was waiting for them to return. Out of the cold damp darkness came three people. Two were women, and one was Red Bear. Little Wolf ran to the younger woman. He put his arms around her, "You are the mother of my dreams. I have seen you often in my dreams.' The younger woman held Little Wolf in her dark copper arms.

Mary asked, "Where is John?" David pointed to Rose's tent. He is very sick. We don't know if he will make it. He is dying," said David. Mary ran to Rose's tent with Little Wolf following her. When she arrived, she demanded for Rose and June to get out of her way. "I will save him somehow!" she cried. They asked, "Who are you? Why should we trust you?' Mary replied, "I am Mary and because John is my husband!"

Mary listened to John's heartbeat. It was very weak. June and Rose were still in a state of shock about Mary's appearance. Was this the real Mary or was she an impostor or evil spirit? Angela surprised everyone. She went into the tent. "I know what you are thinking. Is this really Mary? Look into John's medicine bag, he always kept important personal things in it. There might be a picture of Mary in there." Rose opened John's medicine bag. There was an old envelope in it. Rose opened it. Inside the envelope was a picture of a young Indian woman. She was standing beside John. A great chief was behind them. They had one arm bound to each other. It must have been a wedding picture. Both looked so much in love with each other. The young Indian woman matched the woman holding John's hand before them. On the back of the picture was written, "On our wedding day, Mary is so beautiful."

Angela told them to look after John. There was only one person she knew that could help him. Antonio had told her about a short passage in *The Book of Fall* that applied to her. Antonio knew who the passage referred to. It was the Italian Priest that had practiced the dark arts that had escaped capture by the Catholic Authorities many years ago. Rumors had it that he was sent to a mysterious land in exile.

"How long does John have to live?" asked Angela. "He has only a day or two," replied Rose. "I will be back in time. I must find the Priest that was exiled here. Red Bear will know where to find him. He knows more than he lets on to us."

Angela ran out to find Red Bear. Red Bear was sitting on a log near the campfire. "Red Bear, where is the Italian Priest that dwells in this land? I know you know where he is." Red Bear looked at Angela and asked, "How do you know such a thing?"

Before Angela could answer, Antonio interrupted. "It is said in *The Book of Winter* that an evil Priest could help save the leader of our group. A dark angel will summon his help. She must know his darkness to defeat him. There is only one person here that meets that description here. Red Bear laughed, "Yes, Angela fits that description. What does the passage say?"

The leader of The Keepers of the Yawi might die
An Angel will nccd to find an answer high in the sky
She must face an evil man to stop his death
She must fight evil and match its depth

Only the eagles dare to fly so high
He sees only dark clouds going by
The Dark Angel must find a way to change his ways
To get the medicine to delay your leader's final days

Red Bear said, "I will take Angela to that place. It is not a mountain. It is a Catholic Church with a high tower. The man there is truly evil. He is very dangerous. The evil Priest is one that Angela saved long ago. Antonio was to kill him. He didn't. I will take Antonio with you. The truth will be hard for both of you. I only hope you survive."

Red Bear told them that the old church was only about an hour away. Antonio could see that Angela was getting very anxious as they walked toward the church. You could see the high tower covered by dark clouds. Antonio recognized the church at once. It belonged to a Priest he thought he had killed long ago. It was on the mission with The Council of Religions in which he first met Angela. Red Bear pointed to the large wooden entrance doors to the large old church. "In there you will find more answers than you would ever want to find," Red Bear laughed. "I must stay here."

Antonio and Angela pulled open the large wooden entrance doors. It took all their strength to open only the right side of the double doors. It was dark inside with lighted candles, the only light.

Cautiously they walked inside the church. As soon as they were inside, the door slammed shut behind them. The only thing they could see was a large room that was directly below a domed ceiling. There were many lighted candles that gave them light. There were candelabras by the rounded walls throughout this floor. The floor was white marble with the walls being a slightly darker color.

In the middle of the room was a dark granite table with no chairs around it. Next to the table stood a man dressed like a friar. He had on a black robe with a bright red rope belt around his mid-section. He motioned for them to come to him.

As they approached him, Antonio stopped. Antonio whispered he knew who this man was. This man was very dangerous. Whoever was in front of them must be his spirit. Angela asked Antonio how he knew. Antonio replied that he had killed him many years ago. Angela could hear the fear in the sound of Antonio's voice.

When Antonio was about 3 meters from the man, the man spoke. "Stop there, Antonio." Antonio froze. The man's voice was deep and powerful like a priest's voice about to give a sermon. "Antonio, I commend you for living this long," he said. Antonio replied back, "I had my moments."

"I am happy we could have this one last meeting together, Antonio," the man said. "I have been looking forward to this moment for many years, and now it has arrived!" the man joyfully shouted his words echoing throughout the great room. Angela glanced around the room for other doorways and windows. There were none that she could see. It appeared that the only way out was the way they came. That was not encouraging.

The old man started talking to them. "You see, Antonio knows me from long ago. Many years ago, I was his elder priest in the Catholic Church. My name is Priest Cain. He studied under me to become a priest. Little did I know that he was working for The Council of Religions. It seems that the Council had an idea that I was working for the other side. I think you call them **The Dark Ones**.

Being a cautious person, I didn't trust anyone. I soon found out that Antonio was not who he said he was. Antonio had one great weakness. That weakness was women. I could see the lust in his eyes when he saw a beautiful woman. It just happened that one of my contacts with the **Dark Ones** was a beautiful woman. So, I set him up. I let him see me with her to see if he would follow her. When he did, I knew. Now Antonio can be quite charming with the ladies. It seems funny now that both of us never let on to my beautiful contact that Antonio was a priest. Antonio, my contact is standing with you. Angela was very good at her job.

One day, Angela confessed to me that she had met a charming young man and had an affair with him. She would have to leave me because she had become pregnant. She left her position with **The Dark Ones** soon after that".

Antonio looked upset and alarmed by what the old man called Priest Cain said. Antonio shouted back at Priest Cain, "She never told me that she was pregnant. I never knew." That's when Priest Cain laughed at Antonio. Angela told Antonio to be silent.   She knew how Priest Cain worked his magic.

 "One thing, Antonio, you didn't know is that I delivered her child. I was once a doctor. I arranged for her to have the baby at the Home of Lost Children in Rome."

Antonio asked Cain, "I thought that I killed you in Rome when I tried to take you in to The Council of Religions. We had a fight with swords, and I know that I cut you badly enough that you would die.'

"Yes, you did. I barely survived," replied Cain. Angela found me in time and saved me. She even put a dead man's body in my clothes to fool everyone. When the Council found out you killed me and you had an affair with a woman, I was laughing when the Church defrocked you."

"I know your next question. How did I get here? Well that's a long story. I will make it short. I found out through Angela how to get through to this land. She gave me a sacred book that told me what I must do to get here. What I didn't realize was that I didn't have what it takes to fight my own demons from my past. I was imprisoned here in this church for that. This land has a way of turning your mind inside out. I can't leave here. This land will destroy your mind if you do not guard it closely. I guess Angela had the last laugh. I never thought Angela was so clever."

Angela looked at Antonio. "I must finish what I started with Priest Cain. Antonio, go back to the church's entrance. The Priest and I have some unfinished business to conduct. I must correct a problem. This is now between Priest Cain and me. He has something that I want. You will only be in the way. I need to show Priest Cain who he is dealing with. I am not that naïve young woman that David sent to assist Priest Cain many years ago. Now, go Antonio!"

Antonio was a little confused about what was going to happen. He knew Angela was right. He would only be in the way. This was something that Angela had to do. She would have to deal with it herself. He took a long look at Angela and left. He only hoped that she would survive to meet him back at the entrance to the church.

Priest Cain said, "Angela, I know that you are doing this to protect Antonio and your son. Antonio deserves to die. Didn't he desert you? We can make a deal, and I will save your son, but I must kill Antonio. Some spirits told me that John is very ill. You have come here to get the medicine that will prolong John's life. You know it won't cure him. It will only give him until the New Year, January 15th, to live. I knew the moment I saw you. You came to kill me. You had no choice. I would have found out how to reach you by magic to kill you and your so-called family. I see that you are dressed as White Elk's daughter. I hope you have learned much since I last saw you or this meeting will be very short."

Angela jumped to her left as a fireball was thrown by Priest Cain at her. It hit the wall beside her and knocked down a piece of the wall. Angela smiled. She pointed a gemstone at Cain. A bright yellow light of a laser beam hit at the feet of

Cain. Cain fell hitting his head on the white marble floor. Blood flowed out of Cain's wound on to the floor. "Well now, Angela, I see you have learned much. I have had time to study many more things here," Cain yelled at her.

Cain started to float into the air above the stone table. A large spider appeared directly overhead of Angela. Angela leaped and took a dagger out from under her vest pocket and threw it. It hit the giant spider between its eyes. It fell harmlessly to the marble floor dead. Before Priest Cain could react, Angela jumped up and grabbed Priest Cain's robe and pulled him to the floor. She placed a moonstone on his temple. Priest Cain tried to move, but he couldn't. "I see that you forgot that a moonstone was your greatest threat. I now have you at my mercy," Angela grinned at Cain. "Now where is that medicine I need, Cain?"

Cain replied, "You can kill me. I will never give it to you." Angela watched Cain's eyes. She walked over to a cabinet on the far wall. She opened it. On the middle shelf was a small pouch of herbs and other powders. There was another thing in the pouch. It as a piece of the puzzle that would lead them to the book. "You have one weakness. You always look at the place where you hide things. I learned that working for you," said Angela.

Priest Cain asked, "What are you going to do with me?" Angela replied, "Nothing, I am going to leave you here." Priest Cain stated, "I will do anything to get out of here. You can't leave me in this place." Angela answered him back, "Oh, yes, I can. However, there is one thing that you could do to get out of here."

A very anxious Priest Cain asked, "What is that?" Angela replied, "You must go to the altar and asked for forgiveness for your sins. If you mean it, you will bc allowed to leave here. But there is a price you must pay for that. You will never be able to have any powers. You will become an average man. You will have to live the life of a Religious Priest until you die. Now, I will leave you here by yourself. The moonstone spell will wear off in about one hour. You will never be able to do wrong to me or my family. You will forever be a captive in this church.

I want to thank you for your help delivering my son. There was once some good in you. Using your powers for evil is not power. I have found that using your skills for good and being wise in your actions are a far greater power. I could have killed you today. That would be a waste.   Native Americans do not like to waste anything.

You have great knowledge that you can pass on to others to do good. I hope you think about that. I have shown mercy to you. I hope you can learn from that. I have. This is your chance at redemption. The great spirits of **The Land of the Eagle Feathers** will welcome you.

Forgiveness is a great power of its own. Don't waste your gifts. I hope to see you repay my mercy by helping us. The choice is yours to make. Good-bye, Priest Cain." Angela bent over Priest Cain and kissed him on his forehead. The old Priest looked into her eyes. Nobody had ever been kind to him in such a way. She could feel the sadness leave his heart. She was glad for him. She would see him again.

Antonio was relieved when Angela walked out of the church. He started to ask her questions. "There is no time for that. Never ask me anymore about my past. We have only the future to worry about. I think that is fair," said Angela. Antonio nodded his head.

It wasn't long before Red Bear got them back to the campsite. Angela gave June, Rose and Mary the pouch for John. Mary mixed the contents of the pouch into a liquid potion. They held John down while they forced the potion down his throat. Mary asked June and the others to leave her alone with John. John woke the next morning. He looked up at Mary's face. He could not talk. His eyes told her all she needed to know. Tears of joy were running down his face.

As the fog cleared away from the valley, Moses woke everyone up. He told each one, "We have company. There are at least 30 men dressed like some sort of militia group surrounding us." David had everyone take defensive positions. Mary had to stay with John. He was too weak to be of any help.

A man approached carrying a white flag. Red Bear stood up. He walked toward the man about 100 yards from the campsite. The man was dressed in brown army fatigues. He carried several large combat KA-BAR knifes on his canteen belt. After several minutes of talking, Red Bear returned. Red Bear motioned for everyone to gather around the campfire.

"Don't worry about them attacking us," Red Bear stated. "They only want one of us. They want Nick. They are from a country far away. They fought against Nick in a war many moons ago. Their leader sent them to bring back Nick. Their leader is a great warrior. It seems that Nick and he have a score to settle. News travels fast in The Land of Nightmares. Somehow in this land, word of new arrivals is sent to those who have reasons to know about those new arrivals. They have been waiting for us. They didn't know Nick's real name. I guess it was Nick, they wanted, by the man's description and what Nick preferred to fight with. He said some called him, The Killing Machine. He said Nick was better known as **The Angel of Death**. The name of the leader is called **"The Butcher."** They want an answer by midday if Nick is willing to fight their leader."

Moses asked Nick, "What is he talking about?" Nick had already put on his canteen belt with his razor-sharp large KA-BAR combat knife and his tomahawk. "I was afraid that my real-life nightmares would be here. Some of you know a little about me and that Mideastern war. When "The Butcher" and his militia killed my best friend and most of my command, I lost it. I went on a revenge killing spree.

I killed every one of them. I hunted each one down like they were animals. One night, I made a terrible mistake. I missed my target with a M72 Law and blew up a mud hut. In the mud hut was the family of "The Butcher." Let's say my final fight with "The Butcher" did not go well for each of us. I think I killed him. They never found his body.

The next thing I knew was that I woke up in a hospital. It just wasn't a medical hospital. They transferred me to the psyche ward. I was given a Section 8. They gave me a bunch of medals and released me from duty. Basically, they said that I was too good at killing. I still live with those nightmares. I replay that miss in my mind every day. If it wasn't for most of you including Shanna and my grandparents, I would have never come this far. I have no choice. I must go and fight one last time. I owe him that much."

Antonio asked Nick to recite his passage. "There is meaning in that passage for you."

All the Parts Make a Whole

Be as strong as brother bear
Fierce in battle but always fair
Hunting in the shadows of the night
Looking for food, not wanting to fight

Be as faithful as brother wolf
Beautiful to see but fleet in foot
Howling at its lover in yonder moon
Missing its lover, gone too soon

Be as wise as brother owl
Hidden to most but loving the bough
Watching in the tree, always watching you
Telling you he knows what you do

Be a gentle as brother deer
Harmless to all but living in fear
Hoping they won't be someone's prey
Trying to survive for another day

Learn from the animals that you see
They are all brothers to you and me
Each one has a soul
All the parts make a whole

Moses touched Nick's shoulder. "I am strong like a brother bear. I will go with you to meet this man." One Feather said, "I will go with you. I am your brother wolf. Antonio replied, "I will be your brother Owl." Lo Ming couldn't help it, "I will also go. I am a warrior "Trying to survive for another day." This meeting is for warriors. We will make sure that this is a fair fight." David finally said, "That is enough of us going. I will go to make sure none of you intervene in their fight. The rest of us need to stay here. They will wait for our return. After all, Nick, all parts make a whole."

"Before you go to join Nick you need to know what you could be getting into," I told them. Everyone turned around to see John being helped to a log near the campfire by Mary. "I should fill in parts of the story Nick didn't tell. The unit that Nick was assigned to in the Mideast, had been fighting a group of vicious men led by a man that everyone nicknamed "The Butcher." This man gave no mercy to anyone. He killed everyone and anyone. If you surrendered to him, he didn't care. He just killed you. Many men in Nick's unit were killed fighting him. "The Butcher" always dressed in a distinctive way. He would wear a black skull cap with a white feather. He dressed in a black uniform with a shirt that was black with red plaid. His black pants had two gold stripes running down each side.

Nick makes this man sound better than he was. The reason that Nick wanted to kill "The Butcher' is the way he killed Nick's best friend. After killing Nick's friend, "The Butcher" had left a message on his friend's body that said he would kill everyone in Nick's command until they would meet each other. "The Butcher" had a vendetta against him because Nick was a legend on the battlefield. Nick was known by the enemy as a powerful warrior. The enemy called him the "Killing Machine." Nick was a legend. He was better known as **The Angel of Death** by newspapers' articles about him. It was only a manner of time before "The Butcher' and Nick would have a man to man fight. "The Butcher" knew if he could kill Nick, he would gain more esteem and power in the region. Some say that "The Butcher" wanted esteem more than revenge for the killing of his family.

Nick's unit commanders knew of this vendetta. They wanted Nick to set up a trap for "The Butcher" with him as bait. He was to take a squad and lure "The Butcher" and his men to ambush them. Nick refused to allow anymore of his men to be killed. He went AWOL. He went after "The Butcher" himself.

Nick did hunt down all of "The Butcher's men. Finally, "The Butcher" ambushed Nick. He became surrounded with no hope to survive. A firefight started, and everything looked hopeless. The only thing Nick said he could remember from that point on was that he was fighting and killing everything in sight. Finally, he encountered "The Butcher."

They had a bloody fight. The fight with "The Butcher" came down to hand to hand. The last thing Nick said he could remember was that he was starting to stab "The Butcher" to death, and everything went blank.

Only one of Butcher's men survived the attack. The survivor said that Nick had probably killed at least 20 men himself. The fighting only stopped when Nick killed "The

Butcher." When the Army found Nick, they airlifted Nick and the survivor to a field hospital.

The next day, the army sent men to bury "The Butcher" and his dead men. But when they arrived at the scene of the battle, no one was found. It was like the men had disappeared into thin air. No traces of a battle were ever found. "The Butcher" and his men were never seen of again in the region. Nick was sent home. The army said that he was unfit for combat, and he was given an honorable discharge."

Nick looked at me. He said, 'I bet you know more about this than I will ever know. The survivor said that a man dressed in old buckskins carried me out with him." I replied to him, "Maybe so, but I will never tell you because you should never know what you did there." I looked at the others and then said, "If you go with Nick, give "The Butcher" this envelope. Be very careful, "The Butcher" is a extremely dangerous man. He should honor his truce and give you safe passage back no matter what happens between Nick and him." I passed out. Nick and Moses carried me back the tent. Mary stayed with me.

At midday, several men with a white flag waited for Nick to come out to them. They were surprised to see that Nick had several people with him. "We are to take you to the next valley to fight our leader," they said to Nick. A dark man behind Nick said, "We will go with him to make sure that this is a fair fight. If it is not fair, we will kill each and every one of you." One of Butcher's men laughed, until David looked at his group. They say David's eyes turned bright red. David handed an envelope to the leader of this group. "A man called John said to give this to "The Butcher."

David could see that everyone of Butcher's men had fear in their eyes when David said, "John." "We will do as you say. This is between our leader and the man over there," he said as he pointed at Nick. "We all know that man because he killed us long ago. We have been waiting here for a long time for him." It started to rain as soon as they arrived at the next valley to meet "The Butcher." "The Butcher" was given the envelope from John. He put it in his pocket. He turned to face Nick.

"So, we meet again. I had been waiting for this a long time," said "The Butcher" with a smile and half laugh. They told me that I would have a chance to kill you after they left me here in this strange land with my men that you had killed." Nick didn't reply to him. "I guess that it had to be. We have some unfinished business," "The Butcher" stated sarcastically.

"Yes, I always felt that we never finished what we started so long ago," replied Nick. "But I do have one thing that always bothered me," Nick said.

"I think I know what that is," "The Butcher" seriously replied. "You know the answer to that, but you don't want to come to face it for yourself. You want to know why I hate you so much and want to kill you myself. I know you remember several years ago in that desert village during that firefight. Remember that night that was so dark and windy. You took a shot at me with a grenade launcher and missed. It hit the mud house behind me. You saw a woman run out of that mud house covered in flames and fire. You saw her die in my arms. You should have killed me then, but you didn't. You couldn't because you soon realized she was my wife. All you did was call off the mission and left in a hurry. Need I say more.'

Nick looked at his enemy in the eye. Then he said, "You killed my best friend. You killed my fellow soldiers. I always knew that I have their blood on my hands as well because you always wanted to kill me. I thought that the nightmares would end when I killed you. I knew they wouldn't. The army said I was unfit for duty and threw me away like a piece of discarded thrash. However, I knew we would meet again.

Now in this land, we will end this once and for all. I will give you one last chance for revenge. How do you want to do this?"

"The Butcher" looked at his enemy. Then he said, "I see you have what is called a KA-BAR combat knife and tomahawk in your belt. I have a combat knife and this sword. I think that these weapons are fair enough to use on each other. I have had time to think about this for a long time. I have practiced with these weapons. I will kill you. I will have my revenge. Now let's get started before the rain gets any harder."

Nick pulled out his tomahawk with his left hand and pulled out his large combat knife with his right hand. "The Butcher" pulled out his combat knife with his left hand. He had his Middle Eastern sword with its wide blade in his right hand. Some fair fight Nick thought to himself still it was more than Nick expected of "The Butcher" anyway.

Both men circled each other. The rain was coming down hard making footing very slippery. Nick had removed his shirt. You could see the marks that were left on his chest and back from bullets and knives that had cut him. "The Butcher" noticed them too. The Butcher smiled saying, "This was what warriors do. They settle things among themselves in battle." "The Butcher" made the first move. He struck at Nick's right shoulder. Nick countered with his combat knife. It wasn't enough. The long blade of sword scored first creating a bloody wound on the front of his shoulder.

Nick knew it was only superficial. The blood did flow like it was worse than it was. "The Butcher" laughed. "I thought you were better than that. I will take my time with you. I will cut you up a little piece at a time. I want you to suffer like you have made me suffer," he growled back at Nick.

Nick thought he could use "The Butcher's" confidence. If "The Butcher" thought that this wound was worse than it was, he could catch him off guard and maybe he would have a chance. Nick swung his tomahawk and hit the combat knife blade of "The Butcher." "The Butcher" felt the stinging of the hit in his left hand as it traveled up his arm. He swung his sword at Nick. He missed. Nick countered with his knife slicing at "The Butcher's" chest, cutting his shirt from one end of his chest to the other. Blood was starting to flow down his chest. Now both men had struck for blood.

Both men fought for several minutes. They had cuts from each other's weapons. No one was hurt seriously. Everyone watching this battle were amazed at the skill of both men. They did note that Nick's wound was bleeding badly. It didn't seem to slow him down. The rain had turned the circle of combat into mud. Lightning and thunder added to the noise of their weapons clanging against each other. It was as if the spirits were pleased with the battle.

Nick slipped in the mud, giving his enemy an opening. He thrust his sword into Nick's side. This staggered Nick. He fell to the ground. "The Butcher" could have finished him. He didn't want to. He wanted to take his time in killing him. Nick slowly got up. Nick knew if he didn't finish this fight quickly, he would soon be too weak from loss of blood to protect himself. Nick had to do something fast.

Nick swung and missed. "The Butcher" knew from how much Nick had missed him that Nick was hurt badly. Again, Nick swung and missed wildly with his tomahawk. He laughed at Nick. This time he swung his sword at Nick. The force of the blow knocked Nick down even though Nick had blocked it with his tomahawk. Nick weakly got up. "The Butcher" swung again to knock Nick down. Then he got a big surprise as Nick jumped to the side. Nick swung his tomahawk and knife at "The Butcher's" weapons in one graceful downward swing knocking both of the weapons from "The Butcher's" hands. His enemy was on the ground defenseless. Nick was on top of him with his combat knife on

"The Butcher's" throat. Everything seemed to stop at once. The rain and thunder stopped. Everyone became silent. Nick could kill him with one stroke of his knife. Everyone waited for Nick to finish the job. "The Butcher" knew he was finished.

Nick slowly got off him. Nick told him to get up. "The Butcher" told his men to remain where they were. This was a fight between them. Nick was very weak. He was dying.

Nick looked at "The Butcher" saying, "I will not kill you. You have suffered enough. You have the right to kill me. What I did was an accident. I still did it. I am sorry for your pain. Take these weapons and do what you must. I will not stop you or your men. I only want to die like a warrior. I want to make peace with you before I die. I have learned that killing does not settle anything. It only brings more killing. You had a family. You should have cherished them more than your pride. I hope one day you will realize this. I have."

"The Butcher" took Nick's weapons. It would be easy for him to kill his greatest enemy. But for what, he thought. It wouldn't change anything. His enemy is a great warrior. He respected that. He would not kill him because great warriors have codes. "The Butcher" didn't say anything. He gave Nick his weapons back. The war between them was over.

"You are right. Pride does not replace a loved one. I loved my wife. Life is too precious and short. The wind blows cold from the North. Too bad, I learned my lesson too late. I will not kill you. Your spirit is true as a warrior. Your words are true. Go in peace with your friends from this forsaken land. It is my punishment to remain here. My price to pay, not yours."

Suddenly a bright ray of light from the sky covered both warriors. This white glowing light had healing powers. Nick could feel his wounds heal. "The Butcher's" cuts and wounds healed instantly. Then the light vanished. The two men looked at each other. A female figure formed beside" The

Butcher." Nick recognized her as "The Butcher's" wife. He could never forget her face. She was beautiful, dressed in a white robe.

Tears covered "The Butcher's" face. His wife said, "I forgive you both. Now it is time for us to go home. You have learned much this day." She took her husband by his hand. Nick picked up the envelope that John wanted "The Butcher" to have off the muddy ground. Nick handed it to him.

"The Butcher" opened the envelope. He took out a gold ring. It was a wedding ring. "The Butcher" put his wife's wedding ring on her finger. "I lost this ring in the fight we had long ago. Who gave this to you? Was it a man in a leather coat with a big hat?" Nick nodded, "Yes." "He is the one that sent us here!"

"Does it matter?" his wife asked as she looked at the skies above them. A small child waved at them. They both vanished into the sky above. All the mercenaries vanished as well, leaving Nick with tears of joy flowing down his face.

An old woman wearing a purple dress and hooded cloak walked down the hill behind them. "I see that Nick has learned a valuable lesson. Mercy and forgiveness can be a powerful force. Nick, you have earned this piece of the puzzle to find the last book. Your spirit will be free at last. May you always soar with the Eagles." The old woman walked back up the hill using her long staff with the large crystal on top. Soon, she was out of sight.

The rain had stopped as the group headed back. David had been surprised that none of his group tried to intervene in the fight when it looked like Nick was losing. Lo Ming looked at David, "I know what you are thinking. Why didn't we help Nick?

It is our code as a **Keeper of the Yawi**. We cannot intervene unless we are asked to help. It is also the Warrior's Code. This fight was 'Warrior to Warrior." We would have not stopped it, even if Nick would have died. I hope you understand that Code. We will not stop your fight with John. We know it is coming. Warriors feel such things. I hope that you realize that we will not save you from him. It is our way. John is a Warrior's Warrior. That is why I and the others follow him."

"How do you know that I won't beat him?" said David. "You had your chances. You were lucky once. The next time he will not be distracted by saving his friends. Besides, he has nothing to lose. You have everything. That makes him a very dangerous warrior to face," answered Lo Ming.

Doubt was starting to form in David's mind for the first time in his life. David was always confident when he went into battle. It didn't matter. David was a warrior. He had to know who was better. It was his way. That was the only way David had survived all these years. Too bad, it will happen. He thought. He had to know.

It was getting dark when they arrived back at the campsite. Antonio told them that the next passage was for David. David knew that he must recite the passage for them. Moses and Nick carried John to the campfire to have him eat some supper that Rose had fixed. John was still very ill. He did look a little better. June was worried about John's condition. It would take him at least two days or more if he was to get better.

After they were finished eating, David got up and recited his passage. The title of the passage seemed to say it all.

There's a Bad Storm Coming

There's a bad storm coming
Ain't no use in running
No matter how you try
Can't get away from Father Sky

There's a bad storm coming
Ain't no use in running
No matter where you hide
Can't get away from what's inside

There's a bad storm coming
Ain't no use in running
No matter who you know
Can't get away from the river's flow

There's a bad storm coming
Ain't no use in running
No matter what you do
Can't get away from you

When you hear the thunder's roar
You can't run and hide anymore
There's a bad storm coming
Ain't no use in running

Red Bear stood up. "I know what this passage is about. David is not the only one this passage is about. It is meant for me. I have a storm a coming. I will need to face my mentor. I have felt for several days Grey Fox's spirit. Even though I have been released from my pledge by the Great Spirits to protect the Books, Grey Fox has not forgiven me for not being successful in keeping you from getting the first three books. You may have thought Red Sparrow was sent to The Land of Nightmares to protect him from death. I know better. Grey Fox did it to force me to come here. I will meet him in the Valley of Thunder. I will be leaving in an hour.

Only June and One Feather will be coming with me. It is my turn to face some things. If we are successful, we will bring back Red Sparrow, my other son. If not, June will be the only one that comes back to join you. The Grey Fox will not let Red Sparrow go easily. It will take all my powers to get him released. We will be leaving in an hour. The moon is full. It will give us enough light to see the trail."

"Why is June and One Feather going with you, Red Bear?" asked Lo Ming. David smiled as he answered that by saying, "Red Sparrow is under the influence of Grey Fox. June can break that influence by showing Red Sparrow that she loves One Feather. If Red Bear loses his fight with Grey Fox, somebody will need to lead Red Sparrow back to us. Grey Fox has no real reason to keep Red Sparrow if Red Bear is dead." Everyone noted that David seemed not to care about his father being killed. It appeared David had not changed that much. He still could be cold and heartless.

I could barely stand up. "I see that you have not changed David. You are still that cold heartless man I have fought for so many years. You and I know the real meaning of the title to your passage." David looked at John, "Yes, I do. John, there's a bad storm a coming." I nodded back to David. Everyone knew that there was a bad storm a coming. The only problem was nobody could stop that storm from coming.

Red Bear, June and One Feather left about an hour later. Moses and Nick had carried John back to Mary's tent. Little Wolf had made Mary's tent much bigger by adding pieces of his and John's tents to it. Little Wolf adjusted to the change in Mary's appearance very quickly. Mary's hair was now dark black. Her skin was much darker, a deep dark copper color. Her figure was the same as before. Her face was beautiful. Her dark brown eyes shone in the darkness.

Little Wolf asked, "Mother, why is my father and your father going to fight? I don't want them to fight. I have just got to know my grandfather. I have known John, my father, all my life. He is a good man. He is brave. They shouldn't fight."

Mary answered Little Wolf, "It's a long story. It goes back years before you were born. Sometimes there is no logical explanation why men behave like they do. Maybe, Little Wolf, you can stop them. I tried once. You know how that went. It just might be their destiny." Little Wolf replied, "I will stay here with my mother and father tonight. I am still your boy. I am John's boy until I become a man. That is my destiny for now." Mary kissed Little Wolf on his forehead. Little Wolf watched as his mother kissed his father on his forehead. Little Wolf was happy they were together.

Nick was very tired. His wounds needed to heal. They were still very tender. He went to his tent to rest. He wanted to be alone. Rose was worried about him. She knew he missed Shanna. She knew he was worried about her. Lo Ming filled Rose in what had happened with The Butcher. Rose was proud how Nick had handled that situation.

Lo Ming walked over to Rose. "Give this tea to Nick. It will help him sleep. His wounds are about healed. You need to talk to him. The Red Woman gave me this to give to him. It is a charm. She was concerned about Nick and Shanna being apart. Have him put this necklace on and tell him to think about Shanna. When he falls to sleep, he will become a spirit warrior and be transported to Shanna in his dreams." Rose gave Lo Ming a hug. She ran over to Nick's tent.

"It is Rose. May I come in to see you?" asked Rose. Nick answered by saying, "Rose, I am very tired. I need to sleep, maybe later." "I have some tea to make you sleep. I am worried about you. I think I can help you, if you let me in to see you," she tried to explain. "Well, okay, please be brief," he replied.

Rose was taken back by Nick's appearance. He looked much older than before. "I guess I look like a wreck. The

217

fight took a lot out of me. I am worried sick about Shanna. I wish I could see her. You and she are the only two people that could help me," he told her.

" I don't know about me. You need to see Shanna," Rose said. "Now, how am I going to do that? Do you have some magic potion or something!" Nick said sarcastically. "I know you don't mean to be angry with me. I came to help. Actually, I was sent to help you by Lo Ming. I have some tea and a charm. It should help you solve your problem. Drink this tea and put this charm with its necklace around your neck. Think only about Shanna until you fall asleep. You will then be transported to her bedroom to see her. Hopefully, nobody will see you. Like before, you will be more spirit than man." Nick took the drink out of Rose's hand and drank it. He put the charm around his neck. Before Rose could say anything more, Nick was fast asleep. Rose laughed about one thing. Nick forgot that he had only his shorts on and no other clothes. Now, Shanna will get a big surprise when Nick's spirit gets there.

It was dark in Shanna's bedroom. He appeared by her bed. She had on a loose t-shirt and nothing else. She was lying on her side facing the wall. Nick wanted to lie down next to her. He quietly moved to her bed to get into the bed behind her. As he started to get into bed with her, Shanna moved and hit him with her fist in his stomach. Nick, caught by surprise, doubled over and fell to the floor. The next thing he knew was a foot against his throat almost choking him.

"I don't know who you are. You have two seconds to convince me not to kill you with my foot on your windpipe," Shanna yelled at him. Nick couldn't talk with the foot against his windpipe and the wind being knocked out of him. Nick did the only thing he could. He faintly laughed. Shanna jumped back. "Is that you, Nick?" whispered Shanna to him.

Nick nodded. "Is this the way you greet me? I thought you loved me," he could barely whisper. Shanna bent over and picked up Nick and threw him into bed. Nick was always amazed at Shanna's strength. When Nick landed on the bed, Shanna landed next to him. "I see you came ready to see me. You only have on your shorts. I will show you how much I love you, if you are up to it." Nick replied, "Take it easy, I am pretty banged up. I will just follow your lead if you don't mind." "That's a sorry excuse! You always knew I was stronger than you," she said with a passionate kiss that took his breath away.

Chapter VIII
More Trials Ahead
Will all survive?

After about four hours on the trail to the Valley of Thunder, Red Bear stopped for them to get some rest. "Let's drink some water from our canteens and rest for a few moments," said Red Bear. They sat down on some large rocks to rest and drink. "I know why you really had me go with you," said June. "You need some back up. If you lose, even Grey Fox's spirit would not dare go against me. The Great Spirits would not allow him to harm me. Isn't that right?" asked June. "Yes, that is true. I was playing both ends against the middle as some would say," said Red Bear.

"I don't think that the passage was meant for you at all. It was meant for David. Why would Grey Fox blame you for us getting the books? There is only one person that Grey Fox would blame us for going after the books. David was supposed to stop **The Dark Ones.** He didn't," said June.

"Yes, you are right. June, I knew that you would figure this out. Red Bear can't beat Grey Fox. Only I can," said a voice in the darkness. "Sometimes it takes a little evil to win a battle. Red Bear must not fight his mentor. You know that June. Red Bear is not strong enough to beat his mentor. That is the way it is. I will do that.

Red Bear is too important. He is the only one that knows this land. Grey Fox knows without my father, we would not be able to find the other pieces of the puzzle to obtain *The Book of Winter*. Grey Fox knows that if he kills Red Bear, we will never know where to look for the puzzle pieces. Red Bear is the only one that can guide us around this land." David said as he walked out of the darkness.

June replied to David. "You are right. This is a trap set by Grey Fox. Grey Fox knew that Red Bear would come to fight him. He was counting on that. He wants Red Bear dead. We would be lost in this land without him." Red Bear stood up. "I forbid it. I do not want to be responsible for the death of my sons."

"You are not strong enough to fight Grey Fox. I am," said David. June looked at David, "I don't know whether you want to save your father and brother or just want to make sure that we get *The Book of Winter,* so you get a chance to take it for yourself. Maybe, Grey Fox knew that all along. Grey Fox has always thought that nobody should have the power that *The Book of Winter* contains. He would rather see **The Land of the Eagle Feathers** destroyed than it ever having the possibility its power getting into the hands of evil beings."

"It does not matter. Does it? I see you have no choice. Your group has a saying for this. Once a scorpion, always a scorpion," David laughed. Red Bear tried to stop David from leaving. David put his hands up and forced Red Bear to sit down. "You do not have the power to stop me. Everyone stays here. I can hear the roar of thunder from the Valley from here. I will be back shortly with Red Sparrow," smiled David.

"He is right," said One Feather. "Grey Fox is expecting Red Bear, like a Fox that is expecting a mouse. Grey Fox is not expecting a scorpion that will sting him. We will wait for David."

"June, your man is a wise man," David said as he left. June agreed for the first time with David. "Yes, my man is right. That is why he is my man," she replied to David.

It took David about an hour to reach the Valley of Thunder. Lightning and thunder were filling the valley. It had not started raining. David could see a campfire or bonfire about 100 yards from him. This must be where Grey Fox and his brother must be. Grey Fox would be waiting for Red Bear to come. David guessed it must be close to 2:00 in the morning. David decided to let the cover of the evergreen trees make it easy for him to approach Grey Fox without him seeing him.

Grey Fox had Red Sparrow seated about 10 feet to the left of him. "I see that you have finally come to get your son, Red Bear." Grey Fox could only make out the outline of a man. Grey Fox couldn't see the man's face. David had to smile as he came out of the shadows and saw the look of Grey Fox's face. "Who are you?" Grey Fox asked. David replied, "Somebody that you never ever wanted to see."

"Where is Red Bear?" asked Grey Fox. "Resting up the trail about an hour away. I told him that I would take care of this little matter for him," answered David. "Now, who would you be?" asked Grey Fox. "You have got a lot of questions for a man so great as a medicine man of your standing," answered David with a laugh. "I'm here to settle a little problem that Red Bear has. He wants his son, Red Sparrow, back. So, if you don't mind, let him go with me and I will leave in peace," said David.

David could see that Grey Fox wasn't used to being talked to like that. Grey Fox started getting angry. "I don't know who you are. I will make short work of you if you try to take him away from me," Grey Fox threatened David.

"I guess I should introduce myself to you, Grey Fox. I am the elder son of the man you wanted to kill tonight. They call me many names. Not all of them very polite names. Let me say a few for you: Red Reaper, Soul Collector or just plain David. Tonight, you can call me: "Final." Grey Fox was shaking, "What do you mean by Final?" David laughed, "I will be the Final thing you will ever see."

"My fight is with Red Bear, not you," said Grey Fox. "On the contrary, you made it personal by involving my family," replied David. Grey Fox replied, "I have heard of you. There are legends about how evil you are. We will have to see if you are that good at this as I am."

"I assure you I am much better than you will ever be, Grey Fox. This should only take me a minute or two. Shall we begin, I will give you the first move. It will be your last," smiled David.

Red Bear looked up from his seat on the large rock where David had left him. Red Sparrow ran and hugged Red Bear. June looked at David, "What took you so long?"

David replied, "I had to figure out what to do with Grey Fox. I didn't want to kill him. That would have been too easy. I wanted everyone to know I was better than him. I just froze him in ice. He will thaw out in about a week. He will be alive. His spirit will never be the same. Pride is something once taken will hurt forever. That is what he deserves, nothing less. Now, Red Sparrow, do you have something to say to June."

Red Sparrow bowed his head, "I deeply regret what I did. I am sorry for my actions. I got what I deserved. I will forever be at your beckon call.

Do you forgive me?" June got up, "I forgive you. I know you have learned from your experience. Promise me that you will never follow your brother. You must become a true and brave warrior of our tribe." June could see that David didn't like what she said. Red Sparrow answered June, "You have my word that I will do as you say on my father's name."

"Grey Fox is an honorable man. I am glad that David, my son, you did not kill him. Grey Fox was only trying to stop anyone from getting the books. Anyone with Indian blood would understand why," said Red Bear to David. "I thought that you would say that. Besides, he believed in what he was doing. I may be many things, but I have respect for his beliefs. I have not been gone in the other world that long not to understand our ways. I still remember what you taught me long ago."

Red Bear wasn't totally happy with what had transpired. One day Red Bear would have a long talk with Grey Fox. He owed his mentor, Grey Fox, that much. Red Sparrow opened his hand and gave Red Fox a marble puzzle piece. "Grey Fox dropped this when he was fighting David. I think this belongs to you, father." "No, it belongs to David. He earned it." One Feather looked at David, "It is time we get back to camp. Maybe someday, David, you will remember who you really are."

When they all returned to the campsite, Antonio looked worried. "We need to hurry and find all the pieces. We may be running out of time. I know that the day is growing short. June, you need to recite your passage and go on your journey. June understood. She recited her passage.

Like a Bird with a Broken Wing

Without my tears, I can't cry
Without my wings, I can't fly
Without my voice, I can't sing
I am like a bird with a broken wing

Haunted by love that didn't last
Tortured by sins of the past
Bitten by snakes the devil sends
Betrayed by love that only pretends

A garden cannot grow without the rain
You can't know joy without the pain
A day cannot exist without the night
You can't know wrong without the right

It is time to make a choice
It is time to listen to your voice
It is time to stop trying to hide
It is time to face what's inside

Nothing is right if everything is left
It is time for the healer to heal thyself
You have a voice and you can sing
You don't have to be a bird with a broken wing

June asked Red Bear if he knew of any place in The Land of Nightmares that has birds that do not fly and poisonous snakes. Red Bear thought for several minutes before giving June an answer. Red Bear replied "There is no such place that birds do not fly. There is a valley that has a rock formation on top of a nearby mountain that looks like a bird with a broken wing. It is known as the Valley of a Bird with a Broken Wing. This valley is full of poisonous snakes. They come from a cave at the bottom of the mountain that has that rock formation. This is a dangerous place to go. The poisonous snakes are aggressive. We called them "Devil Snakes." They are known to strike at anything or anyone. I would advise you not to go there."

June replied, "I may sound crazy. I must go there and find something in that cave." One Feather told her if that is what she felt, that is what she must do. Red Bear did not want to take June to that cave. "How will you protect yourself from the snakes?" he asked. Moses replied to Red Bear, "I will go with her. I will talk to the leader of the snakes and explain. If that doesn't work, we will have to distract them."

Red Bear nodded, "I strongly suggest that only June, Moses and myself go to that valley. I will take Moses and June to the cave entrance. Moses will have to talk to the Devil Snakes. We must leave June alone to go into that cave. She must face what is inside like her passage says. She can't hide her past anymore. She is haunted by love that didn't last and tortured by her sins to others. I can see it in her eyes. She must finally confront what she must have done long ago. It is her nightmare to resolve. It will take us several hours to get there. One Feather and the rest of you must stay here. Only a few people will make it appear that we mean no harm to the snakes."

One Feather did not like it. He stayed at the camp. Red Bear led Moses and June up the trail toward the direction of the hidden valley. After about four hours of hard hiking, they arrived at the valley. On the far side of the valley was the rock formation. From a distance it did look like a bird with a broken wing. The rocks had been piled up from long ago, perhaps by an earthquake. It took another hour to get to the cave.

As they approached the cave, hundreds of bright red and black snakes poured out of the cave's entrance. Moses walked up to the biggest snake in the front of all the snakes. He put his hand on the ground before the snake. The snake tried to strike Moses. Moses caught the snake in midair by his left hand.

Moses put his right hand on the back of the large black and white snake's head. He started hissing at the snake. He

225

moved his tongue very fast in and out. The snake hissed back at him. This went on for several minutes. At last, Moses carefully put down the snake on the ground in front of the others. Moses turned to June. "The leader of the snakes will take you into the cave. She says that if you are not successful with who you find in the cave, we will all be bitten and killed. Red Bear had sweat coming down his brow, "June, you better be successful."

Moses made torches for June. The cave looked dark and deep. Moses lit the torches. June followed the large snake cautiously into its main tunnel. After they had gone about 200 meters, they came to a large room. In the room there was an old man dressed in white buckskins with precious jewels covering his jacket. The designs made by the jewels were oscillating and forming into other designs. Each design was a symbol of a constellation of the stars. A fire was in the middle of the room. The leader of the snakes left from a signal given by the old man. The old man pointed to two flat rocks for them to sit down. They immediately seated themselves upon these rocks.

The old man got up and spoke to June. "I have been waiting for you, my child, for many years to come on this quest. I entrusted your care to your parents many years ago. However, they did not fulfill my request. One winter day when you were young, you left the safety of your camp and ran away. You had felt your parents were too harsh on you when they were disciplining you. Let me show you what happened that day."

The old man waved his medicine staff at the cave wall. Visions started to form on the wall. You could see a young girl running into the prairie. Snow was beginning to fall covering everything in a great white blanket. The wind was blowing the snow around. It was becoming a blizzard. The young girl fell into a snow drift and didn't get up. Moments later two people came and picked her up. June recognized them. The two people were her parents. She must have been the young girl. She could see that her mother was terrified. Her father carried her to a cave in a nearby mountain. He quickly built a fire inside to try to warm up her up as she slept in her mother's arms. Her father said that their child was becoming very sick from the cold. You could tell by their expressions that they thought their child was dying.

Her father stood up in the cave and chanted for help from a great medicine man. A form appeared beside them. It was the old man that now was beside them here in this cave. The old man told them that they had failed him. They were to keep the child safe. They did not. Her father begged him to save their child. The old man said to them that the only way he could save the child was that they must give up the child forever. He would save her only because she would be needed for a great quest in the future. If they sacrificed their lives for her, it would give him the power to save her.

Her parents did not even question or hesitate, they agreed at once. The old man told her mother that she must pass on her medicine powers to her child. Her mother took her hands and placed them on her forehead transferring her powers to her. The old man told them that they could hold her one more time before they would have to vanish forever. June could see the sadness in her parents' eyes. They held her tight. Her mother cried out in the pain of leaving her. The old man told them to place June on the ground and step back. He would be sending a man to take June back to the Great Medicine man of their tribe to be raised and taught the ways of the spirits.

June's parents placed her on the cave's floor. The old man waved his medicine staff over their heads. Both her parents vanished never to be seen again. In the back of the cave appeared a man dressed in heavy buckskins. He picked up the child and carried her out of the cave. In the visions on the wall June saw the man's face. June was shocked. It was John who had taken her back to the tribe.

June asked the old man why she did not remember any of this? The old man told her that the spirits had their ways about such things. It was not his or her right to question them. June asked what was to happen now? The old man told her that she must make a choice.

Her choice would be of great consequence to all. For the dark ones to be defeated, June would have to give up everything. She would have to give up her powers of great medicine. She would have to give up her brave and remain here in this land forever. She would have to give up everything that is near and dear to her. She would never see or touch her brave again. She would not ever have the pleasure of having a baby or living a life of happiness. She would have to sacrifice everything. That is what the great spirits want from her. However, she did have a choice. She could go and be with her brave. This would result in the dark forces will win. She could still have a good life, but everything else would be lost. It was her choice.

June looked at the old man. Sadness filled the room in the cave. She held up her arms in the pain of losing everything dear to her. Tears flowed in rivers down her cheeks. The old man did not say anything. It was June's choice to make. June touched her cheek weeping as she thought about One Feather. Her heart was breaking into a thousand pieces.

Her body filled with the pain of her decision. She did not the right to leave. She must fulfill her destiny. She turned to the old man and said that she had no choice. She would sacrifice everything for her friends, tribe and the future of **The Land of the Eagle Feathers**.

June asked the old man what she should do? The old man said, "Nothing." The old man raised his medicine staff. He waved it three times around June's head. A bright flash filled the room. When June's eyes adjusted to the dark cave again, the old man was gone. In his place were two people. She recognized them at once. Joy filled her heart. Her mother and father hugged her.

Her father said that June had saved them. Her willingness to sacrifice everything for others proved to the spirits that they had fulfilled their duties entrusted to them as parents. "We know that you blame yourself for us being lost in the blizzard long ago. We know about your pain about feeling that you had caused us to vanish into the snowstorm. It was our fault that we didn't watch you close enough not yours," her father explained.

June's mind was wondering about her fate. Was she going to have to stay here? The answer to that question was soon answered. A strong voice behind them said only one word, "Come." It was the old woman in the purple dress and hooded cloak. "Child, you have come so far. Several tribes recognize you as a spiritual leader. You have lived up to your destiny. You must go. You will be needed to save **The Land of the Eagle Feathers.** You have a voice, and you must sing. You are not a bird with a broken wing."

The old woman took June's hand. She placed a marble piece of the puzzle to find the last book in it. "All of you are free to go. Your destinies like ours lies out there. You still have much to do. June, your powers were never taken away from you." The old woman led them out of the cave into the light. As the old woman turned to go back inside the cave, she said, "May the spirits be with you. They are pleased."

The day was fading rapidly. "We are lucky to have a bright moon tonight. It will be much easier to see to get back to camp. I see we have some guests to take back with us. They must be your parents. Moses can lead the way back. I want him to be in front in case we encounter anymore snakes. I am not fond of snakes," said Red Bear to June.

Moses turned and greeted June's parents. "Don't mind Red Bear, I am proud to get to meet you. You have a wise and brave daughter. You should be proud of her." June's parents didn't have to say anything. Moses could see it in their smiles. Moses had only seen June this happy one other time. It was when June had first seen One Feather. It will be interesting to see what her parents think of One Feather especially when they meet One Feather's parents, Antonio and Angela.

It was about midnight when Red Bear, Moses, June and her parents arrived back at the campsite. Angela, Antonio and One Feather were the only ones up. They were sitting around the campfire talking. When Antonio saw that they had brought back two other native Indians with them, Antonio asked June, "Who are these two people that you brought back with you?" June replied, "These are the two most important people in anyone's life. Let me introduce them to everyone. This is Running Bear, my father, and this is Evening Spirit, my mother."

Antonio couldn't help it, "I knew you had to be June's mother. She gets her beauty from you. The young brave over there will want to meet you. He is my son, One Feather. I will let his lovely mother, Angela, introduce him to you. We have much to talk about. June can explain everything later. I have a feeling that we will become great friends in the future. I will set you up a tent with some bedding so you can get some rest."

Angela laughed, "Don't mind Antonio. He can't help it. He is that way whenever he sees a beautiful woman." Evening Spirit agreed, "You can tell he is an Italian. I don't mind it at all. Running Bear has some of that in him. He is always flattering me. Don't be surprised if he flatters you." Angela smiled, "I guess your husband has a good eye for beautiful women." Both women laughed at their men, Angela couldn't help it she liked Evening Spirit's sense of humor.

The sun was just coming up over the Eastern mountains. Nick and Rose had finished fixing breakfast. Everyone was sitting on logs and rocks around the campfire eating. John was getting much better. He was able to make it up to the campfire without help.

Running Bear and Evening Spirit asked Mary about John's health, they had noticed that he was so pale. "Why do you ask me about John?" asked Mary. "Because he is your husband. I see your marriage mark on your arm. He has the same mark on his. He always liked butterflies." Mary replied, "Yes, he is my husband. The young man over there is our son, Little Wolf. John is very sick. He has only until the New Year to live if we don't get *The Book of Winter* to save him."

Evening Spirit looked at Mary, "That is too bad! John saved our daughter, June, many years ago. Even in this land, John is a legend. The Winds of Time tell us many things here in this land. You are lucky to have a man that loves you so much that he would give his life for you. His love for you is known even here. We will help you keep this man alive. If you or your son need us for anything, we will come. We owe him so much."

Mary got up and walked away. She thought she heard voices in the wind blowing across the meadow. She walked toward a small brook. She sat down on the brook's bank. The Winds of Time seemed to say, "Yes, you were a very lucky young woman. Love comes full circle like the moon around Mother Earth and Father Sky. You cannot stop it. Time cannot stop it. He needs you more than ever. You have a family. It is your destiny to save **The Land of the Eagle Feathers** with him and his friends. Your son's life depends on it and all that comes after you. Do not waste what is not yours to waste. Do not let love blow away like fall leaves before the winter's snow. Catch them and never let them go!" Mary got up and ran back to the campsite.

Antonio had started the camp meeting. "We are getting close to having all the puzzle pieces. It is Rose's turn now. Rose, please recite your passage." Rose replied, "It will be my pleasure."

Listen to Each Bird's Song

Every bird greets the morn
When a new day is born
Every bird sings its song
They are where they belong

You hear in the song of the sparrow
I know which way you should go
Following the trails of the deer
You will find a place that's clear

You hear in the song of the chickadee
I can see what you need to see
Look for the tree that glows at night
Then you know to turn right

You hear in the song of the red bird
I hear what's already heard
Remember what been taught to you
Then you will know what to do

Remember east is west, west is east
Best is worst, worst is best
Wrong is right, right is wrong
Listen to each bird's song

Before Rose could say anything more, Red Bear got up from the log he was sitting on. "Rose, you don't have to ask. I know where that place is. Your passage talks about birds. There is only one place in this land that has many different types of birds. That place is called Valley of Birds. It is a big flat valley. I once met a man there. He was very sad. I believe his name is Zan. His father is a powerful Warlock called Zorn. Rose, you must be the woman he loves. Zorn has some kind of hold on Zan.

There is a legend that Zorn banished his son there because his son refused to marry a daughter of a rival and powerful Warlock. His son wanted to marry another woman. I guess, Rose, you are that woman.

Rose, it will be very dangerous for you to confront Zorn. He is a leader of a powerful order of Wizards and Warlocks. It is said he has killed many men and women that have tried to defy him. I refuse to be a part of such a foolhardy adventure. I am old and tired. If you insist, I will give directions and draw up a map for someone to help you get there. It will take several hours of hard hiking for you to get there. I will be resting in my tent. Come and get me when you decide what you want to do. You have more than you at stake," Red Bear walked off toward his tent.

Rose got up to go after Red Bear. She walked about 20 feet and got sick. She threw up her breakfast. Mary, Angela, Lo Ming and June ran over to Rose catching her as she fainted. The women told the men to stay where they were. They would handle this themselves. Angela had them take Rose to her tent. Thcy laid Rose down on Angela's sleeping bag. Mary went and got her medicine bag to examine Rose. When Mary came back, Angela said, "I know what is wrong with Rose. You know it, too. We all know that Rose visited Zan a while back. Ever since, Rose has not been eating very well especially in the mornings. Anyone that has had morning sickness knows the signs."

Mary nodded. "I have been watching Rose. I couldn't believe that her traveling as a spirit to Zan could result in her getting pregnant." Lo Ming replied, "I feel that a force much greater is involved here. The spirits here allowed Rose to get pregnant. Rose is getting older. Her time for having children is almost over. It is their gift to her and Zan for the sacrifices she has made for **The Land of the Eagle Feathers.**

Rose is a spirit warrior like most of us have become. Who are we to question the great spirits of this land? Rose and Zan's child must have great things to achieve. The spirits would not allow this to happen unless their child is special."

Rose started to wake up. "I must go to Zan. I must save him from his father. We have a child coming." Mary said to Rose, "You must rest today. We will find a way for you to rescue Zan. Get some rest and we will come up with a plan. Trust us, we will not let you down. Lo Ming will fix you some tea to settle your stomach. Angela will watch you for a little while." Lo Ming went and boiled some special tea for Rose. After Rose drank it, she fell fast asleep.

The men were sitting around the campfire waiting for news about Rose. David didn't say anything. He had an idea what was wrong. He had seen this before. I was feeling much better. I could sense that both David and I knew what was going on in Angela's tent. Nick was upset. I told Nick not to worry. Everything would be all right. The women would take care of Rose.

The men watched as the women had a meeting by Angela's tent. After several minutes, Lo Ming and June walked up to meet with the men. Lo Ming was the first to speak. "Moses, we will need several horses to take Rose to the Valley of Birds. June will send a hawk to find the horse herd. Moses, it will be your responsibility to tame the horses."

Before Lo Ming could say anything more, a female voice behind the men said, "I have already taken care of that. Here are the horses with saddles that you will need to take Rose to the Valley of Birds. Rose should be able to travel by tomorrow morning." The young Indian woman on her painted pony was behind them. She had several saddled painted ponies on a long rope string.

"The women have decided to handle this situation with Rose and Zan. I suggest you men stand down and leave it to them. It's a woman's thing. That is the way it will be. Don't worry, I will be back tomorrow to lead them to the Valley of Birds.

May the spirits be with us. It had been a long time since a child was conceived in this land. It is said that such a child will lead, and the land will prosper. The Winds of Time will blow life into the desert of our souls. Hope is returning to this land. Nobody controls what destiny has for us. I will return at first light tomorrow. Lo Ming, you will have the women ready to ride. Men will only be in the way. It is better for men to stay.

It is written that one woman's wisdom is worth many men much like an apple can grow more than one tree." The young woman turned her painted pony toward the hillside and rode like the wind out of sight.

This gave everyone a day to rest. Tomorrow the women would be leaving for the Valley of Birds. Nick had not had a chance to talk about his meeting with Shanna. I decided to call everyone together, except Rose, after lunch for an update from Nick as to what was going on in Houston.

Nick got up to speak. "Shanna says everything is going as planned. Benita and Raven are doing the logistics to get **The Dark One's Army** to **The Land of the Eagle Feathers.** Shanna was impressed by how organized Benita was. Benita was not leaving anything to chance. Raven seemed to be somewhat distracted. Shanna did not trust Raven. Shanna could feel that something was not quite right with Raven. Shanna said that the feeling was more a sixth sense than anything else.

Shanna said that Benita and Raven were getting along well. She was surprised that Raven took orders from Benita without any complaints. Shanna was going to check to see if Raven may be going to double-cross Benita or David. Even Benita was a little worried about Raven. One night when they were alone, Benita confided in Shanna that Raven couldn't be trusted. Also, Benita was worried about backlash from the Board of Directors made up of **The Omen**. It appears that **The Omen** didn't like how David had grabbed power to become the Chairman of the Board."

David spoke up. "Benita is very smart. She has been playing Raven and myself for years. Raven must be upset due to Benita having more power than her. Raven has always been in power. Raven has always wanted to be Chairman of the Board. I have plans if Raven goes rogue. She has some influence with the Board. I fear more for Benita than Shanna. Shanna knows how to play everyone against the middle."

"That is true. Shanna told me that Benita had approached her about plans if Raven tries to take over. Benita has been doing everything in her power to keep Raven under her thumb. Benita had been entertaining Raven a lot," said Nick.

"You don't have to tell me anymore. I have known about Benita's relationship with Raven for a long time. Benita knows I know. That is one reason we have been able to somewhat control Raven. Raven is a very dangerous enemy to have. Remember, she is our enemy. I will have to take care of Raven later. Benita is another story. She has had my back for years. Do I trust her, the answer is a simple No! But it appears our plans are working out as best as we can expect," David explained.

I got up and told everyone to get as much rest as possible. Things would be getting interesting when the ladies get back tomorrow night. David knew that Shanna was leaving some details out. Benita could be very charming, especially after several bottles of wine. David laughed as he imagined that Shanna could be just as charming. Nick asked why he was laughing. "I do enjoy how the female gender does their work." Nick nodded his head and smiled. He did know more than he was telling David and the others.

The morning sky was bright red. I didn't like the meaning of it. It meant a storm was coming. June had saddled all the horses. Nick had made the women lunches to take and filled each a canteen with water. As June finished saddling the last horse, a rider came down from the hill above us. It was the young Indian woman on her painted pony. The young woman rode over to me. "I see you are getting better. We were worried that you might not recover." I looked at her, "I hate to disappoint the Great Spirits. I will make it to the battle in the valley. It is my destiny to be there."

The young woman replied, "Yes, it is. The time is getting short. You have only a few winter days. John, we are not your enemy. Success is the only way. Your deeds are known. Your spirit is one of courage. I see you brought the leader of **the Dark Ones**. We understand. Scorpions are hard to handle. Are you sure he can be trusted? He was once one of **The Land of the Eagle Feathers**. He has been living in the other world for a long time. That is your problem. I come to shine some truth. Rose is my worry, not yours. We have plans for her and her baby."

"The sky is red. Your storm is rising in the west. I trust you can ride the storm. Rose is a warrior. She has waited for this moment for many circles of the sun. She will finish what Zan's mother started long ago. I will finish **The Dark Ones**. My spirit will live on whether I live or die," said John.

The young woman replied with a serious tone in her voice, "I see your wife has changed back, and your son is here. You have much to protect. Fate had not always been kind to you. Many times, you have challenged fate and won. We of the Great Spirits know that you will do your best. Be careful that you follow the right path to glory." The young Indian spirit guided her horse to where the women had mounted their horses.

All the men watched as the women rode away on their painted ponies. The young Indian woman led the way. Antonio said it best, "Whoever this Zorn is will be no match going against these women. I would love to be there when they come riding in to meet him."

Rose was feeling a little better. The women enjoyed being on these strong ponies. Their horses were a little difficult to handle. They were full of spirit. When they reached the Valley of Birds, the young Indian woman told Rose to get behind her. "Let's have some fun, the horses need to be let loose. They know where to go. Follow me and hang on. We will give Zorn a big surprise." The women spurred their horses and raced down the flat valley. They were on a mission. The wind blew back their hair. June and Mary let out war cries. Dust was flying behind them.

Zorn was standing by Zan's hut. The Winds of Time had told Zorn that Rose was coming. Zorn wanted to end his feud with Rose. He would make her pay. Zan told his father that it would be his father that would pay, not Rose. Zorn looked to the east end of the valley. He could barely make out several riders coming down the valley toward them. There must be several of them judging from the dust their horses were making. As they were getting closer, he could see that they were carrying weapons. That didn't worry him. He was a master warlock.

Zan laughed at Zorn. "You are going to lose. Rose is bringing her war party. I will let them deal with you. I have waited for this moment for several years. It is time that you learn the truth." "What truth is that Zan?" Zorn asked. "The truth that will set us free," answered Zan.

The group of women warriors stopped their painted ponies in a cloud of dust in front of Zorn and Zan. Zorn didn't look so sure of himself. He saw the young Indian woman on the painted pony. He knew he was looking at a strong spirit. Zorn couldn't help but be impressed with the women in front of him. There were six women staring at him.

Zorn spoke directly to the young Indian spirt woman. "I see you have brought reinforcements," he laughed. "I wouldn't laugh if I was you. They are more than a match for the likes of you," she said with a wicked smile. "We are just escorting a woman that wants to talk to you. If you do not let her talk, I will let them have fun with you instead. Do I have your attention, Zorn?"

Zorn nodded. Rose moved her pony directly in front of Zorn. Zorn's face turned red with anger. Rose had her purple blouse and skirt on with planets and stars that moved around. Her arms had silver bracelets on each. Around her neck were several necklaces. Zorn knew that Rose must be very powerful to wear such a dress. "I have come for my man. Before we leave with him, I want to explain some things to you. I know that you have hate for your son. Not only because he wanted to marry me against your wishes, but because of your wife, Zan's mother.

You have blamed Zan for your wife's death. What Zan wouldn't tell you is that he promised his mother to take care of her horse. Zan was afraid you would kill his mother's horse because you would blame the horse for her death.

When Zan and his mother went riding that day, a snake tried to strike your wife. Her horse tried to kill the snake like most horses would do to protect their rider. Your wife fell off and hit her head against a rock as her horse was stomping the snake. Zan's mother was afraid that you would blame her horse and kill it out of revenge. She made Zan promise to save the horse from your wrath as she died in his arms.

Zan kept his promise and took the blame. He told you it was his fault. That he spooked her horse, and she fell off. You took your revenge on him. You never forgave him. You took everything you could away from him. You took the one thing that he wanted the most. You took him away from me because you wanted him to feel what you felt. It took me years to find Zan. I have come for him with my friends for several reasons."

Zorn started to move his hands. Before he could do anything, Zan moved faster. Zan cast a powerful spell on his father. Zorn couldn't move. "All these years, father, you thought I didn't have any power. I have had years to study the arts of magic. I knew you would never let me go from here. So, I waited for Rose to come. She has more to tell you. The young spirit lady told me that my mother's horse had died of old age. You did treat my mother's horse well. I will give you that," yelled Zan at his father.

Rose looked Zorn in his eyes. "I have come to give something that you don't deserve." Rose pointed toward the West to the other end of the valley. Songbirds flew by singing beautiful songs. Zorn could not help it. Tears flowed down his face. They were the birds that his wife loved to listen to each morning. "Look at the white horse in the distance," Rose commanded.

Everyone's eyes looked to the West. A rider on a white horse was swiftly riding toward them. It was an older dark woman dressed in a dark purple dress. Zorn had seen that dress before. It was his wife's favorite dress. Zorn knew who that woman was before anyone could see her face. The horse was his wife's horse.

The white horse stopped in front of Zorn. Zorn was speechless. The woman looked down at her husband. "What have you become? You are not the man I once loved. You have become an old man full of hate. Our son paid a big price for his promise to me. Now, my horse has joined me in the other land. Rose, like me, is very much part of several races. You have forgotten that people from Louisiana have many races in them. My mother was an American Indian. That is why I am here.

You are a foolish old man. You let your love for me turn to hate for our son and his future wife. I am ashamed of you. I can't help it. I still love you. What I don't love is what you have become. You said Rose was not good enough for you. Her blood line comes from a more powerful wizard than you. Her mother is a powerful voodoo priestess. She is more than anyone could want for a daughter-in law. I have watched from afar her deeds and courage. You should be proud of her and our son."

Zorn fell to his knees crying. "I loved you so much. I never realized I was so petty. Only a fool would blame his only son for your death. I was full of anger and grief. I was lost without you. It is not an excuse. I am ashamed. I was never worthy of your love. You were everything to me. I am a foolish old man. To see you again is more than I could have ever hoped for in my life. I will do anything to try to redeem myself to you. I don't blame Rose if she would kill me or worse. I deserve no better."

Zan's mother looked at her husband with tears in her eyes "No, Zorn. That is not why I am here. You can make it up to me. I have a purpose for coming. Rose sent for me. I want you to protect our grandchild."

Rose looked at Zorn in disgust. She was angry. The more she thought about it, the more her anger grew. She pointed at Zorn. Moving her hand, Zorn was thrown about 10 feet back. Zan yelled at Rose to stop. Rose did just that. Her face was in a state of shock. She screamed at Zorn, "I won't become like you. I won't let my hate fill my heart. Life is too short for revenge. I have more important things to worry about than you, Zorn. If Zan can forgive you, then I must do the same."

Zan asked Rose, "Is it true? We are going to have a child." Rose nodded. "It is not my choice to make, Rose. This is your choice and only your choice. I will not make that choice for you. I will do whatever you want."

Rose tried to put her anger aside. She had seen what hate could do. She wanted no part of that side of life. She remembered what her father had said about The Trail of Tears. "Whatever anyone does to you, do not let it change you. They are not worth your soul. Forgiveness is something only you can give. Your mother, Sheba, taught me that many years ago. Many of the brave people from the tribes in **The Land of the Eagle Feathers** showed me that forgiveness can change people. It is not in your heart to hate anyone. Rose, promise me that you will listen to your inner voice."

Rose looked at Zorn. "My mother and father are right. I will not bend toward hate. They taught me well. If you really mean it, Zorn, I will forgive you." Zorn looked at Rose. "Zan was right about you. He said you were an exceptional woman. I should have listened sooner. You have my word."

The young spirit woman said, "I know what Zorn said is true. He called for me to come to him a few days ago. He told me that he was a foolish man. He wanted to make peace with you. He found out before it was too late that he was not the man he should have been. Tell her and the others here why! They need to hear it from you."

Zorn did not want to tell them. "Please tell us, Zorn," said Zorn's wife. "We want to believe you."

Zorn took his time. He looked at everyone. Zan had gone to stand by Rose's horse. He had more of an audience than he ever wanted. "It all started several weeks ago. I was not well. I went to a specialist. I have a rare brain tumor. I will be dead in a few weeks. I came here to give up my powers to my son and die. It's funny that it takes something like that to make you see. I was not going to fight anyone. If Rose wanted to kill me, she had the right. I was not seeking forgiveness. I wanted the spirit here to allow me to say that I was sorry. Nothing more than that. I am sorry, Rose and Zan. I wasted my life in hatred. I am sorry to my lovely wife. Most of all, I am sorry for my grandchild. I will not be around to spend time with her. She will be a lovely baby. I do want to give her one gift. I want to give her my powers if you will let me. She is special. The spirit woman told me that. It will be your choice. I will do as you want, Rose."

Rose looked shocked, "How do you know it's a girl? My special Rose, I am a great Warlock. You know that it is written in the stars. I can read them. Why do you think there are so many women here with you? One of you said, "It's a woman's thing." Do you forgive this old foolish man in front of you?"

Rose said, "Yes to both things. I am glad that I brought your wife here. You will be able to go back with her and be together forever. It would be an honor to have you give your powers to our child. She will always have some of her grandfather in her."

Zorn looked at his wife. "May I be with you?" he asked. Zorn's wife could only nod. Zorn asked Rose to get down off her horse. "Rose, you must lie down. I will place my hand on your body on top of your child. It will take only seconds. Then, I will die. As Indian warriors say, "This is a good day to die" before they die in battle. It is an honor to die among such warriors as are here."

Rose dismounted her horse. She hugged Zorn. The only words she said to him was, "Thank You!" The spirit woman pointed to a spot on the ground. The dead grass turned green. Flowers grew around the grass. There was enough room for Rose to lay down and Zorn to be by her side.

Rose laid down with Zorn lying beside her. He put his hand on top of the child in Rose's body. He smiled at Zan and the others. He looked at his wife. She smiled back at him. He said an ancient saying. A light passed from his body through his hand to Rose's body. Zorn did not move. His hand slowly slipped to the ground beside her. He was dead.

A black horse appeared beside them. Zan recognized the horse. It was his father's horse. He never rode his horse after his wife died. A spirit arose from his father's body. It was Zorn. He mounted his black horse. He rode to his wife's side. Zorn's last words to Zan and Rose were, "Thank You!"

Zorn and his wife rode away into the sky together at last. Zan said he would bury his dad here in the green grass with the flowers around his grave. The young spirit woman said, "I will do it for you, my child. There is a horse waiting for you to ride back. It is a special horse. He is the offspring of your parents' horses. He is yours. You gave him life. He belongs to you."

Rose started to mount her horse. There was something in her hand. It was a piece of the marble puzzle. "Forgiveness has its own rewards. It is time for you to go. I have work to do," said the spirit woman.

Little Wolf was upset. He wished that his grandfather, David, and his father, John, could get along. Everyone knew that David and John would someday have a big battle with each other. Little Wolf decided to talk to David. The women wouldn't be back until about sunset. David was sitting by the campfire. Little Wolf went and sat down beside him.

Neither one said anything for several minutes. "I was wondering. Why do you and my father have to fight each other? Are we not on the same side?" asked Little Wolf. David didn't answer for several minutes. He looked at Little Wolf. "I guess you can say that. There have been a lot of things that happened over the years. Let's say that John and I have had our differences especially over your mother. It may seem somewhat silly now. It was a dead serious matter."

Little Wolf replied to his grandfather, "You have lived in two different worlds. You grew up in **The Land of the Eagle Feathers**. You left this land to go and try to fight the **Dark Ones** from inside their world. Grandfather, I feel that somewhere in your journey to the outside world you lost your way. It is much like the wolf that follows his prey. If he follows his prey too far, he can't find his way home. He may catch his prey. What good does it do if he loses sight of his home? Grandfather, you are home. You have found your way back. Do not get lost again! Not many wolves ever find their way back home."

David didn't say anything more. Little Wolf asked, "My father didn't know I was his son. He treated me like his son. He always told me to do good. One Feather said he always treated him like he was his uncle.

John taught both of us much about our culture. I know John is much older than anyone here. How many people do you know would die for their cause or friends? I don't know about what will happen between my mother and father. I do know that I finally have a real family. I have a mother, father, grandmother and grandfather. That is all I ever wanted. Don't take that away from me! You and my father do not have that right! I know my destiny. I hope you and my father find your way back. You are two lost wolves. You have caught your prey. Will you be able to find your way home?" Little Wolf left his grandfather sitting by the campfire watching the flames dance.

"His grandmother was right. Little Wolf is wiser than his years. Perhaps, wiser than I ever was," David pondered in his thoughts. "My problem is much deeper than that. I have two wolves in me. One that can be good and one that can be evil. I hope that my time with the **Dark Ones** doesn't overcome the good wolf. I have a battle within myself. Years of following the evil one is difficult to change."

The women arrived back with Zan shortly before dark. The young Indian woman said, "You can keep these horses. They are a gift from the spirits. I will be back in two days with more horses for the men. There is only one more puzzle piece to obtain. Little Wolf will be tested. He will need to find the last puzzle piece. It will be a difficult quest for him. I wish him well." The young woman turned her painted pony toward the hill behind them. She galloped her painted pony up the hill. Instead of vanishing out of sight behind the hill, the pony galloped straight up into the night's sky.

Nick and Antonio had fixed the evening meal. As everyone ate, they sat by a blazing campfire. Zan sat by Rose. Nick was happy for Rose. He knew what Zan meant to Rose. Nick knew one thing about **The Land of the Eagle Feathers**. Do not be surprised about anything! This land had a way of directing you to be more than you ever thought you could be. There were several bright flashes of shooting stars that raced across the sky. The night was calm and still.

In the distance, two wolves could be heard. They were howling at the moon. One Feather listened carefully. He seemed to be studying the song of the two wolves. "Snow and Midnight are singing your song," One Feather said to Zan and Rose. "They can feel your happiness. They are saying that you have a child that will change this land. It will not be called The Land of Nightmares in the future. Your child will do great deeds. She has great medicine in her. They say her grandparents are together now. They will be here to guide her. That is all I can tell you about your daughter. The wolves are singing a song of joy."

Antonio got up and asked Little Wolf to recite his passage. Everyone listened to him. One Feather had made a drum for him to sing his passage. Little Wolf took the drum and started to beat an ancient rhythm as he sang his passage. The flames of the campfire seemed to grow with each drumbeat.

A Child of Destiny

Every season has a reason
Every reason has a season
It is and will always be
You are a child of destiny

It takes every minute to make an hour
It takes every petal to make a flower
It takes every rock to make a mountain
It takes every drop to make a fountain

The flowers and trees need sunlight to grow
The rivers and streams need rain to flow
Without the rain, the land cannot give
Without the land, the people cannot live

You are a child of this land
Even though you don't understand
There's something you're destined to do
It all starts and ends with you

You come from the land of the brave
You'll find your answers in a cave
It is written in the North Star's glow
It is hidden in the rivers flow

Little one, don't you cry
Listen and learn, don't ask why
Every reason has its season
Every season has its reason

When Little Wolf beat his last beat, Red Bear got up. "I will not be taking you to that place. It is forbidden. Your song is your song. Look to the North Star, you will follow its glow. You will find a river that flows to a mountain. The river will flow into a cave. You will go in that cave and find out many things. I wish you well. It will be a difficult journey. You have always been a child of destiny. If you come back, you will not be the same. We will see."

Red Bear took some red dust from his medicine bag. He threw it into the blazing campfire. A big puff of red smoke filled the air. As it settled to the ground, an old woman dressed in purple with a purple cape appeared before them.

"I have come to take Little Wolf. I will not be guiding him. I have two wolves that will do that for me. I have instructed them where to take him." She pointed to the darkness in front of them. Two wolves walked out of the darkness. One was white. This one was One Feather's wolf called Snow. The other was black as the dead of night. That one was June's called Midnight. "One Feather and June said I could borrow them tonight. Little Wolf, you must go and follow them to the cave. If you survive the cave, they will escort you back here tomorrow night."

Both wolves walked over to Little Wolf. Little Wolf followed them into the darkness of the night. "Yes, he is a child of destiny. Do not follow them! The wolves will protect him." The old woman walked into the darkness. She seemed to melt into it.

Mary was worried. I was sitting next to her. "He will be alright. He is a smart and wise boy. He will be coming back to us. There is nothing left for us to do tonight until our son gets back. I suggest we get some sleep. We have much to do to get ready for the final task."

I must have got up too fast. I could feel my legs get weak under me. Mary stood up and steadied me. "I will be taking my husband back to my tent. Lo Ming, will you help me?" Lo Ming smiled, "Yes, I will help you and your husband! He needs some good medicine that only you can give. See that star on the left of the moon. In my land, we call it The Star of Redemption. It shines bright tonight. It shines on your tent."

Little Wolf followed the two wolves in front of him. They were on the run most of the night. He looked back to see if the old woman was behind him. She was gone. Little Wolf ran like his name, a wolf. He loved to run. Many braves said he could run as fast as any wolf.

How far they had run, he did not know. It must have been several miles. The hills and streams were getting bigger each mile. Finally, the wolves stopped in front of him. He could hear the sound of a river. The wolves turned North. The North Star glowed in the night sky. They ran for another hour. The sun was rising in the eastern sky. Little Wolf could make out a cave ahead of them. The river ran straight into the mountain.

At the side of the mountain was a small path into the cave. The wolves stopped. They had done their job. He was at the cave. He had to do the next thing himself. Little Wolf walked up to the cave's entrance. He was concerned that the cave would be very dark. He did not have a torch to light. He was relieved to see that the cave had its own light. Diamonds and shiny stones lit the passageway. He went inside.

He followed the path for several hundred feet. The cave was filled with beautiful gems and stones on the walls. Large crystals had formed on the cave's floor, and several large crystals hung from the cave's ceiling. The river vanished into a large cavern below a large room. He walked across to the opening to the room.

In the room was the old woman dressed in purple. Her head was covered by the purple hood of the cape. She pointed to the wall at the end of the cave's room. Little Wolf stepped slowly toward the wall. To his surprise, a large grey and black wolf was tied to a chain in the wall. The wolf was growling and grinding its teeth at him. It was as wild as wild could be. It certainly didn't like strangers or humans for that matter.

Little Wolf had heard about this type of wolf. They were known to be mean. They would bite and claw at anything that moved. They were very dangerous. The only ones that were allowed to exist were here in The Land of Nightmares. Their heads were much larger compared to other large wolves. Their bites could crush or cut off a man's arm or hand. It was said that nobody was ever able to touch one and live. The wolf would tear them apart.

The old woman said, "Little Wolf, you are about to become a man. You have two choices. One is to reach over the wolf's head and untie the last piece of puzzle and take it. The other is to not to do that and remain a boy for the next two years. You must be sure that you are ready to become a man. If you show any kind of fear, the wolf will bite your hand and arm. You could be maimed for life or die from the bite. Your arm and body could be mutilated for the rest of your life. Think about it. You have just met your mother and grandfather. Do you want to risk your life? Nobody has ever passed this test in this land. In that corner over there are several arms and skeletons that tried and failed. Nobody would blame you if you passed on this test."

Little Wolf asked, "Why was I picked to be the child of destiny? The old woman replied, "You have the right to know. Your mother and father are special. Your grandmother is the Red Woman, and your father is the powerful leader of **The Dark Ones**. Your mother is the daughter of those two. She is also a member of **The Keepers of the Yawi**. She is very brave. Your father is special. His bravery and leadership are known throughout this world. His blood is your blood."

The old woman pointed again to the puzzle piece that was tied on the back of the wolf's neck. "Remember, if you have any doubts that you are not man enough to get the puzzle piece, the wolf will tear you apart. Think of all the time you will miss with your new family if you fail."

Little Wolf looked at the wolf. The wolf was pacing around. Saliva was dripping from its mouth. The wolf's eyes were bright red like a demon had possessed it. Little Wolf had to jump back as the wolf lunged at him.

Little Wolf started thinking about how life had been so peaceful and perfect before John had brought the others into this land. He had a great life. He didn't have a care in the world. He had friends he played with and animals that were his pets It could still be a great life for a while longer. He could get to know his mother better. He would have a family. Why should he take a chance of losing that?

Did he really want to be an adult? He was still young. He would be expected to become an adult with adult issues and problems. Why should he be the one that risks everything to get the book? Other people like Antonio and his father were much braver than him. They were already adults. Little Wolf was unsure if he had the will and fortitude to be a man. Was he ready to give it up? He had just become a boy with a loving mother and family. He wanted to have more time to be a boy with them. Did he have what it takes to reach above the wolf or was he too unsure of himself? He thought what life would be like to have those things that he never had.

Sweat was flowing down his brow. His hands were shaking. The wolf was howling for blood. Those teeth were sharp. Saliva was flowing out of its mouth landing on the cave floor. The wolf seemed to be getting more and more upset and angry. It was leaping and pulling against its ropes that held it. Nobody in their right mind would put their hands where the wild wolf could get it. Nobody would live if the animal grabbed them. They would be torn limb by limb.

The old woman said again, "Do you really want to risk your life? You can wait and in two years you would be declared a man. Do you, Little Wolf?"

Something about the way, the old woman said, "Do you?" woke Little Wolf out of his thoughts. He was the child of destiny. He was just as brave as anyone on this journey. Only a boy would not get the puzzle piece. He had come too far to back out now.

The old woman said, "Do not hesitate or you will die?" Little Wolf started to reach in to get the puzzle piece. The wolf growled and bit at him. Little Wolf jumped back just before the wolf would have bit him. He could feel the heat of the wolf's breath on his hand. There was no way that he could possibly get the puzzle piece without his hand being bitten.

Little Wolf studied the wild wolf. He looked the wolf straight in its eyes. They stared at each other for a long time. Little Wolf thought of all of those that depended on him. Images of his childhood and possible childhood moved around his mind like a whirlwind. He knew what he must do to get the puzzle piece. Would it be worth it? He couldn't die. He had to live.

Little Wolf took his left arm. He slowly moved it toward the raging, howling wolf. The wolf jumped and bit his arm. Pain exploded in his arm. Blood streamed out of his arm. He could only move his arm a little. The movement keep the attention of the wolf. The wolf would not let go. Little Wolf took his right hand and grabbed the string that held the puzzle piece. He tore it from the wolf's neck with what strength he had left. The wolf spit out his left arm to bite at Little Wolf's right arm. The wolf missed. Little Wolf fell back and rolled away from the wolf with the string and puzzle piece in his right hand. He had the puzzle piece.

It had cost him most of his left arm. He was in great pain. He held up the puzzle piece. "This was the only way. It may have cost me my left arm. It was worth it. I am a man. I will die a man. They will be proud to have such a brave man for a son and member of the tribe. We will get the book. We will save the land. My arm and my life may be the price."

"Yes, your arm and life may be the price, but not today," said the old woman as Little Wolf fell to the floor of the cave unconscious.

Snow and Midnight returned to the campsite without Little Wolf. It was late afternoon. It was starting to rain. The clouds hung low against the western mountains. The mountains looked like islands surrounded by a sea of water. Mary was worried for Little Wolf. I tried to comfort her. "He will be alright. He is a tough kid. He is smart like you. I can feel it in my bones. He may be a little battered from his experience. We must have some patience."

Mary and I sat in our tent. I was still a little weak. The cold rain made it a dreary day. All we could do was wait. Waiting was never one of my strengths. Mary couldn't help it. Tears of worry were forming in her eyes. I did the only thing I could by taking her in my arms. "Don't worry," was all I could say as we waited.

David was worried. He didn't stay in his tent. Red Bear told him to stay in the dry tent with him. David would not have any of that. He wanted to be the first to know something. Moses went over to June's and One Feather's tent. Moses asked their wolves if they knew anything. The wolves replied with a howl that they were sent back here to wait for a sign. The day seemed to drag on, minute by minute.

Nick had made some hot soup for everyone. Zan had built a small shelter to shield the campfire from the rain. Zan even built a small stove of flat rocks for Nick to use for cooking. Nick was impressed with Zan's skill. Zan told him that he had years of practice to learn such skills. Rose could tell that Nick was missing Shanna. She tried to get Nick to talk about her and how they met. This seemed to help Nick a little.

Nick took portions of his soup to each person. It helped cut the chill of the day. Time was running out, and still there was no Little Wolf in sight. The sunset was a bright red. Antonio and Angela were lying in their tent. Angela told Antonio. "Look at the bright red sunset. That means that Little Wolf is going to be fine. It is the sign I have been waiting to see. I will go tell Mary and John not to worry. Little Wolf will be here shortly." Antonio asked Angela, "How do you know?" Angela answered, "My father is White Elk. I have his blood in my veins. I have learned to trust my intuitions. They have kept me alive through worst situations. Trust me, I know."

The rain had stopped. Angela told Mary and John not to worry. "Little Wolf will be here shortly. He is hurt. My left arm hurts. He is alive. I sense that he is coming back with the young woman on her painted pony. You should make his bed as comfortable as possible. Then come outside and wait by the campfire."

Mary asked me about what Angela had said. "Angela and I rode together for several years. If she feels something, she is usually right. Her father taught her many things. Her intuition saved us many times. I trust her. She wouldn't tell you that unless she knew for sure. I suggest you get your medicine kit ready for him." I could see that what Angela said made Mary feel better.

Night falls suddenly in the winter months, especially in the mountains. It was pitch black. The clouds had covered the sky. We sat around the campfire. Nobody was talking. The horses and ponies seemed to be a little uneasy about something.

"I see that you are all waiting for us," said a woman's voice from the darkness. "I have a young man with me. I need some help. I had to tie him to my saddle to keep him from falling off. He is hurt. It will take him about a day to get over his wounds. Mary should be able to nurse her son back to health. I trust Angela told you that he was coming."

The young Indian's pony walked out of the darkness with an unconscious Little Wolf tied to the saddle with the young Indian woman. David, Moses and Antonio jumped up to lift Little Wolf down off the saddle. They took him with Mary to her tent. She was upset when she looked at his injuries. Angela was right. Little Wolf's left arm was badly hurt. Mary could see the injuries he had were caused by a wolf's bite. She told everyone to go back to the campfire and find out what had happened. She would take care of her son.

When everyone except Mary got back to the campfire, the young woman spoke to them. "Little Wolf is stuff that legends are told about for years around a campfire in the dark of night. He figured out a puzzle that many people died trying. I will tell you about how he did it. It was very painful. He did well. He should be better in another day. The last marble puzzle piece is around his neck. I tied it there so it would not get lost."

The young woman told everyone the whole story about what happened in the cave. After she finished, she nodded to me. "Mary and you have a young man that you can very proud of. He is not a boy any longer. He is a man. He earned that with his blood and determination. He has become a brave of **The Land of the Eagle Feathers**. Here is his head band. He earned an eagle feather for his deed." She tossed it to me. She turned her pony. She rode off into the darkness. It was the first time I ever saw David smile with pride.

Chapter IX
The Puzzle is Solved
Will we finally find the book?

Antonio asked for everyone to join him at the campfire later that night. Everyone was there. Mary left Little Wolf in her tent. Antonio said that all the marble pieces to the puzzle had been collected. There were only two problems left to solve. One was where the puzzle was to begin. Antonio explained that the puzzle was a map to where *The Book of Winter* was located.   The other was where is the book located at the final location on the map?

Antonio looked at John. "John, you have the last passage. It is only fitting that you got that passage. It will tell us where the location of the map will start. It will also give us the location of the book at the last location of the puzzle. It is your turn to recite your passage."

I looked at everyone taking my time. I was proud of all of those here. I even had to say that David was very instrumental in finding some of the pieces. Mary was looking at her father, David. I could see that she had some doubts about him. I knew that they were very close. I felt that the time we spent in The Land of Nightmares had an influence on her. I could only hope that the events of the last several days had the same influence on David.

I stood up and told everyone how I felt. "Our days together will be short. Our mission to find *The Book of Winter* is almost finished. I have gotten to know each of you. I am proud to have known such a group. In less than a full circle of the sun, we have done what nobody believed possible. Some of our enemies have become our friends. We have conquered our fears. We have stood as warriors against our enemies. Now, we start the final chapter or season of our quest. We will not fail. I have traveled many steps to get here. I will travel some more. I am satisfied that these last four seasons of my life have been my best. I have lived many years and done many deeds. I have never had that many friends. Now, I have many. Whatever happens in the next several days, I have found things that I will treasure always. I found my family, not just my blood family, but a much larger family.

David and Red Bear, I will not fight you anymore. David, I cannot fight my family. You must take care of our family. Whether I live or die does not matter, I was given a second chance to live. Fate has always been a stranger to me."

I turned around and took out a bottle of very rare brandy from a supply box. "This brandy is from France. It was given to me by a famous general. Each of you have a small wooden cup that I gave you. Antonio, pour some in each cup." Antonio took the bottle and looked at it for several moments. He whistled. "Go ahead and open it, Antonio. I know it is worth a lot. It's two hundred years old. My family is worth more," I told him.

When Antonio had given out the brandy, I asked for everyone to stand around the fire. "Raise your cups to the sky. No matter where you came from and no matter what you have done, we are all brothers and sisters of the sacred land called **The Land of the Eagle Feathers**. We will always be that no matter what happens. To all that are here today, may the spirits be kind and the days be long. I salute you!" We all took a drink and threw the small wooden cups into the fire.

I had everyone sit down. I recited my passage.

One of a Kind

In the memories of yonder days
Time visits but never stays
Visions of ancestors dance in the mind
Living in today, looking behind

Seasons change as seasons always do
Skies of gray, skies of blue
The river never ceases to flow
Grass will die, grass will grow

Mother Earth has wisdom we don't understand
The answers are hidden in this sacred land
Open your eyes and try to see
The way it is and will always be

Father sky will give you the light
Grandmother moon will give you the night
Mother Earth will give you the dirt
Grandfather sun will give you the earth

You must look beyond yourself
Look to your right, look to your left
Look forward, and then look behind
You will see the white buffalo, one of a kind

"The puzzle map will begin at a cliff that has paintings of long ago of our ancestors. There is the river that never stops flowing there. That means the river must be fed by a large spring. These places are about one day's march back toward the entrance. I saw the cliff myself when we first came into this land. Red Bear and Zan know this land well. They will lead us there. I will find the hidden place once we find the

258

final location. It will take all our powers to raise the book from its hiding place. I am tired. I want to spend some more time with my son and my wife if she will let me."

Mary took my hand and helped me back to our tent. Moses waited until I had left to speak, "John is a very sick man. I hope he has enough strength left to finish this journey." David answered, "He will. I won't allow it. I won't let my son-in-law die. My wife, my daughter and my grandson would not forgive me. John has more reasons to kill me than any of you will ever know. If he can forgive the past, I can too. It is the future we must save. We are all travelers in this time and space. It is good that we travel together. As John says fate is a strange bedfellow. I want our legacy to be told around campfires for many generations."

David got up to go to his tent. Red Bear and Red Sparrow followed him. Lo Ming spoke to the others that remained. "I have known David for many years. He is a complicated man. I find his change of mind very interesting. I also find Mary's behavior to be very interesting.

David can be very devious. That is both a good thing and a bad thing. This fight we are in could use another very devious leader. When evil fights good, I have found the rules sometimes need to be bent. With John and David, we have the best of both worlds.

Don't think John can't be devious. He got us all here. Against all the odds that fate threw at him, he did the impossible. As David said, we are all travelers in time and space. There is more going on under the surface here. Fate and destiny sometimes are hidden just out of sight. For now, we should be grateful to fate. She has been kind to us. Let's hope she remains that way."

The sunrise coming over the Eastern Mountains was bright red. Red Bear and June were very worried. They both studied the clouds behind the sunrise. Those clouds were purple in color. "This is a very bad sign," said Red Bear to June. "Yes, I know. There is a bad storm coming. How long before it will get here?" she asked Red Bear. Red Bear studied the red sunrise for a few moments. "It will come at dusk, tonight. We will have only a few hours to get the book before it hits. We will need to have a strong shelter to survive such a storm. I have seen these before. We must hurry."

We had broken camp. Everything was packed and ready to go. I was feeling much better. Little Wolf's arm was healing nicely. Mary had used some stitches to close some of his cuts. June examined his wounds to see if she could do something more for them. June put some green salve on his arm. "This should heal the wound faster. I am afraid that Little Wolf will always have scars from his wounds. The biggest will be the bite marks of the wolf. Don't worry about that because it will show everyone how great a warrior he is."

Little Wolf had a big smile on his face. Mary had given him his new headband with the one eagle feather in it. Only warriors that did a great deed ever received an eagle feather. "I feel much better. I can make the journey to the book today," he told them.

Everyone gathered around the campfire to wait for the young Indian woman to bring the extra horses. A large thunderclap shook the valley. On the top of the hill behind them appeared the young Indian woman riding her painted pony. In front of her were several horses running down the hill towards them.

It took only a few moments for them to arrive in front of the campfire. "These are the horses that you will need to make your final journey to obtain *The Book of Winter.* You must hurry. A great storm is coming. It is written If you don't obtain the book by the time the storm comes, all will be destroyed. That includes where the book is located. May the spirits be with you!

I see Little Wolf is doing well." The young Indian woman asked Little Wolf to come closer to her. She touched Little Wolf's arm with a gemstone. "The Great Spirits are pleased with you. Your wounds are now healed. Your arm will always have the marks of the great wolf. Little Wolf is not a name for such a great warrior. As is the Indian custom, we can change your name to reflect the deed that made you a man. The Great Spirits have chosen **Great Wolf** as your name. Your sign will always be the marks of the great wolf's bite for all to see on your left arm. The Great Spirits have spoken. Now go, **Great Wolf**, you have one more great deed to do. Take the gray stallion to ride today. He is a gift from us to you. May you survive today!" The young Indian woman turned her painted pony and rode up the hill out of sight.

We got mounted on our horses. The horses that she brought were already saddled. Red Bear and Zan led the way followed by Great Wolf and his mother. I chose to be last. David was in front of me. Red Bear said it would take two hours of hard riding to make it to the cliffs. Our horses were very strong. We soon were in full gallop. All we had to do was hang on and not fall off. I had to say that I did enjoy riding up and down the valleys. It made you feel alive.

We could hear the roar of thunder in the distance like cannons going off before a battle. We arrived at the cliffs faster than we thought. Moses told everyone to dismount. He gave us towels to wipe the sweat off the horses to keep them from getting chilled from the old mountain air. We noticed that the cliff's pictures were of long ago. The river in front of the cliffs was clear. The water was pure and cold.

I went over to the paintings on the cliffs. I told everyone to remain with the horses and wait for me. I looked at the pictures closely. I knew what the pictures were saying.

Open your eyes and try to see
The way it is and will always be

Father sky will give you the light
Grandmother Moon will give you the night
Mother Earth will give you the dirt
Grandfather Sun will give you the earth

You must look beyond yourself
Look to your right, look to your left
Look forward, and then look behind
You will see the white buffalo, one of a kind

I closed my eyes. I opened them seeing visions of my ancestors and how the land was. I looked at the sky and saw Father Sky and Grandmother moon. I could feel Mother Earth in the dirt below my feet. Grandfather sun was high in the sky. I looked at the sun and beyond. Then I looked to the right and the left. I looked forward, and then I looked behind me. I froze. Looking back at me, I saw the sacred white buffalo. Visions of the seasons changing filled my mind.

The white buffalo walked toward me. In my mind, it said, "Follow me, we have much to talk about, John. I have waited many circles of the sun to meet you. The others can't see me, only you." I never looked at anything as I followed the sacred white buffalo up a faint trail by the cliffs. We walked up the hill to the top.

We reached the top of the hill. It overlooked the valleys and hills of the land. "You have done well, John. I see that you have picked your group with care. We are pleased that you are finally here. **The Keepers of the Yawi** are the only ones that can obtain the last book. It took you a while to solve that puzzle. This last part of your journey for *The Book of Winter* will be dangerous. You must find the book and bring it back to the cliffs below before the great storm strikes.

The pieces of the puzzle do not make a map. They must be put together on top of the volcano in front of us. That puzzle will tell you where the book is hidden. Only **The Keepers of The Yawi** are allowed to go with you. You must take Great Wolf with you.

On my back is a bag of red dust, have your voodoo woman, Rose, toss it in the air. The dust will give everyone visions as to what to do. There is only one more thing. You have only, what you call, two hours once you get on top of the plateau of the volcano to find the book. If you do not obtain it in two hours, the volcano will explode. The book and you will be no more. Nobody will have the book and its powers.

If you obtain the book, only Great Wolf will be allowed to carry it. He is to read the first pages. Those pages will tell him what to do with the book. If anyone takes the book from him, you must take it back and give it to him. Use any means necessary to see he keeps the book! Great Wolf is the only one that can control the power of the book. It is written in the stars. The book will either save this land or destroy it and all that is near. Now go back, your time is getting short. Your life may be getting short. I will see you again no matter what happens."

The white buffalo vanished. In my hand was the bag of red dust. I walked down the trail to join the rest of the group. "Great Wolf, you are to gather all the pieces of the marble puzzle and put them in this sacred bag with the red dust. Only Great Wolf and **The Keepers of the Yawi** can go with me to obtain the book. David will remain with the other members of our group here. All of you must construct some sort of strong shelter for us to survive the storm that is coming.

There is one other thing." I pointed to the volcano over the cliffs behind me. "If that volcano explodes, you must leave

The Land of Nightmares after the storm passes without us. You will be safe here from the volcano.

Zan asked, "What do you mean without us?" I answered, "Rose, Antonio, Nick, Mary, Lo Ming, Moses and June will be going with me besides Great Wolf. We would have failed to obtain the book. We would have died in the volcano along with the book.

I asked the group, "Why are you looking at me in the way you are?" Red Bear replied, "The white buffalo changed you. It must have been the white buffalo that you followed up the hill. We could not see it. Your clothes are white with jewels. Your hair is white and long. Your face has a full-grown white beard. Your skin is white almost transparent. Only one that has seen and talked to the great white buffalo looks like you do. We will have to get used to it. It is what it is."

"Time is short. I will give you two hours to say your goodbye to those that are not going with me" I told them.

Zan ran over to Rose. They had set up their tent thinking they were staying tonight anyway. They wanted to be alone. They slipped into their tent. Zan whispered to Rose as they laid down together. "It took us so long to find each other. It is not fair that we may not see each other again," said Zan. Rose replied, "Don't worry, my friends and I have been in tougher spots, I will be back. We don't have time for talk. We do have time for some good old-fashioned lovemaking. There's an old saying in the swamps. Make the most of every day, there might not be a 'morrow. Life is short. Love and memories are forever."

Zan didn't waste any time. Zan stopped and looked into Rose's eyes. He moved down and kissed her stomach. "Please be careful, for her! She is special. She was conceived in love which makes her that much more special. She has a destiny. She will be powerful and beautiful. She has the love of my father and mother inside of her. She will do many great things." Rose said, "Yes, I know. I will be back for you and her. No power will ever stop that love!

Antonio looked at Angela. Angela had a worried look on her face. "Let's go down the river a little-ways out of sight. I can tell there is a hot spring down there by the stream in the air. We could use a little hot bath to wash the dirt away. It will be fun. Besides, you always talk too much before you leave to go anyplace. It ticks me off that you waste perfectly good time talking instead of doing. It must be the Italian in you," Angela said as she grabbed Antonio's arm. "I am glad to know that. I will leave more often then," he replied. Angela kissed Antonio as she threw him into the hot spring, clothes and all. "Now that's one way to shut you up," as she pulled off his shirt.

Antonio could not help himself. Tears flowed down his face. "I must say this. I know we promised not to say that to each other. I love you. I love you with all my Italian heart. I have always loved you. Don't ever leave me!"

Angela held Antonio close to her heart. "Yes, I know. I see it every time you look into my eyes. Antonio, my dear Antonio, I have always come back to you. I am like a moth flying back to the flame of your love. Kiss me and make love to me like there is no tomorrow."

Lo Ming said to Moses, "I guess we don't have to say goodbye to each other since we will be together. We have a great opportunity to live or die as warriors." Moses laughed, "There's still some sunlight shining up the hill. As a man from the Outback, making love outdoors in the sun is a great thing. Are you game for that? Besides, I always wondered if I could beat you in a close hand to hand fight." Lo Ming smiled, "That's a bet. There is only one rule. We must do the fight the Greek way." Moses didn't need to say anything more. He knew what Lo Ming meant. The Greek way meant without clothes.

Moses knew that Lo Ming had trouble saying it. Lo Ming was a true warrior. Moses was a man of the Outback. "Lo Ming, you are my only true love. I love you. You are like a beautiful desert flower in the spring. I can feel and touch how much you love me. I would be a lost soul without you by my side. You are warm and passionate. I love to watch you as you listen to the songbirds in the morning sun. Your love warms me when I am cold. Your love feeds my aching soul. It has been my life's treasure to be with you. You will be in my heart and soul until I die. May the gods of the Great Outback bless our love!"

One Feather was upset. He loved June with all his heart. "Let's take a walk," he asked her. June could tell One Feather was broken up inside. She took his hand. They didn't have to say anything. Their minds melted together. After walking down the trail they came on, June said, "No matter what happens, I will find you. See the clouds in the sky, that pass by, that will be me. Every time you feel a warm breeze on your face, that will be me kissing you on your cheek. I will find you. Don't say anything, I know you love me as I love you. I will survive by knowing that and the strength of your love. Time is only a measure. Stars are bright in a winter's sky. Let us hold each other until it is about time to part. Then we will talk to my parents. Remember, I will find you."

Mary looked at David. She asked David to talk to his grandson. David nodded. "I will be honored to talk to such a brave young man. I have much to say to him." David asked Great Wolf to sit beside him and talk. "If you want to know anything just ask," he told Great Wolf. His grandson asked him one thing that David was surprised about. "Tell me about you and my grandmother." David replied by saying, "I loved her the moment I saw her when we werc little children. I will tell you about her and your mother when we were a happy family long ago."

Mary walked over to me. I could see the sadness in her face. "Let us go and set by the tree over there," she asked me. We sat down by the tree on the winter's dried grass. "I know that there's been a lot of water under the bridge between us. The memories of our love together long ago has come back to me. It had almost been too much for me to take. I am still trying to make sense of it all. Deep in my heart, I can feel love for you. We have a long way to go. It will take time for us. Somehow, I know we will make it. Don't say anything more. Just nod your head that you promise to keep our son safe.

My father will not fight you. He knows that things need time to sort our lives out. There is one thing I must do before we go." Mary stood up. She took my face in her hands. She kissed me passionately. She ran away to the horses leaving me alone. I touched my lips. It was the first time in a long time that I ever felt love on my lips.

I went over to David. "I need to talk to you. Great Wolf, will you let me talk to your grandfather alone?" I asked him. Great Wolf nodded his head. "You need to talk with your mother, any way before we leave in a few minutes," I told him. Great Wolf left in a hurry.

David asked, "Why do you want to talk to me?" he asked. "I need your help. I will tell you why, and you will understand. I only ask for the sake of your grandson and daughter not me," I answered him. "In that case, I will do whatever you need," replied David.

After talking to David, I rounded up **The Keepers of the Yawi**, Great Wolf and One Feather. We mounted our horses and left taking the river trail to the base of the volcano. I took the lead with Great Wolf behind me. It took less than two hours to reach the base of the volcano.

One Feather was assigned to tend to the horses while we went up the trail to the top of the volcano. "If this volcano erupts before we get down, leave for our campsite immediately. Do you have the small pouch that you have been keeping for me?" I asked One Feather. One Feather didn't answer. He opened his shirt and around his neck was the small pouch. He took it off and threw it to me.

I asked June to check to see if the trail was clear ahead of us. June raised her arms to the sky. High above us was a large Bald Eagle gliding on the updrafts of the mountain range. June called to it in her native tongue. The eagle slowly glided down the mountain winds and landed close to us. Giving a command to the eagle, June watched as it rose upward flying close to the mountain trail that we were taking.

We remained silent observing June. She was connected to the Eagle in a mystical, spiritual state. June was in a trance. Her eyes were closed. Her arms were moving much like a bird's wings in flight. When the Eagle was clearly above the mountain ahead of us, June spoke. "The trail to the top of this volcano is clear. I can see on the top of this volcano is a flat plateau with a raised rock platform in the middle. There are several small rock platforms arranged in a circle that surrounds the larger one. This must be the sacred place that holds the sacred book of *The Book of Winter*. However, we must hurry. There looks to be a great storm brewing to the West of us. We have no time to lose." The Eagle disappeared into a black cloud above us.

Moses took June into his arms to keep her from fainting. Her connection with her Eagle Spirit was broken. It took a lot of June's energy to connect with her Eagle Spirit. Moses said he would assist June to the top of the trail. I put Nick and Antonio in the lead. Nick would look for obstacles that could be dangerous. Antonio was to look for any signs or cravings in the rock wall that could guide us.

June asked, "Why were we being so careful? The way ahead looked clear." Antonio looked back at her. He told her that there's an old saying stated in ***The Book of Fall.*** "Even a peaceful road can be filled with unexpected pitfalls."

We picked up the pace to race to the top before the storm would come. As we rounded one bend in the trail, Nick signaled for us to halt. He pointed to some large boulders up ahead.

He gathered some dust from the trailside into his hands. Throwing the dust at the trail ahead of him, he pointed toward the dust cloud that followed. When the dust cleared, you could see a tripwire that crossed the trail. It was attached to a small rock underneath one of the large boulders. Antonio carefully took another larger rock into his hands and embedded it under the boulder by the smaller rock. Then Antonio cut the tripwire to deactivate the trap. Moses nodded his head with approval to Nick. Nick nodded back, recognizing Moses' respect for his skills.

I told everyone that it appeared too easy for us to get the book. There had to be other obstacles involved. The Land of Nightmares wouldn't give up its treasure so easily. We should be careful. I could feel a presence around us.

Moving carefully, we moved at a faster pace. Antonio stopped twice to read some Indian carvings on the rock face beside the trail. Just before we arrived at the mountaintop, June signaled for us to gather close together.

There was a steep cliff ahead of us. At first, we thought we heard thunder in the distance. June told us to wait a few minutes and listen carefully. Each second, the sounds that came from the volcano became louder. Soon we could hear chants from the ancient Indian ancestors. What we thought was the sounds of thunder were not. The sounds became louder and louder. They were drumbeats.

June pointed to the dark sky. The dark clouds were changing into shapes. Visions from the past filled the sky. All types of animals paraded around the volcano. Deer, elk, beavers, mountain lions, bears and bison ran faster and faster. Horses with Indian braves rode behind them. Fire came from the mouths of each horse. They were the spirit riders. They would always follow the herds of the animals but never catch them.

The face of the cliff lit up with symbols. There were bows, arrows, lances, woven baskets, pottery, all types of dwellings from wooden lodges, huts and teepees. Young children played with each other on a peaceful prairie of tall green grass. Women were making clothes from deer and elk hides. Braves were hunting and fishing for food. Councils of various tribes were being held with famous chiefs such as Red Cloud, Cochise, Running Bear, Chief Joseph, Sitting Bull and Crazy Horse.

The visions flashed of the Indian wars. Braves fought with their war lances of eagle feathers and died before being victorious in battle. The sad faces of women and children were from burying their dead from the diseases of smallpox, measles and other white man sicknesses. An image of a medicine woman and great medicine man pointed at us. The drums beat louder, and the chants became louder. Great Wolf walked toward the images. He held out his arms and pointed his fingers at the Great Medicine man and woman. In an ancient Indian language known only to a few people, he spoke to them. Antonio translated to us what was said.

"We had come to save the lands of our sacred home. Some of us are from lands far away across the great seas of time. You honor us with your visions of truth. We are just people of simple blood traveling in a time of great despair. Our trials have been great. Our victories many in our travels.

Now time grows short. Our destiny like the great wanderings of the animal herds have led us here. We mean no disrespect to our ancestors. You, who have come before us, have performed many great and wonderous deeds of bravery and sacrifice. We know we must preserve your life and memory so that they will not be lost in the seas and sands of time. Father Sky and Mother Earth, we hold dear to our souls and hearts.

We ask permission to possess *The Book of Winter*. It is our last hope of keeping the sacred **Land of the Eagle Feathers** from being destroyed by forces of evil. We will only use the book for saving this land and its people." Great Wolf turned and pointed to us. They have been purified by The Land of Nightmares. They have shed their own blood. They are what is written in the sands, on the great stones and walls of the mountains around us. They are **The Keepers of the Yawi**, the people that have come to protect our ancient ways and culture. It is their destiny. It is my destiny."

The Great Chiefs appeared on the wall. Crazy Horse and Sitting Bull pointed at John. Come to us, man called John. You rode with us and ate with us. You are our blood brother. Your deeds and many of your followers are great. You have fought many battles to protect our sacred lands. You have lost much to save this land. Your time grows short as the grass of the coming winter. There is much hurt and sadness in your eyes. It is said that a man's greatness is only known by the strength of his enemies.

You have done well. We will let **The Keepers of the Yawi** and Great Wolf pass into the Volcano of Fire. You have only two of white men's hours to obtain **The Book of Winter** or you will perish.   It is not for us to decide. You must earn that right. Go with our blessings. May the great spirits be with you. It has been an honor to have known and rode with you."

John stood silently for the few moments. "It was my honor to have known such brave men, to have ridden and to have fought so many battles together. We have smoked many peace pipes around the Council fires. I am but a man. I bow to your great deeds. Your bravery in battle and in life is spoken to this day in many lodges and homes. One day, I will join my great blood brothers in the sky. May your legends and deeds be spoken around the Council fires of time." John bowed his head in respect. The images disappeared. You could see the great Chiefs mount their painted ponies. They turned to face us. They held their war lances up to the sky above their heads to salute us. They rode into the dark clouds shouting war hoops.

When I came back to join the others, Antonio spoke about what the Indian carving and paintings on the rock faces said. They say that only **The Keepers of the Yawi** can open the rock that hides the treasure of this fire mountain. If **The Keepers of the Yawi** do not obtain the book in two hours, the volcano will explode into a hundred pieces. The book will be lost forever. All the book's powers will be lost never to be regained, and nothing will be able to destroy the evil that stalks **The Land of the Eagle Feathers.**

"That carving over there on the wall face describes each one of us. It says **The Keepers of the Yawi** consists of the following: a great black warrior from the deserts that are upside down with a great woman warrior from the East, a wise woman of magic, a younger warrior known for his power for killing, a powerful medicine woman that loves a warrior called One Feather, a woman that has healing powers but has a father that is evil, a man that lives by deception and reads many ancient writings, a young man, wise beyond his years, on a vision quest, and finally a man more spirit than man that has traveled through time and space to lead this group of warriors.

Antonio stated that we don't have time to discuss this. The storm is getting nearer. We must act quickly because the carvings state that once anyone steps foot on this mountaintop, the quest starts and cannot stop until the book is obtained. However, the carvings give us two clues for us to succeed.

One was that the women hold the knowledge to obtain the book. The other is that a young man will be in the center. He holds the key. I noted that Antonio had a smile on his face as he looked at my son, Great Wolf.

I asked everyone if they were in agreement to start the last stage of the quest for the book. Each of them had to nod their head in agreement for us to go on to finish this quest. I watched each one nod their head. Then it was my young son's turn. Great Wolf nodded his head and said, "We will become legends in the sands of time. My father cannot participate. He can only watch.

My Grandmother, the Red Woman, told me that you were chosen not because you were all pure. You were chosen for this quest because of your faults and your powers. That is the reason why so many before us failed. My father, John, carefully chose all of you for this quest because you know both sides of the forces of the universe: the good and the evil side. You have walked in both sides. That is why we will succeed when so many have failed.

Most of us are not perfect. We are parts of a whole. We are much greater together than apart like seven spokes in a wheel held with me in the center that will roll over the evil in our path. Remember, it takes everyone to succeed. It is written in the stars. Follow me to our destiny," as he stepped on to the mountaintop.

The bright day was changing fast. The sunlight was starting to be blocked by dark storm clouds coming in from the western sky. Thunder could be heard rolling down the mountain range. Lightning was flashing throughout the dark clouds. The lightning seemed to jump from one cloud to another. Webs of lightning crisscrossed the sky followed by the roar of thunder in the distance. The storm would be arriving in just a few minutes. The wind was picking up speed. This storm was a greeting from the spirits. They wanted to let us know that they would not give up their treasure easily.

Rose immediately gathered the women together. They met in a small circle at the center of the plateau. Rose took out the bag of red dust and the pieces of the puzzle from her medicine pouch. She tossed the red dust and puzzle pieces into the air. The Red Dust covered the air. As the White Buffalo said the dust filled the volcano top with visions. In some ancient language, Rose spoke as she casted the rest of the red powder into the air.

The puzzle pieces broke into a thousand pieces on the volcano top. A bright blinding multicolored flash followed. Smoke of various colors filled the plateau. A gust of wind blew the smoke away. The women's clothes were replaced with colorful flowing silk robes with a hood covering their heads. Each one had a robe that was of a different color with a design formed from precious stones and gems on the back.

June's robe was of shades of purple with a design of a hawk and eagle in flight made from yellow sunstone. Lo Ming's robe was red with the design of a dragon made from bright shiny rubies and pearls. Mary's robe were shades of blue turquoise with a design made of bright red turquoise of a river with mountains and sky. Rose's robe was the color of black Onyx with a design filled with planets and stars made of tiger eyes and red jasper.

The men had their clothing changed into robes. Nick's robe was sky blue in color with the design of a mountain that symbolized the direction: up made from blue topaz. Moses' robe was the color of green with a design of green plants and animals made from gold laced thread symbolizing the direction: down. Antonio's robe was the colors of black and white with a design of a sun made from yellow agate that symbolized: within, the place you are and will always be.

Great Wolf had on a robe the color of white with a design of symbols of the four elements: air, fire, water and earth made out of diamonds of the colors of brownish chocolate, blue, white, with the rarest of all diamonds: red diamonds.

Antonio recognized what this was at once. This is what is called The Sacred Bridge Ceremony that uses chakras. This is a very ancient ceremony that few people know that bridges two worlds; the one you can see and the one that is mystical. It is said you are born with the knowledge of this ceremony. It is passed down through generations to a select few.

Chakra is a vital energy center that resides in everyone's bodies not detectable by modern medicine. Ancient scripts state that great powers can be released by people with especially powerful chakras. Antonio knew that our group was made up of members with strong chakras. Each one of our group had one specific strong chakra part.

Chakras are based on parts of the body. Everyone has seven chakras. These are: Crown or top of the head, Brow or third eye, throat, heart, solar plexus, sacred or ovaries and prostate, and base or coccyx. Antonio knew why John had selected each member of our group. Each one of our group had an especially strong chakra. Another thing he remembered was that most cultures have some sort of chakra base throughout the world.

Antonio knew that if a group of strong chakras were used in this ceremony, the group could unleash mystical powers of unbelievable force. With four powerful women as a base, this would be even more powerful. The one thing that the group must have is an Akasha. An Akasha can combine and direct their powers into one force. That is why Great Wolf was so important. He was the only one here that was pure. The rest of them were not. Great Wolf was the Akasha.

If this was a true chakra ceremony, each member would know their part in the ceremony. One thing Antonio did know was that John was always more than what he seemed to be. To be able to select this group, he had to have the knowledge of the ancients.

As if by some unknown force of nature, everyone went to a specific place on the plateau. There was a circle with a raised platform in the middle. Each of the women went to a specific location on the circle. Mary went to a spot that was the direction of true north. Lo Ming went to a spot on the outer circle that was true east. Rose went to a spot that was true south, and June followed by taking a position of true west. The men took a place between the women in the circle. Moses took a lower space near the lower part of the circle. He represented the direction of low: the lower world. Nick took a place near the upper part of the circle. He represented the direction of up: the upper world. Antonio took a place on the circle between two women. He represented the direction within or the place you are or will always be. Antonio completed the circle wheel. Then Great Wolf went to the raised platform in the center of the circular wheel. From here if he was the Akasha, he could direct the energy that would free *The Book of Winter*.

Time would run out if we didn't get started soon. I opened the pouch that One Feather had given me. I had realized long ago that the marble puzzle pieces would not find the location of where the book was located. They were a diversion to purify each member of our group.

I took out a gemstone from the pouch. It was the gemstone that One Feather took from The Land of the Unspeakables when I was captured by them. It could locate anything that you asked it to find. That must have been the reason the Great Spirits had me captured by them. I was to take the stone to find the book. The gemstone was called The Stone of Discovery.

I held the Stone of Discovery tight in my hands. Pointing toward the sky, I twirled it around my head. "Stone of Discovery find where *The Book of Winter* lies," I yelled. I threw the stone into the sky above me. The stone traveled several feet above the top of the volcano. The Stone of Discovery glowed brightly. A beam of light shot from the stone. It landed several feet in front of Great Wolf. This was where Great Wolf would have to concentrate all the group's energy to lift the book out of the solid rock.

Nick called forth fire forming it in his hands. He lit several torches that were placed outside of the circle. Then he took out of his medicine bag some cedar chips and started a fire with them by Great Wolf. This was a sacred fire. I could see that the fire by Great Wolf was in the middle of an X formed inside the circle. I knew the ceremony was about to begin.

The storm was upon us now. Wind blew the flowing robes against the bodies of the participants. The robes outlined their bodies. Thunder roared, and lightning flashed overhead. I saw the four women at once raise their arms and hands and point toward the woman directly across from each other. In four different ancient languages, they shouted a chant singing it using an ancient mystical tune. They were drawing on the strength of the four corners of the world.

A large beam of light shot from each of the women with the energy color of their chakra into the sky above them: Yellow, Red, Turquoise, and Black. The men's chakra beamed other colors straight into the sky above: Purple, green and orange. Great Wolf took red and white diamonds into each of his raised arms and hands. Like a lightning rod, his gems pulled each of color beams of energy to him. He was slowly one by one, consuming the energy into his body. His body glowed with all the colors pulsating around and through his body.

He was truly the Akasha. His body became like a prism. It was turning all the colors of energy to one. A white beam pulsed from his hands. He put his hands together as one. A flow of energy of white, the strongest beam of all, that takes all the energy colors, flowed out of his stretched arms. Great Wolf directed this stream of white light at the spot on the rock floor that encased *The Book of Winter*. The sounds of rock breaking and cracking echoed throughout the plateau. The rock was turning red and dark blue. Inch by inch, the rock cracked and broke. Great Wolf was straining to hold on to the energy field. His eyes turned red with the flow of energy pulsating through his body.

I was watching carefully. Anything that would disturb this ceremony could be disastrous for all involved. I saw a figure in an orange hood point at Great Wolf. In his arms was a staff with a white crystal on top. He was aiming his staff at a large boulder on the other side of the rim of the volcano behind Great Wolf. Turning I took out a gemstone in my pocket. With all my strength, I threw the gemstone at the figure. As the figure was about to move the boulder with a beam of light from the crystal pointed staff, the gem hit him and exploded in a large cloud of smoke. Luckily, the explosion did not damage the rocks around the figure. It did not cause any one of our people to lose their concentration in flowing their energy to Great Wolf.

Great Wolf kept his focus on the spot where the book was encased in rock. A large rectangular crystal rose from the rock floor of the volcano. Inside it was a large book covered in dark leather with precious gems and stones. The book was glowing bright red. Great Wolf carefully motioned and drew the book toward him. It slowly moved toward him. When he could reach out and touch it, the crystal that encased the book exploded into a thousand grains of crystal dust. The book was finally in his hands. Everybody stopped their energy at once. I could see that the energy it took them had exhausted them. They all fell to the floor of the volcano to rest. Great Wolf had *The Book of Winter* in his hands. He sat down to rest. Nobody said a word.

The storm was getting stronger by the second. The thunder was so loud that the mountain trembled. Suddenly there was a blinding flash of lightning and a roaring loud clap of thunder. Antonio shouted out to everyone and to the world. In a language that was translated to everyone near and far, he said, **"Behold! *The Book of Winter*."**

The vision quest for my son, Great Wolf, was almost over. A figure in a hooded purple robe covered with diamonds that flashed with the lightning strikes from the storm appeared. The hooded figure walked toward Great Wolf. The figure pulled down the hood of the purple robe. Her face was dark red with lines of age. Her long white hair blew about in the wind. In her hand, she held a wooden staff with a large crystal on one end. The stormed suddenly stopped.

She spoke to us in a soft firm voice, "He who holds this book holds in their hands the powers of all that will come or has been. It was written in the stars that a brave young man would someday release this book from its prison. The legend, foretold many years ago, has been fulfilled. Only with the powers of this book could the great evil facing this world be conquered. This is not the end of his destiny. There are many trials ahead of him.

The Book of Winter in his hands is his completion of his vision quest. **The Keepers of the Yawi** have proven themselves. From now until you are no more, you will be always known as **The Keepers of the Yawi**. Remember your powers are greater together than as individuals. Like it or not in order to survive, you must work together. That is your destiny." In the robed woman's hands, she raised her staff in a circular motion. She moved her staff in a circle above her head. "I release all who have come here to this land. This Land of Nightmares will be no more."

We could hear a great cry of relief from thousands of souls who were trapped here. Everyone was being released to return to their homelands. This was good and bad. It meant both the good and evil souls were free. However, I knew one thing. We had the book and the power. We had to get the book to the Council of Elders. Great Wolf would have to carry the book to the Council. He was the only one pure enough to do that. The Council knew how to assess the book's power to strengthen the forces to keep out the evil from **The Land of the Eagle Feathers**. The Council and Great Wolf would be the only ones that could be trusted with the book.

There was only one thing left for us to do. We had to defeat **The Dark Ones** that stood between us and the Council. Wind started to blow around us. Time was short. The Volcano started to shake. Steam was coming out of the vents on each side of the top of the volcano. We had to get moving as fast as possible. I yelled one word, "Run."

Even though the ground was shaking, we made good time going down the trail to the horses. One Feather had the horses saddled. We mounted our horses and galloped down the trail toward our campsite. The volcano started to erupt. Boulders landed just behind us. We were only about a mile from the campsite before I felt it was safe to stop the horses and give them a rest. We dismounted and sat down on some large rocks. The storm was still brewing. The wind was starting to blow harder. I had hoped it had moved on, but it seemed to be coming back.

Great Wolf had put *The Book of Winter* into his backpack. He told everyone that nobody was allowed to examine the book. Antonio asked to see it. Great Wolf said that this was impossible. The backpack that he had put the book into would only allow White Elk to open it. Anyone that tried to open it without White Elk's permission would burn their hands. White Elk had put a special spell on the backpack. White Elk didn't trust anyone. The book contained too much knowledge and power for anyone to handle. It would be better in the hands of the Council and Great Wolf.

Great Wolf decided that he would have to show everyone here what he meant. Great Wolf asked Antonio to come over and touch the backpack. "Only touch the backpack for a very short time like a hot stove or you will get badly burned," he told Antonio.

Antonio walked over to the backpack. He slowly touched the backpack. Antonio was immediately knocked back like he was shocked. He looked at his left hand that touched the backpack. It was bright red. "I see and feel what you mean, Great Wolf. I suggest to all here not to try what I did. Even with my magic, I got a good burn and electric shock. Great Wolf, you can carry the book in your backpack anywhere you want," laughed Antonio holding his burned hand.

"I guess that I will take the backpack with me," said a voice from the brush across the trail from them. As we turned to see who said that, out walked Molden, the leader of the Unspeakables. "John, I see you have been successful in finding *The Book of Winter,*" said Molden with a smile. "All of you can't stop me from taking it. I am too powerful for that. I wanted David for the Stone of Discovery. I would have had him. Why did you trick me? I missed him because you warned him," said Molden angrily. "No, I asked Shanna to look after David. It was her job to protect David. I needed him to help find the book. She did her job well. Didn't she?" I smiled back at Molden.

Molden was getting angry. He took a step toward Great Wolf. "I wouldn't do that if I was you," said a voice behind him. Molden didn't have to turn around. He knew that voice. It was David's voice. "You were not expecting me, Molden," said David. "John is a fair man. He will give you back the Stone of Discovery. Then you can leave this place. If you try to turn around, I will finish you off once and for all. You can't fight all of us. Now promise that you will leave us and go home. I am not a man of great patience," said David.

Molden nodded his head. "Now, John throw him the Stone of Discovery so we can get to camp before this storm," David told me. I threw the stone to Molden. Molden caught it. "Until next time, John. We will meet again. I am surprised that David backed you up." David laughed at Molden. "There is one thing I will tell you. John is my son-in-law. The only one that messes with my family is me. Now go before I forget my manners and kill you." Molden vanished in a puff of smoke with the stone in his hands.

We arrived at the camp shortly. The storm arrived at the same time We didn't see the other horses. "Where is everybody including the horses?" asked Rose. Zan yelled at everyone to dismount and bring the horses toward him. Zan pointed toward a cave. "Get the horses and yourselves in that cave. You will be safe there with us. We have a meal fixed for all of you. We were getting worried after the volcano erupted.

As we got all the horses inside, the storm hit. Strong winds blew dust and small rocks around hitting everything in sight. Hail was next to come. The hailstones were the size of oranges. Finally, the rain came down in sheets while a dark fog covered everything outside. Zan, Red Bear and Red Sparrow took the horses to several horse stalls that had grass for them to eat. The lighting in this large cave was glowing gemstones. "June's parents fixed the meal. They are back in the cave about 100 feet from here," said Zan.

Antonio asked, "How did you do this?" Zan laughed, "I had a lot of help. You don't think you have the only powers here?"

"Get something to eat and get some rest. We will be leaving here first light in morning. I figure that with the help of these horses, we can make the entrance to this land by dark tomorrow. We do not have much time before the New Year. I will leave it up to the others to fill you in about what happened," I told everybody. I started to say something but was interrupted.

The old woman in the purple cloak and dress stood by the entrance to the cave. "I will take care of getting the proper dress for all of you. That ceremonial dress does not do well to travel back in. You all have done well. I did enjoy David's little scene with Molden." The old woman pointed at a bed in one of the stalls.

"John, I brought somebody to see you. Petunia ran over to me. I reached out and tried to pet her. That is the last thing I remember. I fell to the ground and fainted. David carried me over to the bed. "Petunia, John's mule, is the only one that can take care of John tonight. By the way, David, you must sleep in the stall next to John. You have a friend that will keep you company." Old Waco, his mule, ran over to David. David laughed. "I guess someone loves me. I don't know why? I will do as you say," David replied.

"You better, David. John saved your life many times over the years. It is the law of this land," she said. "Why would he do that?" asked David. "You said it yourself to Molden. He is your son-in-law. Only you and him can mess with family. Like it or not, he followed the rules. I made sure of that!" said the old woman.

"Who are you? asked David. "I am someone that knows better!" replied the old woman. "I am whoever you want me to be. I am that voice who speaks to your head and heart. The voice that guides you to do better. David, you can do better. You have heard me for a long time. I am the voice that made you come."

The old woman faded away. Her voice was heard one last time, "David, you and John, just need a little lesson in humility. The mules will teach you that. Mary has medicine for John. How the likes of you, David, could have someone as special as Mary is even beyond me?"

Chapter X
We Have the Book
Will we get back in time?

John woke up with his head hurting. The first thing he saw was Petunia. Old Petunia bent her neck down and licked John's bearded face. "Now Petunia, that's nice but not necessary," said John as he petted Petunia on her face.

"Don't they make a sight?" said Mary to David. "Yes, she has a crush on John. You better treat Petunia well. She might get jealous of you and bite you," said David. Just about then, Old Waco took his head and pushed David. "Now, Waco, I know that you like me. Here are some oats to eat. We will have some hard traveling to do today. Let's go and get some water to drink by the river. We will take Petunia with us. Mary needs to be alone with John," he told the mules. David took the mules by their reins and guided them to the river outside the cave.

Mary was very worried about John. His face was much paler than it should be. He looked like a ghost, being so white. "You need to get Rose. She knows some things about my condition. She can help me a little. At least, she can give me something to make me look more human than a ghost," said John.

Mary sat down on John's straw bed next to him. "I am very worried about you, John. You are weak. Your strength has not come back. I worry that you might die. Great Wolf, our son, would have a hard time dealing with that," she told me. "What about you, Mary? Would you have a hard time dealing with that also?" I asked.

Mary didn't reply right away. "I would. It may be that I have just got used to you being around. I don't know if I still love you like I once did. We have both changed so much. I was a young woman then. I am older now. I will say one thing. The memories I have of you and me in love are wonderful. They were of people long ago. I don't think we can be exactly like that again. Once the water has flowed by, the same water will not flow by again. It was a different time and place. I only know that I feel you are my responsibility to take care of, and you are my husband. I feel the husband part and wife part. I don't feel so much the lover part. I wish I could. Maybe someday, I will. I do want to try. I got to go and get Rose." She left before I could reply. I didn't know which was worse: dying or the pain in my heart.

We broke camp about an hour later. Red Bear said he knew a way around the river that had the dangerous wildlife in it. It would take a couple of more hours to get around it. He figured it would take us about a day and half to get back to what was the entrance to The Land of Nightmares.

I had them tie me on to the saddle of Petunia. I told Petunia to take good care of me. She nodded her head. She had done this many times in our long history together. She saved my life several times by carrying me back from being hurt. Mary traveled behind me in our single file line. David was the last one in line riding Old Waco.

Everything seemed to change about The Land of Nightmares. There were songbirds, eagles and harks flying along the high clouds. Everything sounded happy and relaxed. It was a peaceful land. The darkness that covered the land was gone. It was as if the land was free. Elk and deer herds grazed in the green grassy fields. In the distance, there were people waving at us. We waved back.

We met a young couple about dark. We asked them why they were still here and did not leave with the others. "We have been living here for many years. Like it or not, it is our home. It is written that one of you is with child. That child will become the caretaker of this land. She will make sure that this land is peaceful and safe. We have decided that we will wait for her to return. Many of us stayed for that reason. We hope to see you again. May the spirits be with you on your mission."

The young couple seemed to know it was Rose with child. The young woman asked if she could touch Rose's stomach and feel the child and bless it. Rose dismounted her horse. The young woman laughed as she felt Rose's stomach. "I would like you to feel my stomach. I just found out last night I am with child. It may sound silly but let's touch each other at the same time. Maybe they can communicate to each other. An old woman in a hooded purple cape told me to do that. She said it was written that your child and my child would become great friends and companions." Rose did not say anything. She did as the young woman asked.

"Yes, I could feel them both communicating to each other like they were talking," said Rose to the young woman. Zan said to the couple, "I have lived here for many years in this land. I never thought I would say this. I will be back some day with our child. She has a friend here. It is her right to see him. The old woman told me that many years ago. I just had a hard time believing her. Now, I do. May the great spirits be with you until we meet again." The young man asked, "How do you know our child will be a boy?" Zan looked into the couple's eyes, "Because it is written in the stars. I can read the stars. Destiny is a strange thing. May the spirits be kind to you."

Zan turned his horse back into the line. Rose had mounted her horse. The couple turned and walked toward their home. Rose asked Zan, "Why are there tears in your eyes?" Zan replied, "We must come back here as soon as our work is done with **The Dark Ones**. The young woman might die giving birth to her child. The stars told me that we might save her." Rose only said, "That is what we will do. It is our destiny. I will have it no other way." The only thing Zan said to Rose was, "Yes, dear."

Zan's sadness turned to hope. A smile formed on his face. His father's and mother's spirits were here. He knew that Rose's parents would come. They would want to be near their daughter. "Yes, the pregnant young woman would be alright with so many to help her and her child, " he thought.

It was nightfall when they set up the camp for the night. They let the horses roam the grassy field beside their campsite. Petunia and Old Waco would see that the horses wouldn't roam too far from camp.

After the evening meal, Great Wolf helped me to my tent with Mary. I could see he was very worried about me. I saw it in the faces of others. I just didn't have any strength left. My hair was completely white as was my beard. Every muscle in my body ached. Time was catching up with me. I could only think of one thing. I had to make it to the final battle with **The Dark Ones**. Mary laid down beside me. I was so cold. The warmth of her body helped. I drifted off to sleep. The dreams came flowing through my night's mind like water over a full dam.

Moses and Lo Ming were seated on a log by the campfire that Nick had built. Moses' father sat across from them. Moses asked his father what John was like so many years ago. His father answered, "We met one day in the Outback. He was riding a mule. I was in the middle of the desert. The first thing that struck me was his hat. My Grandfather had told me about a man that he had known many years ago that had done many great deeds of bravery. His description of that man fit him perfectly.

I asked the man on the mule what his name was. He said John. He has never told me his last name. Well, I asked him about the mule he was riding. I laughed when he told me that her name was Petunia. Petunia took a liking to me right away. She licked my face and nodded to John. John smiled and said, "I have got the right man. Petunia just told me that by nodding."

John told me that he needed my help. My grandfather had told him that his grandson was a great warrior and a good man. I must save a land faraway from here. I need a man that I can trust with my life. Your grandfather told me that you are such a man. He also told me that your wife is such a woman.

John dismounted from Petunia. It was getting late, so we made camp. He fixed me a plate of beans and cornbread. I remember it like it was yesterday. The night was much like it was tonight. The stars were bright as shiny diamonds in the dark night sky. He told me stories about my grandfather and him fighting together.

He gave me this. Moses' father pointed to his wedding ring. Your mother has the exact same ring. He said my grandfather wanted me to have them. He said that my grandfather and grandmother wanted to give them to me and your mother."

Moses asked, "How did John get them?" "John told me that one night they came to him in a dream. They said that they didn't need them in the afterlife. They wanted him to take them to me and my wife. John said that when he woke up. The two rings were by the side of his bedroll. John said he never asked why. He just came by to give them to me. Just think he traveled with Petunia over thousands of miles into the worst desert of the Outback to give them to me.

That's how I came to know John. Your mother and I have been with him for many years and fought many battles with him. He has been my greatest friend. He died to protect your mother. I owe him that. You owe him that. I will tell you more stories later. I am tired and need some sleep.

Lo Ming, my wife told me how great a warrior you are. I am glad to meet you. My son is a fortunate man to have a beautiful and strong woman by his side or should I say you are lucky to have such a man by your side," Moses's father said with a smile that lit up his face.

It was about midnight when Mary felt the tent move. She got up to see who or what was doing that. She quickly found out when she opened the tent's flap. Petunia and Old Waco were biting the tent and shaking it. The two mules were saddled. Standing by Petunia and Old Waco were Great Wolf and Moses' father.

"I have come to get John. My grandfather once told me about a time that John was dying after a great battle from his wounds.   I remember what the old woman in purple dress said. She said Petunia was what John needed in the stable in the cave. She also said to David he needed Old Waco.

Tonight, my grandfather visited me in my dreams. He told me that June, Lo Ming, Rose and you must take the two mules to the middle of the grassy pasture. John must be on Petunia. Each of you must be at the four corners of the compass. You must point your eagle feathers toward Father Sky and Grandfather Sun. Great Wolf must beat on his drum four times."

Out of the shadows came Lo Ming, June and Rose to join them. Moses' father petted Petunia. "There are two other things I must say before you go. Angela will be joining you. She will be riding Old Waco. Petunia might die from this to save John. It is up to Angela and Old Waco to save Petunia. It appears that Angela is more than what she seems."

 "What is the other thing we should know?" asked Lo Ming. Moses' father took a minute to speak. "Angela and Old Waco might die saving Petunia and John." A voice from the dark said, "I owe John that much. We once rode together. I rode Old Waco. John rode Petunia. We fought many battles together. John never told you that Old Waco is my mule. It's a long story. I hope to tell you about it someday." Antonio was by her side. He kissed her goodbye. He walked away in silence to sit by the campfire.

Moses came. He went into the tent. He took John into his arms. He carried him out putting John on Petunia. John had enough strength to sit in the saddle. Angela mounted Old Waco. She patted Old Waco's neck. Old Waco's eyes lit up. "If I survive this, I am taking Old Waco back. David will take my horse. He doesn't deserve Old Waco. It took John a long time to convince me to let David ride him. Let's go and save John, Petunia! It is what it is," said Angela.

Mary went in and got her eagle feather. Moses, Great Wolf and Moses' father went over to join Antonio by the campfire. Great Wolf asked Antonio, "Who is Angela besides White Elk's daughter?" David replied out of the darkness as he sat down beside them. "I will tell you that. I know more about her than anyone here, even Antonio. She is older than she looks. I think you all deserve to know who is really is, especially Antonio." Antonio looked at David, "I don't care what you know David. I will listen. I know more than what you think. Go ahead, I will love her any way, no matter what you have to say."

Angela was followed by the women. Angela was dressed in white buckskins with purple gems. In the middle of the grassy field she stopped. Angela pointed to the four other women. She placed each of them at the true directions. Each one was at the four directions of the compass. Petunia knew what to do. Petunia moved to the middle of the four directions. Old Waco moved outside of them.

Angela directed the group, "Do as I say! Each of you point your feathers toward the sky. No matter what happens, don't

290

move.   Don't look at me or anything or anyone! Concentrate on all your energy. Rose, I will give you another eagle feather for your child. She will join in. You will hold two feathers. Point one to the moon and the other feather towards Mother Earth. When this is over, all of you will be exhausted. Just sit down where you are and rest. Rose, your daughter will be alright. June, your wolf, Midnight, will join us. This is a woman's thing. We bring life into the world. We will bring John back to life. He will be himself until his time is over. Then only the Great Spirits can save him after the New Year."

Angela stood in her saddle. She took two eagle feathers out of her dress top. "Point your eagle feathers toward the sky and Rose you know what to do. Every one of you must believe. Close your eyes and concentrate. Do not open your eyes. This will take several minutes. I will tell you when to open them. Do not touch me or any of the mules until this is over, even if we are dying."

Angela took two long breaths. "We pray to you. We need the help of all brave pony warriors. A brave warrior is dying. He needs your strength. His energy is gone. He is a great warrior. I have ridden beside him in many great battles. I have sung his deeds by many campfires. I will give my life for my fellow dog soldier and warrior. I will ride with him one last time if you choose. I would follow him to the depths of the earth or to the mightiest star above. I will follow him into death. We warriors are here tonight to ask you to save him for one last battle. I and all who are here have rode with him. They ask the same."

Midnight howled at the night's sky. A big dark cloud formed above them. Many painted warriors on their horses filled the sky. "Little Elk, daughter of White Elk, you come to us with your prayers. It is true that you rode with him. Are you willing to give your life for him? Is his mount willing to die with him? Is your mount willing to die with him?"

"I am Little Elk, daughter of White Elk. I come before you. I am mounted on Waco, my war horse. My humble request is that we die with him or live to ride to war one last time. That is as it should be. We are warriors. We are one in the same. It is as it shall be. No warrior should die alone. So be it! It is in your hands. We will be judged by you. I, Little Elk, request only one thing. Let our mounts live. They have been loyal. They deserve more than us."

All the eagle feathers shot beams of light into the sky at once. Angela directed her two feathers to move the beams of light into one. She directed the beams down toward John and Petunia. It took all her strength to focus the beams at John. Midnight howled as loud as she could. In the distance, four drumbeats could be heard from Great Wolf's drums. A great flash blinded everything.

Little Elk looked at John and Petunia. They laid in the middle of them. Little Elk guided Old Waco toward them. She dismounted Old Waco. Waco touched Petunia on her head. Little Elk touched John. "It is as it is. Warriors do not deserve to die alone," she said. "You can open your eyes and witness what is to come."

When everyone opened their eyes, they saw John and Little Elk lying together on the ground. Little Elk had John's right hand in hers. Petunia and Old Waco were on the ground together with each of their necks touching.

A thunderous voice spoke from the sky above. "We have witnessed this ceremony. John and Little Elk have shown that their warrior blood is strong. Only warriors that have rode together would risk their lives for each other. Their mounts are loyal. They are legends in our skies. Their warriors' songs have been sung around our campfires. Their song of death would be great. We have witnessed their deeds. Their warrior death songs are not over. So be it! What will be will be. One more battle it will be. Live and go to fight together as one warrior with another. Rise and mount your mounts and ride together one more time. Only the Great Spirits will allow you both to live after the New Year. You rode together. You will die together. It is as it was!"

Petunia and Old Waco slowly got to their feet. They moved over and shook John and Little Elk. John stood up steadying his feet under him. "Little Elk, why did you risk your life for me?" John bent over Little Elk. She opened her eyes. "We rode together many years to many far places. I have always cared for you like a sister to her brother. I once was angry and hurt, but Antonio told me you saved my life.

We were always great warriors together. If you were to die, I would not be the same. I would rather be whole then to miss a part of me. It is as it was."

Raven and Benita were making final preparations for taking their 300 men army of mercenaries to **The Land of the Eagle Feathers**. This was to be the final battle for that land. Raven was a little worried. Not knowing what David was doing in the land was concerning her. If David would get his hands on *The Book of Winter*, he would be very powerful. There would be no way Raven could ever get her power back with **The Dark Ones** and **The Omen**. Ever since David had seized power, all Raven could think of was getting back her position. She resented that David had put Benita in charge. Even though Benita and Raven had been lovers for many years, it was difficult for Raven not to be dominate over Benita. Raven was always the one that dominated their relationship. Raven was wondering about her future. After all, David was married to Benita. If anything was to happen to David, Benita would oversee the whole business empire. Maybe, Benita wouldn't need her anymore.

Raven liked Shanna. Shanna had done some work for Raven in the past. Raven didn't really mind if Shanna had spoiled Raven's plot to kill off several of the group that followed John. If Raven played it right, she had a plan to take *The Book of Winter* for herself and take over everything. Raven had to get *The Book of Winter.* Shanna was the key.

In a few days, Shanna would be leading **The Dark One's Army** with Benita and Raven in charge. She had noticed that Raven was paying more attention to her. Shanna knew that Raven never did anything without a motive. Shanna would play along. Shanna didn't know how this would all end. She would play everyone against the middle. That way she should survive. There was only one thing that would matter. She would do anything to save Nick. In six days, the final battle for **The Land of the Eagle Feathers** would begin.

Red Bear had led the group to the former entrance of The Land of Nightmares. It was midday. The weather had turned warm. All the snow had melted since they had left there. The bison herd was there waiting for them. John was gaining his strength back. He told everyone that they should be back to the Valley of Death in two days. He had Moses tell the bison that they should come along with them. If they wanted to keep **The Land of the Eagle Feathers** away from evil, they needed to help.

After a quick lunch, Red Bear and David led the group back. They were followed by the bison. A large herd of elk followed them. Moses and Lo Ming were left behind. "Why is Moses and Lo Ming not with us?" asked Great Wolf. John answered, "Moses is to gather all the animals he can and lead them back to the valley to join us. This means the bears, wolverines, wolves, coyotes, birds, any animal that could help us including snakes. The animals have more to lose than even us. It is about time they join us in this fight for survival of this land. It is their land as well as anyone's."

 I told everyone that they needed to sct up camp before dark. There would be a meeting for everyone in the large tent for all the leaders tonight. The meeting was to go over the plans for the battle to come. I needed to meet with a few of tribe leaders about when the meeting would start. David asked, "How did all these people get into this land?" I replied, "The Red Woman, your wife, let them in through the North Pass. It was easy. The force that keeps the evil out of this land is so weak that about anyone with some powers can walk in here."

David looked upset. "What keeps everyone else from doing the same?' asked David. "It is up to Shanna, Rico and the old man to play along like the force fields are still there. Shanna and Rico should be at the tunnel with the **Dark Ones** just about now. Shanna is to lead your army through the most rugged terrain. Shanna is to wear down your army before we meet them in this valley.

I gave her a map to follow. They will be very tired traveling the hills and swamps to get here in three days. It's all part of my plan. Don't worry, Shanna will tell Raven and Benita that they need to take the long way. She will tell them she had overheard me say that I have set up booby-traps on the main trail here," I replied.

As John and David were talking, Rico was deciphering the words to the tunnel entrance to **The Land of the Eagle Feathers.** Behind Rico were 300 well armored warriors. They wore black armor and carried swords, crossbows, lances and shields. They had one hundred war horses that had armor shields on their front and sides. Shanna would have laughed at the weapons and armor if she didn't know these soldiers were masters of the ancient art of fighting before guns were invented. Modern weapons were not allowed in **The Land of the Eagle Feathers,** only swords and shields or other medieval weapons.

Rico was not happy about coming along on this adventure. Shanna didn't have any choice. Antonio had said Rico was the only one that could decipher the words to make the tunnel open. The other reason Rico came was to get his prized painting back. Antonio had promised to give his priceless painting back if he helped.

Rico liked playing the part of a helpless museum director. It was a good place to meet rich lovely women. Rico knew how to deal with the outdoors. He was once in the special forces in Italy many years ago. That is where John had recruited him to help him in Houston. John had given him enough jewels and diamonds to literally buy the museum. Rico would have stolen the treasure anyway. Still Rico wanted his painting back. It was worth millions.

Rico didn't disappoint Shanna. He acted like it was difficult to decipher the words. He made a great show of it. Also, he made it known that he was not one to like being in the outdoors. He told everyone that his idea of roughing it was a Holiday Inn. This made even Raven laugh.

Shanna had warned that taking horses would be difficult to travel to the valley for battle. Raven and Benita didn't like to walk that much if they could ride. So far everything was going as planned. Shanna smiled when they got through the tunnel. It was pouring rain. The ground was muddy and slippery. She knew that it would be difficult to walk with all the equipment and rations that the soldiers were carrying. The back of their column would be walking in a mud pit after so many horses and soldiers walked over it before them.

Shanna decided not to ride her horse. She would walk most of the way. It was very dangerous to ride horses in this mud. Rico laughed to himself. He could guess why John had chosen this trail. He had seen John use the same tactic in a war in Hungry and Poland. Rico knew that the soldiers and horses would be exhausted within three days, especially as hard as Raven and Benita would be pushing them.

Shanna had to admit David's army was very well disciplined. There were 300 in total. One hundred men were archers with crossbows and swords. They were in the front of the others. The next group were one hundred men in full battle gear. They carried swords, spears and shields. The final group were one hundred men on horses. They carried lances and long swords. All the soldiers wore black chain linked armor and helmets. Flags were carried in each section to give orders if needed.

Rico whispered to Shanna, "You would think we were actors in a large-scale movie about the middle ages. These soldiers and their horses are magnificent." Shanna replied back to Rico, "There is one thing different from that. These soldiers are killers. I have tangled with them before. They are professionals at killing. They like using ancient weapons. I once asked them why they did this? Their reply was that they liked the closeness of death. They liked to feel the blood of their enemies on their weapons and bodies. Most of them wished they were born centuries ago."

On the other side of the land, we were getting ready to eat. Nick came over to me. "John, our food supply is almost gone." I told Nick and Zan to dig by a big boulder. "You will find plenty of food by that boulder. It is where I told One Feather to bury large amounts of dried fruit and grain. There is that special protein meal that tastes like meat there too. The other people here have brought their own food. We will have enough food until the end of this battle. Then it may not matter."

I met with several of the leaders. They said that the preparations for the coming battle were almost complete. They did as I instructed. They didn't understand why I wanted things laid out the way I did. "You will find out our plans tonight. You may not like it. It is the only way to end this fight. We will start the meeting when the moon is high. Bring as many people as you can to the meeting. They will be able to hear what is said outside the tent."

Nick had fixed a good meal for everyone. I told them they would need to come to the meeting with me. I would need to have them back up what I would be saying. Rose asked, "Why do we need to back you up?" I replied, "You will know why as soon as you hear my battle plans."

The moon was high in the sky when we entered the large tent. There were over 120 warriors there from the tribes. Big Daddy Crawfish and Sheba had brought 20 or so powerful wizards and Voodoo Priests. All these just fit under the large tent. I knew we would be outnumbered by **The Dark One's Army**. I guess two to one was not so bad.

The Red Woman, Great Elder and White Elk were on a small podium. I joined them with Night Panther. The Red Woman welcomed the tribes and other guests. "It is with great warmth and pride to see all of you once again. You know the importance of the coming days. We will be meeting the evil that has stalked this land for many years. In a few days, it will be the New Year in this land. It is written that on that day the final battle for this land will decide our fate. Great Wolf has *The Book of Winter.* If we win the battle, Great Wolf will take the book to be encased in a special chamber to power our land to keep out all intruders. We will finally be safe. The land will finally be safe. We will welcome any and all of you if you want to stay and live in this land. You and your families have earned that right by being here. John and **The Keepers of the Yawi** have done what was once considered impossible. Now, we must do the same."

I got up to speak, "Most of you know me. My name is John. I have fought by your side many times. I have led you to victory. I did not do a good job. Victory in battle has been costly to you and my friends. Many have died on both sides of this war. It is time to finish this war.

The only way to finish this war is to turn the enemy into something else. I have fought many battles through the many circles of the sun. I have won, and I have lost. I have seen much bloodshed. We all have scars from battle. I can only tell you what I have come to know. Bloodshed only gets you more bloodshed.

If we keep doing the same thing, we will be fighting this war for generations to come. I am tired. My days may be numbered. The spirits of this land are tired. They are wondering if this land is worth the cost.

This land is a gift. It is what and shall be, not what has been. In this land, your culture lives and grows each day. Without this land, your culture will die. It will be like the dead leaves in fall. The leaves will fall from the trees. They were once beautiful in colors. Then the leaves turn brown and become dust. The winter winds blow the dust and cover them in white snow.

The spirits have taught me many things. My travels have taught me many things. The wolves howl at the moon. The eagles fly to the heavens carrying messages to the great spirits. Children play and learn from their elders. Life is a cycle of circles of life. It is written that many will come after we are dust in the winds of time. Please listen to my words of wisdom. I will give you a way to stop this.

I will not let my child and loved ones live in fear and worry. If this is my last battle, I will make it your last battle. It is a different type of battle. It is a battle for your souls and the ones that bring evil here.

I have killed my last warrior in this land. You will have killed your last warrior in this land. When you kill, you make more enemies. For every warrior you kill, ten will spring up to avenge their dead. You have seen it in your own eyes. Bloodshed only gives you more bloodshed. Battle only brings you more battles. The cycle goes on and on until nothing or nobody is left to hear the death songs around the campfires.

We will fight the last battle without killing anyone. We will change the evil that comes here. We will be victorious not because we killed our enemy. We will be victorious because we changed our enemy. We know the light of our cultures. We do not need to live in the darkness anymore.

We will battle the enemy with forgiveness, not hate. We will battle our enemy with goodness, not evil. We will battle our enemy with understanding. We will battle their minds with light, not darkness. If one enemy is killed, we will lose. If one of ours dies, we will lose. It takes the greatest warriors to win a battle without killing one enemy.

The brush you circled the Valley of Death with, will be a trap. We will light it. The heat from the fire will make the soldiers drop their armor. Great medicine has been gathered that will be put on the fires. The smoke will cause the soldiers to fall and listen to our songs and visions of the future.

In the next two days, all the large animals and birds will come to help. They will surround the circle of fire. The bison, the large bears, the wolves, the coyotes, the elk, the wolverines, the mountain lions, the wild horses from the far reaches of this land and the snakes will come. The soldiers will be told not to kill any animals. If they do, the animals will seek revenge by killing all of them. This land is as much as for the animals around us as we are to the land.

I know what I say is not what you think a true warrior is. Many of you have counted coup on an enemy. It is the highest bravery to touch an enemy and not kill them. We will be counting coup on our enemy on New Year's Day.

At the end of the day, we will have not an enemy. Our enemy may not be our friends. They will never be our enemy again. They will leave this land without their weapons. They will never come back. David, our biggest enemy, is no more. He has come back home. He is willing to destroy his army. His family means more to him than his riches. We must all agree to my request and to my plan of redemption to our land and those that came before you. I ask your voice vote. If one of you cannot agree and speaks, then all will be lost forever. It must be all or nothing. Only your silence will be your vote. I will do as you wish." I sat down.

All was quiet in the tent. You could hear the wind in the trees. Nobody said a word as the wind blew at the tent sides. Night Panther stood up on the podium. He came to the front and said, "I once thought war was glorious. I am a warrior. I have done much killing. I have seen much bloodshed. I have seen the children cry. Mothers wept for their sons and daughters. I have fought for many seasons of the moon until I grow tired of it. I have many enemies that are strong. I have many friends and family that are gone.

If this is the only way, then I am for it. Nobody here is not a courageous warrior. We have seen many brave deeds in battle here. I ask, how many more battles will we fight until nothing is left of our tribes, and family but death? It is written in the stars that there will be one last battle where nobody dies. All that takes part will be legends in this land until the sun cools and dies. I will follow John. My people will follow John. All that will follow John will make your last war hoop in this land tonight." Night Panther held up his strong bow. As he stretched his right arm over his head, everyone yelled their loudest war hoops. This went on for several minutes until the Great Elder stood up to silence them.

The Great Elder silenced the group. He spoke as a wise man," What John has said he has learned through many generations. The Land of Nightmares is no more. It has been replaced as **The Land of Peace**.

In the spring, this valley has red flowers that grow and bloom in summer. Once only a few grew in this valley many circles of the sun ago. Now the valley is full of red blooms. There is no more room in this valley for more. Each bloom is a dead warrior. **The Land of the Eagle Feathers** needs peace for the children and their children to grow. We need no more red flowers. May the Great Spirits bless you in your battle in two days. May no more red flowers grow in this valley. May this valley be known as the **Valley of Life**, not death. I will go and await *The Book of Winter* on the mountaintop. If it does not come, this land will be no more. I salute my people." The Great Elder held both his arms high toward the sky. A flash of light blinded everyone. He was gone to the mountaintop. The meeting was over.

The Red Woman invited everyone to a feast for the rest of the night. It was like a big reunion. There was plenty of food available. This gave everyone a chance to meet those that they had not seen for many years to be reunited. I told everyone to enjoy themselves. We still had one more day to get ready for the final battle.

Big Daddy Crawfish and his wife Sheba sat by Rose and Zan eating. Big Daddy Crawfish was laughing and carrying on like there was no tomorrow. I could see Sheba elbowing him to try to control him. Sheba told her husband to shut up. Rose had an announcement to make. I was too far away from them to hear Rose's words. I didn't have to. The smile on Big Daddy Crawfish's face told me what Rose said. Big Daddy Crawfish slapped Zan on his back and gave Zan a big bearhug. Sheba hugged Rose. Rose had made her baby announcement to them.

"I see that you have brought back my son and future daughter-in-law in one piece," said Moses' mother to me. Her husband was holding her hand. "I knew if I didn't bring your husband back, you would have kicked my butt from here to Australia," I replied to her.

"I never worried about that. You always keep your word. I am worried about you. Lo Ming said you are very sick. Are you up to strength for this final battle?" asked Moses' mother.

"I can only hope. I am prepared to die. I have met my wife, Mary, and my son. I have had my fill of dying. If this is my last battle, so be it, I will win. There is one thing that you must promise me. If I don't make it, please take care of my wife and son," I told them. Moses' mother nodded her head. She turned and walked away. Her husband stood by me.

"Old friend, we have fought many great battles together all over the world for many years. Evil has a way of always returning. Evil is like a weed. You pull one out, and another takes its place. This is only one battle of what many may come tomorrow and in years to come," Moses' father said with sadness in his eyes.

"Yes, I know. It is written in the stars that there is a balance of evil and good. It is the way of the universe and the spirits of this life of ours. We can only try to keep the balance in check. Evil must never be allowed to come here again. Maybe for just once, we will win this one forever. Don't worry about me. Go and have a good time with your son and Lo Ming. Be happy, in two days, this will be all over for us," I told him.

"I am not one to give advice. You need to spend what little time you have left with your son and wife. I know that Mary is still trying to deal with this. I have seen her look at you. There is still some love left in her heart for you. Don't miss the chance to spend some precious time with her. Believe me, I have been there. Time is too precious to waste," Moses' father hugged me. He whispered in my ear, "I will always be your friend." He turned and left.

I did as Moses' father said. I found Mary and Great Wolf. We sat, ate and laughed with our friends. I was getting tired. I told them that I was going back to my tent to rest. Great Wolf said he wanted to spend the rest of the night outside looking at the stars. "I will go back to our tent with you. There will be no more talking tonight. We have some healing to do. It is something we have to do together," she said. I looked at Mary. I knew that something was different. I had heard her thoughts, not her voice. In this land, that meant only one thing. You only hear the thoughts of those that love you.

As we walked to our tent, the shooting stars filled the dark night's sky. Mary looked so lovely in the light of the stars. She reminded me of the young woman I knew so long ago. Mary interrupted my thoughts. "You look like that striking man that I knew long ago. I remember that butterfly that you once caught so carefully in your hands. You said that it was like our love, so precious and yet so frail. I took the butterfly and told you that butterflies are not so frail. They can travel hundreds and thousands of miles each year. I let it go. We watched it fly high into the air. It was so beautiful in flight. Tonight, I have to know." The only thing I could say back to her mind was, "We both need to know."

The rest of the night was a blur in time. The universe and all the planets and stars came to a stop for us. When I woke up in her arms, I knew. They say tattoos never lie. I remember how her butterfly tattoos shone bright against her dark skin. The energy of our love was still there. Her soft skin against mine was almost too much to bear.

She looked into my eyes. She pulled me to her. "Love is something I thought I had lost. I remember your touch from so long ago. I remember your love from so long ago. Look at the top of the tent, see what I see!" her mind said to me. I turned my head. Above us was a butterfly floating in the air. Mary opened the tent's lap and let it fly high into the morning's sky. That was a sign that we both knew the meaning of. Tears of joy came over us as we held each other in our arms. Moments like this come only once in your life, if you are lucky. My thoughts said that I must be the luckiest man alive. Mary interrupted my thoughts as she started to make love to me again, "No, we are the luckiest couple in the world."

Everyone was busy with their assignments. It was late afternoon when we heard **The Dark One's Army** march to the other end of the valley to camp for the night. Their war drums echoed down through the valley. We watched as they formed battle formations. David had taught them well. Their armor and horses looked magnificent in the bright afternoon sun. It was their way of showing us that they were ready for battle. Benita and Raven knew the rules. The battle would start tomorrow at sunrise. Benita had the army pitch camp. This army was a well-oiled machine.

Moses had been busy moving the animals into the woods around the valley. Nobody would expect the thousands of animals hiding in the dense forest of evergreens. As night fell, Nick slipped out of camp toward **The Dark One's Army**. He found Shanna waiting beside the little pond at the end of the valley.

Nick checked to see if anybody was around. When she signed with her hands that she was alone, he ran and caught Shanna in his arms. She kissed him passionately. They fell to the dry grassy ground together. "Don't worry, Benita and Raven know I am here with you. They will not disturb us. They want to find out what you know about John's battle plans. I told them that I would try and talk you into coming with us," Shanna whispered to him. Nick answered, "I will tell you what David told me to tell you. There are about 150 members of John's army. He has about 120 braves and 30 other people with him. David is acting like he is on John's side. He plans to betray John and the others when you meet before the battle in the middle of the valley. David wants to know if you brought the Omen's small army."

Shanna replied, "Yes, Rico led them here. They are back behind us about a mile away hidden in the dark green forest.

With them are **The Omen's Council**, Raven brought them into this. I smell a trap for everyone. Something is very wrong about this whole set up. It seems that everyone is out for themselves. I just hope that John knows what he is doing."

"I only hope that David knows what he is doing. I don't trust him. I agree with you. It appears that the scorpions are acting like scorpions. No matter what, we will need to protect ourselves. Hell is coming tomorrow morning. We cannot stop it. I do know one thing. If we don't make love, Benita and Raven will know something is up. I know that they are watching us by that tree about 100 feet from us," Nick said softly.

"Why do you think that I picked a warm spring to meet?" asked Shanna with a smile. "Remember, Shanna, we have to make this convincing for our audience." laughed Nick. Shanna got up. She pulled Nick close to her. Before Nick knew it, Shanna had thrown him into the warm spring. "What was that for?" shouted Nick. Shanna smiled, "We both need a warm bath to start. I have brought my favorite soap and oils. I hope you are up for it." Nick started stripping off his wet clothes. Shanna looked at his muscular wet body. She whistled, "I can surely see that you are up for it."

Chapter XI
The Final Battle
What really is John's plan?

Mary woke up. She looked over to where I was sleeping. She discovered that I was getting dressed. "Where are you going, John?" she asked. "I must meet the young woman on the painted pony," I replied. "Why?' she asked. "Things are going from bad to worse. I cannot control it. I want you to remember one thing. Things in this land are not always what they seem. No matter what happens in the morning, everything is going to be alright. Tell our son to run to the top of the mountain if anything goes wrong!

He must put *The Book of Winter* into its proper place to stop this madness once and for all. White Elk will show him what to do. That is all I can tell you. You must trust me. It is the only way to save all of us," I told her as I started out of the tent. "I love you and our son. Please do as I say! It is the last wish I have," I turned and bent down and gave Mary a passionate kiss.

Mary watched me leave the tent. She was very worried. That kiss told her many things. She knew that it was a goodbye kiss. It was a kiss that soldiers gave their wives or girlfriends when they knew that it might be the last one. Mary would do what I had asked. She would tell her son what he was supposed to do early in the morning.

I walked up the hill behind our encampment. The stars were still bright in the night's sky. I could hear the young woman's pony in the distance on the top of the hill. When I reached the top of the hill, I saw her mounted on her pony. "Well John, I am here as you requested," she said with a little hint of anger in her voice.

"I am grateful that you came. I know that you and the other Great Spirits of this land have reason to be angry. As I told you, I am not going to be the same as I was before," I told her. The young woman looked down at me from her pony, "Yes, you told me that. We don't trust what you are doing. You have a plan. We have been watching you. We don't like what we are seeing. What you are setting in motion may not be able to be reversed. If you are going to do what we think, it could destroy everything including this land."

"I have to laugh. I am a man that is half dead. Today is my last day to be alive. That makes me a very dangerous man. I have nothing to lose. Everyone else here, including you and

307

the Great Spirits, are worried about existing another day." I replied to her.

"You think the Old Man will help you. What about your wife, son and the others?" she asked. "If I don't finish it now, I will not be around to save them later. It's all or nothing. I am tired of the killing. When I die, I will know that I did everything possible to save this land. You can tell the High Council of Great Spirits one thing: **I am doing this my way!** I will die as I lived: a free man. Only the soul of **The Land of the Eagle Feathers** can stop me!" I stated back to her in an angry voice.

"So that is it! You are counting on the land to react like it did before. You are much more cunning than anyone thought. You would take the chance of killing everyone to stop the killing. I have been loyal to you for many circles of the sun, John. You have gained much knowledge and wisdom. I tried to change the Great Spirits' minds, but I was overruled. You deserved better. No matter what happens, I want to let you know I agree. It was an honor to know you, John," she softly whispered. Her voice was always like the warm wind on a summer's day that touched your cheek. "I will miss her," I thought to myself.

I smiled back at her, "It was an honor to know you. I respect you and all that you have done for me." The young woman smiled back at me. "Good luck, John. We will meet again. Fate is a strange friend of yours," she said as she turned her pony to ride away. I watched her ride into the darkness. I saw something that I had never seen. She had a wicked smile on her beautiful face. I knew she would enjoy giving my message to the Great Spirits.

The weather was warm for this time of year. The sunrise was just beginning as I arrived back at the encampment. Nick and Rose had prepared breakfast. Corncakes with blackberry preserves and fried eggs were on the menu. I had to admit they could take the simplest ingredients and make it taste better than the best restaurants in Paris. I never cared for the French style pancakes anyway.

I ate with our group. Mary and my son had waited for me to eat with them. I sat down beside them. We ate in silence. The wind was blowing a warm southernly breeze across the valley.

I summoned **The Keepers of the Yawi**. I told **The Keepers of the Yawi** to be ready in three hours. We will meet at the head of the valley. You are to ride your horses with me to meet **The Dark One's Army**. "Wear what you want to be remembered by, it is possible that things could go wrong. We are dealing with **The Dark Ones** and **The Omen.** Anything can happen.

One Feather, you are to stay by Great Wolf. If things get out of hand, you are to make sure that Great Wolf makes it to the mountaintop to give the book to White Elk. That would stop any madness. It just might save all our lives."

I pointed to David. "David, I trust you to take charge if I die today. It is up to you to save this land. It has been written in the sands of time that my greatest enemy will take my place. I don't know what exactly that means. I only know what I have been told by the Great Spirits."

I sent word for everyone to come for a final meeting. When they arrived, I stood up to speak. "You all know what to do. We have planned this well. As the saying goes: It is a good day to die. I will live until sunset. Don't cry for me! I am a warrior. I have lived long. I will die proud of all who rode with me. No matter what happens, I have loved you all. Today is that day. We are dealing with our enemy. Many things can happen both good and bad today. If things turn bad, you must protect each other. Look at the bright sunrise that meets us, it is a sign." I took off my hat. I waved it for all to see. I raised both of my arms toward the sky. "I salute you all. Now go and take your positions! May the Great Spirits be with you!" The whole camp erupted into three final war whoops. The whole valley echoed back.

About 150 of our group left to go to their positions. It would take them about three hours to get around the valley to their positions. Moses had hidden **The Land of the Eagle Feathers'** animals in the dark forests at the edges of the valley floor. No one could see the thousands of animals surrounding the valley. Moses had convinced the animals of what to do. It would be their day as well as ours.

The Dark One's Army started to line up at about 8 o'clock. The sun was bright. Its warm rays shone down on the valley below. I sent for Nick. Nick, take this white flag and ride over to **The Dark Ones'.** You tell Benita we will meet them at noon instead of this morning to settle this. I will bring David with me and **The Keepers of the Yawi** for one final meeting to try to stop this. Don't argue with Benita or Raven! Just come back and give me their answer." Nick mounted his horse and nodded his head.

He rode to the middle of the valley with the white flag. Benita rode out with Shanna and Raven to meet him. Benita looked at Nick and asked, "Where is John's army? I thought we were supposed to start this morning." Nick replied, "John said that he wants you to think about this. He wants to meet you and discuss this at noon. He will bring David with him and his group. We have the book. What is your answer, Benita?"

Raven didn't like the change of plans. Benita knew that disappointing look on Raven's face. Benita replied, "We will wait. I will bring my men with me. We will meet in the middle of this field by the small cedar tree over there. I will wait for my husband, David. He is still in charge. I hope he is well." Nick looked at Shanna and back at Raven before answering. "Oh, he is very well. I can see why you married him. He is a strong leader. I can see why you miss him," smiled Nick as he looked quickly at Raven.

Nick looked at Shanna. Shanna was dressed for work. She had her throwing vest on full of sharp knives. She always wore black tight leather pants and a red loose see thru blouse. They said that if you saw her in that outfit someone was going to die. "Are you coming back with me, Shanna?" asked Nick. Shanna shook her head. "I like this side of the field better. The company is more like me. I think I fit in better over here. I hope you will change your mind. We have much to offer you. You know me, I don't like to lose to anyone. I will give you until we meet at noon to come over to us. If not, like a spider, I will kill my mate," laughed Shanna.

"I always knew that winning was more important to you than anything," Nick said to Shanna. Shanna laughed and replied, "No, it isn't! Money and staying alive are the most important things to me. It's a great shame to waste a man like you. You have been a great lover and friend. But as they say, this is not personal, it is only business, Nick."

Nick looked at Benita and Raven, "I will give John your answer. We will meet with you when the sun is straight up at noon. Benita, I ask only one favor. If I do not change sides, let Shanna and me fight it out to the death. If I die, I would like it at the hands of a lover not a stranger," Nick said looking at all three of them.

Nick turned his horse and rode back to the encampment to meet John. "Do you think he means what he said? said Raven. Shanna answered Raven, "Did you see what he had on? It is his old military Special Forces uniform. He knows what I am wearing means that I will probably kill someone today. I know what he is wearing means he will kill many people today. He came to send us a message. Never underestimate Nick, he is a cold-blooded killer. In fact, he likes killing."

"Well then, Shanna, we will give him his wish. You get to kill him. I have seen his kind before. He will kill you if he feels you betrayed him. You will not have any choice. I hope for your sake he changes sides," said Raven. "Don't worry, Raven. I have an edge. He loves me. He will hesitate a second before he kills me. That will be time enough for me to kill him. It was fun as long as it lasted," Shanna said with a wicked smile. Shanna was cold even by Raven's standards.

"Too bad, these two were made for each other. Maybe, I should get rid of Benita and take Shanna for a partner," Raven thought. Benita didn't like the look that Raven was giving Shanna. Benita had seen that look before. Raven had found someone more like her.

I watched as Nick crossed the field in front of me. We had two hours before the meeting was to take place. Antonio and Angela were busy with two teams of oxen pulling two old wooden wagons filled with bags of gold and precious gems. The soft dirt and mud made it difficult for the oxen to move the wagons. Moses signaled two of the biggest bison to get behind the wagons to help push them into the middle of the grassy field. It took them about an hour to place the wagons there.

The sun was drying the field out. Antonio couldn't believe it was getting so hot. Sweat was pouring from Angela and his face. He sat with Angela on top of one of the wagons. They could see that the heat was causing problems for the army of **The Dark Ones**. Many of their men had taken off their protective armor. "I can't believe it is so hot," said Angela. "Somehow, I think this is part of John's plan," said Antonio.

"I think so too. John never does anything without having an ace up his sleeve. He always tries to have an edge. He knows how **The Dark One's Army** fights. Their army always uses some type of protective clothing. If it gets much hotter, it will be very difficult for them to fight with any protective armor or clothing. They will get heat stroke or heat exhaustion in a few minutes of hand to hand combat," said Angela.

"Yes, the Americans beat the British in one of the battles of their Revolutionary War by that tactic. The poor British soldiers wore their hot red uniforms on a very hot day. The American commander had his soldiers wear only light shirts and no dress uniforms. Many of the British soldiers couldn't fight because of the heat. They fell in their ranks of heat stroke," said Antonio.

"How do you know so much about that?" said Angela. "You know me. I never missed a good fight. Besides the French were always willing to pay advisors to assist the colonists," answered Antonio. Angela laughed, "I never know whether to believe you or not. You do tell some very tall stories. Let's get back to the others. I need to change into something more revealing and get out of this hot black leather."

Antonio smiled, "I agree. You learned a lot from John. Your beauty always gave you an edge whether you faced a man or woman. I know I am distracted by you."   Antonio picked up one of the small bags. He opened it. He saw that one of the scouts for **The Dark Ones** had crawled up several yards away from them. Antonio dumped the contents of the bag on the ground.

The scout saw what was in the bag. The bright gems and gold coins spilled onto the ground just feet away from her. "Don't worry! We won't kill you. We have hundreds of these bags on these two wagons. I would say each bag is worth several hundreds of thousands of dollars. Here take a couple back to your friends. Tell your fellow soldiers that if they don't fight and leave, everyone will get a bag. If you fight, you might get one. You will have to live to spend it. I know the **Dark Ones'** leaders. Even if you win, they will take all of it for themselves. Are they worth dying for?" asked Antonio.

Angela threw several of the bags to the scout. The scout took the bags and crawled away.

Angela smiled saying, "Yes, John always has an edge. I think our work is done here. We need to get back. Within two hours, the word about the bags should be all over their camp. We will soon know if it has the desired effect on the other soldiers. Remember, they are mercenaries. They fight for money. There is only one other thing they like as much. Some of them just like a good fight." They jumped off the wagons, unhitched the oxen and led them back to camp.

David watched with me on top of the hill behind their camp. Nick rode up the hill and reported that the meeting in the middle of the field was agreed to. Nick rode back to the base of the hill to wait. David asked me, "Why do I think you have something else planned?"

I answered David, "Why should I trust you to do your part? I find it hard to believe that you want to destroy what you built. It would hard for anyone to give up the power you have. I know you started this to destroy the enemies of this land. I also feel that you have a plan of your own, David."

David paused for a few moments before answering. "Yes, you are right. I will find it hard to destroy everything that I had worked on for years. You know that I have destroyed many evil organizations that could have tried to take over **The Land of the Eagle Feathers** throughout the years. This protected the land in some ways. It also gave **The Omen** more power to be able to take over this land. You know that I could only do so much. Now, I have the power to somewhat control **The Dark Ones and The Omen.** You know that if **The Dark Ones and The Omen** are destroyed, others will take their place. That is a problem without a solution."

I looked at David staring into his eyes. "Yes, you are right. We do have a problem. There has always been a balance of good and evil. That is how the whole world exists. I must

314

stop this war once and for all with **The Omen and The Dark Ones.** I will do that today. The rest is up to you," I told him.

David smiled. "I figured you had that in mind. John, you put me in almost an impossible position. I must protect this land and my family. You also know that I must remain in control of **The Omen and The Dark Ones.** *The Book of Winter* will give **The Land of the Eagle Feathers** power to keep everyone out for many years. There was one thing that you always knew. You needed someone to help keep the other evil powers at bay. That is why you never killed me when you had many chances. I always wondered why I was able to survive all those attempts on my life. I thought I was just lucky. It was you all the time. Wasn't it, John?"

"Believe what you want, David! I only have today. What you do after today is your business. David, you are a strong and ruthless man. You started this journey in life many years ago to save this land. Now, you can have it all. I will leave the rest for you. The only thing you must do is to finish what I started long ago. The only thing I ask of you is to protect our land, our people and our family," I asked him.

"I don't know how I will do it. What you are asking could cost me everything including my real wife and family," replied David. "It has always been your destiny to save this land. I am sorry that you will never get to fully enjoy living here. You will figure it out. I wished our lives could have been different. Fate has strange partners. Later today, you must go with the flow of the events. Act your part no matter what happens to me or the others. You know that things are not what they always seem to be. Just remember that you must trust me. It is time. Destiny awaits us today!" I assured him.

David thought about John's plan as they walked to the base of the hill. It was simple enough. The valley was surrounded by two streams with deep sides. John had hidden over 200

315

people to cover the whole valley at various places that would cover anyone in the valley with bows and arrows. To back the people up, Moses had hundreds if not thousands of various creatures from **The Land of the Eagle Feathers.** These creatures were large and dangerous. Herds of bison, elk, bears of all types, mountain lions, deer, wild horses, wolverines, skunks, bobcats and many others would fill in the gaps in the line. The most dangerous were the snakes. Moses even summoned his friends, the rattlesnakes. The warm temperatures allowed them to come. There were thousands of these creatures by the stream beds. In the air would be all types of birds from eagles to hawks and vultures besides owls and falcons to attack the invaders.

John had hoped that this show of force would make anyone think twice before attacking them. If that was not enough, John had 30 of the best shamans, warlocks, witches, voodoo priests and priestesses not to mention medicine men and other mystical people. These people could do about anything.

David knew that Raven had her plans. She would be bringing other soldiers more dangerous than Benita's. They would be accompanied by **The Council of Omens**. These were very dangerous people schooled in various types of magic.

With over 450 facing their less than 300, then it could be a blood bath if fighting broke out between the two sides. David knew that John's select special people could take care of **The Council of Omens. The Dark One's Army** of mercenaries was another thing. They were killers that like fighting and killing. Being outnumbered would be a big problem for John's group. David knew that John's warriors would easily win if the numbers were equal. That was not the case because of the additional soldiers. John was smart to include the wild animals. Those animals would even up the odds against them.

The snakes would be enough to scare the most hardened warrior.

The stage was set. It was about noon. The sun was high in the sky. Benita had assembled her army. They were in rows of twenty for the foot soldiers. The first four rows carried bows and arrows and swords. They were the archers. The next 8 rows were infantry carrying spears and swords besides shields. The final three rows were cavalry on horseback carrying spears and swords. All the men had heavy armor on to protect them.

As they came across the field, their drummers drummed a marching cadence. Everyone marched in step to the tempo of the drums. The flag carriers were on both ends of each row. The hot gentle breeze caused each flag to wave. David had to say he had trained these soldiers well. They looked magnificent in their black uniforms and shiny armor with their weapons at the ready. In front of the army were Shanna, Raven and Benita on their horses. When they had reached the mid-point of the valley by the small cedar tree, they came to a halt. Benita and Raven looked at the two wagons filled with gold and gem bags. David knew what they were thinking. They would win the battle and take all of it for themselves. They didn't care if anyone got hurt or killed.

John and David mounted their horses. John was on his white horse. David was on his black stallion. It was time to meet Benita and Raven in the field. David was dressed in black. His long black hair with streaks of gray gave him a very distinct look. A heavy gold necklace interspaced with precious gems and a large diamond hung against his black shirt. His black pants were worn with the legs inside his high black diamond snakeskin leather riding boots. David had that look of a powerful, dangerous man that nobody would want to challenge.

David looked at the other people who would accompany them to meet Benita and Raven. Mary rode up beside him. She had on a short white deerskin dress covered with gems. On her neck was a necklace of precious gems with a bald eagle feather hanging down between the dark skin of her breasts. She had white leather high topped moccasins on her feet. In her hands were her bow with a quiver of arrows on her back. Next to her was Nick. He had his black opts uniform on with two KA-BAR knives in his web belt. Nick's eyes got David's attention. Nick's eyes were killer eyes.

John was on the other side of David. David was surprised by what John was wearing. Instead of the Roman General uniform he usually wore, John had on his old union scout's uniform with his white cavalry hat with the faded seven on it. John's pants were blue uniform pants with fur mountain man boots. His shirt was red plaid under a light leather coat. Around John's neck was an Indian necklace of beads and turquoise carvings of butterflies and with a bald eagle in the center. In John's leather belt was a bowie knife.

Next to John were Lo Ming and Moses. Lo Ming had on a loose silk martial arts robe. It was bright red with a large dragon embroidered in gold and silver. She had her fighting stick in her hand and a sword in her black cloth belt. Moses looked the part of an Australian Outback guide. His brown leather vest hung on his bare chest. His brown canvas pants were tucked into his brown hunting boots. A whip and large hunting knife hung on his crocodile leather belt. His face and broad chest were painted with animal shapes and dots of various colored paints. On his head was a black Australian Bush hat with a headband that had a bald eagle feather in it. David noted that all **The Keepers of the Yawi** had a bald eagle feather somewhere on them.

On the other side of Nick were Antonio and Angela. Antonio was dressed in fine Italian leather pants and dark leather boots. His bright colorful expensive shirt was unbuttoned on the three top buttons. He had a broad red hat with a hatband with an eagle feather in it. On his side, he hung a fine Italian fencing sword with two jeweled draggers in his waist belt. His hands were covered with black fencing gloves. He looked like a sixteenth century nobleman. Antonio knew what David was thinking. "Yes, I was once a great Italian nobleman. If I die today, I want to die dressed in my best clothes. I would have worn my red coat, but it is too hot," Antonio said with smile.

Angela, riding next to Antonio, had on dark tight pants and black soft high-top moccasins. Her dark hair hung down her back with Indian braids and a headband with a bald eagle feather in it. She had a low cut tight backless black blouse embroidered with planets and stars. Her blouse showed off lots of her dark skin.

In her left hand was an Indian Lance lined with eagle feathers. On her right shoulder was an Indian buffalo shield covered with mystical paintings. What was interesting about the Indian lance was it did not have a spear point. Instead of a spear point, it had a large crystal on that end. Angela's father, White Elk, must have given that to her. She also carried a steel headed tomahawk hidden in back of her black leather belt. Under both of her eyes were two lines of black and red paint to protect her eyes from the glare of the sun.

June and Rose were on horses behind David and John. June was in her medicine woman's mystical dress. She had her bow and arrows as her weapons. Rose was in her mystic arts dress. Roses' low-cut purple blouse was covered with stars and planets. She had two bags of exploding beads tied to her waist belt.

I turned my white horse around to face them. "Rose, this is too dangerous for you and your baby. I want you to go back and join Great Wolf. Take Petunia with you for Great Wolf to use to ride up the backside mountain trail if things get too intense here. June is to go with you. Rose give your beads to Zan. He will take your place beside us. June, it is very important for all of you to get Great Wolf up to the top of the mountain to White Elk. No matter what happens, you must promise me that you will do that. Remember, no matter what happens, you must get Great Wolf to White Elk or all could be lost.

We lined up at our end of the valley. Before us was **The Dark One's Army** lined up in battle formation. There were 15 of us on horses with David and me in the middle of the line of horses. Following us on foot in a line behind us is our group of mystical, magician and medicine warriors. In this group were: Big Daddy Crawfish, Sheba, Red Bear, Red Sparrow, Nick's grandfather and grandmother, White Owl and several others prominent in the arts of illusion. There were 30 of them in all. **The Council of Omen** would recognize them as masters of the mystic arts and ancient arts. **The Council of Omen** would not want to fight with them. Many of our group were known as dangerous people to challenge.

I told this group to line up in front of us when we reached the middle of the field to meet with Raven and Benita. I reminded them that **The Council of Omen** would be here to greet them within 30 minutes after the meeting started. I could see by the expression on their faces they had been waiting for such a moment. There was no love for the Council. Many of our group had bad experiences with members of the Council for years, if not centuries. I only hoped that they could contain themselves from settling some old scores.

Raven and Benita with Shanna were waiting by the small cedar tree mounted on their horses. The sun was at high noon. The heat of the sun was getting almost unbearable. David looked at the first rows of the mercenaries. He could tell that the heat was bothering them. They did not hold their weapons at ready. It wouldn't be long before some of them would start dropping from the heat. John was right. Benita and Raven wouldn't think about the effect of the heat on their soldiers. They could only think of one thing: fight this last battle. Their greed would color all reason.

I stopped our line in front of Benita and Raven. "I see that we outnumber your followers, John," said Benita with a smile. David looked at them and replied, "John and I have reached an agreement. It would be foolish for us to fight over *The Book of Winter*. His people will fight to the last man. They see this as their final chance to be rid of us. They are very possessed with the idea of not giving up the book. The book is almost a religious relic to them."

"Then what do we get out of this if we leave? We did not come here for our health. What could be so important that you would make such an agreement?" an angry Raven shouted.

"We will receive one billion dollars in gold and jewels and priceless ancient relics such as the Sword of Alexander the Great. Everyone here will receive a bag of gold and gems worth hundreds of thousands of dollars if we do not fight. We will not have to pay out anything. We will be able to keep our mercenary army intact. See it as a business deal. We will make a huge profit in the long run. Doesn't it make sense to you?" smiled David with a wicked expression on his face.

Raven spoke, mocking David, "You are some leader. We could take that now without losing too many men and equipment. We outnumber John's followers. I see only a few people in front of us. We have many more coming. I brought the rest of our reserves including our powerful Council. Nobody can stand against their power." Raven gave a nod to one of the archers. They shot an arrow with a smoke bomb on it to signal for Raven's reserves to march into the valley.

"You see. David, I am more cunning than you. They should be here in about 10 minutes. I will take over after I kill you.

You are too weak to be the leader of us," laughed Raven. Benita turned to address Raven, "Raven, you are going too far. David is still the leader. He must have reasons for what he is doing. Give him a chance to speak, before this gets out of hand."

I walked my horse up to Raven's. I looked her in the eye saying, "Let's wait until your Council arrives. They may have different thoughts about this. Dying here gets you nothing. When they arrive in front of us, I will show you what you are facing. I think you may have a change of heart. Right now, I have ten of my best archers aiming at your heart. They will fire if I signal them. I told them it did not matter if some of us get killed. It would be a small price to pay to kill you, Raven. I am a dangerous man. I will be dead at the end of this day no matter what I do. How does it feel to face a dead man?"

Benita realized that her leadership was fading away if Raven got her way. "We will wait until the Council and our reserves get here. Besides, what do we have to lose? We will let the Council decide what to do. Our mercenaries still see David as their leader. We cannot chance them turning on us. They have already been promised bags of gold to not fight and leave. There is only one thing they are more afraid of than David. That is **The Council of Omen**," said Benita. So, we waited in the hot sun for the Council and reserves to arrive.

Benita, Raven and Shanna had noticed how much Mary had changed. Benita and Raven still recognized Mary. They knew her before her accident in the jungle. Shanna did not. If Nick had not informed her about Mary's change in appearance, Shanna would have never guessed it was her.

It did not surprise Benita that Mary changed back to her true self. Benita had worried for some time that this could happen. She had prepared for that to happen. **The Land of the Eagle Feathers** had the power to change Mary back. The little girl she helped raise was here before her. Mary did notice Benita looked troubled as she looked at her. Benita had the look of someone that had lost something that was precious to her.

Soon drums and bugles could be heard coming over the far hill behind Raven and Benita. David sent one of his mercenaries to send for the Council to come. It did not take long for all the Council to arrive on horseback. I counted sixteen of them.

David said to them, "I have made an agreement with John to not fight. We will receive over a billion dollars in gold and jewels plus many priceless relics for not fighting and leaving this land forever. On that hill behind me is *The Book of Winter*. I want it just as much as you do. We can fight and maybe obtain it. It will cost us men and equipment. It may even cost you your lives. I, for one, would like to be alive to live another day. This land has cost us too much in money and treasure. I figure we have only a 50 per cent chance of winning any battle against John's followers.

I risked my life to assist John and his followers to find the book. I want it as badly as you do. John has one thing on his side. His followers are fighting for their homeland. They do not care if they live or die. That makes his followers hard to beat in a battle. I will leave the decision up to you. I will lead our army to battle or we can take the treasure and leave. It is up to you."

One of the oldest Omen asked, "Why do you think we will not win such a battle? We have them outnumbered by many men. The members of the Omen here could take what little men John has."

"l am John. You know who I am. I don't lose battles. I have learned from the best generals and leaders throughout history." I stopped and took out an old cigar from my coat pocket and lit it. "Oh, this was a gift from one of my friends. They called him President Grant. He gave it to me for some missions I helped him with many years ago. You see the sword at my side. Lee gave that to me in Mexico before Grant. I have learned to fight. The greatest generals are who are known as Native Americans. I learned about tactics from Sitting Bull, Crazy Horse, Chief Joseph and Red Cloud to name a few."

"Get to the point," Raven shouted at me. "This land is sacred to the Indians and me. The first thing I will show you is what **The Council of Omen** will face in a battle with us." I motioned for the 30 men and women behind me to move to the front. "I brought a few of my friends to greet you. You know who they are? They can't wait to deal with you." David smiled he could see that **The Council** was taken back by who they saw in front of them. Nobody could have guessed they would be facing some of the best masters of the mystic arts. One of the Council said, "John has made his point about us. What about the fighting army?"

"You are surrounded by over 200 of the best archers and fighters in this world! Besides the group in front of you, they are called **The Keepers of the Yawi.** I imagine you know how tough they are." I told them.

Raven interrupted me by saying, "We still outnumber you by many times. We can take everything. I don't see why we should stop this battle." I looked at Raven and the others. I motioned for Moses to call out the creatures of the land. "These are who you should be afraid of just look at the movement near the streams. That is not grass blowing in the wind. It is thousands of rattlesnakes at my command. Look at the edge of the forest around us. You will see my reserve forces. Every dangerous creature in this land is here to protect their land. The bears, mountain lions, wolverines, wolves, wild boars and many others are waiting in the forest to attack. They will rip you and your army to sheds."

As if to make a point, all the animals started making loud ferocious cries. The echoes of their cries filled the valley. David could see the expression on the Omen's fearful faces. He could hear their thoughts. "We came to fight men. We did not come to fight poisonous snakes and other dangerous animals especially thousands of them."

"There is one more group of animals that you need to be aware. See those dark clouds over to the east behind you. Those dark spots are not storm clouds. They are the birds of this land. This is their land. There are all types of birds coming for you. You cannot shoot all these birds down. The eagles, vultures and hawks will cut you up. What they don't finish, the other birds will finish. Your bones will be picked clean. Your white bones will be all that is left of you," I hope I have made my point."

"John, this fight was supposed to be us versus your people. There was no mention about bringing into this fight all types of creatures," said Raven. "I wouldn't talk about what is fair or not, Raven. You brought in more than 300 warriors and **The Omen** besides. There is a small postscript in the passages about this battle that we were supposed to follow. It states that whoever does not follow the rules of engagement will suffer. Because we broke the rules, we will have to pay the price if someone starts the battle today.

You see, I will win either way. I have told my people to hold their fire no matter what happens. This means if you start anything, the land will rebel. If that happens, you will regret it. We all may regret it," I firmly stated to her.

"I don't believe you, John. You wouldn't put your family in danger," Benita pointed out. David finally spoke, "I believe him. John has become more unstable lately. He is fanatical about killing every last one of you. He would rather see both **The Dark Ones and The Omen** destroyed. He cannot bear the idea of us taking over this land. If we are destroyed, then there is nobody left to take over this land. He feels that some of his followers will live. He thinks it is better to start this land over than give it to us. He told me that he would rather get something than nothing. That is why I say to the Council. That it is better to get something than die for nothing. What does the Council say? You have seen what could happen."

Raven did not want to wait for the Council to decide. It was all or nothing for her. "David, you are too weak and afraid to be the Chairman of the Council. I declare my right to challenge you. I will make you pay. I won't kill you. I will hurt you more," Raven yelled out of her mind. Raven took out a knife and threw it at Mary. Benita knew what Raven was going to do. She moved her horse just in time to stop it. Raven's knife hit Benita instead. Benita fell off her horse with the knife sticking in her chest.

Raven jumped off her horse and ran to Benita. Raven was in a state of shock. Raven yelled out in the pain of losing her mate. The soldiers in back of the columns thought that was the signal to attack. Everything became confused. The columns rushed forward to attack. Everyone reacted, and the fighting began.

Arrows filled the air. John and David yelled for the Council and the other mystical people to destroy the arrows on both sides. Many of the ranks of **The Dark Ones** started attacking **The Keepers of the Yawi**. They knew that they were the most dangerous and best fighters that John had. John yelled for Mary to go to Great Wolf. Mary rode off toward the hill.

Nick had at least 10 soldiers attacking him. He jumped off his horse and took out both his KA-BAR combat knives. Even though he was outnumbered, he managed to kill at least 5 of them. One man that had gotten behind him was about to strike him with a spear when a knife hit him in the heart. Shanna jumped off her horse. She ran over to Nick to fight beside him. "This was not part of our plan," she yelled at him.

Nick yelled back, "I know. We can't fight all of them. There are too many even for us."

Antonio and Angela had dismounted their horses to fight. They had several men attacking them. Angela pointed at Shanna. "She saved my life. We must save them. It is a point of honor," Angela yelled to Antonio. Antonio nodded in agreement. They both cut their way to the side of Nick and Shanna.

Antonio yelled at Shanna and Nick, "You must get back and help protect Great Wolf and the others. Antonio said he saw several of Benita's men circling around the hill that June, One Feather and Rose were trying to protect Great Wolf. "He must survive to get the book to the mountaintop. Please protect our family, June and One Feather! We will cover you." Antonio and Angela fought as Nick and Shanna ran to the hill. As they looked back one last time, they saw Antonio fall with a spear point sticking out of his chest. Angela was still fighting to try to save him. An arrow had hit her in the back. She fell near Antonio.

The soldiers stopped. They looked at the two on the ground before them. They couldn't believe that these two had killed so many of them. They were dying from their wounds. They were truly great warriors. The soldiers would not inflict any more. They deserved to die together as great warriors should.

They watched as Angela crawled over to Antonio. "I have always loved you," she whispered. Antonio pulled Angela to him. "You are the most beautiful woman in the world. I regret ever leaving you. If only I knew about One Feather," he cried. "Don't regret anything. I knew you loved me. We just chose different paths," Angela said to him. Angela reached into her pocket. She pulled out a necklace with a ring on it. Antonio whispered to her, "I see you always kept it." Antonio reached out his hand. Angela could barely touch his hand with her hand that held the wedding ring. "You are still the most beautiful woman I ever met. I love you," he whispered to her. Both of their hands closed over each other's. In a few moments, their hands went limp. They died looking at each other. Even the darkest of hearts had been touched by what they had witnessed. The men surrounding Antonio and Angela dropped their weapons. They picked up Antonio and Angela and carried them off the field of battle to show their respect for them.

On the top of the sacred mountain, the old man and his dog watched the forces attacking each other. The old man looked at his dog saying, "We have no other choice. Both sides broke the rules, we must do as what is written. We must destroy both sides. That is the rules. We cannot stop it. John chose this, and David did not try to stop it. John knows what the punishment will be." The old dog started barking at the old man. "I know that you don't like this. We have no other choice," said the old man. The old hound dog barked several times again. The old man understood what the old dog was saying to him. "Yes, I agree. We do not have any other choice. We must do it," the old man heard in his mind from his trusted companion.

The Old Man raised his hands to the sky. He took his walking staff. The Old Man pointed his staff to the sky. Then he took the staff and pointed it downward. He hit the bottom of the staff three times against the ground as hard as he could. The old hound dog barked three times at the ground where the staff had hit the ground. This was a signal to **The Land of the Eagle Feathers** to rebel against those that did not follow the sacred rules.

The ground shook and waved like a ribbon. Deep fissures cracked the ground. Soldiers and horses fell into the deep fissures. Lava shot up into the air. Everyone ran to anywhere they thought would save them.

I pointed to some of the others that were left. I told them to run to the sacred mountain. I got off my horse. I patted his neck and whispered to him. "You have been a loyal companion. Fly away as fast as you can. Save yourself. I must stay here. I picked up Zan and put him on my horse." I hit my horse's shoulder. My horse ran to the mountain trail to be safe.

Lo Ming and Moses had stood side by side and fought. Moses' mother and Father were by their side. When the earthquake started, all the fighting stopped. Everyone was running to escape. A large crack in the ground opened. Moses' father and mother started to fall into the crack. Lo Ming and Moses grabbed them by their clothing. They pulled them back to safety. They turned and ran.

Soon it was only a few of **The Dark Ones** and a few of **The Omen** were left alive. Some people made it to the sacred mountain. Red Bear and Red Sparrow died together when a big boulder rolled over them. David ran over to them. David started pounding the large boulder with his fists. "I only found them a short time ago. I thought I had lost them a lifetime ago." He held his bloody fists towards the sky. "Have not I suffered enough for this land? I have given my all to save it. They did their part. Why? Why?" he shouted at the sky as he fell to his knees in grief.

Many of **The Omen** tried to ride their horses. They were bucked off. Most died as they hit the ground or fell into the deep lava pits. As far as I could see, there was destruction. The whole army of **The Dark Ones** was dead or dying. Either the lava pits or the boulders killed them where they stood.

Raven looked at me. I didn't think it was possible for her to cry. She still held Benita in her arms. "She was the best of me. I am such a fool. Benita loved Mary like she was her daughter. She raised her. I should have known that she would never let anything happen to her. Benita was the only person

I ever loved. John, you can have this land. It is not worth the cost,' Raven said bitterly with tears in her eyes. I took out my sword and pointed toward the sacred mountaintop. "Raven, I should kill you. I think that you have suffered enough," I told her.

Nick and Shanna got to the mercenaries before they were able to get to Rose, June, One Feather and Great Wolf. They told them to take Great Wolf to the mountaintop. Nick and Shanna would try to hold off these men until they were gone.

Rose was on old Waco. Angela had told Rose to take her mule. Rose would need a surefooted animal to ride such a difficult trail up the mountain. Nick shouted at them to leave. Nick told them that Antonio and Angela wanted them to live. They had given their lives for this. One Feather couldn't believe what Nick had said. He did not question what Nick said. He knew only one thing. He would obey what his parents requested of him. Great Wolf jumped on Petunia's back. Great Wolf had *The Book of Winter* in his backpack.

June and One Feather had a difficult time riding up the mountain trail. They were dodging rocks, trees and boulders. Their horses were not as good at traveling rocky mountain trails as mules were. They wondered how Nick and Shanna were doing with so many mercenary soldiers to fight.

About half-way up the mountain, a large boulder rolled down the mountain. Petunia tried to get out of the way. The boulder hit Petunia's leg. The boulder broke Petunia's leg as it bounced against her leg. Petunia fell to the rocky mountain trail. Petunia tried to get up. She couldn't stand. Old Waco ran over to Petunia.

He licked Petunia's head. Old Waco gave out the most mournful cry. Rose tried to get him to move from her. Old Waco refused. Old Waco would not leave Petunia. Rose got off Old Waco. "Yes Waco, you belong with your friend, Petunia. Nobody should die alone. She has only a few hours before that happens. We will be back for you," said Rose as she petted Old Waco. Old Waco sat down beside Petunia on the rocky trail. Petunia licked Old Waco. Old Waco put his head on Petunia's neck. That was the way they left them. It was the way that it should have been.

Rose got up behind June on June's horse. One Feather grabbed Great Wolf and pulled him into his saddle. They left Petunia and Old Waco on the side of the trail. Nobody said anything. The tears in their eyes said it all.

One Feather's horse was getting very tired. One Feather and June dismounted their horses. June looked back and saw four of Raven's men following them on horseback. "We need to stop them. You must go," shouted June. One Feather told Great Wolf to take his horse and get to the mountaintop.

Great Wolf did not want to leave. June looked at Great Wolf saying, "I promised your father that I would make sure you got to White Elk. He said that you are our only hope. You must go. Rose will help you. You must keep her and her baby safe. Now go, Great Wolf. Travel like the wind!" shouted June. Rose took the reins from June's horse and pulled Great Wolf's horse behind her. Great Wolf looked back to see One Feather and June had turned to fight the four men on horseback.

On the side of the hill where Great Wolf had been, Shanna and Nick were battling several of **The Dark Ones'** mercenaries. The uniform that these men wore had a spider symbol on the left arm. Shanna and Nick knew what that meant. These were the best of the best. They were Raven's handpicked killers. They were as good as it gets. It would be difficult to defeat two or three of them. It would be almost impossible to defeat at least 10 of them. Shanna said to Nick at least we can detain them until the others can get away. I'm afraid that is all we will be able to do. Nick stabbed the men in front of him. Shanna threw her knife and killed another one. Nick tossed the dead man's sword to her. The fight was a little more even now.

Nick was busy with two men when he heard a moan from Shanna. Shanna was holding her left shoulder. A swordsman had been able to get behind her and stab her in the shoulder. Blood was running down Shanna's blouse. Nick's eyes turned completely red. He became a wild man. He killed two men in a matter of seconds. He threw one of his knives and killed another that was behind Shanna. It was too late. Shanna had another mercenary cut her in the leg. She fell to the ground bleeding. The man was about to finish her. Nick knew he could not get there in time to stop him. As the man started to swing his sword, he suddenly stopped. An arrow hit him in the neck. Mary stood behind him. "Shanna won't die today." She said to Nick. Two mercenaries fell in front of him. He looked to see who killed them. "Mary, you are right," Lo Ming laughed. Moses was standing right beside her. "Let's finish this," said Moses' mother and father.

Mary ran over to Shanna. She was badly hurt from her wounds. Mary was able to stop Shanna's bleeding. Nick and the others finished off the rest of the attackers shortly. Nick looked at Mary, "Nick, Shanna will live. You should have a wonderful life together." Just as Mary finished her last words to Nick, Mary fell to the ground. An arrow was sticking in her back. Moses turned and threw his large knife and killed the man with the bow instantly. The Red Woman appeared. She saw what happened and rushed to her side. The Red Woman pulled out the arrow very quickly.

Moses' mother shouted she would go and get John. Lo Ming stopped her. This is a job for me. I will go. It would be best for me to get him and David. Lo Ming ran like a deer being chased by wolves. She found John in the middle of the battlefield. John was trying his best to comfort David. Lo Ming shouted at them. When they didn't answer her, she went over and hit them on the back of their heads. "I don't care what you are doing. Red Bear and Red Sparrow are dead. Mary is not, but she is dying. Go to the hill!" Lo Ming didn't have to say anything more.

Red Woman was doing her best to save Mary. She was bleeding badly. She looked at David and me and shook her head. We knew if Red Woman couldn't save her, nobody could. David bent down and touched Mary's cheek. Tears were running down his cheek. David was out of his mind with grief. David couldn't talk. He was too upset. Mary reached up and touched her father's face. "You know I always loved you and mother. Benita deserves a proper burial. She was always kind to me. Please make sure my mother takes good care of my son and teaches him well. I know you must go back. It is as it was written. Let me talk to my husband," Mary said so softly. All David could do was nod his head.

David motioned me over. I sat down on the ground next to her. "I wished it could have been different. My memories of you loving me is more than I deserve. It took me a long time to come to terms with you. I know your time like mine is short. I will see you over the rainbow bridge soon. Tell my mother and son I died loving them. Don't talk, John, my husband. We were so close. Just kiss me goodbye for now." she whispered. I kissed her. I looked up at the setting sun. I kissed her one more time. I whispered to her. "It is as it was written. We would die together."

I died at sunset as foretold. David laid me beside her. Lo Ming took Mary's hand and put it in mine. David sobbed and cried like a man that had lost his soul. The Red Woman appeared next to him. She took David in her arms. The rest of the others walked away. They left us all alone.

Moses noticed that Lo Ming was not back. Where could she be? She had told John and David about Mary. Moses asked his mother to come with him. Something told him that something was very wrong. Moses and his mother ran back to the battlefield. They saw Lo Ming fighting four mercenaries at once. They were too far to assist her. Lo Ming was like a whirlwind. The men that she was fighting were laughing at her. Moses could hear them shouting at her. "We will finally finish the Great Lo Ming. We have been waiting years for this chance," shouted one of the men. As if to make a statement, Lo Ming jumped over the man and killed him with her fighting stick. That left three of them. Moses and his mother felt helpless. His mother knew who these men were. "Moses, we have got to get there quickly. Those men have been trying to kill her for years. They are good. They are better than good. I don't think she can kill them all," his mother shouted. Lo Ming looked at the three before her. She studied them. She thought out every move. She would kill them all in one great movement. She knew if she didn't, she would lose. Moses and his mother would get there too late.

Lo Ming waited for them to attack. They rushed her all at once. She jumped over the first man cutting his throat. She landed on the second man with a kick to his neck breaking it. The third man swung his sword just missing her. She took her small dragger and stabbed him directly in his heart. They were all dead.

Moses and his mother shouted for joy. She had won. They stopped running. Thunder could be heard in the distance. Lo Ming picked up her fighting stick. She raised it above her head. A lightning bolt flashed. It hit the fighting stick. Lo Ming looked at Moses in disbelief. She fell to the ground. Moses called her name as he ran to her. His mother shook her head. She tried to stop him. He pushed his mother to the side.

Moses' mother knew she was dead. When she got there, Moses had Lo Ming in his arms. Moses was calling Lo Ming's name as he held her. He held her lifeless body in his arms. Moses kept saying, "I love you. Please wake up! We had such plans. We were to go to my home in the Great Outback. You would have loved it there. It is Summer there now. The Spring rains would have come. There would be beautiful flowers growing in the desert. We would have been married by my grandfather on the sacred mountain. Lo Ming, you cannot be dead."

Moses' mother's heart was breaking for her son. She put her arms around him. "Carry her to the middle of the battlefield, my son. She would have wanted that. She was never defeated. She told me that she loved you very much. I had thought of her as the daughter I never had. She would have made you a good wife. Moses, please do as I say."

Moses stood up with Lo Ming in his arms. He took her to the middle of the field. Red poppies were starting to grow all around the field. Moses' mother asked Moses to lay Lo Ming down. She had taken Lo Ming's fighting stick. Moses found a bed of flowers growing. He laid her down in the middle of it. His heart was broken. His spirit was lost. His mother gave Lo Ming's fighting stick to him. Moses put her stick in Lo Ming's arms. He stood up. He started to fall to the ground in sorrow and despair.

A strong hand caught him and held him. "Moses, you are a lucky man to have had a woman like her. She died a warrior. She would have liked that. You must not despair. She would not have wanted that for you. She once told me to give this to you if she died in battle," said Lo Ming's uncle. Her uncle gave him a necklace made of jade. "She liked green. She wanted you to always think of her as alive. Never think of her as dead! Remember her as she should be remembered: a great warrior. That is what she would want," Moses nodded his head. He heard the cry of an eagle. He looked at the sky. He saw a Bald Eagle fly overhead. It dipped its' right wing out of respect. They watched together as it flew to the heavens above.

On the mountaintop, Rose and Great Wolf had arrived to give the book to White Elk. White Elk was waiting for them. White Elk told Great Wolf to dismount. He pointed to a large crystal platform. Great Wolf took out ***The Book of Winter*** from his backpack. There was a place large enough for the book in the crystal. Great Wolf placed the book in that slot. The crystal closed and encased the book. All became silent, the earthquakes stopped. The ground became still.

White Elk motioned to Great Wolf to follow him. White Elk told Great Wolf that **The Land of the Eagle Feathers** was now safe. The book is finally home. Many have died today for that book. They gave their lives to save this land. Your father and mother are dead. I am sorry to tell you that. Many of your friends are dead. Don't cry, it is not over. There is someone that you will have to meet.

Great Wolf turned around. The old man and his dog were standing a few feet away. "You have done well, my child. I am pleased. There is one more thing we must do. Come with me to the great cliff! Maybe all is not lost!" said the old man.

Great Wolf could not help it. Tears rolled down his face. He had seen too much death today. Antonio and Angela died helping Shanna and Nick escape. His father had saved Zan, Big Daddy Crawfish and Sheba. Rose would be grateful for their sacrifice. The only thing that Great Wolf didn't know was whether his grandfather was alive. At least, Rose and her child would have a father and mother.

Rose watched as the old man led Great Wolf to the great cliff. The Great Cliff overlooked the valley below. The old man and his dog stopped at the edge of the Great Cliff. "Tell me what you see, Great Wolf," asked the old man.

Great Wolf looked down at the destruction on the valley floor. "I see many dead people and animals. I see my father lying dead on the ground with my mother. I see my grandfather and grandmother alive by that big boulder. I see only a few people alive. I see death," Great Wolf whispered.

"Yes, you see what man can do to himself. You see what happens when good and evil are not in balance. There has always been good and evil as long as man has traveled the earth. I want you and Rose to take your horses down to the valley. I want you to go to the middle of the field. When you get there, take your father's sword and point it at me. Don't move a muscle! Whatever happens, don't move! Perhaps, a miracle can happen. Whatever happens will be the destiny of all those that lie below us. Now go! Brave young man and do as I said," the old man reminded Great Wolf.

Rose and Great Wolf mounted their horses. They rode carefully down the mountain trail. Rose stopped her horse where they had left June and One Feather. She told Great Wolf to dismount his horse. Rose and Great Wolf slowly walked about 100 yards down the trail. Against a large tree were June and One Feather setting holding hands. In front of them were four dead mercenaries lying face down on the trail. Rose stopped Great Wolf from running to June and One Feather. "Do not go to them. They died holding hands. It is what it should be. We will come back for them later. We must get back to save who we can find," Rose told Great Wolf. "They died together protecting this land. They deserve a warrior's burial."

Rose and Great Wolf mounted their horses. They continued down the trail. They found Petunia dead on the side of the trail with Old Waco resting his head on Petunia's side. Old Waco was dead. He had two spears in his side. Two mercenaries lay dead on the trail several feet away. Great Wolf could only say, "Old Waco protected Petunia as well as he could. They would have had it no other way."

It took a while to get to the bottom of the mountain. Great Wolf looked at the survivors. "Everyone needs to go to the place where they were at before the earthquake. It is our only chance to save this place and its people," yelled Great Wolf. For some reason, both John's followers and what was left of **The Dark Ones and The Omen** moved to the field. David and Moses had carried John and Mary to the center of the field. The ground had somehow mended itself. There were no deep fissures or lava. The animals had returned. The rattlesnakes moved toward the streams. The horses moved to the center of the field.

"Everyone must not move. Do not move! When I point to the mountain, make sure you listen," shouted Great Wolf. Everyone froze in place as Great Wolf reached down and took his father's sword and pointed to the mountaintop. A great rush of wind and dust covered the valley. It was as if time stopped. It was like time turned backwards. Great Wolf could feel it in his soul. Time was moving but not forward. The wind blew in from the North. The dust settled to the earth. The bright sun came out.

Great Wolf looked at the scene before him. Everyone was still frozen in place and time. It was the moment before Raven tried to kill Mary. A large voice could be heard coming from the Great Mountain Cliff. "Don't anyone move! I have a message for you." That's when everyone became alive again. Everyone turned their heads. They saw an image of an old man and his dog projected on the great cliff.

"I have come to tell you that only you can change what happened. I will show you what will happen if you fight in this valley. What you see on this cliff will be what has already happened. Many of you died today. Now you have a decision to make," said the old man. During the next several minutes, scenes of death and destruction filled the cliff. Death was everywhere. People on both sides saw their death or those they love die. Finally, the images stopped, and images of the old man and his dog returned.

"You have seen what has happened. Every one of you must decide whether to live or die. The offer to have riches and live is still on the table. You can leave this land. You can never come back. You will die if you do. *The Book of Winter* is now in its rightful place. I can erase all of you from this place like you were never born. Will you be able to control your greed and selfishness? David is the only one that can answer the question. What do you say David? Can you restore the balance of good and evil?

David was still on his horse. Mary was still beside him. He looked down at the ground beside him. John lay dead on the ground. "I speak for all here today. We will leave this land. We will take your generous offer. I will take all that is here today with me. I have only one request. We will only leave if you restore John's life back. He was a great warrior. Great Warriors die for others. He died for everyone here. How say my men and **The Omen**!" shouted David. Every man, woman and animal cried for him to live. The cheers for John echoed like thunder before a storm.

The image of the old man and his dog looked back at the valley before them. "So be it! He will live. Only the greatest of warriors could win a battle, have both sides praise him and nobody died. His destiny and fate have been fulfilled. It was written in the stars. Now go and leave this land and remember what you saw today," said the old man.

An old mule appeared by John. David dismounted his horse. He picked up John and told him to ride around his army. John didn't understand. He got on old Petunia. All the army and his followers cheered him. John rode old Petunia around the valley to the cheers of his enemies and his friends. It was as it should have been. It was written in *The Book of Winter*.

On the sacred mountaintop, a young woman watched the scene below. She said, "Fate was always your friend." The young spirit woman turned her painted pony and rode into the sky. There was a smile on her face.

Chapter XII
The Battle is Over
What will happen next?

Later that night everyone sat around the campfire. Nick and Rose had fixed a meal. They insisted on it. The group ate in silence for several minutes. They were all still digesting what had happened to them. Everyone that was involved in the events of this day would remember everything that happened to them. This included those that were here, and all the other people involved. The old man said it was **The Land of the Eagle Feathers'** way of reminding you of what could have been.

Our group was a little saddened that this would probably be the last time for such a meal. There was a wooden box. Shanna had Nick and Moses carry it in from **The Dark Ones'** camp. Nick got up and got his KA-BAR knife. He used it to take off the wooden top of the box. Inside he pulled out several bottles of wine, whiskey and other beverages. He gave everyone a silver cup from inside the box. "You can thank Shanna for this. She brought it with her. Each silver cup has your name engraved on it. It also has a bald eagle stamped on it. She thought it would make a nice keepsake. You will see there is one bottle of your favorite drink for every one of us. She even included non-alcohol drinks for some of you. Here's your bottle, Rose!" Nick said as he handed it to Rose.

Rose unwrapped the white paper around her bottle. Rose laughed. She got up and ran over to Shanna. Rose gave her a big hug. Rose showed everyone her bottle. "I have not had this soda since I was a little girl. Big Daddy Crawfish and Sheba bought me a bottle of this when I was a little girl. They

brought it to cerebrate my first time visit to New Orleans."
Rose asked, "How did you know?"

"You are not the only one with a crystal ball. Your mother
told me to get it for you instead of your favorite wine. She
said something about you not being able to drink wine at the
end of this adventure. I don't question mothers," laughed
Shanna. Rose replied, "Well, I'll be--." Zan interrupted Rose
saying, "Don't say it. We shouldn't be saying such words
around our child." Rose laughed and patted her stomach. "I
guess I will have to change some of my ways for this little
one."

Nick asked everyone to stand up for a toast. "Raise your
cups high: To **The Keepers of the Yawi** and their friends and
relatives. May we find peace and happiness in the years to
come!" Everyone shouted, "Here, here!!" as they toasted each
other. Nick sat down next to Shanna.

June got up to speak. "It is hard to believe that we have
been together for about a year. Many of us have found things
that we thought we had lost. I found the love of my life and
more. As you know, One Feather doesn't like to give
speeches. We want you all to be at our wedding. It will be a
traditional Native American wedding. We will be making
The Land of the Eagle Feathers our home." Everyone
congratulated them.

Antonio got up to speak. "I am a lucky man. Some say a
handsome man at that. I did the traditional thing. Today, the
most beautiful woman I ever knew gave me this ring on this
silver necklace. She had kept it for many years. I thought she
had tossed it away many years ago. I guess it is never too late.
When you are on your death bed, you think about what you
should have done. I hope I have not stepped out of line. Your
father, White Elk, gave me permission to marry you, Angela.
That is, if you still want me.' Antonio had a hard time getting

341

the last words out. His voice cracked as tears flowed down his face.

Angela's face was filled with a smile with tears flowing as well. She looked at John and Mary. "Yes, I will only on one condition. John and Mary will have to give me away. John to make sure that I don't run away, and Mary to remind me how lucky I am." There wasn't a dry eye around the campfire. Angela got up and kissed Antonio. June and One Feather couldn't have been more pleased.

Lo Ming and Moses stood up together. Lo Ming proudly said, "I will tell you the most beautiful speech I ever heard. It may surprise you that Moses said it. I had just died. This is what he said, "I love you. Please wake up! We had such plans. We were to go to my home in the Great Outback. You would have loved it there. It is Summer there now. The Spring rains would have come. There would be beautiful flowers growing in the desert. We would have been married by my grandfather on the sacred mountain." I told Moses I was holding him to his words. I hope you will be able to come to our wedding. I will promise you that it will be an adventure. I think we like that sort of thing." They sat down to a round of applause.

Zan asked Rose, "Will you please stand up?" Rose, being somewhat perplexed, did as Zan asked. "As you ladies are aware, my father died in The Land of Nightmares. Before he died, he slipped me a small ring on my finger." Zan held up his hand and slipped a small golden ring off his little finger. Zan got on his knees and took Rose's hand. "My dad told me to give this to Rose. He said my mother gave it to him in a dream. Rose, I want our child to be born to us as a married couple. I am a bit old fashioned that way. We have a family. The people here are our family. So in front of our family, Rose, I am asking you to marry me." Rose looked deeply into Zan's eyes, "I most certainly will. It took you long enough.

You know that I searched to the end of the world to find you. I will never let you go. I have loved you for many years."

Red Woman's voice could be heard in the darkness. "White Elk will be busy with all these weddings around here. I suggest that you think about when you would want to get married. Don't rush into anything! Black Panther and his tribe will rejoin this land. June's tribe and White Owl will rejoin us as well. The Others in the Southwest will have several members come to stay with us.

I know you know the story of *The Wolf and Raven*. David and I have much the same relationship. David is the Wolf, and I am the Raven. Each of us cannot change for the other. David will go back to Houston, and I must stay here. We have different lives but love each other. I must go now."

David asked to speak, "I will be going back early tomorrow to take **The Dark One's Army** and the **Council of Omen** to Houston. Every one of them agreed to take the gifts and never come back. My duty is to see that the balance is kept between good and evil. As many of you know, I am legally married to the Red Woman. I talked to Benita. We will have a divorce. I will give her a good settlement. She will be able then to be free to be with Raven. Benita has agreed to be my second in command. Raven will do anything Benita agrees to. I know Raven is Raven. I will need someone like her to help me destroy other evil organizations and cults.

Without Benita's assistance, my wife would have been killed. Benita helped me raise Mary. She kept Mary safe. I never knew that until lately. She promised that to my wife. I owe her that much. I will visit here from time to time. This is my fate and my wife's fate as well. It is the way it is written in the stars. I must be going to rejoin the others. John, I do have one satisfaction that you can't take away from me."

I asked, "David, what is that?" David answered, "It is simple. I will always be your father-in-law. Isn't that right, daughter?" Mary laughed, "Yes, you have a point. Don't forget, father! John has to call my mother, the Red Woman, mother-in-law, also." Everyone laughed at me, I had to say I had never thought about that.

Shanna gave David some expensive and rare wine. She also gave David a silver cup. "It has your name on it and the Bald Eagle emblem. John said to give it to you. It is time for that he said." David looked at the cup and laughed. "I guess, I didn't get the last laugh."

David handed a shoebox size gift to Mary. "Mary, this gift is from Benita. She said that she knew you probably would not be coming back. She wanted you to have this." Mary opened the box. It was the Indian doll toy that Benita had given her when Mary was a child. "Benita said you would know what to do with it." Mary said to David, "Tell her I will never forget her." David replied, "I think that is the best gift you can ever give her is for me to tell her that."

Rico has been invited to come to this meeting by Antonio. He stood up and asked, "I did my part. Where is my favorite painting that Antonio and Nick stole from me in Houston?" Antonio answered, "Now Rico, where is the best place to hide something?" Rico thought for a few moments. "My mama always said to hide something that is valuable the best place to hide it is in plain sight."

Antonio answered, "Exactly!" Rico replied, "You hid it in my office. It's behind my office desk on the wall. You said it was a fake painting of the painting you stole. That way I was protected from anyone thinking I stole it. That fake painting is the real one. It never left the museum. You took the fake one so if you got caught, they couldn't charge you. Very smart of you, Antonio! You made me come when I didn't have too."

"Don't lie to us, Rico," I told him. "Rico would have volunteered to come anyway. Rico was working for me. In fact, he was also working for Shanna. Wasn't he, Shanna?"

Angela laughed, 'Why he was working for me, too?" Antonio smiled, "Rico was working for many people. How many people were you working for Rico?"

Rico had been caught double dealing with several people in front of him. Rico answered, "Private or government agencies! There is a difference. I am just a little Italian boy trying to make it in a hostile world. Besides, someone had to keep you from getting the attention of other organizations and government agencies.

Isn't that right, Lo Ming? Lo Ming told me that long ago when I worked for her Uncle in China. When Lo Ming went and sold some of her antiques at the Houston Art Museum, she saw me talking to Antonio. You can say that she gave me an offer that I could not refuse.

As bad as I would like to, I will not tell anyone about my dealing with anyone. I will let you all sort it out. You are all what I call: scorpions. I am a businessman. I don't tell about the people I have deals with. If I did, I would go out of business or be dead. Please forgive me, I will not charge you anything. David already paid me handsomely."

Mary stood up to talk next. "Of all of us, I guess that I changed the most during this year. I'm not that light brown-haired white woman you once knew. I was so surprised that each of you accepted me when I changed back to my true self. I am still trying to sort everything out. Rose, you have been a true friend to me. June, you helped me find my way back to our ways. Lo Ming, you are a good spiritual guide. Angela and Shanna, you two, always kept me guessing of what you would do next. Antonio, you were always a gentleman. Moses, you taught all of us about nature and respect for animals. I hoped that I held my own with all of you. Nick once told me that he never had a soldier so skilled and a medic so good. I take that as a compliment.

Things don't always turn out the way we thought they would. Fate has a way of its own. If someone had told me that I would find that I had a husband and a strong young son, I would have wondered what they had been drinking or smoking. I will be staying in this land for a long time. I want to teach my son about many things. I want to be with my mother and my people.

John and I are still working it out. I know he is more of the outside world than here. He will be visiting us time to time until we settle everything. We are much like my father and my mother. He is the Wolf and I am the Raven in this story. It will be difficult for either of us to change into the other's form. There is one thing that I want to say. I love each one of you. You will be welcome in my lodge any day."

It was my time to speak. "It took me many years to put a group like you together. You first came to know me by my first name: John. You have done what nobody ever thought anyone could do. You found the four books. You saved this land. You preserved the culture and people of this land for many generations to come.

I am lucky. I got to live. The reason for that is the people that started with me about a year ago. I thank you for saving me and this land. There are those among us that have lived many years. The old man recognized that fact. He has granted a very long life to each of you: **The Keepers of the Yawi.** He has also granted that to your relatives and special friends. The only thing that you must do is return here once every 3 circles of the sun or every 3 years for this to continue.

Shanna and Nick will be doing some work with me. We have some work to finish. Moses and his family need to settle some things down in Australia. Some of you might want to join us. Angela and I never dissolved our business partnership. Like it or not, I will have to put up with my blood brother, Antonio. As Lo Ming says, it will be an adventure.

I forgot one thing. In the brown leather bags behind you, the old man left you some parting gifts. I am sure that Rico can get you a good price for those items inside of them. Enjoy the rest of the evening. Let's not make any more speeches tonight."

A large puff of smoke filled the air covering everything. White Elk appeared in all his glory. His white elk skin coat glowed by the campfire. "I come to send you greetings from the **Great Council** of this Land. The Great Elder has summoned **The Keepers of the Yawi** and John to meet with them tomorrow night. David, you must take your people, Shanna, Angela and Rico back with you. You must start at sunrise. You can take the southern trail and use the old pass to get out. I will see that that pass is open. It will cut two days journey off leaving this land. If you hurry, you will be able to get out of this land by sunset tomorrow night. Please do as I say! Remember, this meeting is only for **The Keepers of the Yawi and John**," said White Elk as he disappeared into a white puff of smoke.

The next morning, David took all of **The Dark One's Army and The Omen Council** with him. Angela and Shanna were a little upset about not being included in the meeting with **The Council of Elders**. They were somewhat relieved when I told them it had no reflection on them. White Elk wanted to make sure that David got everyone out. Their mission was to make sure that nothing happened to David. Antonio and Nick were to join them in Houston in about a week. They were welcome to come back to **The Land of the Eagle Feathers** anytime. It was extremely important to have someone watch after David.

It was nightfall when we reached the sacred mountaintop. This meeting was to be held around the sacred campfire. One Feather and Great Wolf would be allowed to attend. The Red Woman had the evening meal fixed for them. They ate talking about the events of the last year. The weather was still very warm. The sky was dark full of stars. The moon had moved toward the eastern horizon. The moon was pink and reddish in color. We could see the whole encampment in the valley below of the groups that had took part in the events days before that fought with us. Their campfires were bright filling the valley.

We were sitting on logs facing west. It was starting to get a little colder. As the temperature fell, the sky became clearer. On a dark winter night, the stars are always brighter. June and Moses were pointing out all the constellations of the stars to the others. June got excited. "I see the Seven Sisters. Doesn't it look like a bear is chasing those seven stars." Moses replied, "Yes, I agree. That big bear is trying to get to them. He just cannot quite make it to get them." As Mary was about to say something, the campfire in front of us began to start growing. Soon it was so large we had to move back from it.

The fire started to die down. "Welcome to **The Keepers of the Yawi**," a voice said from the darkness in front of us." A bright light from somewhere above shone down. It was the Great Elder and **The Council of Elders of The Land of the Eagle Feathers.** They were seated across from us.

The Great Elder stood up. "We are here tonight to honor you. You have done what nobody could have ever done. Many failed before you in finding them. You found and obtained the four sacred books. Less than a cycle of the sun, you came here. You worked together and fought together. Many of you were injured and hurt in the progress. That did not stop you. You are all great warriors.

We know that others helped you such as: David, The Red Woman, and Angela. Shanna was not even one of you, but she risked her life and almost died. They are needed elsewhere tonight. We heard you talking about Rico. He has been one of us for many years. We call him **Little Fox that Howls too**

Much. John gave him that name. We honor them as well. You and they will always be welcome in this land.

You are now legends in this land. People will sing songs of your adventures and exploits for many moons and cycles of the sun. You have completed a circle: the four seasons of the cycle. You have the mark of the Bald Eagle on your arms. Nobody but you will ever have the honor to be called, **The Keepers of the Yawi**. Our culture and ways of life have been saved for many generations. These precious things will not be forgotten in the dust of stars and the sands of time. Tonight, we will honor you as you should be honored. The others not here with you will see this in their dreams."

White Elk rose beside the Great Elder. They both pointed their sacred staffs toward the sky. Two bright laser beams of light flashed into the darkness of the winter's night sky. An outline of a great large Bald Eagle appeared overhead. It flapped its wings and flew to the heavens above.

Everywhere the campfires stopped and lost their fire. It was complete darkness. Not a sound could be heard except two wolves howling at the night's sky. The wolves became silence. An old man's voice could be heard in the distance. He was singing an ancient song of joy. A single drum and flute accompanied him.

His voice was like the sound of the wind flowing through the waves of grain in the summer. It was soft. It was calling for the ones who had been lost so long ago. The soft song of the one lonely old voice was calling for the spirits to come and join him.

Slowly his old voice started to build. He was saying what many wished to be said. His lonely voice was eerie and yet touched your heart. The voice drew you into it. Its meaning was clear. A chorus of soft voices started joining him. A face of the old man filled the night's sky above the mountaintop. The old man was singing. The drum became more drums.

The flute became more flutes. The chorus were spirits singing their songs of life and death. They filled the sky behind the old man. These spirits singing were warriors, women and children. They were dancing and rejoicing as they sang.

As the voices became louder, the old man's face started to change. Slowly, his face changed from an old man to a great old warrior's face. A head dress of many Bald Eagle feathers was on his head. We saw a great flash in front of us. The whole **Council of Elders** of this land became spirits. They arose to join him in the sky singing and dancing. Great warriors on horses rode around the stars above.

The old warrior stopped singing. Slowly the chorus' singing faded away. Everyone stopped and watched the old warrior in the sky above. "I am the Spirit of this land. I am the Spirits of Spirits. I am what you could call the Spirit of the Yawi. We are pleased. Our culture and ways have been saved for all.

The four seasons of the cycle of the sun has completed its circle. A circle has no beginning or ending. The circle of life has no ending. We have only beginnings. This land will endure as long as we believe in this land. Our spirits are strong again. We will endure. Let us celebrate our new beginning. We are part of the past and the future. The circle will come again and go again just as the seasons. Let us rejoice in our land. Without this land, there is no tomorrow for us. We must hold our spirits close to our hearts. Our souls and spirits live within us. This land lives within us. We must protect it and guard its sacred values forever!"

The old warrior started to sing again. At first, it was only him and a drummer. Then a flute joined in with him. The song was one of sadness for the past combined with hope for the future. More spirits joined in song. Soon all the stars in the sky turned into bright shining spirits. The heavens lit up into a chorus of song. Thousands of spirits sang. Finally, when the heavens seemed to be full of joyful music. It became silent.

 The silence was followed by great explosions. Fireworks shook the heavens and skies above the mountaintop. The great chorus faded. The fireworks continued for several minutes until the whole sky filled with bright eagles flying between the exploding stars. Suddenly everything became dark except for the old warrior. He sang his song with one drummer and one flutist. You could hear his words of wisdom as he sang.

For each ending, there is a beginning
For each beginning, there is an ending
For each reason, there is a season
For each season, there is a reason

It was written many moons ago
In the stars hey, yi, hey, yi, yo
For few to see, less to know
The gift of life hey, yi, hey, yi, yo

In the land where deer and buffalo play
For every night, there is a day
For every day, there is a night
For every wrong, there is a right

The two wolves will fight for your soul
It is written hey, yi, hey, yi, yo
Everything is a part of the whole
It will always be hey, yi, hey, yi, yo

Everything's a circle going around
From the sky above to the leaves on the ground
Few to see, less to know
Everything's a part of the whole hey, yi, hey, yi, yo

The drummer stopped drumming. The flute stopped its music. They faded into the stars. The old warrior slowly sang the last words to his song: **hey, yi, hey, yi, yo.** The old warrior looked at the great crowd below and smiled. He turned and mounted a great war horse made of stars. His war horse reared up. A dog appeared beside his war horse. The old warrior galloped away with his dog running beside him toward the heavens until they faded into the dark starry night.

After a few days, I had returned to the Eagle Train Station. Antonio and Nick had left the day before. Everything was going well in Houston. I was getting ready to board the old steam locomotive train. I looked back like I had did many times before.

The old man and his dog were sitting on the station's porch. The old man said to me, "Well now, John, you must know that each year a circle is completed. The four seasons completes or as we say it begins a cycle again. That is the way it is. We will be waiting for you, John," said the old man with his old hound dog barking in agreement.

As I was getting on the old black train, I looked back at him, again. "Yes, you are right. Everything comes full circle like the four seasons of each cycle of the sun. You can defeat them, but more will replace them," I replied to him. The old man laughed, and his old hound dog barked. I looked back at the two standing on the porch as the old train pulled out. I understood what the old hound dog was barking. The old hound dog was saying, "We will be seeing you."

About the Authors:

Joe G. Morin was born and raised on a small rural southern Indiana farm. He currently lives in East Tennessee where he taught Adult Education for several years. His ancestors came from France, Scotland and Ireland. His current publications on Amazon.com are *Why Men Have Problems with Women and An Angel in the Kitchen.* He loves to tell stories. He is from a family of story tellers. He would listen to his Grandfather tell his stories about being a rural schoolteacher and farmer for hours. You may contact him at joegmorin@gmail.com

Jo Ann Bullard was born in East Tennessee. Having been a professional entertainer, she traveled all over the world. There is no place like East Tennessee. She lives and writes in the foothills of the Smoky Mountains. Her ancestors were Cherokee, Blackfoot and Scotch-Irish. Her current publications on Amazon.com are *The Problems with Men, and An Angel in the Kitchen.* She has written several articles for professional publications. She is currently working on a volume of song lyrics. You may visit her at ja2bullard@gmail.com

Special Thanks for the assistance of June Henley Haney and Little Lucky.

This Book is final book in the series: The Quest of the Land of the Eagle Feathers.

This is the fourth book in a four-part series.

The books in order are:

The Quest of the Land of the Eagle Feathers: The Book of Spring

The Ouest of the Land of the Eagle Feathers: The Book of Summer

The Quest of the Land of the Eagle Feathers: The Book of Fall

The Quest of the Land of the Eagle Feathers: The Book of Winter

All of the books are available on Amazon.com. To find each book, you must put in the whole title such as: The Quest of the Land of the Eagle Feathers: The Book of Spring. These books are the same as the more Adult version of The Land of the Eagle Feathers but without the adult scenes.

www.ingramcontent.com/pod-product-compliance
Lightning Source LLC
Chambersburg PA
CBHW062011170626
46813CB00001B/115